A SPI

THE
OUTGOING

Published by Mission Point Press
2554 Chandler Rd.
Traverse City, MI 49696
(231) 421-9513
www.MissionPointPress.com

Design by Sarah Meiers

ISBN 978-1-958363-64-5

Library of Congress Control Number 2023900510

Printed in the United States of America

A SPINNERFALL THRILLER

THE OUTGOING

THOMAS A. BUHR

MISSION POINT PRESS

To Kathy and Rick,
not just family but best friends.

What fates impose, that men must needs abide;
It boots not to resist both wind and tide
—William Shakespeare

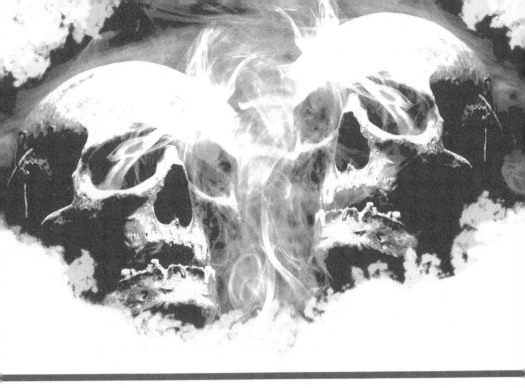

CHAPTER 1

Lost in the Woods

I remember the sad story of Donny Massengale and Roland Parrish. It came screaming through the haze of my day-to-day existence back then in the spring of 1984. I was watching the evening news in my apartment in Orlando, while nursing a hangover and lighting another smoke when Peter Jennings told me.

"There is now an extensive search for two college students who went on a fishing trip in Northern Michigan and have not been seen in over a week," the network anchorman said in that eloquent, continental delivery of his.

I cracked a beer — hair of the dog — while Jennings kicked it to a reporter in front of the Michigan State Police Forensic Lab in Grayling, Michigan.

"Donny Massengale and Roland Parrish are faces in the crowd," the reporter said with grim professionalism while pictures of the young men appeared on the screen (one short and stocky with short dark hair and plenty of facial stubble, the other tall and lean with longer blondish hair). "We all have a Donny and Roland in our lives. They were taking a break before summer classes at Central Michigan University to fish Michigan's famous Au Sable River. The few folks that remember seeing them on April 29th said the boys were friendly but not very knowledgeable of the area. No one has seen them since. It's been ten days."

No one, save the pizza delivery boy, had seen me in three days. I'd stocked the frig with Miller Lite, bought a quart of Jack and negotiated a deal for a gram and a half on Monday. The last three days had been wash-rinse-repeat with plenty of tunes — The Who always led off a binge while Neil Young always finished it — and the TV as living wallpaper, interspersed with periods of blackout. It had become my thing.

"Nobody's fucking looking for me!" I shouted at the screen. "What about me?"

The reporter went on:

"Instead of fishing the night of April 29th, the pair went to several bars in the area. A neighbor heard Donny's red Blazer pull into his uncle's cabin sometime around midnight. It was gone by seven the next morning when the same neighbor came out to walk his dog."

A parade of locals and law officers flashed across the screen, each speaking stoically into the reporter's mic while adding another dark stroke to the story.

I could relate to the boy's behavior. I loved to fish but did a helluva lot more drinking than fishing back then. Still the news intrigued me beyond shared affinities. I knew the area, had canoed the Au Sable as a kid at summer camp, camped in the nearby forests, even caught a few trout on a Mepps spinner and a Zebco rod and reel. I was a native Michigander and downstate kid to boot, charmed by Northern Michigan's Big Wild. It would turn out they were as well.

I sat in a trance, sipping that beer and hot boxing my smoke, as the facts were laid out.

The red Blazer never appeared again. The neighbor thought nothing of it until the uncle showed up a week later. He asked about the boys, frowned at the reply, went into the cabin to find dirty dishes in the sink, uneaten food in the frig, duffle bags barely unpacked, and beds hardly touched. He called the police. A search was underway involving county and state cops, U.S. Fish and Wildlife, and Department of Natural Resources law enforcement officers. Michigan National Guard units from nearby Camp Grayling helped with the effort. The TV had shots of boats dragging lakes and military helicopters sweeping over the stands of aspen, pine and oak in hopes of finding a clue.

"They're out there somewhere," the uncle told the reporter. Then it was back to the anchor desk and the day's next story, something about Jesse Jackson's campaign.

I got up, took a piss and went back to bed.

There were follow-up stories over the next week. Even *The Orlando Sentinel* had a couple of articles on The Missing Michigan Trout Fishermen as they were now being called. It was big news until it wasn't. Something took its place, but I can't remember what.

After that first story I lost interest because I was getting lost myself. Another night on the town in the seediest bars possible with cheaper drinks, better jukeboxes, and easier women. Another gram or two, or an eight-ball if I could find folks to chip in. Another long night of craziness and debauchery. Another long day of shame and regret. Who has time for other people's problems when they are too busy creating their own? It's a full-time job descending the long and winding trail to the gates of Hell.

Then a couple weeks later I almost made it. My dad found me OD'ing on the couch in the living room, gasping for breath, sweating like a pig, and scared out of my wits. I'd decided to bolt from O-Town, where I was pretending to go to grad school, and come home to Stuart to lay up for a bit and figure out a way to con the Old Man out of some more cash. Being a drunk and doper is expensive. Instead, I ended up in an emergency room and, by day's end, a treatment center in West Palm Beach.

That began my journey from lost to found. There was little room for Massengale and Parrish in that new world. But the hunt for them went on all summer long across the vast stretches of state and national forest land and festered in stops and starts that autumn until the first big snowfall in December. Even a psychic was employed that winter. They never found the Blazer or a trace of Donny Massengale and Roland Parrish.

"They are out there somewhere," the uncle said in an interview that Christmas. "We just want to bring them home." He would repeat that phrase in interviews until his death in 1995 from cancer.

Twenty-one years later, they were out there still. Law enforcement stumbled and bumbled from the get-go. Those first few critical days of investigation were lost while police agencies argued over ownership of the case. The FBI came in a few days later and only muddied the waters. Part of the problem was a serial killer stalking Michigan in the mid-1980s known as the Bigfoot Killer. Those in charge were certain that the boys' disappearance was another Bigfoot murder. Few officers challenged that assertion and those that did were ignored.

By 1990 the case of the Missing Michigan Trout Fishermen was so cold that the file was frosting over in storage like a leftover package of peas from some forgotten Thanksgiving. Nobody wanted to touch it and law enforcement did their level best to sweep it under the rug — out of sight, out of mind. Because of this mindset they would miss at least one great opportunity to break the case wide open.

I didn't know any of these things until much later. In those two decades I got sober, grew up, found my career, married my soulmate, and trudged the Road of Happy Destiny. Those years were the best years of my life. But all things must pass.

A personal tragedy started a cascade of events that put me on a different road: one that would lead to the truth about Donny and Roland. Along with two colleagues — one my oldest friend, the other my newest friend — we followed the tragic path of Massengale and Parrish to the bitter end by doing what no other law enforcement agency had considered by focusing not on the night that the fishermen went missing but on what had happened before.

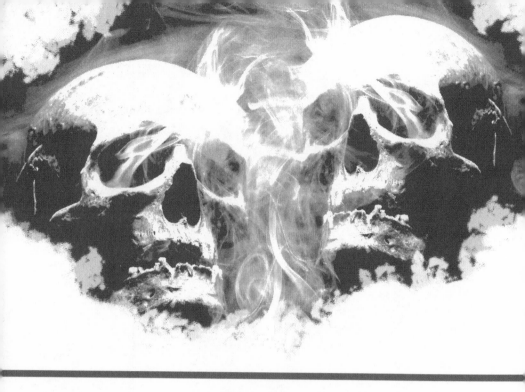

CHAPTER 2

Lost in the World

Before all of that could begin something had to end.

The love of my life, Paula, my wife of ten years, dropped dead one pretty May morning in 2004 after playing her weekly tennis match. She'd just come off the court after winning in three sets.

Paula always took Thursday mornings off from her veterinary practice to enjoy the game that she'd always loved. It was a deserved midweek ritual, since she worked six days a week, and more if necessary. There were plenty of Sundays when she'd be spending a lazy day poolside reading her romance novels, listening to her smooth jazz or fussing with the garden. And then she'd get a phone call.

"Dammit!" she'd say. "A beagle got clipped by a car. I gotta go to the hospital, Art."

And off she would go to try and save the poor thing. When she came home hours later, I had only to look at her expression to know how it went. A smile and gentle sigh suggested a good outcome. Silence and a stone face said otherwise. Paula brought her work home every night.

On that Thursday, she was in fine spirits and had left me a note suggesting I go fishing that afternoon since she'd be working late at her hospital (All Creatures Great and Small).

Arthur The Great,

Go catch some fish, preferably snook, of course. Bring one home to eat if you'd like. Be very nice to the rest. I should be back by 8:30.

Love,
Paula The Even Greater

Jan Casey, her tennis partner, said that they had been discussing the final rally for match point while making their way to a shaded table for ice teas and Cobb salads. Paula had been an exceptional tennis player since childhood. In high school she was on the way to a scholarship at some major school, but injuries to both knees had robbed her of that chance. Paula played on and learned to place returns with an almost supernatural sense to run the opponent ragged and make up for her own lack of mobility.

Jan was saying something like "Florida summer's here now, dear," and Paula gave her a startled look and gasped and just dropped, dropped like a stone to the court.

Paula fell so freely that her nose fractured on impact. She had died almost instantly, the result of a congenital heart defect waiting for its moment.

I identified her that afternoon — a horror that can't be erased.

A piece of flesh-colored bulbous playdough had replaced her petite, slightly upturned nose that fit with her blond-haired, blue-eyed elfin countenance. There were nasty bruises on her forehead, cheek and chin as well as crusts of dried blood in her nostrils. It was a nightmare of pale sunken stillness, especially in the eyes, deep sockets now that her blood had stopped keeping those baby-blues buoyant. She was cold and stiff to the touch.

I confirmed her identity, signed the paperwork, collected her clothes, and made some arrangements with a funeral home. After that I went home. It was dark by then.

I was greeted by our "family." The two dogs, Shamrock, a Heinz 57 that favored beagle, and Samantha, a shepherd-collie mix, led the charge with yips, figure eights, paws on legs and licking of hands. Wally, our brown-and-orange tabby, glided in as the dogs settled down then sat at the usual distance, about five feet, before batting his eyes and revving up the purring machine. He was named for a mythical alligator that supposedly lived in a pond by the golf course in the subdivision that Paula and I had called home back when we first met. We had gone on an expedition one night to find Wally but discovered a couple making love on the 7th green instead. It had all been part of our crazy teenage years.

I called Paula's older sister, Adrian, first because I knew that's what Paula would have wanted.

I got a glass of water, lit a cigarette, and punched in Adrian's number.

There was a gasp, silence, groaning and then a series of "Nos" that sounded like aural projectile vomiting.

"Adrian," I said after a while. "Adrian, I don't like telling you this anymore than you like hearing it. Please, please, I'm sorry."

The "No" chanting stopped.

"How?" Adrian asked. Her voice soft, even childlike.

I told her what had happened.

"Do my parents know?" I could hear a lighter being sparked and some shuffling.

"You were my first call," I said.

"Thank you for that."

"It was never in question."

"She was eating?" It had to be asked. Paula had problems with bulimia since adolescence. It became so severe in her late 20s that Paula was hospitalized for several weeks and ended up in a treatment center like the ones for drugs and alcohol.

"Yes."

"And?"

"There was none of that. She'd put on a couple pounds over the winter and described herself as a 'pleasantly plump 40-something sex kitten.' I didn't see any evidence of a relapse."

"Art, I gotta arrange some things with my secretary and a couple of colleagues, but by tomorrow afternoon I can be there," Adrian said with a sniffle. "I'll cross my fingers that the call to Sherm and Fran is not too...taxing."

The call to Sherm and Fran was ugly.

Frances screamed "Oh, my God!" several times and then started wailing like a banshee.

"Paula's dead! Sherman! Paula's dead!" she shouted.

There was a rustling noise, then a fumbling of the receiver.

"What the Hell happened?" Sherman said in a voice that sounded more angry than aggrieved.

I started to explain, but he kept interrupting with questions ("Why was she playing tennis on a Thursday morning? It's too hot to play this time of year, what was she thinking? Was there a medical professional on site?"), all framed in an accusatory tone, as if I or someone had done something wrong and now his daughter was gone as a result.

"This will kill her mother, Art, just kill her," he concluded.

All through Sherm's performance I could hear cries and wails in the background from Frances Howard. It was as if she was the chorus in a Greek tragedy.

I sparked my second cigarette of the call and told him what funeral home I picked. He didn't question it, didn't push back. There may have been fashionable funeral parlors around but who among us has them on speed dial?

"Well, keep your chin up," he said after I finished, and hung up.

"Fuck you," I said to the dial tone, once I was sure it was a dial tone.

In-laws!

I had one more family call to make. It was a much easier one.

My brother, Nick, and I had always been close. That was partly the result of our tyrant father but also because our mother raised us to be brothers, not siblings. She felt that there was a difference.

"Oh, no, Art, no," Nick said. "What happened?"

Nick and Paula were not birds of a feather. She was an extrovert, happy go lucky to the point of being corny at times. I found it endearing. Nick kept his thoughts to himself. It wasn't that he didn't like her. He did, probably as much as he could. My brother was a quiet, intense man with a sizable chip on his shoulder and a penchant for long chilly silences. Most people took this for anger and disapproval. Some of it was, but I knew better. Nick was the oldest son of Frank Jenkins and that was a chore on par with any labor Hercules ever tackled. Our father was a bear of a man — seriously, he was about as big as one — with an outsized personality to make up for a microscopic sense of self-esteem, a gift from his own father.

Frank Jenkins did everything he could whenever he could to pass that gift along to Nick. According to our father, there was nothing that my brother could do right. The rule applied to me as well, but my punishment was to be largely ignored.

But Nick Jenkins did just about everything right. He was cutting everybody's lawns in the neighborhood by age ten. Some weeks he made fifty dollars. Dad complained that it was way too much cash for a kid his age to handle. He was certain that Nick would only spend it foolishly on "baseball cards, comics and candy." The truth was much worse; Nick was smoking Lucky Strikes by age 11.

The bulk of Frank's bile involved football, the family's official religion, even though we occasionally went to church. Very occasionally.

Nick was a good athlete despite the nicotine habit, and as a junior, his gridiron star rose. But all Frank Jenkins did was talk about *his own football exploits* at a military school in Kentucky.

"I remember going up against a guy at end who had 40 pounds on me," Dad would proclaim after the game to all the tables around us at Bill Knapp's — the family's official spot for Friday dinners. "I kicked his country ass. Not a lot of passing in those days." Pointing a finger at Nick, who sat there stone-faced and glassy eyed in his purple-and-white letter jacket. "No, Sir-Ree-Bob! We ran the ball, Nicko, right down their redneck throats!"

Our father exorcised his demons on Nick, and me as well, until dementia robbed Frank of that fire, then death took him in the last December of the century. This left Nick with deep scars but also forged a steely resolve in him as well as a spirit to prove the son of a bitch wrong. He accomplished that with a string of successful restaurants, but the stress and rage took its toll. Nick had a bad heart attack (are there really any good ones?) in 1998 and made a whole bunch of life changes: no more 15 cups of coffee, no more late-night Grand Slams at Denny's after pulling a Friday night shift, no more operatic rages after Michigan coach Lloyd Carr ran the same play for the umpteenth time with the same mixed results or another putt ran way too wide of the mark. He learned to eat better. He exercised (speed bag was his favorite). He learned to laugh at himself, occasionally. But most importantly, he traded those smokes for gum, lots and lots of gum.

As a result, Nick began to resemble the fearsome end and hard-hitting safety of his high school football days. But the fire wasn't extinguished, just reduced to a steady flame, all one had to do was notice the passion with which he popped and cracked those many sticks of Juicy Fruit.

I explained the events to him. Nick lived in our hometown, Ann Arbor, Michigan. "I can get down there tomorrow afternoon," he said.

We said our good-byes and I hung up the phone. It was almost 10. I stared at Shammy and Sammy; both were lying in front of me with intent faces.

"Fuck guys," I said. "I forgot to take you out."

I gathered up the leashes, hooked up the dogs, turned on the backyard light and clicked through the screen door.

Standing there in the night, I felt a new and terrible form of loneliness come creeping toward me.

· · · · ·

Adrian was there by mid-morning. She had rented a blue SUV and arrived with two suitcases and a laptop as well as bringing a much-needed sense of solidarity.

"We'll get through this, Art," she said with a long hug. "We will, together."

Paula and Adrian had not been close growing up. In fact, they hated each other. The Howard home was, at arm's length and first glance, a palace of right-minded abundance. Their father, Sherman, was a Wall Street wheeler dealer who could always smell blood in the water and money to be made. Their mother, Frances, was a cold-hearted queen to her daughters demanding a certain look, a certain attitude, a certain polish and shine to match the beautiful furnishings and artwork that adorned the Howard home. It was the way things ought to be.

It led Adrian, tall, brunette, and awkward with a troubling secret inside, to rebel and go proto-Goth while exploring drugs and coming to terms with impulses inside her that she knew made her different, wrong, unwanted. At seventeen, she ran away to get lost on her way to being found.

Paula embraced the call to be The Golden Child. For a while, the tennis, the grades, the prom-queen-in-the-making look with the spot-on Palm Beach boyfriend in high school had both parents beaming. Then came the tennis injuries, the falling grades, the breakup with the heel boyfriend, the clay feet possessed by all of us.

Adrian despised Paula for playing the game and winning. Then a miracle occurred, not overnight, but over a long stretch of time.

Paula was bruised and broken, her romance crushed, her tennis dreams dashed, her favored-child status forever gone. She tracked down Adrian, who was working in a record shop in Fort Lauderdale and living with her first true love, a dark-featured beauty named Marjorie Haygood, who went by the name Naomi, just Naomi.

A reconciliation of sorts began over a series of lunches at Wolfies on U.S. 1 in the very heart of Liquordale.

The surprise of all surprises was Paula's acceptance of Adrian for who she was. That was the difference-maker Adrian would tell me years later. Paula even promised to "work on Mom and Dad," but Adrian begged her not to:

"It's not your battle."

"I want to help," Paula said. She was willing to earn her sister's alliance.

"You already have," Adrian said.

They did not become tight after that, but the hate was gone, and the sisters kept in touch. Adrian moved to Colorado about a year later with Naomi. I'd guess that would have been late 1977. By then Paula was plumbing the depths of her own darkness at the University of Florida in Gainesville, the only college left that would take her. It would be another dozen more years before each one could really be what the other needed. Adrian had her challenges, not the least of which were finding a career path — she manages a software firm now — and surviving a toxic staccato-like breakup with Naomi that took up most of early 1980s. In the same period, Paula would make another stab at being the Golden Child before crashing to earth in a disastrous marriage and eating disorder. I was grappling with my own demons as well.

Adrian Howard was 48 now and had aged well. She was a vegan before anybody knew what that meant. She practiced yoga when it wasn't cool. There were still a lot of cigarettes, but some habits are hard to break. Adrian was taller than Paula by nearly a half-foot and slim, with short cropped brown hair: a handsome woman who got hit on by men and women alike.

Adrian and I managed the arrangements while Nick took over

the domestic activities, arranging the gifts of food and keeping the house tidy.

The Howards showed up with enough chow for a softball team including an array of cold cuts, condiments, salads, plastic containers of conch chowder, as well as key lime and blueberry pie.

"This should help," Sherman declared. He had several opinions on the situation ("We've been dealt a bitter blow" — No shit!) that he thought everyone should know, and not just about his late daughter.

"It seems 43 has underestimated the Iraqis," he said. "That could cost him the election."

"I never bought the whole greeted as liberators thing," I said. "Those folks may take our help from time to time, but they hate us, and don't want us around."

"Ah, but if we don't fight them there then we'll fight them here. What does your friend Eddie think?"

"Oh, my, God," I said. "He doesn't know."

"How can that be?" Sherman said.

There were two reasonable explanations for why Eddie Fletcher didn't know.

The first is common to everyone who has ever experienced sudden loss; it confounds the mind. There is a shock like a blind-side hit on the football field. Then comes both grief and panic. "How do I handle this? What do I do next?" The thinking process begins to resemble a whirlpool. There is so much to do and, at least it seems, such a short time to do it all.

"Shit!" I said, "He should have been one of the first calls. I am such an asshole!" Then I beat my fists against my head.

Adrian was there in a moment. "Artie, it's OK. Look, it's not like he's, uh, accessible right now."

That was the second, and probably the real reason. Eddie was nowhere, and that was by his own choice.

Eddie Fletcher was my oldest friend and, after Paula, my best friend.

We had come together in August of 1970, each on the doorstep of teenaged wasteland. There was a common bond, the three of us were from somewhere else — Eddie and I were from Michigan, Paula was from Ohio — and now resided in Boca Raton, and because our parents had money no one was complaining. My dad had retired, but Eddie's and Paula's fathers were still working.

Eddie and I had a separate connection; our fathers had known each other for years. Frank Jenkins and Vince Fletcher had business dealings through the machine-tool industry. Eddie and I had met a couple of times as kids at Michigan football games or company picnics.

The three of us were the rarest of combinations: a tween triangle sans sex, but dripping with drama from time to time. Eddie showed off to Paula from the get-go. Despite braces, she was "hurt me" cute even then. Paula would flirt right back until he showed serious interest then she would gravitate to me. There were occasional wrestling matches between Eddie and me involving a hard foul in a game of one-on-one, or who was better on *Star Trek*, or a song or something. But it was about claiming Paula. She would always run off crying when we did it.

In college, Paula and Eddie had a one-night affair during their freshmen year. Eddie was at Florida State but came to Gainesville for the Gator Growl, a true bacchanal in those days when Florida was just a party school. They ran into each other at a bar, drunk and dealing with the anxiety of that first semester away from home.

We all ended up not speaking to each other for years, and Paula never mentioned that night again.

There were several times I figured that Paula was out of my life completely. I even wished for it once or twice. It never got that way with Eddie, but I was pissed at him for a good long time after the Gator Growl incident.

Despite the teenaged kerfuffles and years of icy silences, when Paula and I decided to marry, Eddie was my Best Man. Had we ever given kids a shot — we discussed it and decided animals were better — Eddie Fletcher would have been the godfather or executive parent as he'd have seen it.

Eddie came from a military background. Vince had served three years in the South Pacific in World War Two. His older brother, Donald, did two tours in Vietnam with the 82nd Airborne and put in 20 years before retiring as a colonel. Service was expected in the Fletcher Family. Eddie was ROTC at Florida State and went into military intelligence. During the 1980s his job was to keep an eye on "The Bear That Walks Like a Man."

But that's not where the threat developed. When Saddam Hussein invaded Kuwait, Captain Eddie Fletcher was on a transport within 24 hours as a company intelligence officer.

Eddie would escape without a scratch, having spent most of the time reading field reports, giving his analysis, and venturing out every now and then to see for himself. The shooting was all but over by the time he was rolling in a Humvee to a forward position. There would be no crowded hour for him, just a firsthand account of the ravages of war from the carnage on the battlefield to the wounds one couldn't see.

Eddie ended up debriefing a lot of soldiers to see how this army had performed. The first Gulf War had been a textbook victory, but some soldiers were suffering, nonetheless. Battlefield trauma, soon to be known as PTSD, was apparent in many interviews. It got Eddie in touch with his own childhood battle.

Vince Fletcher could be a great dad, but he was a strict disciplinarian who had a 19th century view of raising children. He slapped and punched and kicked Eddie and Donald sometimes for something as innocuous as not eating their broccoli.

Turns out that Vince had been part of a war crime at Okinawa. He and his destroyer crewmates had machine-gunned a group of Japanese floating helplessly on the surface after their submarine had been depth-charged into submission. Vince and company sang a racist chant while leveling their guns at the stunned submariners and turning the ocean red.

The boys only knew because they had spied on Vince and his war buddies drinking beers and telling war stories one night after the two boys were supposed to be in bed.

So when Eddie conducted those interviews from *his* war, he could suddenly understand his father's fits of rage. Eddie had his own struggles with rage, too: he'd fly off the handle, he'd stew, he'd snap. When Eddie was at FSU, for instance, he'd gotten suspended for a semester after beating the shit out of a graduate student for wearing a Mao cap. The pot boiled over again when Eddie listened to the stories of all those combat-weary soldiers. Eddie wanted to grab his AR and finish the job, killing every last Republican Guard, every last Saddam sympathizer and then turning the gun on himself. It didn't make sense, but then again, it did.

After wrestling with these impulses, Eddie had to go see the same doctors that he'd been recommending for some of his men.

He left active duty in 1992 and decided to become a lawyer to defend the laws of a land that he loved so dearly. He started at Florida State, then parlayed his veteran status to transfer to Michigan. He graduated in 1996 and started a career representing veterans and veteran organizations on health care issues.

There's nobody that I ever loved more than Paula. There's nobody that I ever respected more than Eddie.

When Eddie got married in 2001, I was his Best Man, and everything seemed fine. But when the towers fell in New York, he went back on active duty to coordinate logistics. He's always been tight-lipped about what he did in the Afghan war. It was too much for his wife, Donna, that's for sure. She divorced him in 2002 after Eddie came home from a year in service. He barely had time to restart his law practice when the Army came calling in the fall of 2003. They needed experienced intel officers to counter a rising insurgency in Iraq.

"The package was good," he told me at Christmas. "That's all I have to say."

He was gone after New Year's.

I sent a long, detailed email to Eddie's military address, but he was deployed, and who knew when he'd see it?

• • • • •

We had all agreed to cremation, but Frances wanted a chance to see her youngest daughter one more time. She wanted a viewing. I thought it was barbaric, even disrespectful. Adrian was with me on this, but she saw her mother's pain, the eyes cried red, the dark circles from restless nights, the slack face from defeat and a thin, monotone voice that suggested Frances was now as lifeless inside as her youngest daughter. Sherman was right, Paula's death was killing his wife. So, he supported the viewing, too.

Adrian went through Paula's cosmetics, picking the right hues. Paula had never worn a lot of makeup other than for special occasions. She didn't have a lot of jewelry either, which had to do with her first marriage. Her husband, the scion of a wealthy real estate magnate, had draped her in diamond earrings and broaches and necklaces and bracelets. But Paula figured it out in the end. In her first husband's eyes Paula was a possession that needed to be properly managed, and the shiny stuff was like an owner's tag.

She got all the bling in the divorce and sold every piece to fund her tuition at Florida's veterinary school. Some of the bling-money paid for our rent and food in that first year at Gainesville.

Adrian picked out a pair of topaz earrings that flashed traces of pink, Paula's favorite color. The necklace choice was simple because she only had one that would work. It was a silver pendant with three pink sapphires, which she called "Trinity." I'd used Jan to determine a good gift for our fifth anniversary. Paula had seen it at a local jewelry shop when accompanying Jan, who was getting a bracelet repaired, and she absolutely loved it. The piece was expensive, but Paula was priceless. Thank goodness, my one and only book made money.

"You, me, us," Paula had told me when I put it on her. "Can you see that?"

"I can, but you're going to have to take it off now," I said.

"Why?" She frowned.

"Because you're not going to be having any clothes on soon."

"Ohhhh, well, here, help me with the clasp."

I stared at the necklace in my hand while remembering that night.

"Art?" Adrian's voice yanked me from a far, far better place than here.

"Yeah?"

"How's this one?" she asked.

It was my favorite, a simple but elegant linen dress, knee length with a pleated taper for airy comfort in a Florida summer, cut to show her shoulders and upper back as well as offering more relief from the heat but modestly falling over her chest and giving room for Trinity as well. The color was a swirl of pinks and corals. She loved it and wore it as often as any special event allowed.

"There's a complication," Adrian said.

"Complication?"

"Mom says she has the perfect dress," Adrian said.

"It's not here so it can't be Paula's dress," I said with a snap.

"She was planning on giving it to her."

"Is it Frances's dress because…"

"…Mom bought it in Paris for Paula. She was waiting for the right moment."

"Jesus!"

"She's bringing it by tomorrow."

Frances and Sherman showed up around 11 in the morning. She held out the dress, a cool aqua that went to just above the ankles, sleeveless and likely clingy. "What do you think?" she asked. Paula was not a big fan of clingy. Her shoulders, back and neck were more covered, but not too much. It could have worked in the cooler winter months, which didn't matter because it wasn't Paula's dress. She had not picked it out and gone through the long and involved process of deciding, as women do with almost all clothes but especially the important ones, about whether it was for her. She had never *seen it*. She had never *worn it*. She knew nothing *about it*. It had no connection *to her*.

There was one thing I knew, it was expensive, probably as much as a decent used car, maybe more than that. Suddenly, I knew everything. There was more going on here — a statement by Frances and Sherman. A statement that their youngest had died young but died rich. My choice would have been too common, too bourgeois. It was bad enough that Paula was a career woman. It was bad enough she was the "pet doctor." That had not been their plan. She was supposed to marry into wealth no matter what number husband it was, but she chose an outdoor writer with no ambition to pursue lucre. Now they could dress her up like the rich girl she was, had always been, and don't you forget it!

"Who's the designer, Mom?" Adrian asked.

"It's a variation on Eileen Fischer's work that we found in a dress shop off Rue de Rivoli," Frances said. For the first time since Paula's death Francis was engaged. She even smiled.

"Don't you like it Art?" Frances asked.

"Art?" Adrian said. "It matches Paula's eyes."

"Kinda," I said. "I never saw bluer eyes than hers."

I got up and walked out to the pool deck. Sherman was on his cell talking to extended family, an uncle.

"Stay at the Marriot on the Island," he said. "See you soon."

Then he sat down beside me. "What did you think?"

"It's a nice dress."

"But it's not Paula's dress, in another month or so and it would have been."

"For what occasion?"

"Frances would have invented one." Sherman refreshed his cup of coffee and took a bite of bagel. Then he leaned toward me. "It's not a monstrosity, Arthur. Paula would have liked it."

I sighed like a tire deflating from a nail.

Sherman got closer to my face than he had ever been, then whispered in my ear:

"Frances looks and sounds better, but that's just medication, Arthur. She hasn't been well. You know that." Frances had been down in the dumps for a few years. She'd already weathered menopause. Paula thought it was age.

"She needs this, Arthur," Sherman said after a sip of coffee.

"Paula was her favorite. I don't like this viewing thing. It's from another time, not here, not now. Funerals are for the living. Let Paula wear the dress. Do it for Frances. She's always liked you, always. Please, Arthur." He was practically begging. Sherman Howard doesn't beg. No, his life objective was to make others beg.

My mother had suffered from terrible depression over the last decade of her life. The rise of her symptoms correlated with our arrival in Florida. Her problem became so bad after Nick had moved back to Michigan and gotten married, that my father feared she might kill herself. My dad was part of the cause for Mom's melancholy, but, to his credit, he tried to make things better — and with some success, too. Then cancer knocked on Mom's door and took it all away.

And Frances Howard had done as much as anyone to make my mother happy in the Florida years. She'd been a true friend to her.

"I'm OK with the dress," I said after some time. "I want Paula's necklace on her."

"Of course," said Sherman. "That was never in doubt."

It was settled. I would keep Paula's pink and coral dress for longer than I should have, longer than maybe was healthy, but that's the place I was headed.

Paula's visitation was set for one hour on Friday evening. The memorial was the next day. She was ready on Friday morning, but we waited till just before the scheduled time to see her.

As bereaved widower, something that just did not sound right at 46 years of age, I was given the first chance to go into the room and have a moment alone with my wife, my late wife.

Her display casket was silver and trimmed in garlands and sprays of white, blue and yellow flowers. There were other arrangements that had been sent to us over the 15 days since her death. The ones that were still fresh had been tastefully arranged around the bier. There was a dearth of pink, her signature color. I never got an explanation for that, but it fit with the theme of an unexplainable death. The funeral directors had done a magnificent job anyway, but I would not personally thank them for it.

I walked slowly, cautiously toward the bier. I could see the white satin lining in diamond crisscross design, the folded-back shroud, and then, Paula.

The restoration of her face was uncanny, high quality wax museum work, Tussaud's would be impressed, but there was still a lot of Paula there. It was not a good idea to dwell on how much. I crept close enough to see Trinity on her bosom. It fell just onto the gown and the color scheme of silver flash and shimmering pink on aqua cloth worked, but I got too close and saw the flaws. Her beauty had been painted on. She became less a person and more a product of Duvall's Mortuary Services. I got the hell away and retreated to the first row of chairs.

I prayed, first the Serenity Prayer, and then the Lord's Prayer. Despite four years in a pew while attending Boca Raton Episcopal High School that was all the liturgy I knew. It wasn't enough.

Then I remembered something that Paula used to give her clients after the death of a pet. It was an essay, almost a free form poem, called Rainbow Bridge. The thought was that all those dogs, cats, birds, horses and whatever went to a place of rolling meadows and friendly trees where, fully restored to their prime of health with limbs intact etc., they played together in bliss while waiting for the day when their humans came to claim them. In that moment, dogs would sharpen their ears, raise up their heads and run with tails wagging, cats would prance with feline grace and start the purring machines, birds would swoop and chirp before carefully landing on a kind shoulder, horses neighed and galloped to waiting strokes, and all the other creatures from boas to geckos did whatever the heck they do in such a moment.

The reunions were bathed in love and rejoicing, then human and animal went off to their slices of heaven together. I imagined that was where Paula would be now, playing with the animals, refereeing squabbles, if any even took place, and waiting for me, not as a pet but because she loved *them* so. She'd spend most of the time there with her own departed pets: Maggie, our first dog, a cocker spaniel, that we put down during the week of 9/11; Copper, a runt-of-the-litter cocker (Paula had loved cocker spaniels ever since seeing *Lady and the Tramp*) that lived her short life with us in the late '90s; and Mango-Jango, an orange cat who had passed from feline leukemia just last fall. Paula would tell each of them gently that "We'll stay here now until Art comes along, now go find your squeak or go get that ball. Let's have toss." She'd be happy in an old red "Boca Episcopal Girls Tennis" tee and a pair of pastel plaid Bermudas, her "knock-around-the-house" favorites, restored to whatever best self she chose. There would be some peace, and part of me wanted to be there now. That was unsettling.

I dropped out of the chair to my knees and implored God to put Paula in charge of Rainbow Bridge. The question of her command could be revisited when I showed up. Perhaps we could run the place as a team for eternity.

Then I ran for the door.

My expression must have been alarming because Frances and Sherman were on me in an instant with hugs and words of support. This was the first and only time that Sherman and I ever embraced. I was moved even though I would never forgive them for this circus.

After Paula's parents were finished, Adrian grasped me tightly for several seconds while stroking my back. Then she whispered in my ear a sentiment that was the only good thing that came out of this bad time.

"Love is doing the hard things," she said. "Love is doing the hard things."

Amen.

• • • • •

By noon the next day, my house was cleared, and Adrian was leaving before breakfast.

"Tell me that I won't lose you," she said in the driveway.

"You won't," I said. "You came here two weeks ago a sister-in-law, but you leave a sister."

Nick and his wife, Susan, were leaving mid-morning, and they asked about me coming up to Michigan as soon as I felt up to it.

"You need to get away from here," Nick said.

"Not yet, but yes, I do."

I spent the rest of Sunday robotically cleaning and organizing a house that had seen a whirlwind of traffic over the last two weeks. There was food that needed to be thrown out, bedding that needed washing, ashtrays to be cleaned, etc. The dogs had been angels. Wally, being a cat, went on as if nothing had changed.

By sundown everything had changed. Paula was everywhere and nowhere in the house. I sat and chain-smoked. Paula's death had ended four-plus years being cigarette-free. Then a thought popped into my mind.

I wanted a drink. I needed a drink. I've *earned* a drink.

I'd called my sponsor, Roger, a lanky, affable ex-Marine the day after the incident. We chatted a couple of times since, but the question of my sobriety had been put aside because Paula's death was too important. I made up excuses to miss my usual meetings. I'd lied about going to other meetings. I'd lied to other friends in recovery as well.

I did everything wrong. All that I'd been taught in recovery, all that I'd taught to others in recovery, faded in an instant.

I got this, I thought. But I didn't, and now the piper was playing in my head.

I got in my SUV and drove to ABC Liquors to buy a fifth of Jack Daniels and a carton of smokes, and when I got home, I got a tumbler out of the dishwasher and poured two fingers into it, then raised the glass.

I didn't know what to toast to.

Certainly not Paula, because she would not approve of this.

Certainly not life, because I didn't believe in it anymore anyway.

So I summoned the dark side of my Irish blood to find the right words.

"To the end," I said. "To the end."

Then I drank, remembering the warm bite, surprised that I didn't choke, and poured round two as the first glow spread through my body, three fingers this time and down the hatch they went, making me gasp at the end of the draw, spilling some and feeling the head rush.

The Jack Daniels bottleneck was clear now, and the bourbon was sloshing around in that block of glass below it.

I climbed down that bottleneck and splashed around in the brown water for the next five days.

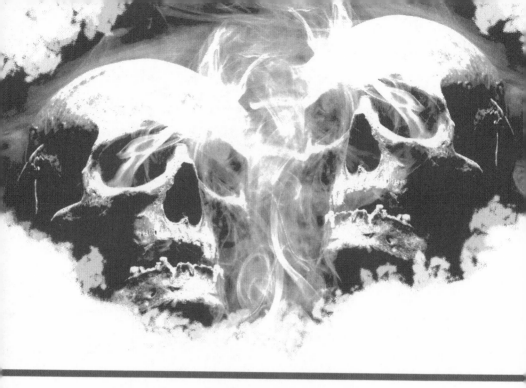

CHAPTER 3

The White Rose

"Hello, Mr. Jenkins, I'm Katherine LeClair." The tall, willowy woman entered the office where I was waiting. She closed the door and extended her hand.

"Hello, Doctor," I said shaking that hand.

"You can call me Kate," she said with a pleasant smile and an accent that suggested Britain. Her doctor "uniform" was a white blouse and a navy-blue skirt: professional but not stiff.

"Are you from the U.K.?" I asked.

"Scotland," she said, as she sat down behind her desk. "Kincardine, Fife, a little town near Edinburgh."

"Oh, Canada has a Kincardine."

"Those Canadians," she said with twinkle in her brown eyes, "always stealin' things. Oy."

"I once got in a fight with a Canadian." The boy inside me wanted to show off to this pretty woman.

"Didja' win?" She tilted her head and raised an eyebrow with playful curiosity.

"It got stopped before I could. The guy got a hand free in the struggle and was about to roundhouse me then my brother stepped in."

"Stepped in?" she said while putting on her glasses. Tortoiseshells.

"Yeah, he put his foot on the guy's hand."

"Well," Kate shrugged, "what are brothers for anyway."

She went about organizing some papers. I looked at her degrees on the wall: BA from Kenyon, MA from Cincinnati (psychology), PhD from Ohio State (clinical psychology). There were also three certifications in addiction counseling and chemical dependency training. Kate LeClair from Kincardine, Fife, wasn't just another pretty face.

"Ya' looking at the artwork?" she said.

"You have credentials. How come all in Ohio?"

"My father taught at the University of Edinburgh, 19th century romantic and Victorian literature. He took a sabbatical to the University of Dayton in Ohio back in the 1980s."

"Why there?"

"Dunno to this day." She raised her hands in mock surprise, then gave me a sly grin, "Coulda' been the weather? If so, he got that a bit wrong."

Kate LeClair went on to explain that the family enjoyed their year in Ohio, and her father, Daniel, made a big enough impression that the nearby University of Cincinnati offered him a position. So, at 14, Kate had to fully adjust to life in America.

"I had to learn to talk like I was from Ah-Hi-Ah," she said in the perfect flat nasal sound of the Midwest, "or else get teased, and I got a good share of that fer being so tall."

"That's very good, but I like your regular accent better."

"Meh, tew," she said with some exaggeration, then laughed. "Let's get to it now, shall we?"

I liked Kate LeClair immediately. She had both a friendly manner and a kind face. It was round and creamy with some freckles on her cheeks and nose, accented by the sun, which she otherwise must keep at bay given her ultra-fair complexion. Her lips were thin, almost invisible, and her teeth were straight but a bit gappy. It was easy to see because she laughed a lot. Her hair was a shiny shade of auburn, tied off in the back to keep the neck and shoulders cool in the steam bath that was Floridian May.

It was Kate's eyes that made her so disarming. I've always found brown eyes to be warm, but hers radiated hyper awareness as well.

My feelings for her were enhanced by the fact that Kate had been the first person in my eight days at the Whispering Palms Detox Unit to have treated me as a person and not damaged goods.

"I have read your intake," she said while glancing at a sheet of paper, "and apologize for not getting to you sooner, but I was out of town. How are ya feeling?"

"Much better in the last three days. Thank God it was only a five-day bender."

"Really, the notes on the intake say you were coherent with a BAL below legal intoxication, .02."

"I think that I sweated it out the night before."

"How so?" she asked.

"I had been drinking since about noon and listening to music. After dark there was a full moon. I went out to sing a Neil Young song to it and left the door open. Our cat, Wally, ran out and I closed the door to prevent the dogs from doing the same and went looking for him."

"Did you find him?"

"Yes, about two hours later. He was lying in the street dead. A car hit him."

"Oh, no."

"I buried him the backyard. Then I went in and poured the

rest of my supply down the drain, then washed out the bottles. At eight the next morning I called Roger, my sponsor, and asked for ride here."

"What about your dogs?"

"I had them boarded at my wife's hospital."

"She's a vet."

"She was a vet." I explained what had happened.

"I'm sorry to hear that, Arthur." Kate looked at me for a long time before writing down some notes. "Take me through your relapse."

"There's never a reason for alcoholics to drink," Kate said when I finished, "but any reason will do if they forget who they are."

"I fucked up."

"I understand that feeling," she said carefully, "but it's time for some perspective. You're in grief and shame right now. What I want to do is look at why you chose not to get to meetings, be honest with your sponsor and work the program that had been working very well for 20 years. I think there were things going on before your wife's death. They were waiting, perhaps growing."

"Do you think I need long term?"

She made a face while considering my question. "I'm not sure. Your empty house is a trigger."

"I hate that house now."

"I think you hate what happened."

"I don't want to stay here any longer than necessary."

"You've been in detox probably two or three days longer than necessary and you didn't leave. Why?"

"They offered a chance for a clinical assessment, so I stayed until you were available."

"Tell me about you and Paula."

I told her about how I met Paula at Royal Palms in Boca when we were both 12 years old, our high school years, the tumultuous college years, her ill-fated first marriage, her divorce and eating disorder, the rejuvenation of our friendship, a night at the Howard's seawall when we realized our feelings for each other and the sprinkler system interrupting our first kiss, the Gainesville years, our marriage, the return to Stuart and the happiness of that time.

At the end Kate gave me a soft smile before writing on her notepad.

"I don't mean to be flip, Arthur," she finally said after a sigh, "but it's storybook in a sense, very touching, and I understand you so much better now."

"Paula and I joked that it could have the title 'Splendor in the Sprinklers,' like the film with Natalie Wood and Warren Beatty."

"Oh, I've seen it," she gave me a stone-faced look, "a powerful one that is." Then she softened her gaze while bobbing her head slightly. "You should be grateful for what the two of you shared."

"There's gratitude tangled up somewhere in all the anger."

"That's not necessarily a bad thing. You *should* be angry. Now let's get to work. You want to leave here then show me that you're serious about staying sober. What's going on beyond losing Paula? The more that we can find out here right now, the better prepared you'll be out there."

"A problem shared is a problem cut in half."

"Yes, I know the term. Do you need time to think?"

I didn't because at least two issues were always hovering in my mind. The first one was the decline of Florida with an accent on the environmental problems to be sure but the whole state had been going to Hell for a long time. I ranted about it for fifteen minutes.

Kate checked my intake form on her desk. "That makes sense. You are an outdoor writer. How long?"

"Almost nine years. I loved it here for years but now, Florida has become a poisoned land filled with poisonous people."

"And how did your wife feel about it?"

"She noticed it, but it didn't seem to bother her, not like it did me."

"Did you talk about it?"

"Not much."

"Why?"

"It was like the hum of the refrigerator. Sometimes you don't hear it when something else is going on or it turns off for a while."

"Now it's all you hear?" she asked.

"It's come to the forefront."

"OK, what else?" Kate LeClair was making furious notes.

It was a related issue. I'd written a book entitled *The Outgoing Tide: How we are losing Florida's wild places and what we can do to stop it*. It won awards. It made a reasonable amount of money. But I felt that it should have kickstarted some effort to stop the destruction. That was undermined by attacks from the business community and the "right side of the aisle." I could weather the old trope that environmental reform could be bad for business and cost some jobs because there were a few grains of truth in it. My work had always endeavored to find a middle way, but that wasn't good enough for some. I was branded a tree-hugging, Godless environmentalist and un-American to boot. That stalled out any action.

"So your book didn't change anything. What about the magazine that you work for?"

"The book landed me that gig. I'm a field editor, mostly on conservation issues, but I still write a lot of how-to-fish pieces. I can practically do it in my sleep."

"Do they know about this?"

"On leave because of Paula, not sure about going back."

"Why?"

"Bored and frustrated, have been for a while."

"Did you talk about this with Paula?"

"No, not really."

"Why not? Was she supportive of your work?"

"Yes," I said, then paused to find the right words. "Paula didn't like all the threats to the land and water, but, especially, the wildlife."

"That makes sense given what I now know about her. What did she think of your book?"

"She liked it, but…she never read it," I said, hating the words as they came out of my mouth.

"She never read it! Did she read the other articles? Any of them?"

"No," I could feel a bubble or two of rage boiling up. "No, but she *liked* them. She *thought* they were good."

"Was there ever any contention between the two of you about this?"

"No, she told everybody all the time how great a writer I was and how proud of me she was, but…"

"She never read a word."

"She heard some of them. Quite a lot of my articles. I'd read them out loud to see how they sounded and catch typos."

"I did that with term papers. It's a good trick. So, she was exposed to the work and…"

"She liked it. She always liked it, nothing more, nothing less."

"Did you argue about anything?"

I stopped to think, mostly to process a safe response. I didn't want marriage counseling with a dead wife.

"Oh, the usual things," I finally said.

"So here we go, huh, Arthur?"

"Whaddya' mean?"

"Blown' smoke up meh arse."

Silence, staring eye to eye.

We waited to see who'd blink first.

I did.

"Blown' smoke up meh arse. That must some new therapeutic lingo."

"Older than the hills," Kate gave a slight grin. "Come on, I'm trying to save your life."

"I thought that I was supposed to do that?"

"Helpin', OK. Beyond finances, house chores and sex, did you argue about anything, particularly these things because they were clearly botherin' yew." The more Kate became animated the more her Scot came out.

"We didn't argue much about anything, ever."

"So ya kept it all inside."

"Yup."

"Why?"

"Partly because none of it ever was that big a deal. I mean, yes, she wanted to go out with other couples on the weekends and have dinner parties or brunch by our poolside, and, and…"

"You wanted some peace and quiet, or to go fishing."

"Some of it was fine, but there was too much."

"And you didn't dare push it?"

"It didn't seem worth it to rock the boat."

"Why?"

"Not worth the trouble."

"Why?"

"I don't know. It was, we were, why upset things?"

"Why? Come on, ya know, say it."

Bubble, Bubble, Bubble.

"BECAUSE I DIDN'T WANT TO LOSE HER!"

After a very long time Kate finally spoke:

"She loved you. Would that ever happen?"

"I always worried that it might. I was always concerned that she'd wake up someday and tell me it was over, that she'd realized that she could do better."

"Were there ever any signs of infidelity?"

"No, she was pretty straightlaced. I think Paula would have just separated or divorced me rather than run around."

"So, you never felt good enough?"

"Sometimes."

"Is there anything else?"

"That's enough."

She frantically jotted down more notes. I started shuffling my feet and added a couple of sighs.

"You know your issues now. We can talk about them more if you wish, but I think your sponsor and the Steps will be the best remedy."

"That's surprising coming from a PhD in clinical psych."

"New breed," she said, then took a deep breath. "Hmmm, Arthur, do you think that you deserve a life?"

"I wouldn't be here if I didn't."

Kate nodded approval and her glasses slid halfway down her nose. "Do you deserve to be happy?"

"Not sure about that yet. But again, I haven't stormed out of the room."

"Oh, a half-hour or so ago Ida' let yew. But now I'd hafta' knock ya down."

"Medical malpractice. I'll be rolling in dough."

"Not a chance boyo. I'll charm the jury. Now seriously, how much do I have to worry about you going back out?"

I was enjoying some of this exchange. Kate LeClair was a different type of shrink using both honey and vinegar to effect. There was something else as well. She was a bit too playful, even flirty at times. In any other circumstance that would be fine, but I was not going to fall for my therapist. There were enough issues in my life without adding a cliché to the pile.

"How many meetings a day? With signatures of confirmation I'd imagine," I finally said. "Do you want me to piss in a cup every day as well?"

That creamy freckled face tightened, and those friendly brown eyes became sharp.

"How many would you like?" she asked in a loud voice, "because it really doesn't matter. There's nothing legally binding here. Your employer didn't send you here. Once you leave you can do what you bloody well please and there's not a damn thing I can do about it!"

This stunned me. She could go from warm to cold in a beat. What's more, Kate LeClair clearly cared. I wasn't just a client, or maybe she feels this way about all of them. Either way, it was powerful.

"I wouldn't do that to you!" I said matching her volume and regretting the words immediately.

I think this stunned her as well. Kate became quiet, pensive, then jotted more notes on that pad.

"Don't do it to *you*, Arthur Jenkins. Where would you go? Not that house, I hope."

"I'd visit my brother in Michigan."

"I'd want updates via email. Two meetings a day, honor system. Are you an honorable man, Arthur Jenkins?"

"I don't think anybody ever asked me that."

"Indeed, but do ya think you've passed some type of test?"

"No, I'm still talking the exam."

"You are, and you will be."

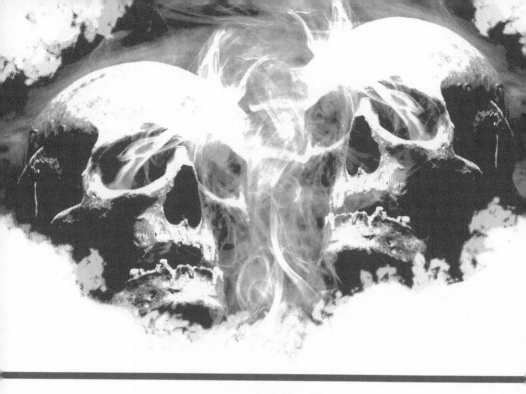

CHAPTER 4

A Sea of Maize

Our home in Florida was a $700,000 house, with a pool, hot tub, all the latest appliances, central air, solar panels, three bedrooms, four bathrooms, two sunken marble tubs, three car garage, beautiful screened patio, three majestic live oaks in the front yard with two matching gumbos in the backyard, three different types of citrus trees (orange, lemon, key lime) and a lush garden of native plants that attracted scores of butterflies year round.

Four months gone from that life. I found myself in an almost sixty-year-old split-log cabin: one bedroom; one bathroom with shower; no AC; fireplace with an occasional bat; propane heat as a backup; no dish washing machine; no washer/dryer; mouse infested if the dogs aren't quick on their paws. All surrounded by miles and miles of southern Michigan corn.

It turned out that this arrangement wasn't all that bad. And there was hope it might get better.

My journey to The Corn Palace started when Nick suggested after two weeks of staying at his house that I rent a place in the country to get some peace and quiet. It was a mutual thing. He already had enough commotion with his two teenagers: Bart, stir-crazy in his summer between high school and college; and, Katrina, now 13 and featuring a new crisis each day. A grieving little brother with two friendly but rambunctious dogs had Nick Jenkins chewing cartons of Juicy Fruit and muttering profanity pretty much nonstop — another Jenkins trait.

"An old friend of mine has a place near Chelsea," he said one morning. "It's farm country, but he has several lakes stocked with fish, bass mostly, and you'd have access as part of the deal."

I met Nick's friend, Cameron Krenshaw, at his place in the farmlands west of Ann Arbor.

"Arthur Jenkins, welcome," he said, "Call me Cam."

Cam was a big, square-headed, broad-shouldered man in his early sixties. He was wearing blue jeans and matching work shirt. His skin was dark brown from the sun and wrinkled. Cam's nose was bent, there was a scar on his right cheek, one incisor was missing, his jawline was strong, and he had light green eyes. He was a fourth-generation farmer whose family had settled near Chelsea, Michigan, in the 1880s. They owned a sizable amount of farmland in scattered parcels that ran from just west of Ann Arbor to almost the city limits of Jackson. There was a clan of Krenshaws who'd homesteaded where they could and consolidated what they could. Ultimately, the family broke into specialties. If it grew, clucked, oinked, or mooed, a Krenshaw likely raised it around here.

"Hello, Cam," I said and extended my hand.

He smiled then turned toward the house. "Hey, Kody! Come out here!"

In a moment, a young man, probably late teens, came running

around the side of the house. He was a smaller, wiry version of Cam.

"Yes, Dad?" the young man said.

"This is Arthur Jenkins. He might be renting the Mother-In-Law."

"Yes, sir," Kody said, "Nice meeting you, Mr. Jenkins."

The place in question was a piece of Krenshaw family history; Uncle Eb's Mother-In-Law cabin. The story goes that Ebenezer Krenshaw came home from World War Two, married his sweetheart, Denise Slocum, and built the cabin in one summer while tenting next to the dwelling in progress with his new bride. In time, Eb and Denise moved into the main house, but so did Denise's recently widowed mother, Dorcas, who gave meaning to the term "Battleax." Eb suggested that Dorcas move into the cabin for some privacy.

The plan worked and Dorcas lived there for almost 20 years until her death in 1980. Since then, the "Mother-In-Law" cabin has served as a guest house for many Krenshaw visitors, especially malcontents, as well as a trysting hideaway for at least one family member.

Now Cam rented it out on occasion.

"Mostly to deer hunters. I might put it on the market next spring, but it's smack dab in the middle of my land," he said. "Let's take your truck."

We traveled down a potholed asphalt road that split two massive fields of Krenshaw corn. There was a small colony of birches that marked the turnoff into the Mother-In-Law's driveway. Old Uncle Eb Krenshaw's cabin was nestled in a modest valley and surrounded by mature oaks and maples which created a canopy of sorts and shaded the area for much of the day. That dirt road meandered around for about 100 yards before ending in front of another giant cornfield — the Mother-In-Law's front yard. The house and its stands of trees were an island in a sea of maize.

The cabin was in very fine shape, given that it was born when Give 'Em Hell Harry was stopping every buck passed his way.

It had a small porch out front that had a bench swing set up and in good working order.

The inside had recently been redone with oak panels. It was not much bigger than our old living room. There was a couch, coffee table, big boxy television, small dinner table set to the side, kitchen with stove and refrigerator, and that bedroom. There were two pictures on the walls: one was of a man reading by a fireplace with a spaniel sleeping by his feet, the other was of a meadow alive with wildflowers on a mid-summer day. There was a touch of a musty smell with the hint of ancient smoke.

"Nobody's been here since New Year's," Cam said, "but we cleaned it up and aired it out a bit. Your dogs might catch a mouse if they are quick. That's good eatin'."

He shot me an impish grin, which contrasted with his hulkish frame. He motioned to a door between the kitchen and living room. It opened to a back porch with freshly cured concrete. There were about a dozen bird feeders with black-capped chickadees, golden finches and a couple of mourning doves flittering about just on the edge of the tree line. A downy woodpecker swung on a suet cage hung from one platform tapping at a brick of fatty, nutty goodness.

"The cardinals must be taking a break. We get all kinds of birds, don't be surprised to see some pheasants at dusk or dawn. There's a sack of feed in the closet by the front bathroom. You like birds?"

"Love 'em."

"Well, then you can sit here and watch 'em all day long."

I did just that for most of June and July with some nightly trips to one of seven farm ponds in the Krenshaw Empire of Maize. The fishing was good, plenty of bluegills and some fine largemouth bass. I brought dozens of bluegill fillets to Cam and there were fish fries and cookouts.

I was trying to keep things moving along, and let time heal all wounds. The dogs were a big help. Sam and Sham settled into changing locales easily, probably because I knew how to handle them when traveling.

"Stick close to your pets in new locations," Paula always told clients. "It's very hard on them, but if they trust you and you remain attentive to them it will be OK."

I wasn't OK but wasn't drinking either. There was a recovery clubhouse in Ann Arbor and some meetings in Chelsea. I made at least two each day and sent Kate weekly emails.

"Keep up the good work young man," she usually wrote back. "When are you coming back?"

That was a good question because the longer I was here the less I wanted to go back. It was nice to see Nick — we always had at least one lunch each week at his restaurant, *Baron von Pizza*. It was nice to make friends with the Krenshaws. It was nice to walk the dogs along the edges of the cornfields, to watch them scouting the birds, and running those same edges each morning. I had returned to my roots and started to feel all the possibilities. I'd left here at age twelve and never really returned to see it — but now I had and liked the lay of the land.

There were still a lot of dark moments lying on the couch or in bed late at night with the dogs snoozing away.

What am I going to do now? I pondered that thought and prayed for insight.

I didn't want to go back for any longer than it took to pack up my things and find a realtor. By early August I asked Cam just how serious he was about selling the place. He said to give him a few days. He came back with a number. I consulted with Nick.

"Offer him cash," Nick said. "Farmers love cash."

"Everybody loves cash," I said.

"Do it." Nick saw the writing on Florida's wall long before I did, and he was calling me back home.

I did it. Paula's life insurance helped, as did selling her part of the business to Dr. Irene Bennet, her partner at All Creatures. I instructed Ambrose, my realtor, to price the house to sell. It did in a fortnight. While Kody stayed at the Mother-In-Law to take care of the dogs, I hopped on a jet to take care of loose ends.

• • • • •

Letting go of my Florida house was easy. I didn't even stay there, choosing that Marriot on Hutchinson's Island instead. Still, there were some very difficult tasks to navigate.

Irene Bennett had a sister, Imogene, who had a consignment shop in Lake Worth. After talking with Irene, Jan and Adrian, I decided to sell Paula's clothes and most of her jewelry and give my cut of the proceeds to the expansion of the pet hospital's boarding facilities — known as the Bark Park and Paw Palace. These services at All Creatures were designed to create pleasant surroundings for the animals, in line with Paula's philosophy that dogs and cats, all pets, in fact, were sentient beings and not just accessories. This would be a practical tribute to her and also make some amends to Wally.

The important jewelry items, Trinity, those earrings she wore at the viewing as well as a pendant fashioned from her engagement ring and wedding ring were in a safety deposit box. Paula's pink and coral dress was also kept. I could not bear having anyone else ever wear it.

The second chore involved Kate LeClair. She was not happy with my actions and met me with an icy stare. Kate had cut her auburn hair to just below the ears. It made her look strikingly younger, like a college girl.

"Too bloody hot fer long hair," she said. "You look like you lost weight?"

"I started running again in Michigan."

"Are you gonna run away, Arthur Jenkins?"

I shuffled in my chair. "What do you think?" I asked.

"I'm asking yew."

"You said the house was a trigger, and you know my feelings about the damn state."

She stared at me with a flat expression. "You got it all figured out now, right?"

"You know better than that."

"Indeed." She wrote on her pad for a very long time, then looked up, adjusted her glasses, and cleared her throat. It made me feel like a defendant about to hear the judge pass sentence. "You know about geographic cure?" she asked.

"Familiar with the concept, but I think that this is the right plan."

"Do ya now?" She asked coolly. "All the expert now with your, what 90 days of sobriety? What do they call that? Ninety Day Wonders?"

"How did I piss you off?"

She put down her pen and scratched her chin. "You didn't. I don't want to lose you in a flight to greener grass because grass never stays green forever. Getting away for a spell was good. You made the best of it. Now you, we, must come up with the right course forward. The grief is still there. Ya know it is." The Scot in Kate bounced in and out of her voice.

"It didn't leave, but keeping busy helped, and it's a fresh start."

"Trew. Keeping busy treats the symptoms but not the disease. Time is a good medicine. Your meetings, sponsor and program are good medicines, tew. But let this period of intense emotion settle before making this big a decision. Don't think that the decision cures you, Arthur, slow down, young man." She stood up, put her hands on the desk and leaned over toward me. "I'm on your side, but I'm gonna speak my mind with no coat of sugar."

I suppressed a laugh.

"What's so funny?" Kate's expression suggested that she might punch me.

"Sugar coating, it's sugar coating."

I thought that Kate might tell me to get the fuck out of her office, but she got it and smirked.

"Aye, you Yanks have a different phrase for everything."

The tension between us went down a couple of notches.

"I imagine that Whispering Palms will not allow you to counsel a client from 1300 miles away," I said.

"I can recommend somebody," Kate said sounding conciliatory. Then she looked down at her desk while her hands shuffled my paperwork. "A woman from my class at Ohio State. She's working at a facility in Brighton, big treatment center."

"I know the place. Thanks."

"Let me show you something, Arthur Jenkins," Kate said softly. "Just to make my point." She held out a brochure for Whispering Palms and flipped to a page featuring a half-dozen smiling clients. All, according to the copy below the picture, "had been relieved of the bondage of self."

Kate tapped one person, "Relapsed, in treatment now," she said, then pointed to another, "Relapsed, still out there," then another, "Doing time in county jail for third DUI," and finally, one more, "Blew her brains out two weeks ago."

"You're not gonna lose me, Kate."

"Better keep that promise, Arthur Jenkins, or there'll be Hell to pay."

The final task was the toughest one. The night before leaving, I drove out to the House of Refuge on Hutchinson's Island to scatter some of Paula's ashes. The rest would return with me to Michigan.

The old sanctuary for shipwrecked sailors had seen 120-plus years of storms. The rock formations out front of its beach had stemmed erosion. Sensible building codes — I had helped champion those regulations — had prevented the House from being torn down for a fancy beach home. It was the rare instance of Florida honoring its heritage. The House of Refuge endured while much of the rest of the state fell to the wayside for strip malls, theme parks and community developments.

This was a special place for me.

It was here that I walked the beach until dawn in May of 1991 after the sprinklers had dampened my first kiss with Paula. There was another woman in my life at that moment, but by dawn I *wanted* a future with Paula. In December of 1993, I proposed to her on the beach by the rocks with the House of Refuge above us.

"It was that turtle that convinced you to give me a chance," Paula said after she'd said "Yes," and we'd embraced as the surf curled in our toes. I'd told her about walking the beach that night and seeing a giant Loggerhead laying her eggs. It had always been her favorite part of the tale.

"Well, she was on your side," I said.

"Knew it!" She danced around in her crazy little happy twirl. Most folk would have found it geeky or weird, but I adored it. "Animals like me."

"They're not the only ones." I suggested that we make love right there.

Paula liked sand in her toes, but nowhere else. Her choice was comfortable, bold, and familiar.

"How about IRP golf course?"

"What if we get caught?"

"I'll show 'em the ring?" She flashed the engagement ring, which she loved so much it would become her wedding ring with a bigger diamond. This diamond would be set in that pendant.

"Come on," she said and tugged on the beltline of my trousers. "You know people do it."

"Yeah, but we interrupted them."

"We'll be fine. Besides, we're much better looking naked than they were."

We parked in one of the condo parking lots and snuck onto the course.

"We have to be quiet," I said.

"No, we don't," she answered in a very sexy voice. "It's Christmas and time to open some presents."

Uninterrupted, we decked the halls, or at least the blue tee box at Hole 7.

I thought about that and many other events, from the first time I met Paula, in braces and pink braids, to the note on the table that morning last May.

It left me drained.

I opened the bag and sprinkled the powdery ashes until every grain was gone, mixed into the sand and sea by a light offshore wind.

There was a desire for dramatic moment. In my mind there was Paula walking the shoreline, in lasting glory, and surrounded by wags, purrs and chirps. It was a perfect vision except for one thing…she was wearing that damn aqua dress.

But the beach was empty. That was OK because now the path was clear.

My Florida Years were almost finished, but the tide was still going out.

· · · · ·

After a fitful sleep I turned in my rental at Palm Beach International Airport at six a.m. and settled into a four hour wait before boarding. In an airport shop I saw the headlines across every newspaper:

Michigan State Police Believe They Have Notorious Bigfoot Killer in Custody

The Bigfoot Killer was so named because he moved through the state leaving a trail of bodies and vanished people with few clues other than an occasional footprint, usually in size 15. He was even more ephemeral than the legendary ape man. There were never witnesses, never any unidentified person talking to the deceased or missing near the time of the event. It smacked of the supernatural. The Bigfoot Killer was believed to be responsible for up to 29 unsolved murders and disappearances starting in 1979 through at least 1999. He was Michigan's version of the Bogeyman.

The suspect in custody, Carl Lee Tobias, fit the bill of a serial killer. In fact, he could have come directly from central casting. A little rat of a man, Tobias, 46, a native of Hastings, Michigan, was about five and a half feet tall and 140 pounds. He had long, stringy hair, a receding hairline, bug eyes, bent nose, weak chin, bad teeth and a surprisingly large shoe size for a pipsqueak. The suspected slayer had been a part-time fishing guide, outfitter, construction worker and convenience store clerk.

Technology had caught up to BFK on August 5, 2004. A tourist trying out a new digital camera caught Carl talking to Cora Lynn Jepsen at Ferry Beach in Charlevoix. Jepsen, 17, went missing the next day. Her body was found near the Jordan River three days later.

Cora Lynn would have started her senior year at Traverse City Central the week the case broke nationwide. She was blond, pretty, popular, a cheerleader, and hoped to go to Michigan State University to study biology.

A statewide manhunt went into gear. A picture of Cora Lynn was everywhere from telephone poles to websites with these questions: Did you see this woman on August 5th and if you did, then where and with who?

Che Foster, a 35-year-old office manager from suburban Detroit, did see Cora Lynn. He focused on her with his new digital camera because she was so very pretty in her blue shorts and white halter. The man she was talking to was incidental, but he got caught in the frame, too. Foster turned the data card over to police on the 9th.

The pictures appeared on every news station and digital news platform in Michigan and the adjoining states of Wisconsin, Indiana, and Ohio. Blowups of the man talking to Jepsen were on front pages everywhere.

And a whole bunch of people knew who the man was. The Charlevoix County Sheriff had 50 calls by the end of the first day. All but 12 of them identified Tobias, who was living in East Jordan, but working part-time on a commercial fishing boat running out of Charlevoix.

Carl Lee Tobias had some type of attraction that helped him lure a beautiful young woman — who should have known better

— to go somewhere with him. It turns out that it was drugs, ecstasy at a good price. Jepsen was with some friends and there were plans for a shoreline bonfire on Lake Charlevoix that night. Carl said the drugs were in his Jeep. They needed to drive a short distance away just to make the deal out of the sight of prying eyes. Once parked, he had chloroform ready and quickly overpowered Jepsen.

Police arrested Tobias at his apartment in East Jordan on August 12th and found the chloroform, a hammer and Jepsen's underwear. The Michigan State Police Forensics Lab matched traces of blood and DNA matter to Jepsen. In addition, five witnesses, three fly fishers and a couple hiking, recalled seeing Tobias's yellow Jeep near where the girl's body was found. They were able to identify the vehicle in part because it had a Montana license plate on the front bumper.

Michigan State Police Detective, Stosch Wynarski, laid out the evidence to Tobias on the 19th.

"We got you, Carl," Wynarski said.

"Oh, I don't think you know just how big a fish you have in your net, detective," Tobias said, then smiled through those brown teeth.

After arranging to get some chewing tobacco and several McDonald's cheeseburgers with fries and shakes, Tobias told his tale of terror. It took two eight-hour sessions. Between cheeseburgers with breaks for chew, Tobias confessed to eleven other killings going back to 1979. They were all young women between the ages of 15 and 20, mostly with blond or light brown hair, petite, pretty and very naïve. Five had been cheerleaders, one had done some modeling. Because the killings stretched back over two decades, DNA and blood analyses were not always reliable, but Carl gave details that only the killer would know. Nine of the bodies had already been found. He gave locations for the other two. Searches would turn up skulls and dental records provided IDs.

"It was ghoulish," one officer said, "and he seemed to enjoy it."

I devoured the information on the case while white-knuckling my way across the friendly skies to Metro Airport in Detroit then riding back to Chelsea for a reunion with my dogs.

"Glad you're home, Mr. Jenkins," Kody said. "The dogs were great. Crazy thing about Bigfoot, huh?"

"America loves a serial killing," I said. After unpacking and a quick microwave meal of meatloaf, I turned on a cable news station to watch a replay of the press conference by the Michigan State Police at the courthouse steps in Charlevoix.

"We believe that we've solved the Bigfoot Killer murders," Assistant Chief of Detectives for the Michigan State Police, Darwin Moon, said. "It's likely that not all the murders attributed to Bigfoot were done by his hand, but Carl Lee Tobias is responsible for the bulk of these unsolved crimes."

"Is there any evidence that he was involved in the missing trout fishermen's case?" one reporter asked.

"No," Moon said, "he has an alibi for that one."

It was a rock-solid alibi. Tobias was in Montana from 1983 to 1986, working for Big Sky Outfitters in Bozeman. On both April 29th and 30th of 1984 he was working an eight-hour shift in the main shop. There were a half-dozen witnesses as well as employment records to support this claim.

Moon indicated that the Montana State Police wanted to question Tobias about three murders of young women in their state during this time. He vehemently denied their charges, perhaps because Montana had a death penalty.

The media frenzy lasted all week since true crime was drawing more eyeballs than the lack of proper armor for Humvees in Iraq or the continuing drop in math and reading scores for middle schoolers. It included a familiar face. A writer that I'd known of for twenty years.

Asa Fountain was a freelance writer who had cut his teeth on grassroots Michigan history such as the sinking of the Carl D. Bradley, the fire of 1911 that destroyed Oscoda/AuSable and the migration of the Amish and Mennonites to northeastern Michigan. With those pieces appearing in historical quarterlies and various local periodicals, he had a good reputation but a small reader-ship. Then Fountain discovered true crime, writing a long piece on John Norman Collins, who killed seven women in the Ann Arbor-Ypsilanti area in the late 1960s. The article was published in the *Detroit Free Press* in 1990. His readership soared. Thus began his journey into the dark side of The Pleasant Peninsula.

On a Wednesday night prime time show Fountain was ques-tioned about the Bigfoot case. He had been proposing that Donny Massengale and Roland Parrish were victims of Bigfoot. According to Fountain's initial theory of the crime, the boys woke up early on the 30th to get a head start on the day's fishing. This was despite a night of heavy drinking that Fountain dismissed because the boys were young and could handle such things. They were interested in fishing remote spots and Massengale, experienced in the area, knew just the place. Fountain believed that location to be near 4001 Bridge, which crossed the Au Sable River in an area that was nothing but National Forest.

And little Carl Lee must have been waiting for them.

In Fountain's scenario, the fishermen were quickly subdued, likely by a baseball bat. The Killer had used a bat on other victims. Then BFK, as Fountain called him, drove the Blazer somewhere even more secluded with the bodies to dispose of them. The truck was then repainted or hidden until things settled down and later sold to someone who wouldn't ask too many questions — the writer believed that the deep woods of rural Michigan allowed for such things.

"It was, always, the primary theory of the case, a simple one, Occam's Razor, if you will," Fountain told a reporter during a segment wedged between stories on cleaning products that cause cancer and John Kerry windsurfing. "Of course," Fountain said, "there is another alternative theory that, now, ah, takes on a greater weight, much greater, indeed."

"What is that?" a comely reporter asked.

"In good time," Fountain said.

"I understand that you are writing a book about the case that will go into detail about these revelations?" the reporter followed up.

"Yes," he said. "Yes, it will all be, laid out, in depth. I have everything that is known and much that isn't. More will be revealed."

"How soon can we expect it?"

"It should be ready in the next few months, right in time for Christmas," he said, then Asa Fountain smiled for the camera.

• • • • •

Labor Day came and went, and I began my first Michigan autumn in 35 years. Sweet September was working its magic on me. The dogs got a nice long midday walk plus an evening stroll before I headed out to my nightly meetings. Sammy and Shammy loved all the new smells. They were both picking up every stick they saw and insisting on bringing them into the Mother-In-Law (sticks were in short supply in our Florida neighborhood with the strict Association rules on lawn care). After the sticks were sorted, there were stereo belly rubs and tag team wrestling matches — Sammy mostly refereed by sticking her nose in to lick me or her sister at times. At night, we all slept together sprawled out like a happy pack of friendly wolves.

The fall fish fries featured bull sessions about fishing (Cam was going to stock walleye in his biggest lake next spring), hunting (there was a need to kill a lot of deer come season because of crop damage) and the election (neither presidential candidate gave a shit about farmers, but Bush was better on guns and taxes). Cam would invite his brothers, cousins, and friends. There would be beans, slaw, potato salad, and plenty of pie.

"You gonna have to run extra miles after this spread, Jenkins," Cam said.

"Gladly," I said.

"Try not to trip in front of a tractor."

As the days passed, I could begin to feel the distance between

Then and Now. There had been a point when I would tally the hours since Paula died, using 11:30 am on that day as my starting point. Then I counted the days, weeks and months. One dark night, I even calculated the minutes. These things still happened, but less and less. I wasn't necessarily happy, but there was a real sense that the worst of it was over.

And something new was coming.

It was a cool morning in the third week of September with a touch of mist in the fields that had been freshly harvested, leaving only a stalk of corn here and there. I went for a run without the dogs. The ground was slick with dew and glistened in the fresh sunlight and I was running along a lane between the bare fields and an ancient tree line of oaks, maples, willows and sycamores — all of them beginning to show fall colors. Around a bend I came upon a section of crops that had yet to be cut. The rows and rows of corn stood as sentries at attention, waiting for the final battle and bathed golden by the new day. Every stalk towered over me.

Suddenly a pheasant darted out from the cornfield. It hurried along in front of me with legs spinning like two wheels and tail high on point, not unlike the old cartoon Roadrunner. I chased the bird with all my might as it zigzagged between the corn and trees. It was a moment of both release and connection. Here was a thing completely unexpected not long ago and yet totally in tune with where I was now. This was fall in the Midwest, my birthplace, not spring in Florida, the land where I had lived for so long. It was simple, natural, and revelatory. The beautiful creature, a symbol of the uplands in the Heartland, played tag with me for a minute or so before disappearing into the woods. I raised my hand in tribute as it faded into the underbrush and continued my run through the gilded morning air while listening to the hum of distant tractors harvesting what had been sown the previous spring.

There were still some lonely nights and depression found me when the weather turned toward late fall a week before Tricks and Treats. Golden September as well as October's Indian Summer of yellows, oranges and reds faded to gray as the nights grew very cold and frost blackened all those smiling pumpkins. Paula was still dead, and I wasn't through with her loss. Some days were spent lying on the couch talking to her, asking what she thought about the move.

"There was nothing there for me, Bluebird, now that you're gone," I said to the room while our girls slept by the fireplace. "You were Florida, my Florida. Please understand?"

I waited for a response, likely in a dream, but there was none. Oddly, there had not been one dream about Paula since her death. No sightings. No scenarios where I learned that she wasn't dead, just living across town. No wild chases to track her down. Nothing.

I emailed Kate LeClair to ask if this was unnatural.

"No one knows what dreams may come. People grieve in different ways," she wrote back.

• • • • •

While I was going through my grief, Asa Fountain was making hay.

Just after Halloween, Fountain released a book on the Bigfoot Killer with the title, *On the Trail of the BFK*. Overall, the book was supposed to be a comprehensive review of the case, including a psychological profile of Tobias.

"He was a pathetic little man who couldn't make it with the pretty girls, so he killed them," Fountain wrote.

It made some sense. But Fountain's chapter on Massengale and Parrish, perhaps included to try and wipe some of the egg off the writer's face for getting it so wrong, landed him in very hot water.

First, it was the new claim that the boys had been victims of a drug deal gone bad: that Massengale had brought a "large quantity of marijuana" to northern Michigan to sell to a "shady connection." Furthermore, Fountain had reported that Donny had stolen $500 from the safe of Little Caesars, where he had been the assistant manager, to finance the deal.

It was common knowledge that Donny had purchased some

pot for the vacation, but only a small amount. The theft of money was new.

The families of Donny and Roland were outraged.

"My brother has been dead for 20 years and now this writer is killing him all over again," Leah Massengale, Donny's sister, said to Kim Gold, star reporter for Detroit's NBC affiliate, Local 4. There was talk of a libel suit against Fountain.

Asa's case wasn't helped by the fact that several people who were quoted in his book came forward to claim that they never said what Fountain attributed to them.

"He made this shit up about Donny," James Wagner, who had smoked pot with Donny the night before Massengale went to the Au Sable, said to Gold in the same report. "It was barely a nickel bag."

Others challenged their accounts as presented by Fountain and demanded to hear the tapes.

Fountain told Gold that he didn't use recordings, just notes.

Several, including Wagner, agreed to take lie-detector tests.

Victim's rights groups started protesting appearances by Asa Fountain and demanded that bookstores, including Amazon, pull *On the Trail of the BFK*.

Finally, the publisher did pull the book and then reissued a copy without the missing trout fishers chapter.

It was clear to me that Fountain had rushed the book out to ride the wave of interest in the case. The work was subpar, even by the standards of most murder porn. By the spring of 2005, he was hounded out of the state, and relocated to Seattle to begin a book on the Green River Killer.

And the case of Donny Massengale and Roland Parrish grew even sadder and colder. It needed a proper investigation rather than a half-baked ploy to make a fast buck.

• • • • •

It was a snowy night in early 2005. I had the TV on one of the cable news stations as I folded and arranged my laundry from the laundromat. Sam and Sham "helped" a bit by sticking their noses in piles of clothes and sniffing.

The TV was going on about a huge scandal in Iraq. This was beyond "Hillbilly Armor" and the cost overruns of rebuilding the country that we'd destroyed. It involved an engineering company called Smutek. They specialized in remediation of oil and gas facilities. Smutek, a major contributor to President Bush's campaign, had received a huge no-bid contract to work in Iraq, specifically at two sites called El Hamar and El Baghi, the Donkey and The Mule. That smacked of scandal, but it was even worse.

Smutek had been at both sites since mid-2003. In that period 58 employees, contractors and soldiers had fallen ill with cardio and pulmonary issues. Nine had died, including three soldiers who were all 22 years of age or younger. At first, the problem had been covered up, but Reuters had broken the story of the mystery illnesses over the weekend. Now the media frenzy was on.

A press conference was being held at the U.S. compound in Bagdad's "Green Zone" where the "Liberators" could feel safe. A general had just gone on and on with double talk concerning a couple of questions. I was only half listening. Then a reporter asked if this could be the result of terrorism or the insurgency?

"Let me get our specialist to answer that," the general said.

The was a shuffling at the podium. I glanced at the screen and dropped my pile of laundry.

The officer at the mic was dressed in his desert kit. His cap was snug, and he wore those wrap-around sunglasses that all the troops over there were wearing. He rubbed has hands together and then flicked at his right ear. It was a familiar gesture. I'd seen it hundreds of times.

"All of our chemical analysis at both sites indicate that there are no traces of sarin, VX, mustard gas, chlorine, phosgene or any other military grade chemical weapon that is known to us," he said.

"So, it could be a new one?" asked the reporter, an NBC firebrand who dressed in khaki with shoulder epaulets. "No, sir," the officer said. "The chemicals we found, Chromium-6, PCE, TCE among the most prevalent, are common by-products to both production of hydrocarbons and activities designed to clean up those facilities, such as in the case of oil spills. There was also a substantial presence of Btex and other VOCs at both the Donkey and the Mule. These alone can cause illnesses on par with what we've experienced."

"So, they were already there?"

"Perhaps," the officer said. "Or we brought them with us."

"What is your name?"

"Lieutenant Colonel Edward F. Fletcher, G-2 Intelligence Liaison Officer for the 3rd Infantry Division, United States Army."

"Holy Shit, Eddie," I said, "you just stepped into a mine field."

CHAPTER 5

Seeing the Elephant

After a late night of fishing, I was planning to sleep in. But the phone rang just after seven.

"HOOAH, Motherfucker!" the voice on the phone said. This immediately cleared the last vestiges of sleep from my mind. The dogs had barely stirred at the phone ringing. Both had become late sleepers just like their human.

"Eddie?" I said, "is that you?"

"Copy that," he said.

"Where are you?"

"About 1500 miles due north of your position."

I thought for a minute, trying to remember my geography.

"You're in Hudson Bay?" I finally said.

"Huh? What? Where are you?"

"Chelsea," I said while giving Sammy a belly rub. Her

expression suggested that I should hang up and we all go back to sleep. Shamrock was still snoring lightly.

"Michigan?" His tone sounded like I had mentioned something preposterous like the Negril or Katmandu.

"You are correct, sir," I said. "Now, for the bonus round, where the Hell are you?"

"Spinnerfall," he said, it rang out like a declaration.

"What?" This sounded like the name of a space station or strip joint.

"Yeah, I keep forgetting that you've never been here. Remember the place I bought into a few years back up by Grayling?"

"With your Army buddies."

"Roger that, Blue Leader," he said, then there was a spitting sound. Was he dipping again, at seven in the morning?

"How long have you been back?"

"A little more than a month."

"How are you?"

"I'm OK, just needed to square away some things. We moved Mom to Seattle to be near Donald, so I was out there. In DC for a bit to debrief and settle accounts."

"Are you going back?"

"No, I'm out, retired. Retired a colonel."

"Congratulations," I said, relieved. "I'm so glad that you're home safe."

"Why are you in Chelsea?" he asked.

I explained the move from Florida but kept it as brief as possible. There was no need to rehash the whole drama now.

"It makes sense. Ida' done the same thing, but Chelsea?"

"I came up to Michigan last fall to get away for a while and Nick's friend rented me a family guesthouse out off Scio Church Road. We hit it off, now we're pretty good friends. I fish a ton with him and his son, Kody. The guy's a farmer, Cam Krenshaw, got about six farm ponds, small lakes really, full of bass and bream. He's raising a crop of walleye in one. Next year they should be big enough to eat."

"Krenshaw Dairy? I drank their milk as a kid."

"Probably his cousin, Barney. Cam raises corn, lots and lots of corn."

"So are you wearing overalls and a straw hat?" he asked with a bit of a laugh.

"Every fucking day. Hell, I'm wearing them now in bed."

He laughed harder, choked, then produced a cough and spit.

"You OK?" I asked.

"Outstanding, got time for a visit?"

"Up there?"

"Sure, you'll love it. I'll teach you to fly fish. Bring the dogs. You still got the dogs?"

"Sure do, when?"

"Anytime. We gotta big hatch coming."

"I know how to fly cast."

"Oh, that saltwater shit isn't real fly fishing. You gotta use a dry fly. Besides, we can go popper fishing for bass if you want."

"Smallmouth?"

"Absolutely, and largemouth, although not Florida size mind you. We need to catch up. We need to relax, long overdue."

"I could get up there Friday?"

"Sounds perfect. I have a cabin, several, out back. I'll get the best one cleaned up. Here's the directions…"

I scrambled out of bed, bumped Shamrock in the process. She moaned and gave me a sleepy-eyed look. I found a pen and pad of paper on my desk and took down his instructions.

"I gotta thing that I want to ask you about when you're here," he said.

"OK," I said.

"It's pretty interesting. You follow all that Bigfoot shit last fall?"

"How could I avoid it?"

"Yeah, we even got the story over there. We'll talk about it. I gotta go put in my miles, see you Friday." Then he hung up.

• • • • •

In time, Eddie would tell me the whole story about the place that he called "Spinnerfall."

It wasn't really a cabin. The place was built in the 1920s as a hunting and fishing lodge. It was an outgrowth of Northern Michigan's evolution. For nearly 50 years, much of the area had been the base of operations for a booming lumber industry but by the end of the First World War the trees were just about gone. The fish and other animals except the grayling, which was extirpated from the Au Sable by then, were still there. In fact, deer populations were booming. The white pine, green gold to the lumber barons, had kept the forest floor in shadow and limited the growth of other plants and bushes. With the tree canopy gone, generations of aspen and alders, and berry bushes, were sprouting up everywhere. The white-tailed deer flourished with all this food, and so did grouse and woodcock. It was a hunters' paradise, fishers', too, because the brown, brook and rainbow trout had adapted far better than the grayling.

The swells of the Roaring '20s came up from Chicago, Detroit, Cleveland and other big cities to rough it in the wild and fill their blood lust. These fine men would need a place to stay. The lodge, originally called Parmalee Lodge, was one of many that sprang up in the region around this time. It had seen the likes of Henry Ford and his Vagabonds including Thomas Edison and Harvey Firestone, George Mason, Robert Downey, William Durant and other captains of industry. But by the late 1960s things had changed. The rich folk started buying their own cabins or just going somewhere else, somewhere more exotic. For them, the woods of the Au Sable Valley had lost their charm.

The place went bankrupt and fell into disrepair.

Then, a decade later, Gig Esch and three other men bought it for a song. They were familiar with the area due to their training at nearby Camp Grayling, which had come into existence just before the First World War and eventually become one of the biggest military bases in the country. All of them were ardent outdoorsmen. Esch, a sergeant major in the signal corps, was an expert deer hunter. Two others, Jerry Remy and Gareth Peters, both in the Michigan National Guard, were master carpenters in their civilian life. The fourth, Chief Warrant Officer 4 Avar Grant, was a quartermaster and wheeler-dealer. He got supplies and materials at a discount while Remy and Peters refurbished the place. It was said that Esch sat back, drank beer, and did the cooking.

The result was nothing short of a resurrection. Upon completion in 1980, the four soldiers renamed it "Spinnerfall" for the mayfly mating stage, considered to be the prime time to catch the biggest trout while they sipped on the spent bugs floating like crosses on the water.

Remy and Peters sold their share of Spinnerfall to the other two in the late 1980s. Their terms as guardsmen were over and the Go-Go Eighties had them working overtime back home.

The place had always been a bit of a party palace in addition to a hunting and fishing lodge. There were legendary bacchanals in the summer as part-time soldiers from Michigan, Ohio and Indiana rotated into the National Guard Camp for their weekends or fortnights of training. The local talent, mostly waitresses from Spike's Keg-o-Nails, Shoppenogens, Red Barn, Big Boy or other bars and restaurants supplied the companionship. The outcomes were strictly don't ask, don't tell.

Eddie became familiar with Spinnerfall on his second tour of training at Camp Grayling in 1984. He was there for a winter survival/recon exercise designed to mimic an operation somewhere in the forests of Eastern Europe. Eddie would spend a week alone in the woods of Northern Michigan, in full winter kit, but with only three days of rations, spying on troops who were conducting their own winter operations designed to thwart The Bear That Walks Like a Man. The troopers and tankers didn't know specifically that Eddie was there, but they were supposed to be watching for scouts. Each side was essentially competing against the other.

Eddie would win, but not without a cost. By the end of the

week, he'd plotted out troop strength, make and type of armor, artillery, HQs and movements. In addition, he made all the intel drops via pre-designated relay spots — literally trees and other landmarks in the woods — as well as two dead-in-the-middle-of-a-January-night coded radio signals. Eddie would call it the best game of hide and seek that he ever played. But the day before the end Eddie was crossing what he thought was a frozen wetland. It was, in fact, a pond, about four feet deep. There had been a thaw, Eddie broke through, got out safely, but was sopping wet. The low that night was zero. There was an SOS signal that Eddie could have called in, but that would have meant he had to do the exercise all over again. No way! He knew how well it had gone, and it was still a ball-buster without the pond incident. So Eddie spent the night trying not to freeze to death.

He trudged through a foot of fresh snow — a relative snowless winter to that point had aided in his covert operations — to the pickup point on the morning of the eighth day. He was already well into hypothermia. The field doctor recognized this immediately. A helicopter came to evac Eddie to the camp hospital. He would spend three days in sick bay, but all he wanted to know was his exercise grade.

"You're lucky that you didn't lose any fingers or toes, Fletcher," his commanding officer, a major, said.

"What was my grade, sir?" Eddie asked.

"We're docking five points for the pond incident," the major said. "We don't need a corpse out there for the enemy to find, that's FUBAR, Lieutenant!"

"Yes, sir," Eddie said, but he was relieved that it wasn't a larger demerit. "So?"

"You gotta 95, highest grade I've seen," the major said. "With your intel we'd killed them all, an entire battalion. You're a natural born field rat, Fletcher. Sharpen your combat skills and you'd make a great sniper. They'd never see you coming."

"Sir," Eddie said, "the goal is for them to never see *us* coming."

"Outstanding. Anything that I can get you?"

"Three cups of coffee," Eddie said. "Two to drink and one to pour over me. I still can't get warm."

After release Eddie went to Spike's Keg-o-Nails, ordered three cheeseburger platters, two baskets of onion rings and a pitcher of Molson's. He was into the second platter when Esch came striding up to his table.

"Are you the swinging dick that lifted the skirts of my beloved battalion?" Esch asked.

"That would be me," Eddie said between chews. He'd never been hungrier.

"My asshole is going to sting for three days after the reaming I just took."

"You look like a man that needs a drink, Sergeant Major," Eddie motioned to an empty chair. "Sit down, I'm buying. Grab that third platter. I'm getting more anyway."

Esch sat down, took a bite of the cheeseburger. "Jack Daniels?"

"Sure, make it two."

"What's your name?"

"Eddie Fletcher, second lieutenant, First Infantry Division, The Big Red One, Sergeant Major. If you're gonna be a one be a Big Red One! Gonna get a silver bar for sussing you guys," he said, then shot Esch a shit-eating grin mixed with bits of cheeseburger.

"I heard they're gonna leapfrog you to two silver bars for that, fast track."

"Hell! I'm ready for the War College and charm school. Give me three stars and an army with kick-ass armor and proper air support. I'll run the Bear to Moscow and wrap it up by Labor Day. Gotta avoid the Russian winter, Sergeant Major, learn the lessons of history."

"Just one army, Fletcher?"

"We'll be well-trained. I'll see to it."

"What about tactical nukes?" Esch asked, marveling at Eddie's bravado. The sergeant major knew the trait could win battles, but also get soldiers killed if not properly developed.

"Well," Eddie gobbled down an onion ring. "We got 'em, too, Sarge. I'd have a plan."

"Tell me how you really feel, Fletcher," Esch chuckled.

"Just did. Pass me the ketchup, will ya?"

The two men ate and drank until near closing, swapping scores of stories along the way. Then they walked over to a park nearby and vomited much of that food and drink into the flowing water of the Au Sable River.

"Nice looking stream," Eddie said between pukes. "Any fish in it?'

"You gotta be crazy, Second Lou," Esch said. Sometime during the festivities Esch started called Eddie "Second Lou," after Sweet Lou Whitaker, the star Detroit Tigers second baseman. Eddie liked it but felt it would soon need to be amended to at least "First Lou," if not Lieutenant General Fletcher. "This is one of the best trout streams in America."

"How do you catch 'em?" Eddie asked.

"Fly fishing," Esch said. "I'll teach you, in fact. When are you shipping out?'

"Staying around for some classroom stuff, but it's a daytime gig, office hours, learning to read satellite shit, stuff like that. I'm here till March, maybe longer."

"On base?"

"Yeah."

"Any chance they let you quarter off base?"

"Fuck, they'll let me do anything now."

"Maybe not anything."

"I'll check, why?"

"I gotta place about 20 miles east," Esch said. "In the woods, plenty of privacy. Own it with three other guys. It's our getaway. Better than the base by a country mile, plenty of room. Hell, Second Lou, you can have your own cabin."

"I deserve it."

"You're a cocky son-of-bitch."

"Gotta be, Sergeant Major. It's how I survive."

Eddie ended up spending the rest of the winter at Spinnerfall, and would stay there during two additional training deployments, including a summer version of the winter operation where Eddie got stung by yellow jackets and contracted poison ivy after taking a piss in the wrong set of bushes. He would still score a 93.

He couldn't afford an ownership share in those years. But by the late '90s, others were ready to move on and Eddie's success as a lawyer — he was a master at cross examination — had given him the money to buy in.

Around the turn of the millennium, Grant, fighting colon cancer, sold out to Esch. By then Gig's serial womanizing caught up to him, leading to an ugly divorce, and he needed to sell. Eddie was on the doorstep of being named a partner. Furthermore, he lived well within his means and had invested wisely, and "Second Lou," now a major, was rolling in dough. And Eddie didn't want another partner at Spinnerfall.

In August of 2001, while the country wondered about Chandra Levy and Mohamed Atta learned how to pilot commercial aircraft, Eddie Fletcher bought out a desperate Gig Esch for a fair price. On Saturday of Labor Day weekend, Eddie married Donna. Their honeymoon lasted ten days, then the world turned upside down.

• • • • •

Chelsea was located between Ann Arbor to the east and Jackson the west. I-94 gave access to each city, and from there separate pathways to the North Country. It was hardly a case of two roads diverging with the choice making all the difference, but there were considerations.

Going east meant catching US-23 to merge with I-75 just south of Flint — an armpit of a city even in its glory years. It also meant more traffic until one crossed the Zilwaukee Bridge near Saginaw because of the growing suburbs north of Ann Arbor and west of Detroit.

Going west to Jackson was a much easier, if slightly longer, choice going up US-127 to I-75 just three miles south of Grayling. There was the ten-minute ride through Lansing — enemy territory for a blue-blood Wolverine. But I didn't have any identifying marks on my vehicle other than a faded "Florida Gators" bumper sticker that Paula had insisted on. She loved the Burnt Orange and Blue. Otherwise, the trip rolled through the farmlands of Central Michigan which turned to the pine, birch, and ferns of Northern Michigan around Clare — the Gateway to the North.

While Frank Bascombe could have provided insightful commentary on either choice, he would not be riding with me today — probably showing some property. I decided to go through Jackson, ignored Lansing to the best of my ability, and let the rest of the trip soothe me. Going Up North was always an adventure for Downstaters and it never lost its magic.

Spinnerfall was right where Eddie said it would be, but few could miss it anyway. There was a sign by the driveway with the lodge's name in freshly painted yellow letters plus a couple of bugs and imitation trout flies painted in the corners.

The lodge itself was a complex nestled in the pines. There was a big, long building in the shape of an L. The length had to be 40 yards. Back behind the main building, which was retrofitted in Permalog, a carefully crafted concrete molding designed to ape logs, were three cabins, all redone in split log, and two newer, smaller structures that turned out to be storage sheds. The parking area was big enough for a mini strip mall — there's a story that an M2 Bradley Fighting Vehicle was parked there once. There was a wood-plank porch by the main door with a grill station, picnic table and several chairs. I noticed a metal fire ring and two foldout metal chairs next to the nearest cabin.

Eddie's brown 2000 Jeep Cherokee was parked close to the main door. It had Ohio plates because Eddie's firm had been based in Cleveland. He never warmed to the city, but he was never there much anyway. Most of his cases were tried in Virginia due to plaintiff's standing. There were several stickers for military bases and other federal facilities on the windows and back bumper.

"HOOAH!" Eddie said as he stormed out of the main door and ran to greet me. Long ago he had "cleared me for the honor" of that greeting, strictly an Army thing otherwise, because I was part of "his army." (Some folks say they had stolen it from the Marines, but it was best not to bring that up.)

"HOOAH, you fucker!" I said and embraced him. It was like squeezing an oak tree.

"Let me get a look at you," he said and placed both hands on my shoulders while giving me the once-over. This was a standard action with him after any length of time. Eddie Fletcher was an observer. He paid attention to detail. Nothing got past him. I think he first learned the skill dealing with his father, trying to read the signs and avoid conflict. The Army only improved it.

I, of course, studied him in return. The fitness was there. Eddie didn't go to seed after leaving active duty in 1992. Instead, he became a middle-distance runner while in law school, using the time to stay in shape and deal with the stress of classes and aftermath of what he'd seen in Gulf One — the terrible place that war could take good men even in the best of circumstances. Running 10 to 15 miles wasn't possible during his recent deployment in Baghdad or Fallujah. Soldiers trained at gyms on base when they had the time. It was clear that he'd been hitting the weights.

The rest of him was not quite so robust. His hair was military short, but thicker on top. That was a popular style in the armed forces, an oval patch on the top of the head with the sides shaved clean. But the striking thing was that he'd gone completely gray. When Eddie married Donna less than four years earlier there was a fleck or two of silver in his jet-black hair; now his roof was covered in snow.

His face was longer, thinner, tired, but the eyes were worse. Eddie's emotions and intensity could make them pulse like electrodes, but in those moments between the orbs were flat and hollow. It wasn't exactly haunting as much as lifeless.

"A little frosty on top," I said.

"At least I got hair," he said. "Let's see those dogs."

Sammy and Shammy were both glad to see their Uncle Eddie. He had treats for them.

We went into the main building, which wasn't quite what I had expected of a retreat for soldiers. I figured that there would be mounted rifles, swords, division, battalion and company insignia and, at least, pictures of war and the machines of war. Instead, there were three mounts of trout on the wall over a large fireplace. The brown was better than two feet long. The rainbow was not as long but much thicker with a body like an overinflated football. The brook trout was barely half the size of the other two but seemed to have every color in the rainbow save pink. It was the one that my eyes kept going back to. There were five pictures all done in the same style with a common theme: songbirds, woodpeckers, raptors, wildflowers and pollinators, all of North America, all presented in loving detail by the artist, each bird, flower and butterfly almost popping out of their weathered-wood canvases.

There were two couches with a common end table plus one coffee table set in front of the fireplace. A big-screen TV was wedged into the corner. A small table, set near the entrance to the kitchen, had a laptop and legal pads on it. On the hearth were three ancient duck decoys; one was missing its head.

"Let me get the pup dogs some water," Eddie said and headed in to the kitchen. "I got four dog dishes in case you didn't bring any."

"Why is one decoy missing a head?" I asked.

"Oh, good story. Supposedly, Soapy Williams shot it off."

"The governor?"

"Yup, mistook it for the real thing," Eddie said while running the faucet. "He wasn't a bad guy for a Democrat." The blood of Eisenhower Republicanism coursed through Eddie's veins, but he was no ideologue. "We named it Mennen."

I laughed then looked down the long hallway off to the right.

"How far back does that go?" I asked.

"Oh, the hallway? There's four bedrooms, full bath and a tying room."

"Tying room?"

"For flies," he said and put the dishes down. "Need lots and lots of flies. Another shitter behind you near the front door. Pretty conveniently located not far from the kitchen and chow hall. Esch wasn't a great cook. Coffee?"

"Sure."

He returned with two piping hot cups of Joe then produced a pair of dog bones.

"Are these acceptable?" he asked.

"Yes, sir." Paula was a stickler about dog bones. She vehemently opposed rawhide having seen too many dogs choke to death from them.

"Hey pups!" he said, "Come and get it!" The dogs stopped drinking and hightailed it over to where he was sitting. He gave each a bone and they settled on to the rug and began chewing contentedly.

"Safe at last," I said.

"Safer."

"So," I said after a sip, "I saw you on television back in January."

"Yup. My fifteen minutes of fame."

"Did you get in trouble for that?"

"Oh, no. I wasn't gonna get a medal or anything, but we needed to get in front of the story. It was kinda falling on the grenade."

"Is that why you're home now?" I asked, my recollection was that Eddie had signed on for a two-year stint.

"No. My time was up."

"No stop-loss?"

"Not for me," he said while shuffling on the couch and fingering his can of Skoal. "So, is there a memorial to Paula? I remember an email about scattering her ashes."

Eddie had sent a brief reply to my email concerning Paula's death. "I am heart sick and wish that I could be there," he wrote. But there had been no replies to any of my others. That was understandable because of his situation. I explained what had occurred.

"Probably the best place to pay respects would be the House of Refuge, huh?"

"Yeah," I said, but hoped to drop the subject.

Eddie saw this and brought up fishing. He always knew how to read the room.

The plan was to go fly fishing that night. Eddie insisted on teaching me how to cast using plates in the parking area with a fly rod and a piece of yarn. The goal was to hit the plates consistently. After a few tries I started making the marks. I think it surprised him. Next was fitting me to some waders with the proper felt boots. My Red Ball waders with plastic soles would not do the trick.

"Art, you'll be slipping and sliding," Eddie said. "Put these on."

He had an old pair of stocking-foot waders that fit fine. They had been patched up extensively with Aquaseal on the seams and crotch. The boots, equally worn, were a couple sizes too big. I walked like Frankenstein's monster. The dogs thought the whole thing was crazy.

"It'll do for tonight," he said. "Summer flow, gentle water. There might be a leak or two, but water will be about 67 degrees and it's a nice summer night. Consider it air conditioning."

"When do we go?"

"After chow, hot dogs and beans?"

We hopped in his truck after dinner and headed east on Cherry Creek Road. The road cut through second or third generation white pine plus plenty of red and jack pine as well. The stands of trees crept right up to the road's edge to form walls of green needles on either side. There were a couple of two-track dirt turnoffs leading to who knows where.

After a few minutes we came to a major road, M 33-72, and turned right.

"Welcome to the burg of Mio," Eddie said and then took a left. A blue sign with yellow letters indicated it was F-32.

"Glance over your right shoulder and you might see the dam," he said.

"Where are we going?" I asked.

"It's a secret. I should have blindfolded you."

After a couple of miles, Eddie made another turn off into the woods and we rumbled and bumbled along a bumpy trail for a few minutes before parking in a notch in the trees.

"Get your shit on," Eddie said, and packed his lip with Skoal.

Then he led me to a path in the tree line, just a crease between two spruces, that would be easy to miss unless one knew it was there. We spent the next 15 minutes wandering through a maze of trees, past underbrush and deadfall in what could only be described as perpetual shadow. I doubted the rays of the sun ever made it to the ground here. It was tricky to maneuver in what passed for daylight.

How the hell would we get out at nightfall? I wondered.

"When do we get there?" I asked.

"Looking for the mark right now. Oh, there it is."

"What?"

"Pileated Tree."

"Pileated Tree?"

"There," he pointed to a monarch white pine, now dying and pocked with marks from the giant woodpecker. "Duck through here. Careful of the rod."

I did, and then found myself in an opening free of the constant brushing of tree limbs, tag alders and skeletal branches of long-fallen pines.

"Look to your left," he said.

I did and saw the river. It had just appeared out of the seemingly impenetrable brush.

"Where did that come from?"

"It's always been here."

"But how did you find it?"

"Magic, and a shitload of trial and error."

He motioned me to an easy access spot into the river lodged between two sweepers. After a few feet of wading, we entered a huge open area, a pool, easily two hundred yards long and about half as wide, bracketed by two sharp corners, the upper going hard right and the lower hard left. There was a braided disturbance on the surface at the top end, maybe a quarter of the run, that suggested riffles. I imagined that looking from above it could be construed as hair on the head of this quiet water. On the far side a ridge, almost 50 feet high, stretched above the river as far as the eye could see. It was topped by pines standing about six stories tall, several of them in stages of falling down the highbank due to the slow crawl of erosion. Access from that side would be akin to jumping off a cliff.

"Can you wade all this?"

"This time of year, for sure," Eddie said. "Let's get around this leaning cedar. There's a bunch of logs by the bank that are perfect for setting up and hanging out."

We did that, assembled the rods, broken down to two pieces for easier travel in the woods, strung up the line and rigged our flies. Eddie had on an emerger, which I would learn was the life-stage of a mayfly just as it broke the film of the water and exited its nymphal case.

"The bug is very vulnerable at that point," Eddie said. "Fish know it."

"Then why am I putting on a nymph?"

"Because you need to learn to mend line."

For the uninitiated, fly fishing appears to be all about the cast. Volumes of prose and poetry have been written about proper fly casting, and one film practically made it a metaphor for life. But to those who fish, mending the line — making tiny adjustments to give the fly a natural drift in the water — is far more important. Without a good drift all hope is lost.

"A buddy of mine teaches fly fishing at one of those lodges upriver, ex-firefighter, great guy," Eddie said. "He always says 'no mend, no bend,' so remember, plenty of trout are caught on bad casts, but none are caught on bad drifts."

Truth was that pitching a nymph was not the same as casting a dry, but Eddie said that drift still mattered underneath the water, and nothing was rising right now anyway. We headed up to the wrinkly water and I stepped out to cast.

"OK, cast across," Eddie said. "Good, now with your wrist, flip the rod tip back upstream." I did, and it resulted in a section of fly line being picked up off the water and deposited a couple feet upstream from where it had been floating. This created a bow in my line and effectively slowed down the speed of my fly in the water. In this case the fly sank deeper. I was using a bead-headed hare's ear. It looked like something that a barista might have for an ear piercing. Eddie claimed that the bead was tungsten and the same type used in submarines. I continued to refine my casting and mending under the watchful eye of Coach Fletcher until it was interrupted by a bend in the rod.

"Teacher, should I reel that in?" I asked sarcastically.

"That's a small one. Just strip it in."

I did. It was a rainbow, not ten inches long and largely silver with just a hint of a red stripe.

"That's a planter," Eddie screamed over the gurgling of the water. It was only about to our knees but moving quickly. "They need a year in the river to get any color."

I released the fish and caught another on the next cast. It was a carbon copy of the first. This happened on four of the next five casts. I had not even moved ten feet downstream.

"You appear to be getting it," he said.

"Yeah," I said and missed a strike in the process. "This is like fishing for ladyfish or jacks in the Indian River Lagoon."

"No, it's much harder."

"Why?"

"Because it's fly fishing. Come on back in. We'll sit, rest the water, and wait for the evening hatch."

"I passed the course?"

"We'll see."

The set of logs above the leaning cedar was tailor-made to sit on and wait for hatches, spinnerfalls or signs of rising fish. There was plenty of room for our rods and Eddie produced two canteens, from where I don't know, plus some beef jerky.

"Did you arrange these logs?" I asked.

"Beyond my skill set. River God did it. I've thanked him several times."

"Very comfortable."

"Room to piss or shit back there," he pointed to a clearing behind us. There was an indentation in the bank from where he'd gotten out and back in. "Sometimes I bring a book when it's Hendrickson time and you have to wait and wait. They never start soon enough, but mostly I just watch the river and the woods. It's a great place to unwind."

"It reminds me of the Everglades," I said. "Not the same terrain at all, but the same spirit."

"Copy that, just don't take a dump near a gator." Eddie had mistakenly done that once near Nine Mile Pond and came scrambling back to the boat holding up his loose trousers while cursing up a storm. We barely launched off the bank in time to escape an alligator that has grown in length with each retelling but was probably only six feet long.

Several birds were flying across the river, dipping and twirling in the late day sun. A couple of them landed on nearby branches. I recognized the species but checked with the expert.

"Cedar waxwings?" I asked pointing at one sitting on the end of the log.

"Yes, sir. The bandit bird, they are eating small olives."

"It's beautiful out here."

"Copy that, and it gets even better. I love the twilight. I love the night."

"You're just a dark guy."

"Incorrect, I'm a ray of light in a murky world," he said, but shot me a playful grin.

"Oh, I forgot."

It was good to see him act this way. Given all that he'd experienced through life it was no surprise that Eddie could be wound too tight at times. He could be too much of an Army man, but he seemed to know that. A lot of his rhetoric was purposely over the top and much of it was tongue and cheek. It was another way that he blew off some steam from that pressure cooker inside.

"Sixty-six degrees," he said after holding a thermometer in the water for a minute or so. "We should see something around 8:30 or so. Intel says no hatches yet of Ephrons."

"Ephrons?"

"White fly."

"You're speaking Latin now. Where are your jodhpurs, tweed coat and dickie?"

"Dry cleaners," he said and then explained the white fly cycle, which included the fact that they hatched and spun, mated, all in the same night.

"They molt in midair rather than go to the trees for a day. You'll see them shed the tail section while flying around. It's pretty cool."

But 8:30 came and no white flies. The tree line grew darker. The light breeze dropped. The air cooled. A mosquito or two buzzed in our ears. The waxwings went to roost. Eddie peered into the twilight but did not see a bug.

"Not even Cahills or Isos," he said. Those were other mayflies that were still around but not in the numbers of earlier in the summer.

We sat in silence and hoped.

"What was it like in the days after she died?" Eddie asked before popping another wad of dip into his mouth.

"I went into shock pretty quickly," I said then gave a condensed and sanitized version of those first two weeks. He didn't need to know about the viewing having had his own horrible experience with a fellow soldier after Gulf One. ("He looked like a wax dummy," Eddie had said. "Had to, been burned up in a copter mishap.")

"It had to be Hell. I wish I could have been there to help."

"I ended up drinking, after everybody left."

"I wondered. For how long?"

"Five days, but I came to my senses, got well over a year now."

"Good, I'll throw out my scotch and beer if you want."

"No need, but thanks. I see Nick all the time at The Baron, and Cam drinks a couple when we fish. If you're working the program it doesn't matter."

"Where did you get help?"

"Whispering Palms, to detox and get some counseling."

"A shrink?"

"Addiction Specialist, and a good one. She was also easy on the eyes."

"A woman?"

"Yeah, and from Scotland."

"What?"

I gave Eddie a briefing on Kate LeClair.

"You know," he said. "I'm slated to date a Scot."

"Huh?"

"I shared quarters with a Major Douglas Oswald, 3rd Battalion of the Royal Regiment of Scotland, the old Black Watch," he said then spat into the night. "He was attached to us out of Basra. The Brits were pacifying that shithole. Anyway, their intel guys came to see what we were doing and vice versa. Hell, we were all looking for an answer! Anyway, he was from Glasgow and we hit it off. Good man, you'd like him. He called me a 'proper bloke,' by the end. Showed me a picture of his kid sister, Clara, cute as a button, brown doe-eyes, short black hair. Douglas said he'd fix me up with her if I ever get over there."

"What's stopping you?"

"He's still deployed," Eddie said. "I think it's his third go. The Black Watch is getting the shit kicked out of them. Tony Blair is a stupid git. Of course, W isn't much better."

"Surprising to hear that from you."

"There's a reason why soldiers, warriors are often the best peacemakers. It's because we've seen war. You know this, Art. Look, some wars are necessary and must be fought. But war should be the last option. In this case, it seemed like the only option. Jesus! I love Colin Powell, but what on earth was he thinking by backing this fiasco?"

"I remember that discussion after the UN speech." Eddie had been down in Florida, licking his post-divorce wounds, and we had him over for dinner. He'd said that the substance of Powell's speech was iffy, but he trusted him.

"I've never seen the elephant in the flesh, but I've heard his stampedes both in the distance and a block or two away, and I've witnessed the aftermath of his rampages." Eddie dropped his wad of chew into the dark river. "They should be in zoos, only released when all reasonable avenues have been exhausted."

"I'm glad that you are home," I said, trying not to sound too emotional.

"Ya know, Art," he said then rubbed his hands and brushed his right ear, "right now, on this river, with you and the cedar waxwings, I'm glad to be home, too."

An owl hooted upriver, then another one just across from us answered it.

"And those guys, too," Eddie said standing up and pointing in the direction of the hoots. "I love those guys!"

"This is a good place."

"What's mine is yours," Eddie sat down and composed himself. "I can come here and lose things. Yeah, I find them again but over time, not so quickly, and they don't feel as heavy…know what I mean?"

"I gotta cornfield like that."

"A cornfield," Eddie stood up and looked bemused. "A fucking cornfield?"

"You ever play tag with a pheasant?" And I explained my occasional encounters with them while running.

"Hmm, I'll never see cornfields the same after that…Not even cornflakes, because, well…"

"I never know when to take you seriously."

"I'm highly trained to keep you off balance."

"No, you come by that honestly."

Eddie looked at me and smiled. "No bugs tonight. Let's go. I'll show you my foolproof way out. You'll love it. I'm a genius, a visionary."

Eddie had created a system of gates marked with plastic thumb tacks with light-reflective heads. They were stuck in the trees along the path that we came in on. It was like a slalom course. We traveled in silence other than the snapping of branches at our feet and Eddie's occasional shouts of "Hey Bear!"

"Gotta let the monsters know that we're on the trail," he said when we got back to the Jeep.

When we got home, I took the dogs out on leashes. Eddie had recommended it.

"Too many critters at night that could hurt them," he said. "Porcupines are the worst for dogs, coons aren't much better."

I was staying in the cabin, but the dogs spent the day in the main building. Eddie wasn't too concerned about accidents on the hardwood floors or throw rugs.

"There's been a ton of puke and other bodily substances spilled here over the years," he said on the ride home, "Including projectile diarrhea because, seriously, Esch wasn't a good cook."

He had their bedtime snacks and Milkbones ready when I came in. When the girls were settled at their dishes, crunching away, he produced a plate of cheese and crackers.

"Tea?" he asked.

"Sure," I said, "I wonder if Clara would approve."

"She'll be too smitten with me to notice."

"Oh, right, foolish me."

He came back with a cup of Earl Grey Green then sat down with a tumbler of scotch, Glenfiddich.

"OK, Let's get to the mystery," he said and reached down under the end table and produced a paperback book.

"On the trail of the BFK," I said. "You read it?'

"Yeah," he said. "I got this from my brother when I was in Seattle. Did you?"

"No, but I sure heard enough about it."

"Bigfoot is solved but it's chapter nine, 'What Happened to Donny and Roland?' that I'm interested in."

"That intrigues me as well," I said. "The whole drug dealing thing was bullshit. He's lucky not to get sued."

"I need your opinion, and maybe your help."

"It happened right around here?"

"Yes, sir. The cabin is just a couple of miles west of here."

"I guess that would be right. Where were you then?"

"I left Grayling about two weeks before they went missing. I'd been here for nearly four months but shipped out to Benning in mid-April to work with the One-Five-Oh." Eddie fiddled with his can of Skoal. "They tore down the original cabin that the boys were staying in. The uncle sold it in '86 or so. Couldn't stay there."

"I can relate."

"Yeah, and the new owners sold it two years later. I think it switched hands again twice before the current owners rebuilt in '98 or so."

"That's a lot of turnarounds."

"Rumor is that it's haunted."

"Do you believe that?"

"There's literal and figurative, Art," Eddie said between sips. "I doubt the ghosts of Massengale and Parrish are rattling chains. But the vibe? It must be unsettling with people always asking you if that's the place or what's it like at night and so on. That would play with your mind. All houses up here make noises at night, you'll see. The creaking of wood. The skittering of mice."

"There's more gravy than grave about you," I said, quoting *A Christmas Carol*.

"Exactly."

"What do you need me to do?"

"Read chapter nine and we'll talk in the morning. I'm not liking the weather forecast for tomorrow."

I finished my tea and took the dogs to the cabin. It was clean and cozy with a queen-sized bed, nightstand, small dresser, bathroom with a shower not much bigger than a closet, and very little room otherwise. There was one picture on the wall. It was an osprey hanging in the air with wings stretched and tail feathers splayed. The head was looking down in search of prey. I guessed that Eddie had brought it here to remind him of the bygone days of bygone Florida.

The next morning, I walked the dogs out behind the cabin and then headed to the main building. The air was crisp from a typical northwoods nocturnal cooldown. It probably got in the 40s last night after an 80-degree day. That made for good sleeping.

I heard music emanating from the open widows of the main building. It was bagpipes!

I let myself in and unhooked the dogs who immediately went to Eddie and pranced around him as he marched back and forth in the living room using the butt end of a fly rod as a baton.

"That's a nice touch," I said after he turned it off.

"Sure is," he said with a glow to his features. "It's *Pipes and Drums* by The Scots Guards. Last night's conversation got me in the mood for it. Douglas used to play it before missions. Fired us the fuck up."

"Kinda like *Apocalypse Now*."

"That movie was bullshit. Coffee? Toast?"

"I thought that you might have scones. Yes, that would be fine."

He shot me a finger then went to the kitchen.

"You read the chapter?" he asked, returning with a pot and mug after popping some bread in the toaster.

"I did."

"This thing with Massengale and Parrish has been fucked up from the get-go," Eddie said.

"And it's twenty-plus years now, right?"

"And begging to be solved," he said.

"Yes, it needs a serious investigation."

"I'm thinking about looking into it. We talked about it for years out here during cookouts and bull sessions. Gig Esch was part of the search team. He said it was a clusterfuck."

"What about your law practice?"

The toast popped. Eddie went and got it, then grabbed some butter and blackberry jam.

"I'm a little, ah, radioactive for the courtroom, Art."

"Smutek?"

"Yeah," he said making a fist and lightly pounding the coffee table. "It could be used against me by a clever counsel, especially given the fact that they have yet to confirm what the cause of those illnesses was."

"What about your partnership?"

"Lost my place in line." He rubbed his hands before balling them into fists again. "It might not have been as close as I believed back there in 2001. I mean, I thought I deserved it."

"Did they not hire you back?"

"I am assisting on some cases, going over records, depos. It's first year associate stuff and not even full-time." He looked across the room to a spot outside the window. "I go down to their Detroit office for a couple days each week. It's a start but I got plenty of free time and solid cash reserves."

"What's my role in this?"

"A sounding board. But most importantly, you know how to investigate things, leave no stone unturned."

"Yeah, but that went nowhere."

"Not because of you," he said. "It's on them, the powers that be in batshit-crazy Florida. Well, in this case, law enforcement screwed the pooch." He looked at the dogs. "Sorry girls, no offense."

"What's the goal Eddie? We're not the police."

"Get justice, closure."

"Through the proper channels."

"Of course," he said. "Of course." He finished his cup of coffee and poured another. "Hey? The weather is iffy for smallmouth tonight. How about a big cookout? I got some friends that I'd like you to meet. If you can stay through Sunday, the weather should be fine tomorrow night."

"Sounds good. Give me a list of things to get in town. I'll take care of it."

"Outstanding," he gave me a thumbs up.

Six guys, ranging in ages from the early twenties to mid-fifties, came by to feast on burgers, ribs and all the other fixings. Most of the conversation was fishing-related and centered on the Hex Hatch — the Super Bowl of dry fly fishing around here — as well as the coming white fly hatch. It turned out that Eddie knew these men from fishing the Au Sable and Manistee rivers. One was working in a fly shop in Grayling and another had been a guide but now managed a lumberyard near Mio.

I learned a lot about fly fishing while listening to the conversations, but the night became more interesting after the four younger guys excused themselves around 8:30 to go bar hopping.

"I think Mattie's really going mousin'," said Earl Gamby. He was a sturdy looking man, a few years older than me, who ran a plumbing company in Grayling. "He'll never show up at Spike's, be somewhere on the South by ten."

"Mousin'?" I asked. "With mouse flies?"

"Yeah," Earl said, "although he uses a gurgler, looks more like a frog. Trout eat mice, but mostly frogs at night this time of year."

"Big fish technique," Eddie said while packing a chew. "I need to learn it."

"Right up your alley, Fletcher," Earl said.

"Copy that," Eddie said, then poured another scotch. How he would dip and drink at the same time was a marvel.

"So I understand that you wanna talk about May '84 and the events around it?" Clem Haskins, another 50-something asked. He was a short, wiry fellow with the features of a friendly Leprechaun.

"Yup," Eddie said. "My friend here is interested."

I nodded my head.

"Well, Eddie," Earl said. "As you know both Clem and I were part of the search."

The two men took turns explaining what happened back then. Both went on several searches that year covering an area all the way from Maltby Hills to Pigeon River Forest from May till just before rifle season.

"Then again when the snow cleared the following spring," Clem said, "By then we figured to find some skeletons, but we never did."

"Never found a Goddamn thing," Earl said. He pulled on his bottle of Molson's. "Nobody did. Bupkis."

Instead, they found plenty of old campsites, fire rings, illegal dumps, lots of refrigerators, car tires, a rusted engine from a '68 Pontiac, spent shotgun shells, and even several kitchen sinks. But no bodies, no Blazer, no blood, no scene of the crime.

"But that's not the interesting part guys," Eddie said.

Earl and Clem looked at each other.

"Not hardly," Earl said.

"What's the interesting part?" I asked.

"What we found the year before, and the year before that," Clem said.

"Go on," Eddie said, then spat before taking a swig of amber.

"Well, like I told you before, there were those circles," Earl said.

"Altars," Clem said, reaching for his can of Copenhagen.

"Altars?" I asked. This had never been in any information that I'd read.

"Yes, sir, Arthur," Clem said. "Circles made of stones or traced in the dirt and sand, plus some stick figures hanging from nearby trees. All of it carefully arranged. How many did we find in '82 and '83, Earl?"

"Five or six," he said, then described places where someone had camped or spent a lot of time. These areas were beaten down, ferns and bushes flattened, littered with beer cans, bean cans, cigarette butts, used toilet paper, even a tampon or two.

"Plus, the rubbers," Clem said, "Don't forget the rubbers."

"Werewolf parties," Earl said.

"What?" I asked. This piqued my interest.

"Those were parties in the deep woods, usually around the

full moon," Eddie chimed in. "Young kids, mostly in high school, not that common anymore."

"They cracked down on it after the murders," Earl said.

"Massengale and Parrish?"

Earl nodded.

"Lotta shit going on in the woods back then," Clem said.

"But you guys have buried the lead," Eddie said.

Earl and Clem looked confused, and Eddie continued: "Tell Art about the rest."

"Yeah, I'm still not comfortable with all that," Clem said, "even now."

"Tell it!" Eddie's eyes glowed in the two lanterns that he set up earlier as darkness fell.

"They killed animals out there, dogs, cats, coons, maybe a fox or fox pups." Earl finally said after fixing a stare at Eddie. I surmised that neither he nor Clem were at ease.

"To eat?" I said but knowing better by now.

"No," Clem said. "I think they were tortured, sacrificed."

"You're fucking kidding me," I said and looked at Eddie.

"OK, and what else did you find?" Eddie asked coolly.

"Alright, if you want me to say it I will," Earl said in exasperation. "The worst site we found was fresh, done the night before I'd guess. There were three stakes, each had the head of a cat on them." He stopped and swallowed hard. Earl was back there in that place in time. He looked like he could smell the decay. "We found their bodies, gutted, entrails hung up in the branches of a tag alder."

"This is awful!" I said, thinking of every pet that I'd ever loved.

"What was carved in the oak nearby?" Eddie asked. His tone was as chilling as the story.

"Some letters," Earl said, "Never forgot 'em. They spelled W-Y-V-E-R-N."

"Wyvern?" I said.

"Yeah," Earl said. "You know what it is?"

"It's a dragon with a poisonous barbed tail," I said. Sophomore year, my roommate was into Dungeons and Dragons. He'd recount campaigns while getting high. Wyverns were a common foe.

"This was in 1982 and 1983?" Eddie said. "Did you see any of this in the years since?"

"No," both men said.

"No ritual sites, no sacrificed animals in 1984 or since?"

"No."

"Thank you, gentlemen," Eddie said and got up to check the gas on the grill station.

It started raining and we all quickly gathered things and moved them inside. Shortly after that both Earl and Clem said their good-byes. Eddie sent the extra burgers home with Earl and some pie with Clem.

"Thanks, Fletcher," Earl said. "My barn next time, maybe we fish after."

Eddie smiled and nodded.

"Sure thing," Clem said. "Next time let's play Euchre and leave the ghost stories alone."

I took the dogs out for a quick pee in the rain. When I came back Eddie had their dishes filled and was sitting on the couch nursing another scotch.

"Whaddya think?" he asked.

"Great food," I said. "Unlike Esch, you are a good cook."

"You know what I mean."

"Look, it's powerful to hear from two men who were part of the search only hours after reading about it in the book."

"And the rest?"

"OK, it was the 1980s, the era of the Satanic Panic," I said. "It's not hard to imagine a handful of misguided losers who'd listened to too much Ozzy doing something like that. It's horrifying and I'd like to kneecap all of them with a baseball bat before shattering their hands to splinters."

"Sexy."

"Shut The Fuck Up!" I said and stood up. Sammy ran over from her dog dish. Shamrock stopped eating and sharpened her ears.

"OK, sorry," he said, "Sorry, sorry, sit down." He got up and went to the kitchen and poured his drink out in the sink then came back to the living room rubbing his hands. "I want you to see."

"Eddie," I said sitting down. "I do see, but it's a very long walk down the hall from backwoods rituals to a double murder, let alone by some satanic cult, a very long walk."

"So, we follow that path."

"How do we even start?"

"Already have. You know any of that before tonight?"

"Nope. How could the police miss it back then?"

"Esch always said that it was Bigfoot, Bigfoot, Bigfoot back then."

"We need to get the casefile. Is that possible? Isn't it still open?"

"Yup, but I gotta guy."

"A guy?"

"Can you come back in a week or two? At least the hatch should be going."

"I suppose. This is a nice place and I'm glad to see you, but, Eddie, this must feel like a serious effort and not just a couple of guys fucking around because things, things are..."

"Fucked up right now," he said sheepishly. "I agree about that. For me, this is something that has always been in the back of my mind. One of those 'if I had the time, I'd do it' things. I got some time now. How about you?"

"Who's your guy?" I asked.

"He's a master of investigation, 25 years in military intelligence, pioneered computer surveillance, cracking and hacking. He knows how to find the buried body." Eddie scratched his head and flicked that right ear. "His named is Zachariah Phoenix, but we call him 'Black Zac.'"

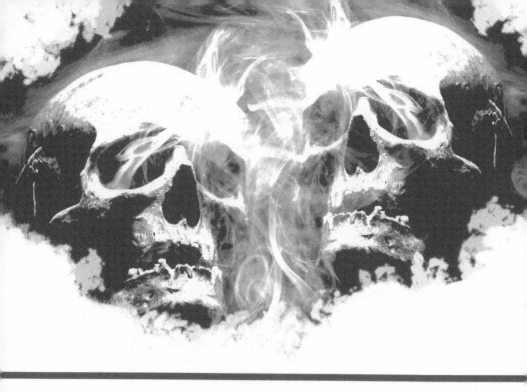

CHAPTER 6

Phoenix Rising

The rain fell overnight. There would be no smallmouth fishing. I decided to hear out Eddie's friend on this thing. The Massengale and Parrish mystery had a narcotic feel that so many of these cases have. What the hell happened to them? Plus, I had the time and was looking for direction anyway now that the move to Chelsea was complete. More importantly, I sensed that Eddie really wanted me involved.

As a result, over coffee on Sunday morning I committed to getting a LexisNexis account through the University of Michigan. I would do a sweep of every newspaper article on the case from May of '84 to the present and access the archive of broadcast news stories at Vanderbilt University. The information would likely be redundant, but Fountain's sloppiness in part of his account of the murders suggested that some key nuggets might be unearthed.

"Stories in the local papers will likely not be in the Lexis database," I said while hooking up the dogs.

"I'll draw up a list," Eddie said. "The local libraries probably have some on microfilm, or the offices for the papers?"

"Yup," I said. "That'll take time."

"Thanks," he said.

I drove home in a steady rain all the way through Lansing.

• • • • •

I spent my fortnight between visits to Spinnerfall wisely. In addition to the research, I finished off a piece on fall spinnerbait strategies for *Michigan Fishing and Hunting*. It was my second piece for them since moving to Chelsea. My letter of introduction to the editor, Bob Wills, had garnered a phone call in return. He was excited at the prospect of me writing for them.

"You'd have to be a contributor for now," he said. "My field editor staff is solid at present."

"That's all I want, Bob, but I'll need some direction on topics."

"Would you be willing to delve into some conservation issues?" he asked.

"I'll need time to get up to speed."

So much for taking a break from outdoor stuff, but writers write, and I was itching to make words and chisel out stories. The pay covered groceries and utilities for the month. It was satisfying.

Eddie let me take one of his fly rods home to practice on Cam's lakes. Kody was intrigued and I tried to show him how to cast in the Krenshaw's front yard. He picked it up and the next thing I knew Kody was catching 'gills in every lake. We had a couple of fine fish fries as a result.

"Good thing he still doesn't mind cleaning fish," Cam said one pleasant summer evening on his deck in the backyard.

"Yeah, I don't know how long that'll last," I said.

"Probably until he gets a girlfriend," Cam said.

"Already bird-dogging one," Callie said as she cleared the

table and brought us another pitcher of sweet tea. "Takes after his father." She shot us a sly face.

Callie Krenshaw was an attractive woman in her late fifties by my guess, but she looked at least ten years younger with light brown hair and a trim figure. She had been a cheerleader at Michigan State in the late sixties and had stayed in shape over the years. The Krenshaws' oldest son, Joel, was a junior at State. This was a Green and White house, so I treaded lightly at times.

All of this was going on while Kody played "press coverage" with the dogs. The game involved Kody pretending to either go out for a pass or cover Sam or Sham while they did the same. Cousin Lennie Krenshaw, only 10 years old, played quarterback with a tennis ball. Kody was trending toward the Maize and Blue, despite his mother's protests. It was creating a house divided, something every Michigander understood and dreaded.

"Cam," I said then carefully arranged my thoughts. "What do you remember about those missing trout fishermen?"

"Oh, the college boys from Central?" he said. "Well, it was a big deal. Sorta been resurfaced with the Bigfoot thing and that book."

"Shitty book."

"I guess he's in some hot water. That happen much, Arthur?"

"Only when you lie or make stuff up."

"Well, I could have told him something useful."

"Really, what?"

"I had a great uncle, Paul Krenshaw. His side of the family has a deer cabin up by McKinley. They've had it for 85 years."

"How's that?"

"Paul had some building skills. He was a self-taught engineer you could say. East Michigan Power was building the dams on the Au Sable back then. Paul went up there to work on them, good money. He lived in a tent, did his job and also supplied the camps with fresh venison and some trout. The man was a hunting and fishing machine."

"Kody might be headed in the same direction."

"Oh, the boy won't hunt. Wants to play football but loves fishing as you well know." Cam finished off another bluegill fillet then took a swig of tea. "Anyway, Paul bought some land around 1916. He went to France the next year. Didn't get back up there until the spring of '20, built the cabin then."

"Near McKinley?"

"South side of the river. You were off Parmalee Bridge?"

I nodded.

"About 20 miles due east. Anyway, he told me once that people up there were close-knit with their own rules and code for living. Most of them felt that whatever happened to you, well, you probably had it coming."

"You think there's a local angle to what happened?"

"Yeah, I sure do, especially now that we know that Bigfoot thing was bullshit."

"My friend is looking into the murders. He wants me to help him."

"Be careful if you do."

• • • • •

I arrived at Spinnerfall on Monday afternoon, the last week of August, in effect the last week of summer. Labor Day was right around the corner.

Eddie was sitting on the couch reading a book, *Europe's Last Summer*. It seemed in spirit with the day.

"How's that book?"

"Very straightforward and very good," he said.

"Does the Archduke still get assassinated?"

"He always does, and they always fuck it up."

"Well here's some lite reading," I said and dropped several files of articles on the coffee table.

"How many?"

"One hundred and twenty-seven articles, two-hundred and twelve pages in total from the *Ann Arbor News*, *Detroit Free Press*,

Detroit News, Lansing State Journal, Grand Rapids Press, Bay City Times, Traverse City Record-Eagle, Toledo Blade, Cleveland Plain Dealer, Chicago Tribune, New York Times, Washington Post, Associated Press and *Reuters*," I said. "I'm waiting on a CD of broadcasts from Vanderbilt."

"How many?"

"Fifty-three," I said. "I need to transcribe and return the CD in sixty days."

"Why?"

"It's their policy."

"Find anything?"

"I have yet to go through it in detail."

"OK. Great work! I'm gonna go on a run. Zac should be here around 1700 hours."

"Five o'clock for us civilians."

"Let me brief you on Zac."

I got the dogs squared away. Then Eddie gave me some background on Phoenix.

By the end of a highly detailed account by Eddie, including several "incidents" during a joint training mission involving observation drones and attractive women that got both in hot water, I could speak chapter and verse on Black Zac.

Zachariah Phoenix was from Youngstown, Ohio. He went to Youngstown State and joined the Reserve Officer's Training Corps before ever setting a foot on campus. It was the only way that he could afford college.

Zac went on active duty in 1978 and had pursued a path in military intelligence on the recommendation of a commanding officer. He was interested from the start. Mysteries had always intrigued him. He preferred spying on his friends rather than playing with them, at least some of the time but Zac was always ready for games like capture the flag or hide and seek. He loved plotting ways to win. On a promise to his mother, Zac chose domestic intelligence. She had lost a brother in Vietnam during Tet and an uncle in Korea from the Chosin retreat.

The United States Army had a domestic intelligence unit because of the need during World War Two to monitor defense facilities for Nazi espionage. The Cold War only made it more necessary. It was not a glamorous posting. Some soldiers and officers felt that it was cowardly rearguard bullshit. Zac was unfazed by that. He knew that the Cold War was a multifront chess match with the Soviets that was likely to be won by whoever kept their secrets best. With billions of dollars being spent at hundreds of companies to develop superior weapons there were plenty of places for The Bear to poke around. It was a difficult assignment in an open society. The soldier with a rifle at Checkpoint Charley was able to see his mark, but for Zac it could be anybody.

This was not the stuff of a James Bond film. Zac Phoenix didn't have any fancy gadgets. His tools were pen and notebook. His beats were endless interviews with prospective employees at companies with defense contracts as well as their friends, relatives, co-workers and even teachers going back to junior high. School records were examined as well as membership in any groups from high-school glee clubs to fraternities, sororities, 4-H, optimists clubs, Rotarians, unions and so on as well as any causes the "target" in question might have supported such as civil rights or banning the bomb. It all mattered because any group or cause could potentially be avenues for access by the other side. Bank records were perused as well and continually monitored. Sometimes targets were tailed and surveilled, but rarely.

He became a master at digging for information. Per Zac, there was always another interview, always another record to examine and, most importantly, always another person in the target's orbit that needed scrutiny. As computers came into more use Zac's skills only improved. He had taken all the computer classes that Youngstown offered and even commuted to Pitt and Ohio State for additional courses. It was the era of key punching, but the training got him ready for the information revolution to come.

In the 1980s, Zac was part of the first Army unit to begin using computers to monitor potential targets. A decade later, he was working with a new generation of "whiz kids" to hack into emails and personal files, crack passwords, and install spyware, all while learning how to defend against the other side doing the same.

It led to a solid if not particularly spectacular military career. Zac never captured a Russian operative let alone turned one. There were never any grand operations straight out of a Ludlum or le Carre novel. Zachariah Phoenix was not Jack Bauer, although he sometimes worked as many hours in a day. Instead, most red flags he turned up pointed in an entirely different direction: the unfettered free market and unchained lust of capitalism. The bulk of spying in America was corporation on corporation, industrial espionage. As a result, Zac practically had the FBI and Justice Department on speed dial.

But it wasn't all for naught. Declassified files released by the Russian Republic in the late 1990s, when there was a flicker of romance for democracy and a free society over there, indicated that Phoenix's work had chased away many operatives. They chose to concentrate wherever his eyes, or his charge's eyes, were not looking. Had every intelligence officer been so thorough, The Bear might not have won the spying battle while still losing the Cold War.

Despite all of it, Zac never got to go to the Army War College for that Gold Star. He retired a colonel and was awarded the Distinguished Service Medal. It was still a slap in the face that had roots as pedestrian as his choice of service (it was the slowest promotion track of them all), dramatic as a brawl in a bar (where he got the name "Black Zac") and as dark as the country's original sin.

· · · · ·

I was playing with the dogs when a black Ford Expedition pulled into the parking area around quarter after five. Both Sammy and Shammy darted for the picture window, put their paws on the pane and let out a couple of barks.

"Relax, girls," I said. "It's a friend." Then I went out to greet him.

A man in a black suit with a light blue shirt and navy tie got out of the SUV. He was a light-skinned African American wearing those wraparound "Terminator" sunglasses that were all the rage. He moved toward me with a crisp pace and then took off those shades.

"Arthur Jenkins," he said, "I'm Zac Phoenix. It's a pleasure. I've heard a lot about you over the years." He extended his hand.

"Mr. Phoenix," I said and shook his hand.

"Zac, please."

Zac had a smooth face with short-cropped hair showing a bit of frost on the sides. The eyes that were deep set but still sharp as a hawk's while they darted from me to around the front yard and back again: absorbing, processing and concluding. His nose was aquiline and the jawline strong, adding to the raptor visage. If he had wings, I could see Phoenix flying around coast to coast looking for vermin in the fields. The frame was military grade, wide shoulders, narrow hips all standing a bit beyond six feet. By Eddie's account, "Zac was knocking on the door of 50," but he could have passed for a robust 30.

"Eddie made up a room for you in the lodge. Can I help you with anything?"

"Sure, there's a couple of boxes in the back seat. I'll grab my briefcase and bag. Long day, Arthur."

"Where did you come from, Cleveland?" I asked, figuring Zac might be an investigator for Eddie's firm.

"No," he said, "Chicago, with a stop in Grand Rapids." Zac pressed the lock button and the Expedition chirped. This caused some barking by the girls.

"Oh, that's right, Leapfrog mentioned dogs. Let's get the introductions over with out here."

"Good call, Zac. Dogs respond better to strangers in the open."

"I always play the odds, Arthur Jenkins," he said with the soulful tone of a deejay on some smooth jazz station letting the listeners know the last song was *Breezin'* by George Benson with *Street Life* by Randy Crawford coming up after the break.

By now, both dogs could be trusted in the daytime not to run off. Still, I brought them out on leashes. Zac set his bags down and held his hands out.

"I come in peace young ladies," he said, then slowly bent his knees to their level. "See, smell, I want to be your friend." In a few moments, Sammy licked one hand and Shamrock did the same with the other. Within a minute he was rubbing their bellies.

"Now, my fine, new friends," he got back up, "may I enter your home?"

Sammy went to the door and wagged her tail. Shamrock was nudging his left hand for more petting.

"You must be a dog person?" I asked.

"I've never had one. My daughters had cats, and a fish or two."

"But you like them?"

"Most of them. I've been to thousands of houses in my line of work. The majority had dogs. I had to learn how to…pacify them."

"I see."

Zac instructed me to put the boxes by the coffee table. He put his briefcase next to them. Then I showed him to his room down the hall.

"Can I get you anything?"

"Oh, coffee would be nice."

I made a pot while Zac settled in on one of the couches.

"I finally get to see Spinnerfall," he said when I came back with a cup.

"You know about this place?"

"Sure, I've been to Camp Grayling, let's see," and he rolled those eyes to an upper angle while recalling. "at least seven times in my 25 years of active duty. Some of it was training and some of it was instructing, always stayed on base. I knew Esch, we were not close. Avar wasn't a bad guy. God rest his soul."

"I guess this place had a helluva reputation."

"Party central in the 1980s. They parked a couple of Strykers here one time, shit to pay for that stunt, but the ladies loved it, I'm told."

"Almost a monastery now."

"That fits, where is Leapfrog?"

"Eddie's on a run. Is that his military handle?"

"He's had several. But that's what I call him."

"How'd he get that one?"

"By being bumped from second lieutenant to captain in only six months. Rarely happens, especially in peacetime."

"I remember that." Eddie had sent me a copy of an article on his fast-track promotion from *Stars and Stripes*.

"How's he doing?"

"He was a little manic when I first saw him up here two weeks ago, a bit moody, too."

"That makes sense after 18 months in the sandbox. Plus, the extracurriculars."

"You mean Smutek?"

"Roger on that, Arthur."

"He says that went OK."

"No, FUBAR." Zac made a sour face. "Major FUBAR. He talked out of turn in class."

"He made it sound like he saved the day by getting out in front of the story."

Zac sighed. Then padded his suit pocket.

"Let's step outside for a smoke. I never smoke inside."

We went to the porch.

"There's something to getting out in front of the story," Zac said after a couple of draws on his Camel. "It wasn't his call, and he shouldn't have used such a quotable phrase."

"Or we brought it with us?"

"Yes, it made for a handy headline. Practically a bumper sticker. Look, Arthur, I am not as old a friend of his as you are, but, trust me, I love the man. Listen, he did a good job over there. It was tough going. Eddie was part of a recruitment of personnel to clean up a mess, and it's all of that and then some, but I know this...he came home early."

"That's what I thought. Zac, this thing with Massengale and Parrish, do you think he's trying to, ah, find a path to redemption?"

"Interesting take on it," he said then sent those eyes on tilt in thought. "I know that his firm did not welcome him back with open arms. That's Bullshit! The public loves us in public you know. It's all, 'Thank you for your service,' but when it comes to actions, well, the vet doesn't always get the same in process."

"Could the Smutek thing be involved? Eddie thinks so."

"In perception, yes, in practice, no. They did not have a hand in that. Smutek and their allies, like Halliburton, just want loose cannons gone. His firm, however, might see potential vulnerabilities because of what Eddie said. My sense is that they have him wandering the wilderness, so to speak, until the dust settles. He likes a challenge. He can't sit still. It made him a great soldier. This might be something to keep him busy and, it happened practically in his backyard."

"Is there anything to it?" I asked, but before Zac could answer there was the sound of foot beats.

"Breech on your right flank, C-2!" It was Eddie.

"Ah, shit!" Zac yelled. "Forward position already sussed your ass, Fletcher! Machine guns cut you off at the hip five seconds ago. HOOAH!" He stubbed out his smoke and ran toward Eddie.

"Too agile for your sorry-ass gunners!" Eddie screamed back.

"Fuckin-A to that!"

The men embraced and started screaming "HOOAHS!" then started chanting "Ugha! Ugha! Ugha!" while bouncing up and down.

The dogs went crazy inside with their own barking cadence.

It was chaos for nearly a minute.

I stood with hands on hips and waited for the commotion to settle.

"You wanna drink?" Eddie asked Zac.

"No. I am still on the clock."

"Well, I'm gonna have a beer," Eddie said. "Off the scotch for now." He gave me a look.

"You're off the scotch?" Zac asked, "Now, Fletcher, since when?"

"Oh, you know what they say, C-2. Scotch makes everybody a genius. I'm already a genius." He headed inside to greet the dogs.

"And so, it begins," Zac said with a smile. "And so it begins."

Zac arranged some papers on the coffee table while Eddie fixed a plate of smoked whitefish and crackers. I refreshed our coffees. The dogs set about chewing on their bones.

"Give me a moment to check on the steaks," Eddie said, "still marinating."

"Yes, dear," Zac replied then smirked.

I looked over the dossiers that Zac had brought on both Donny Massengale and Roland Parrish. Donny was from Dexter, just north of Ann Arbor. Roland was from Jackson, the next county to the west. They were boys of that time and place, the 1960s and '70s. They collected baseball cards, went to summer camps, joined the Boy Scouts, played little league, did "OK" in school, had summer jobs once the summer camps were done. Donny cut lawns and flipped burgers at McDonald's. Roland worked at a machine tool factory in town. They loved the outdoors, especially fishing.

Donny was a tad short and stocky and was a fair wrestler. He had black hair, already receding in his senior photo, hazel eyes, and a ruddy complexion that he tried to hide by shaving only now and then in hope that the black stubble would smooth his features. He was popular. Friends remembered him as smart, funny and industrious.

Roland was well over six-feet tall, whipsaw lean and ran cross-country but wasn't all that fast. He had soft blue eyes, a pale patrician face, and fine reddish-blond hair. His few friends described Roland as quiet in nature with a tendency to go his own way. Even his parents felt that Roland was enigmatic, especially by college. If he wasn't tinkering with his prized 1970 Camaro,

Roland was hiking the Kalamazoo or St. Joe rivers for small-mouth bass.

They had long hair, did some drinking, smoked some pot, listened to rock n' roll, had girlfriends and so on. I knew lots of guys like them way back when.

They became friends in college during their sophomore year at Central Michigan.

Donny was studying history, but like many undergrads he had little idea how that would help him after school. Roland was more practical, majoring in marketing. The two boys shared plenty of interests — fishing and the Detroit Tigers topping the list.

In the spring of 1984, both Donny and Roland were on schedule to graduate on time with a better sense of their futures. Donny, who had impressed a number of faculty in his field, was going to pursue a masters degree somewhere, possibly the University of Michigan. He told his parents that a scholarship or even a fellowship was possible. Roland was already looking at advertising and public relations firms in Detroit, Lansing and Grand Rapids.

They had planned to stay in Mount Pleasant that summer. Donny was an assistant manager of the local Little Caesars pizza shop where he'd worked since the start of college. Roland was going to be a delivery boy for Little Caesars while taking summer courses in computer science hoping to bone up his resume for next year's job search. Donny had been dating Melissa Sasso, a redheaded sociology major from Ferndale, on and off for over a year. Roland didn't have steady girlfriend, but really wanted one.

They had about ten days before spring term, so Donny and Roland took off for that ill-fated week of fishing on the Au Sable River. Donny had learned to fly fish as a young boy on the Au Sable thanks to that uncle who was immersed in the sport. Roland had only tried it out the previous summer.

They would spend most of the week at that uncle's cabin near Luzerne.

Except they wouldn't.

"Ok," Eddie said after setting down the plate and his Labatt's Blue. "Whaddya got?"

"A couple of hundred pages of reports on the case, plus some maps and names of those who were interviewed," Zac said. "These are from the State Police files, most of the counties are not digital."

"How did you get them, FOIA?" I asked.

Zac looked at me for a moment. "Can't do that," he said. "It's still an open case."

"Oh, I see. You...*hacked* them?"

"We procured them." Zac looked annoyed. "Fletcher, didn't you brief Arthur on this?"

"Didn't get to that part," Eddie said. "I needed your help in explaining it."

"Isn't that illegal?" I asked. "Can't we get in trouble?"

"We are not going to get caught," Zac said. "The State Police database is practically an open book. Besides, we were careful, very careful."

"But still, it feels wrong."

Zac sighed and rolled his eyes.

"Art," Eddie said. "We're not doing this for the Russians or the Chinese. We are not gathering oppo work for some political campaign. We are not going to sell this to some tabloid. We need to know what the authorities did or did not do."

"We could have obtained it old school by greasing a palm or two," Zac said, "but that's how you do get caught."

"It happens?" I asked.

"Oh yes," Zac said. "Sometimes people can get talked into it. How do you think some of those true-crime books get written? You could ask for permission, get denied and spend the next ten years spinning your wheels. You got that time, Arthur? I don't and neither does Fletcher."

I stared back at him then said, "And why do you think reporters use anonymous sources? Yeah, I get it because it happened with my book, but I didn't have to pay. People wanted to help." This was all conciliatory on my part.

"And they slipped you internal memos and records," Zac said. "Nobody sued."

"There were threats," I said. My book had some information on sweet deals between developers and politicians that were possibly illegal and certainly untoward. In a couple cases laws were likely broken. I approached the proper authorities, but nothing was ever done. "You read my book?"

"I did my homework," Zac said coolly. "Are we good, Arthur?"

Eddie was rubbing his hands while I considered it. The truth was that if we were serious about this then we needed to know as much as possible as soon as possible. I wasn't interested in riding hobby horses to fill a void in my life, but, for now, I would stay on board.

"Yes," I said. "Can you give us a summary before going into any details?"

"Of course," Zac said appearing relieved. "The bottom line is that whoever killed Massengale and Parrish had a significant head start, caught a break due to the elements, benefitted by the inexperience of local law enforcement as well as the hostility of the community toward them and were shielded by an even bigger crime. The killers were extraordinarily lucky, but they also had some experience in these matters and the temperament to handle the situation."

"That's a lot," Eddie said. "Break it down."

"First," Zac said. "We can assume that the boys were killed in the early hours of Monday, April 30th. They were not reported missing until Monday the 7th of May at just after noon. That allowed for an entire week to dispose of the bodies without anyone aware of the crime.

"Second, the area received about four inches of rain starting on Tuesday morning and continuing until late Friday night. It was a cold rain. The river went up two feet. This cut down on traffic in and around the suspected area of the killings and covered up evidence like blood, footprints and tire tracks."

"Where's the suspected area?" I asked.

"Here," Zac said and brought out a map of the area with a blue circle stretching south to Roscommon, north to Gaylord, west to Grayling and east to Glennie. "An area of 3500 square miles, almost all of it dense woods, some of it very remote."

"Much of it is National Forest?" I asked. Because of the scars of lumbering, Michigan had been among the first states to have large areas set aside as refuges for the replanting of trees, particularly pines.

"Almost all of it," Zac said.

"Initial response from law enforcement?" Eddie asked.

"Crawford, Alcona, Roscommon, Iosco and Montmorency sheriff's departments plus U.S. Fish and Wildlife and Department of Natural Resources law enforcement." Zac produced a roster of the entities plus numbers of officers involved. "They get an A for effort but a C minus, at best, for execution."

"Where were the State Police?" I asked.

"They did not show up in numbers until Wednesday."

"Why?" Eddie asked.

"There's the inexperience part," Zac said. "That plus a turf battle. Most of the land was federal."

"Ridiculous," Eddie said and produced a can of Skoal. "And FBI?"

"I'll get to that."

"You mentioned inexperience," I said.

"Most murders in this neck of the woods are pretty straight forward," Zac said. "A husband kills a wife or vice versa. A simmering feud between neighbors turns violent. A drunken brawl ends up going sideways. A drunk driver gets in a hit-and-run. There are clear antecedents to the crime or lots of witnesses. The perps are not hardened criminals or psychopaths. They crack quickly. There are complete confessions. It's over in a day or two. There are rarely prolonged investigations.

"Sometimes bodies are found in the woods. A deer hunter has a heart attack. A snowmobiler hits a tree. There's no sign of foul play. It's easy to solve. This case was entirely different. The training was not as thorough back then for rural law entities. The resources were just not in place. They weren't ready for something like this."

"Hostile community?" Eddie asked.

"This was directed at the Fish and Wildlife as well as DNR. They are not well thought of around here. People wouldn't talk to them."

"That's true," Eddie said. "DNR means Damn Near Russian for many of my friends."

"This is the land of militias and sovereign citizens. A place for outliers. People don't like the state and federal governments. Plus, there was that diseased cattle thing in the '70s."

"Oh, yeah," I said. "The PBB thing."

"Correct," Zac said. "The state forced a burial of the cattle north of here. Really pissed off the citizens. They ended up winning a court case to prevent all the cows from being interned. It went all the way to the Michigan Supreme Court."

"And people are still pissed today about that," Eddie said. "So, the Staties show up. How'd that go?"

"The Michigan State Police Department has a reputation as one of the best in the country," Zac said. "Then and now. They had a forensic office in Grayling. They had their top staff ready to examine evidence. After some confusion, State Police took over the case, recanvassed the locals with county cops, got the feds and DNR to run the searches and drag the river and lakes."

"Sounds about right," Eddie said before packing a chew.

"What evidence did they find?" I asked.

"Nothing in reality. Garbage dumps, old clothes, animal bones, none of it new or related to Massengale and Parrish."

"Their truck?" Eddie said then spat into a paper cup.

"Oh, what a clusterfuck that was," Zac said shaking his head. "First, they got both the model and color wrong. Second, they did not issue a correct license plate until Friday afternoon, twelve days after the murders likely occurred."

"How can that happen?" I asked. Fountain never mentioned this in his book.

"They went by the neighbor's recollection instead of checking with the family. Finally, one of the fathers noticed the mistake."

"I can guess what the big crime was," Eddie said.

"The Bigfoot murders. They'd found seven bodies in the previous six months, eighteen in all by that point, going back to late '79. Now, of course, we know that none of those most recent bodies were victims of Tobias because he was in Montana, but back then he was getting credit for every unsolved homicide. BFK was the Bogeyman in Michigan that spring and for years and years afterwards."

"Any of his victims found near here?" Eddie asked while scratching Shamrock's head.

"Most were on the west side of the state," Zac said then shuffled through some papers. "The closest were two up in Cheboygan County, 1980 and '81."

"Fee Bee," Eddie said, "What about those assholes?"

"They sent two agents from the Behavioral Sciences Unit in mid-May. They stayed for two days and then went to Lansing for a week."

"Why?" Eddie said.

"To work with the Bigfoot Task Force. This was the early days of profiling. I think they were more interested in gathering data on Bigfoot for their files."

"What were their conclusions?" Eddie said.

"I don't have that at present," Zac said. "I think that we should go FOIA if we need it." Then he looked at me. "Federal data sets are a tougher nut to crack."

"I'm sure that you could do it, C-2," Eddie said. "So let me guess, the Fee Bees believed it's Bigfoot or a copycat. They influenced the direction of the investigation."

"You are correct, sir. There had been thoughts about a carjacking gone wrong, but, surprisingly, there was little follow-up. *As their eyes turned to Bigfoot the local focus was lost.*"

"Any concern with those werewolf parties?" I asked. My trepidation about Zac's methods were abating as the case came into form.

"The Oscoda sheriffs were very concerned. But it was April, a Sunday night, cold, and werewolf parties were summer events. Interestingly, there were internal memos on the lack of evidence for any parties in that summer or the next one. The conclusion was that there were too many 'eyes in the woods' so the kids stopped doing it or found another spot. The parties resumed in '86, but the sheriff cracked down. They raided one, found a lot of underage drinking."

"Any arrests?" Eddie asked.

"None on record. No other mention of parties in the files I obtained."

"Anything on ritual sites in the woods, animal sacrifice, devil worship?" I asked.

Zac looked confused. Eddie filled him in.

"That's new information," Zac said. "Entirely new, no record in anything I have. It's a reasonable lead to follow...But..." He swung those hawkeyes to the corners and tilted his head in consideration. "Interesting," he sighed. "But let's not get ahead of ourselves in that regard."

"Why?" I asked.

"Arthur, you're a media guy," Zac said, "do you remember the McMartin preschool case back in the late '80s?"

"I do, what a clusterfuck."

"Fill me in," Eddie said. "I was busy keeping us free back then."

"Thank you for your service," Zac said with an exaggerated smile.

Eddie shot him a double-barreled bird. We all laughed then I told Eddie about the McMartin preschool case of alleged massive child abuse, animal sacrifices and devil worship, among other lurid details, that was the Flagship of the Satanic Panic Era. It was sensational. It spawned nationwide concern about satanists corrupting our youth. It fed the media three square meals a day for years. And it was a complete lie based on the ramblings of a mother mired in schizophrenia, improper interviewing of the children, poor police work and the rise of hyperbolic TV talk shows on the prowl for the next big story.

"Leap," Zac said after I finished, "I wonder if your friends might have been influenced by all that. Coulda been some creative campfire thing that they mistook for deviltry."

"Those guys are pretty straightforward," Eddie said. "Besides, Art said all that McMartin crap was in the late '80s."

"Mid to late," I injected.

"My guys saw this in the early '80s, all gone by '84, the year of the killings."

Zac pondered this.

"Look, Ramirez is an avowed satanist," I said to break the silence. "Berkowitz now claims to have been part of a cult and there's strong evidence to support that." I had studied media coverage of The Son of Sam killings while working on my Doctorate at Florida. "It can happen."

"Both have mental illnesses," Zac said. "Gentlemen, if we start claiming 'the devil made 'em do it' then we'll be laughed out of any meeting with law enforcement."

"But what if he did?"

"It's a case of what came first. The serpent or the egg. It could be bad people trying on those beliefs as a fashion statement rather than the beliefs turning them bad. They were a murderer waiting to be born regardless."

"They killed animals out there," Eddie said after a spit. "That's a hallmark of psychopaths and a roadmap to murderers. Screw the whole devil thing. The altars are a solid lead."

"They are worth a look, Leap," Zac said. "Maybe whoever built those things and did those deeds might be connected to the case or know somebody involved, but we bury the word 'satanist' because is too charged, too much baggage."

"Not if they open the door."

"Tread lightly on that, Leap," Zac said looking concerned.

"I will. What's your theory of the case, C-2?" Eddie asked.

"A carjacking gone wrong makes sense," he said. "Or they stumbled into something that they were not supposed to see. A row with locals is less plausible. It goes back to a brawl going sideways. It's sudden, unexpected and almost always involves witnesses and individuals unlikely to execute the clean disposal of the bodies, keeping them hidden for 21 years with nobody talking. The new angle with the altars should be investigated, but I still think that this was likely folks with criminal backgrounds and more than a drop or two of cold-bloodedness. Those boys are gone, completely gone."

We sat in silence pondering what that meant.

"I'm ready for that drink now, Fletcher," Zac finally said.

After dinner we sat on the porch. I played fetch with Shamrock while Sammy sat by Eddie and Zac's feet chewing a bone.

"Are you still thinking about a security branch, C-2?" Eddie asked. Zac had filled me in on his private investigation firm while we were eating. He started it within months of leaving the service back in 2003. The company had five employees, a case manager and four field agents, all licensed private eyes. There were also some "off the books" operatives. ("Trust me, Arthur," Zac had said between bites, "It's more cloak than dagger. I haven't been knocked out by a sap in over a month.")

"Still figuring out the details," Zac said. "There's overhead in the equipment necessary to do it properly. Cyberspace is three-dimensional chess when the big boys are involved."

"You're the biggest boy of all, C-2," Eddie said.

I froze at the comment. Zac shot him a dirty look, but thankfully in jest.

"I'm the blackest Zac of them all, homey," he said, and they both burst out laughing.

"Can I ask a question?" I said.

"Well, I don't know, Art," Eddie said. "You only have

assembled in front of you the very heart of U.S. military intelligence during the latter quarter of the 20th century."

"Don't pin that bullshit on me, Fletcher," Zac said, but he was enjoying it.

"You call Zac C-2 and I understand that is the designation for a company's intelligence officer."

"He's the lynchpin in the field gathering raw intel," Zac said.

"But Eddie said that your nickname was 'Black Zac.' I'm confused."

"Well, disinformation is the new superweapon."

"Tell him the fucking story, C-2," Eddie said.

"1984 NBA Finals, the big showdown between the Lakers and Celtics. I'm sitting in a bar in McLean, Virginia, called 'Roosters' with nine other guys, all Army, getting ready to watch Game One."

"I know the place," Eddie said. "Catered to our branch, but a couple of Fee Bees sometimes showed up."

"Yes, sir, slumming with the proletariat," Zac said with a twisted smile.

"Musta been a Monday," Eddie said. "The country club was closed." I would never understand why Eddie and Zac hated the FBI. Maybe it was tribal.

"Anyway, this peckerwood of a sergeant named Milford says, 'It's Laker talent versus Celtic character' and I lose my shit. This guy is always pulling that crap. I stand up and start shouting because it's a noisy bar, 'Excuse me, Sergeant, but this is Black Zac telling you that the Lakers have character, too, and the Celtics have talent, too, and both teams have grit and heart and intelligence, too. You obviously know nothing about either team. This is Black Zac telling you to stick to watching NASCAR, you simple motherfucker!' I'd had a few scotches by then."

"What happened next?" I ask.

"Some guy behind me stands up and yells, 'Sit down and shut up, nigger,' so I turned around and decked him. One punch, out cold before he hits the floor, jaw broke in three places, but the floor did that last part."

"And?"

"Place broke out in a big brawl. Lots of damage, lots of injuries. We all got arrested. It was like something out of a western movie with glasses, pitchers and chairs flying around. A couple guys got thrown over tables, just a huge donnybrook. I got busted back to a gold bar, lucky not to do jail time. Somebody said the guy who yelled at me had a knife. They never found it."

"You were lucky," Eddie said, "and you had a new handle to boot."

"Shit, Fletcher. Ruiz knocked out two guys and threw another one into a wall. That one had a fractured skull. Ruiz didn't get busted."

"God, he was a force of nature," Eddie said. "Whatta warrior."

"He told the police and our CO that he was looking out for his fellow soldier. Just doing what he was taught, following our code. Ruiz would have been a great general."

"You would have been a great general," Eddie said.

"I guess that star wasn't in my stars," Zac said then finished his drink. "I miss Gilberto, more than any of them."

"What happened?" I asked.

"Iraq, first time," Eddie said, "sniper, the odd, angry shot."

• • • • •

The next morning, I found Eddie at the dining table with a cup of coffee and a pile of case files.

"When did Zac leave?" I asked.

"Around O-Seven Hundred."

"And how long have you been at that?"

"Since O-Five Hundred," he said. "Off to the library?"

"After some toast. Where's that thermos you have?"

Eddie pointed to a cupboard above the stove.

"You got the dogs covered?"

He nodded.

"My range is from 1982 to 1986," I said. "Any burglaries,

assaults, auto theft, fires, vandalism or other strange happenings, correct?"

"You are in compliance with the directive," he said. "We know a lot about what the police discovered concerning the murders, which was hardly anything, but little about what was going on in the area leading up to the murders or afterwards. If it's local then let's understand the locality in the early 1980s, copy?"

I saluted. He gave me the finger. The day began.

"Thanks for the baloney sandwiches," I said and passed Eddie the plastic baggies.

"More water?" he asked. I took one of the canteens.

My day at the Crawford County Library had been a long one. The microfilm projector was not functioning properly and some of the newspaper pages printed in unreadable smudges no matter what I or the library assistant tried to do. In some cases, I just took notes from the display. By day's end I was all the way through April of 1984. The "good stuff" was next.

Beyond some articles about werewolf parties, including several Letters to the Editor about them that can best be described as "Kids These Days!" there wasn't much. The biggest disappointment was no reports of vandalism or ritual sites being found in the woods.

"That was in Oscoda and Alcona counties," Eddie said. "Not sure if *Crawford County Avalanche* would have covered it." I had been debriefing him while we sat on those logs at his spot along the Au Sable.

"They covered cats being rescued from trees by the fire department, meetings of the local Rockhound Club and had 100 pages on the Canoe Marathon every one of the summers," I said.

"Those are big deals around here," he said.

I had met Eddie at the notch in the woods after he'd given me detailed instructions on how to find it even though I'd already been there once (he did those things). He was there waiting with all the equipment and a 'field dinner when I pulled in at 6:30. Happily, the food was not Army MREs since I usually didn't shit for a week after eating one. By "nineteen hundred hours" we were at our position, rigged and enjoying a feast of baloney and ham sandwiches plus beef jerky. Eddie loved beef jerky.

"I had a better day with the files," he said while chewing some jerky.

"OK?"

"The clerk at the Shell station just down the block from the bar where Massengale and Parrish were last seen was open until midnight that night."

"That's surprising," I said. "April in sleepy Mio."

"Main street is M-33. That's the main artery on the east side of the state to I-75 so there's lots of weekend traffic. Remember, it was Opening Weekend of Trout Season. That was a super big deal back then."

"A lot more year-round water now?"

"Sure. So about 11:30 a middle-aged woman stops for gas but needs help with the pump. The clerk, James Kruger, 22, goes out and helps her. He sees someone using the pay phone by the edge of the parking lot. He can't see the person, but he hears the voice. It is a man's voice."

"Young, old?"

"Not the point."

"What is the point?"

Eddie's features brighten. "Staties do a phone dump on the calls that night from that booth. They catch a break because that call, at 11:40 p.m., was collect person-to-person," he said with the glee one might express when describing a pretty girl.

"I remember those."

"It was from Wilbur Marshall to his wife, Joan. Wilbur had been fishing up around Onaway. He was running late getting back to Flint. Joan was seven months pregnant. He didn't want her to worry."

"He has an alibi. Did he see the boys?"

"No, but after Marshall completes the call a 'young woman between 16 and 20' according to his interview comes up to him and then says, 'Oh, I thought you were somebody else,' and turns to walk away. Marshall asks if he can help her. She says to him 'I'm just waiting for some guys,' and walks away."

"Any further description of the girl?"

"No."

"Any follow-up on the girl?"

"None so far in anything I've read."

"Is Marshall still around?"

"There's a number and an address in the file. I called C-2. He's looking into it. I have assembled a question list. If we can find him that's our first interview."

"Sounds good," I said and then noticed a fish rise in front of us. "See that?"

"Yup," Eddie said. "Go out there and get him, Art. Remember, the fish is lying a couple of feet in front of that ring. Cast six or seven feet above it and mend that line."

I shuffled out in my Frankenstein boots, stripped out line and made my cast. The emerger landed short of the mark but as it drifted by where the rise had been there was a violent splash. Eddie had told me to wait a beat before raising the rod. "Think, 'Oh, he ate it' then set the hook lightly," he had said to me.

I did that. The rod bent and throbbed. The line went downstream then a trout jumped. I stripped it in. Eddie was there in seconds with a net. It was a rainbow on par with the best I'd caught before while nymphing.

"Great job!" he said. "Your first dry-fly fish!'

"There's another one," I said and pointed to a ring out farther in the stream.

"Go get it, but let me dust your fly." He produced a tube of white powder, not unlike cocaine, put the fly in it then shook it with his thumb over the opening. "There," he blew the excess powder off the fly. "You are ready for number two."

It took a bit of maneuvering to get to the spot and I wasn't exactly sure where the ring was by the time I got there. Several casts floated by but on the sixth or seventh one the fish took it. I hit it too hard and the hook came out.

"Slower! Oh, there's bugs hatching now!" he said. "See?"

I did. There were several white bugs flying past me in straight lines about ten feet above the water. A couple turned in neat 180s and came by me again. Then I heard a yell.

"Fish on!" Eddie said and I turned to see him with rod bent. He played the fish for about 30 seconds and brought it to net. "Another rainbow," he unhooked it and was quickly shaking his fly in that tube.

I heard a splash in front of me, turned around, and scanned the water. There was just the slightest dimple right next to me. I dropped the fly nearby. It disappeared. I set the hook and the rod bent and line shot upstream. This was a bigger tug, but it came loose in a blink. I retrieved the fly, blew on it and cast at another rise where I think the splash had come from. There was a strike as the fly landed. I set the hook and another rainbow started jumping across the surface. Eddie was too busy casting to another fish. I landed mine with my hands after fiddling around. This one was bigger than the last one and had speckles and a deeper shade of red on its sides. I quickly unhooked it and made my way to Eddie.

"I'll need more flies or some of the powder," I said.

He was unhooking another rainbow.

"Here's the dry shake and here's a container with a couple emergers and spinners."

"When do I put the spinners on?"

"In about 40 minutes. Watch the bugs in the air, some of them will start to shed their tails. You'll see it. Also, they will float like T's on the surface. Switch then. Good luck. This is going to get crazy." I hadn't seen him look this happy since our reunion.

Eddie loved fishing, especially when the bite was on.

The bite was on. It became a three-ring circus of piscatorial fun!

Things were happening too fast everywhere around me. The air was full of white specks, not unlike snow flurries. It never got as bad as Eddie had warned me. ("There can be blizzards of ephorons so thick that you cannot fish!") Instead, it was just the right amount. It seemed like every fish in the river was feeding. There were splashes, rings, dimples, boils and surface ripples of every type I had ever seen short of gamefish running schools of mullet or pilchards.

Eddie was right about the mayflies molting in midair. Their exoskeletons trailed behind them like the signs that planes tow around stadiums with messages like "Eat at Joes" or "Get a Coppertone Tan." White bugs of every life stage were floating by: shucks from nymphs, essentially grayish brown tissue; emergers popping through the film with wings expanding like highspeed films of flowers blooming; duns riding high on the water like sailboats gliding on a soft wind, some taking off then flying in straight lines up stream and joining others in an ephoronic rush hour over the river; and, finally, the spinners splayed out spent on the water from depositing eggs or fertilizing females, their short lives now complete. It was intoxicating in a very, very good way.

It was a clusterfuck for the most part. There were too many fish rising. Which one to cast to? I was paralyzed at times and became a tad manic. Then there was hooking them. Eddie's instructions got lost in the white noise of excitement. This was a new form of fishing! That alone had me reduced to the mindset of a five-year old. I just wanted to catch them all at once! Oh, and remembering to dry shake my fly, or change it, or make sure there weren't any wind knots from casting too fast, or not grab the line when a trout refused to come to my hand or not...slowing...down...and... thinking. Nope! Nope! Nope! I just could not do it.

ThereweretoomanyfishandIwantedthemall.

As result, I missed twice as many as I caught, seven in total. But the last one was the best, a brown trout, heavily freckled on a golden canvas, blue spot on the gill plate, and prominent lower jaw (it was a male) that reminded me of that linesided quarry of days gone by. It fought the best of any trout so far, jumping twice, but finally coming to hand and easily releasing. I'd give the fish 15 inches and with it I became hooked on casting fur and feathers far and fine.

Eddie did even better, a John Wayne Night or close to it. By his estimates, and for all of Eddie's bluster he was the most honest angler I'd ever known, he'd put 17 in the net, mostly rainbows and most under a foot. There were five browns to his tally, all over 14 inches. It helped that he had the only net.

I got to watch the last one. By then the bugs had thinned. Most of my flies were either gone, likely in some fish's jaw, or mangled beyond use. Besides, it was full on night. I could not see well enough to find risers or cover them very well. That would only come with experience.

Eddie was casting to a sound. It was sometimes a bloop and sometimes a gurgle. I couldn't see it, but he kinda did. Eddie would make a couple of casts, stop, wait, hear a noise, adjust his line, or move a step up, down, out, in, over and over like a dance, a very slow dance.

All the time Eddie was talking, mostly to himself, sometimes to me and occasionally to the fish, "Oh, the fucker moved." "Where'd you go?" "Did you see that one, Art?" "Oh, I thought you ate mine there, cocksucker."

And then the cocksucker did eat his.

There was a sucking sound just out in front of Eddie. He swung the rod above him. "Yes!" he cried. There was a pronounced displacement of water. The reel began the whine that for all fishers is sweet, sweet music.

"Gotta go full white, Art?" Eddie said, meaning he was turning on his headlight to the max setting. That would end any further fishing for the night, at least in this area.

"Whaddya need me to do?"

"Stay the fuck outta the way!"

Just as he said that the fish came out of the water. I couldn't see anything beyond a silhouette flying above the river for a few feet, but the splashes it was making were readily apparent. There were a lot of those. The fish jumped three more times. It took out a bunch of line. Eddie moved into the middle of the stream and then down river to gain some of it back.

"Art, flashlight, turn it on!" Eddie screamed.

"Oh, yeah, sorry," I said and got it out of my wader pocket.

"Keep it out of my fucking eyes!"

"Will do."

The fish started slashing on the surface. Eddie was walking it out of the river's main current and into the soft water. This allowed him to get back all the line. I backed up as he moved it to below the leaning cedar in a spot with no current.

"Here we go," he said, and snapped the net off its magnet on the back of his fishing vest. "Come 'ere, baby, come 'ere," he said as if he was coaxing one of the dogs over to the couch. "Alrighty. Alrighty." The fish made a sudden move throwing up a sheet of water. "Oh, now relax, relax." Then Eddie lifted his rod as far as his left arm would go above him, slid that extended arm back behind his ear and with his right arm reached out and scooped the fish into the net. The trout thrashed around violently inside the net for several seconds drenching Eddie's vest with water in the process.

"Art, take the rod," he said. I came over and did so.

"Oh, what a pretty girl," Eddie said looking at the fish in the net. It was a brown trout with fewer spots and some in different colors than the one I'd caught. My fish had uniformly dark brown spots. This one had some red and orange ones mixed in and even a couple with white circles around the blemishes. I mentioned this.

"Different strain," Eddie said. "So, your guess at length?"

"Better than 20 inches," I said. "That's the number you all are obsessed with in this sport. I'd say five pounds."

"Copy," he said. "All of five, probably 21 inches, 22 at outside. I don't tape em. Don't like to handle them much. Would like a picture. Waiting on a waterproof digital that takes something better than the shit that's out now."

"They are coming out next year," I said, "Not much bigger than a pack of smokes."

"See where the hook is," he said, and pointed to the corner of the mouth. "That's the sweet spot, hardly ever comes out, no lasting damage to the fish." He reached down and gently removed it. The fish fidgeted but only a bit. "It was 63-degree water when we started. OK, let me move her here so we can watch her after the release." Eddie stepped over to an area about a foot deep and carefully guided the fish out of the net. It swam a short distance over to a log, stuck its head underneath and remained motionless except for the lite feathering of its side fins.

Eddie reeled in his line, clipped off the fly, a spinner, now chewed to a stick of threads, and produced his can of Skoal.

"We'll watch her for a second," he said. We had both kept many fish in our lives from bream to bass, snapper to snook. In recent years there was a lot more letting go. When Eddie first started fishing the Au Sable, he kept trout because everybody did. Now he released all of them but made sure to do it correctly.

"Big fish burn a lot of energy in the fight. Too many people just plop them back in the water," he had told me while driving to his spot that first night. "That's lazy bullshit, but most people are talking the talk and not walking the walk." Eddie Fletcher could certainly talk, but few folks could match his stride.

We stood in silence and watched how the fish finally swung herself around to be parallel with the log, then moved several inches away from it, and finally swam off. It took about almost ten minutes.

"Let's go home," Eddie said.

We stumbled happily through the gates of flash tacks and then Eddie suggested a marching chant. "Which one do you like?" he asked. He'd taught me all of them.

"Always liked the three-day pass, sir," I said.

"Asked my general for a three-day pass," he sang, "A couple of whores and a bag of grass, sound off!"

"One, Two!" I shouted.

"Take it on down!"

"Three, Four!"

"Once again!"

"One, Two, Three, Four, One-Two, Three-Four!"

"Outstanding!" he said. "If I die on the Russian Front…"

We were all the way to the Girl from Kansas City by the time we got back to the trucks. It was like old times. We weren't two world-weary forty-somethings trying to make peace with our diminishing lives. No, we were young again, strong again, everything seemed possible again. For a couple of hours that night we had life by the ass again. It was wonderful, truly wonderful!

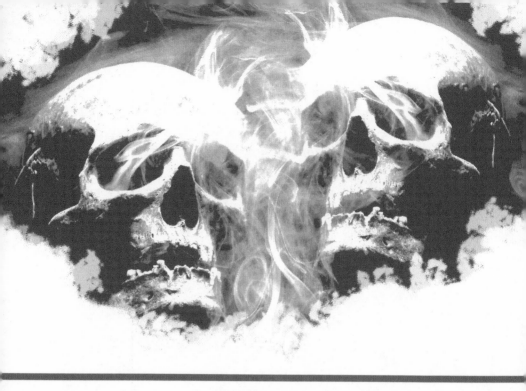

CHAPTER 7

The Girl in the Tree

Local Girl Found Dead in Woods
-Parents say she was troubled teen-

It was not the headline that I expected in the May 9, 1984, edition of the *Crawford County Avalanche*. Hanna Grey, 17, was found hanging in a tree off County Road 604 by two women hunting for mushrooms. The location was east of McKinley and south of the Au Sable River, not far from the 4001 Bridge, cited by Asa Fountain in his "account" of the deaths of Massengale and Parrish.

Grey's death was the big story of the issue. The search for Donny and Roland was in the right corner of the front page. The effect of the rainy weather on the early season of fishing, turkey hunting and mushroom picking received more coverage. My guess is that Massengale and Parrish broke as the paper went to press. It was a different era, and *The Avalanche* likely did not have the resources to turn on a dime as the news dictated.

The next edition was dedicated to the search with four full pages. Grey's death, now labeled an apparent suicide, did not appear until page three.

I followed Hanna's story through to her obit and funeral notice while I gathered the local pieces on Massengale and Parrish. She offered the only new angle. Almost everything on the missing trout anglers had appeared in the other bigger newspapers.

There was no speculation about a connection between Grey's death and the missing boys in any of the stories or the dozens of Letters to the Editor in those editions. Those letters spoke of a dark cloud over the area and mentioned the tension between locals and folks from downstate on several matters including: fishing regulations; too many rental canoes; wargame activities at Camp Grayling disturbing the peace; and efforts to enact federal regulations making the Au Sable a "Wild and Scenic" river.

"All these folks from somewhere else telling us what to do with our homes is an act of war," wrote one disgruntled citizen.

I hurried back to Spinnerfall around five p.m. in a light rain.

Eddie was on the phone with Zac. I took the dogs out then came back in as he was just hanging up.

"We found Marshall," he said, looking like the cat that ate the canary. "He's agreed to speak to us tonight."

"Already?" I said.

"Zac did his magic, but he doesn't like it when I use that term. Zac prefers 'elbow grease.'"

"Get him back on the phone," I said then set down the copy of the May 9th front page.

Eddie's eyes widened and he punched a number on his cellphone.

"Yeah," he said. "I'm putting you on speaker."

After making sure we could hear him, and he could hear us, I told Zac about the sad story of Hanna Grey.

"You're shitting me," he said after a moment. "This was the headline on May 9ᵗʰ?"

"I think Massengale and Parrish had just broke. They may have had more information on Grey."

"Do you have her obit?" Zac asked.

"Yes."

"Give me names, locations and relation of the survivors. Somebody's still alive, and we need to talk to them."

I went through the list.

"Hey, Art, while I have you on the phone," Zac said, "what do you think about this scenario, you hire my firm for one dollar to investigate this and I make Fletcher an Associate Investigator?"

"Why?" I asked because this was unexpected.

"Here's why. Marshall is a lucky break. He wants to talk but given the widespread publicity of the Fountain fiasco, plus the local's distrust of folks from somewhere else poking around, we need to have a good cover story. An investigation by a reputable private investigation firm to correct the erroneous accounts in the news and Fountain's book is our best shot at getting whoever is left to talk. We can make it sound like we're on their side."

"Are you willing to be public about your role in this?"

"Yes. In fact, our in-house discussion, including legal counsel mind you, came to a decision that it would be good for the firm."

"And you're not worried?"

"No, it's very unlikely that we will be doing anything more involved than we have already done. Doing searches on people and background checks are all perfectly above board."

"Doesn't Eddie need a license?"

"Not as an associate investigator. He's already overqualified with a JD."

"My job is to ask questions," Eddie said. "I know the law."

"An ID card and business card, letterhead, etc. should open some doors," Zac said.

"I'm not going to be breaking into houses or roughing up guys in alleyways, although I'd like the second part."

"Hands off, Fletcher," Zac said. "Liability issues."

"Copy, Art, this gives us credibility. If you and I, together or separately, just show up somewhere and start quizzing folks on this, well, how far do you think that's going to go?"

"Why do you need me?" I asked.

"Because of what you just found," Zac said, "and at the end of this we will need to present it in writing to the proper authorities, or beyond."

"Hold the phone!" Eddie said. "Hold The Fucking Phone!" Ever the multitasker, he'd been carefully reading the article while we chatted on the phone.

"What now, Leap?" Zac asked sounding a bit peeved.

"I think that I might know the son of one of these women," Eddie said. "The ones that found the girl."

"No shit," I said, Zac made some type of noise of surprise into the receiver as well.

"A guy from a fly shop, big-time guide."

"You got his number?" Zac asked.

"I can find it or ask around. He's got a cottage on the North Branch."

"Do it!" Zac said, and it sounded like an order.

"What about your law firm?" I asked. "Can you juggle all this?"

"I'm in full-time on this until they agree to put me on cases that lead back to the courtroom," he said. "I can swing the shit they have me doing now and this with no problem."

"And with Fletcher working for me it cuts costs to almost nothing," Zac said, getting back on subject.

"You are foregoing pay, Eddie?" I asked.

"Yes, this was all my idea anyway."

"And I am splitting costs as well," Zac said. "Because I am interested and if we do find useful information it will be good for my firm."

"My out of pocket beyond one dollar?"

"Let's cap it at one thousand for now," Zac said. "With Leap working for free and a friendly discount that means about 50 hours of digging. We can renegotiate when that's reached."

"Can I think about it for a week or so?"

"Let's go through the Grey search and possible interview with the sister who found Hanna. Hopefully somebody is still alive," Zac said. "After that I will need a decision. Everything is free until then."

"That's more than fair," I said. My interest in the case was piqued enough to go a full yard if we found something worth the hunt.

After a dinner of cold cuts, we dialed Marshall at 7 p.m., and he picked up on the second ring.

Eddie asked to put him on speaker, and after introductions we got right to our question list. Eddie established the nature of Marshall's call to his wife. Wilbur's memory of it fit with the police record.

"I was worried about Joan," Wilbur said. "She was kind enough to give me that fishing weekend knowing there wouldn't be much time once the baby was born."

"It all worked out?" Eddie said. We already knew that it did. The Marshalls' had a heathy baby girl named Melissa. Zac did his homework.

"Oh, yes," he said, "and now she's engaged!"

We offered our congratulations.

"About that night," Eddie said. "The young woman who came up to you after the call to your wife, what do you remember about her?"

"Well," he said. "She was certainly late teens. I figured she might be in college given that it was a Sunday night and late. I thought a high school kid would be home. You know, some colleges are out by late April."

"That's true. Can you describe her?"

"I can. Even in the streetlight I could tell she was attractive, tall, good figure, statuesque you could say. Being six foot five, I liked tall women."

"How tall?"

"Oh, five foot seven or so. My wife is five six and this woman was taller than her."

"Do you remember how long your hair was?" Eddie asked.

"Short, I worked at GM by then."

"That's interesting," Eddie said. "What's your hair color?" He seemed in deep thought.

"Brown."

"Can you describe the woman's face?"

"She was white, but the light wasn't good enough to see much beyond that."

"No eye color?"

"No."

"How was she dressed?" Eddie asked and started shuffling some papers on the table.

"Tight blue jeans. That was for sure, and a brownish spring coat. Oh, she had boots on. I remember the sound they made on the concrete. That might have made her taller, I guess."

"Her hair color?" Eddie asked, still searching for a folder on the desk.

"Not brunette and not blond. I'd say light brown or honey blond, and to the middle of her back. It was a nice look."

"And her voice?"

"Midwestern, just like yours or mine."

Eddie laughed.

"What was her disposition?" I asked. "How did she act?"

"Well, not rude but dismissive," he said, "like she was in a hurry. After she said that she was 'Looking for some guys,' she turned and walked away quickly."

"Back toward the bar?" Eddie asked.

"Bar?"

"Big Water Bar & Grill. That would be north of the Shell station."

"Yes, I watched her for a moment and that was that."

We said our good-byes and confirmed the possibility of a follow-up. Marshall agreed and thanked us.

"I am glad that somebody finally asked about the girl," he said then hung up.

Eddie found the folder.

"Here's a picture of Donny Massengale," he said while handing it to me. "He was 5 foot 7, stocky as you can see, a wrestler in high school."

"When's this taken?" I asked.

"Cocoa Beach," Eddie said, "Spring Break, March of '84."

It was a black and white of Donny in jams grinning back at the camera, young, carefree, and likely sunburnt, with less than two months to live.

"Here's Roland during a fall rush party in '83," Eddie said.

Parrish towered over a group of revelers with beers in hand, boys and girls buzzed and mugging for the camera.

"How tall was he?"

"Six foot five inches, short reddish-brown hair," Eddie said.

"Are you thinking what I'm thinking?" I asked and felt some excitement.

"I believe the girl was looking for Roland," Eddie said. "Now who the Hell was she?"

• • • • •

The next morning, I drove east on M-72 toward Mio retracing the route that Donny and Roland likely took on the last night of their lives. It was a solid avenue of trees for several miles. Eddie had finished all the police files and was drawing up a master list of people to interview. Zac would then begin the process of tracking them down.

The Oscoda County Library was a simple white cement-block building. The librarian, a woman slightly older than me with red hair and glasses, helped retrieve all the necessary cannisters for the *Oscoda County News*.

"An interesting time around here back then," she said. "Everyone was mad at everyone."

"Why?"

"I think the area was changing too fast. It was like the sixties finally caught up to us. Some kids were smoking pot and wearing longer hair. A whole bunch of people were concerned about the environment. There were bikers around. Some of them squatting in the woods."

"That was all new?" I asked.

"In 1980 it was still closer to 1950 around here," she said, "then, boom, it changed."

I began my sweep in 1981 and found plenty of stories on break-ins, bar fights and suspicious fires. There were articles on werewolf parties and illegal camping as well. Several Letters to the Editor voiced concern about vagrants living in the woods.

"If we don't watch it, some 'Manson Family' types could be around us waiting to strike," wrote one person.

I got back to Spinnerfall around 4 p.m. to find Eddie pacing the living room with Shamrock in his wake while Samantha watched them from the couch.

"We fucking found her!" Eddie shouted at me. "One of the sisters, and she's up here!"

"Which one?" I felt my pulse quicken.

"Mildred Deacon," Eddie said. "I know her nephew Josh Hall. We're going to their cabin after chow." He grabbed his cellphone and made a call while I took the dogs out.

The North Branch of the Au Sable River has long been considered the Uptown of the area. Many of the cabins go back a century or more. Like the original lodge at Spinnerfall, the area was the headquarters for the High and Mighty in those days. By midcentury, the burgeoning middle class gobbled up the estates as the American Aristocracy grew bored with the gentle Au Sable and set their sights on more exotic locales.

Such was the case with the cabin of Mildred Deacon. Along with her sister, Iris Hall, she had been coming to the Au Sable Valley since they were kids, first on weeklong camping trips with their parents in the 1920s. Back then their father lashed tents and gear to his Model A for a seven-hour drive from Dearborn. In about 1950 the family bought the cabin near Lovells.

After a good five-minute meander down a two-track snug with pines on either side, we met Josh in what passed for a driveway.

It wasn't much of a cabin per se, just about the size of a double-wide trailer with weathered split-log siding in need of some tender loving care.

"Eddie Fletcher," he said. "Been a while, huh?"

"Three years or so," Eddie said, then handed him two fly boxes.

"Thanks, man," Josh said while examining the flies that Eddie had tied for him, likely over the course of today. Hall was tall with short black hair and a lot of facial stubble. His eyes were like mine, a bit blue, a bit green, all depending on the light.

Eddie introduced me then asked Josh if his aunt was up to this.

"She is," Josh said. "Nobody has asked her about it in years."

"How much does she remember?" I asked.

"All of it," Josh said. "Come on, she's waiting."

Mildred Deacon, now 84 years old, met us inside with a smile and an offer of coffee. We returned the smile and accepted the offer. She was tall but stooped with a taut face and a sharpness to her eyes, also consisting of bits of blue and green.

"It was mushrooms that brought us here that week," she said as we sat down. Then she elaborated on the virtues of the morel mushroom:

"It is a delicacy of the North Country, turning every dish from an omelet to a souffle into a gourmet event. Oh, my goodness, how I love the taste. Iris did, too."

"Ever use it in soup?" Eddie asked. It turns out that he'd spent part of the afternoon, in between tying all the lifeforms of the Hendrickson mayfly for Josh, Googling morels to prepare for the interview. The truth was that Eddie didn't like any type of mushroom but spent the next ten minutes talking about the sundry ways to use morels in cooking. I looked at Josh and he just smiled back. My sense is that he was a co-conspirator in the matter.

The "witness" properly massaged, Eddie got to business.

"When did you get up to the cabin that week?" he asked.

"I think that it was Friday," Mildred said. "It rained like the dickens all week, but we knew when it stopped there would be a bounty."

"I would agree," Eddie said.

"But there wasn't, you see."

"What?"

"That was why we ended up where we did…that Monday," she said. "There just weren't many morels in our usual spots. It was queer."

"That can happen," Eddie said, then he started tapping his temple. "Now what day did it stop raining?"

"Oh, it had to be Saturday," she said. "The weekend got fairly nice, sunny, warmer." She stopped and closed her eyes for a moment. "And muddy!" She laughed. "Very, very muddy."

"Why did you go all the way to 4001?" Eddie asked. "I mean, hardly anyone goes down there now, but then it was…"

"…Indian country," Mildred said. "That's what Iris called it. That's why we went there. It was a long ride, for sure, but we were a couple of widows in our 60s. We had the time, Eddie. We had plenty of time."

"And nobody looked there."

"Oh, some did, but not many and there were huge stands of poplars."

"Still are," Eddie said and smiled.

Mildred smiled back but then frowned for a moment.

"Not a minute after getting out of the truck I found a huge wad of about 20," she said and then looked down for a moment before staring at Eddie. He sensed what was going on.

"And it wasn't long after that, right?"

"I hear this scream. It was Iris. 'Millie! Come quick! Oh, my God! Oh, My God!'

"I dropped my sack and hobbled as quickly as I could, arthritis in my knees. 'Oh, Dear Jesus! Dear Jesus,' Iris is screaming but now it sounded like she might be crying.

"I wondered what's going on. Iris might have stumbled. She was a bit clumsy or, heavens no, was having chest pains or something. I'd had CPR training at the Senior Center back home and I was trying to think of the nearest hospital when I had to dodge a bicycle laying against two aspen trees."

"A bicycle," I said, then wrote it down on my legal pad.

"Yes, it was a surprise but then the smell hit me." Mildred stopped for a moment and took a long drink of coffee. "I knew right away what that odor was. It was the scent of death. Perhaps Iris had stumbled upon a dead deer or bear. She'd always been the squeamish one."

Mildred paused for a moment, and those blue-green eyes began to glisten.

"It wasn't a deer, bear or any other woodland creature," and her voice broke. "It was the young girl.

"'Oh, sweet Jesus, Joseph and Mary,' I said. 'What happened to you dear child?' Iris had stopped screaming. Now she was bent over vomiting."

Mildred sat in silence and stared across the room, then cleared her throat.

"She hung from a big pine and dangled slightly in the morning breeze. Oh, my God how her head was bent down." After a long sigh Mildred went on. "Her face was swollen purple with a dark stain coming out of the corner of the mouth...The eyes were filmy and bulged out like that of a frog or lizard. There was a pile of ooze on the pine straw just below her feet...One shoe was off, exposing a pink sock. A yellowish-brown liquid was dripping from the pant leg...I knew what it was and that was too much. I started puking until there was nothing left inside."

There was a long silence after that. Mildred Deacon just sat there with a far-off look. Josh was giving Eddie a hard stare. I think he regretted this.

"Thank you for that," Eddie finally said. "It can't be easy thinking about it again."

"No," Mildred said softly. "I haven't told anyone this in years. Years."

"Did you drive back to town to get the police?" I asked.

"Mio, Oscoda County Sheriff."

"Did they question you?" Eddie asked.

"Yes, but not for long."

"Any follow-up from them?"

"No, never. No reporters bothered us either. That was a Godsend." She looked at Josh. "Your mother didn't take it well. She was in bed for a couple of days afterwards."

"I know," Josh said. "She had nightmares about it the rest of her life."

"Iris was a gentle soul," Mildred said. "So, you two think this is tied to those missing boys?"

"It's never been properly investigated," Eddie said. "What do you think?"

"There was lots of talk and lots of promises back then by the police, and those boys are still out there."

We left not long after that and retraced our path through the white pines.

"You sure did your homework on morels," I said as we hit the main road.

"Lots of stuff on the Internet," Eddie said.

"Phillip Marlowe trotted out the chessmen, and you surfed the Web."

"I wonder what he'd think of the Web?"

"We'll never know. His time and place are sealed off forever from high tech."

"Maybe he's immortal?"

"Only in used bookstores. Look, I respect your effort but that was fruitless."

"Incorrect. You didn't listen."

"The bicycle? How is that a clue?"

"You really didn't listen."

"Enlighten me."

"She confirmed Zac's report," he said. "The investigation was a botch from the start. About the time that Mildred and Iris roll into Mio Donny's uncle is calling about the boys' disappearance. Two suspicious events occur within a short time frame and there is no record of anyone trying to look for a link. That's mind-boggling."

"We kinda knew that already Eddie."

"Now it has additional support," he said. "Trust me, Art, one can never have enough corroborating evidence, never enough."

"OK."

"It means the field is wide open," he said. "There's information out there. If we can find somebody who knew this girl at the time of her death, then I think we'll find something useful. Or it might be someone else, but it's out there. It's time to hunt so a-hunting we will go."

• • • • •

I went back to Chelsea in the morning. Eddie would spend the weekend at his firm in Detroit doing grunt work. From Friday through to Monday he would maybe sleep ten hours, right there on a couch in the lounge.

"I've crashed in worse spots," he said, "and gone longer on less sleep."

The dogs were glad to see the Mother-in-Law. They ran around outside chasing butterflies while I unpacked the truck. After a trip to the store and refilling of the bird feeders, I sat on my back porch and watched the chickadees and doves have a free-for-all while Sam and Sham snoozed inside.

"Curiouser and curiouser," I said to myself. In less than three weeks I'd gone from someone who kinda knew who Donny Massengale and Roland Parrish were to someone who had exclusive knowledge and had possibly unearthed new leads on their case. It had been surprisingly easy. That made me wonder just how real the whole thing could be. How could we be the ones finding these things after 20 years?

"I'm a law-and-order guy," Zac said at the end of our debriefing on the Deacon interview, "but they shit all over this case and now it lies stinking in the cold-file drawer. No one wants to touch it. Fletcher's right, we hunt."

I took a long walk with the dogs along the edge of the corn-field after dinner. The sun was starting to have that low fall angle and the tassels on the stalks looked like spun gold in the warm glow. A red-tailed hawk flew above us hunting the easement for mice and even a careless pheasant. Shamrock watched the bird intently as it passed over.

"You like being home?" I asked her.

She swished her tail slightly while staying focused on the sky.

That night I called Kody to confirm our plans for tomorrow's game. It would be his first time ever at The Big House.

"Mom may never speak to me again," he said on the phone. "But I think Dad wanted to go, too."

"Next time I'll get another ticket," I said.

I needed advice on my new hobby of junior detective and whether Massengale and Parrish were just a couple of windmills on my journey.

I called Adrian but she didn't pick up, so I left her a message. She had become a tough person to get a hold of because her soft-ware business was going great guns. Apparently, the company had developed a menu of products designed to facilitate political campaigns by refining the targeting of voters.

Nick was too busy dealing with students at The Baron to consult. It was move-in weekend plus the first football Friday night of the season. He was likely chewing gum by the pack and swearing like a longshoreman.

Kate LeClair would have to wait until Monday, and that wasn't a sure thing. We were in a frosty period in our relationship. I had decided not to seek counsel from the woman that she recommended. We sparred over it in a string of emails.

"You're being pig-headed, Arthur Jenkins," she wrote, "and too smart for your own good."

"I like your advice just fine," I wrote back. "Bill me by the minute or the word."

We had managed to stay in touch over the last year, and I hadn't received an invoice yet.

I was left with the one other choice.

"I'm sure that you've been watching what Eddie and I have been doing, Bird," I said while sitting on the couch. Shamrock sharpened her ears at the word, "Bird." She still remembered that it was short for "Bluebird," my nickname for Paula.

"Those boys never had a chance to experience half of what we've seen. They didn't know that their end was near," I said to the air in the room. "Whatever happened, they never saw it coming. You know a thing or two about that."

Paula had not been a great advisor to me. She listened. She cared. But she lived in a world that was right in front of her. For Paula, things were practically binary. There were right answers and wrong answers and never a lot of in between. She'd research facts, for sure, but moving beyond a mainstream, in-your-lane directive was not her thing.

I imagined what she would think about the investigation.

"Oh, Art," I could hear her say, "Why would you bother with all that? You're not a policeman. It's not your job. It's terrible what happened to those boys, but isn't there another tract of land to be preserved? Another stretch of water being polluted? Didn't you say there was some new way to catch snook the other day? Those are your things, sweetheart. Do that instead of being Sherlock Holmes."

"But I need something different now."

And there was only silence.

On Monday I emailed Kate LeClair in detail. Twenty minutes

later my phone dinged. It was a text message, something rare for me in those days.

"Can I call you right now?" It was from Kate. I replied with a "Yes."

Thirty seconds later the phone rang.

"Well, Arthur Jenkins," Kate said. "You're clearly out of your gourd."

"I've missed your Scottish lilt," I said.

"And this is how you get my attention, hey, boyo?"

"It's my co-dependency."

She laughed. "So, you're a detective now?"

"I value your opinion, Kate."

"I'll take it as a compliment, but I won't hold back."

"Tell me something I don't know."

"I read your book," she said with a chuckle. "After getting to know you I wanted to read you."

"What did you think?" I asked because what people thought of my writing was a central aspect to my being.

"I understand your rage much better now. I've been here about two years and grown fond of the manatees and dolphins, but the Florida you describe must have been paradise."

"It was."

Kate sensed that I didn't want to discuss it and moved on. "Now what about these missing fishers. I saw that Fountain fellow on TV. Oy, how he speaks!"

"It's disjointed and disingenuous. Didn't picture you as a viewer of tabloid television."

"A guilty pleasure," she said robustly. "Always been a fan of reading the whodunits, now I get to watch 'em, tew."

"Let me guess, Agatha Christie?"

"And Conan Doyle, Sayers, Chandler, Hammett and all the spying ones…Don't get me off track, Arthur."

"Friendly banter."

"What we're friends now?"

"I haven't received a bill for services."

"Aye, ya won't," she teased. "It's all part of the aftercare."

"OK," I said, and then went into detail about why I was looking into Massengale and Parrish.

"You've given up on the outdoors now," she said after.

I told her about the work for *Michigan Hunting and Fishing*.

"I'm having to learn things and adjust what I know about fishing to how it's done up here."

"That involved?"

"It would be more so going from Michigan to Florida. But I know nothing about trout fishing and now I'm learning to fly-fish for them."

"We invented all that. I have an uncle in Aberdeen who knows everything about sal-mon."

"Perhaps someday I can meet him," I said, sounding a bit snarky.

"Aye, we'll have haggis," Kate answered, giving as good as she got. "A friend of mine did say that you were the foremost expert on the snook fish."

"I wouldn't go that far," I said, but this was music to me. Ever since I was 12 snook have fascinated me. It was the fish that everyone talked about in the Florida bait and tackle shops. It required its own set of rules. There were fishermen and then there were snook fishermen. I came to see it as *sui generis*, pure Florida.

"Well, he's not the only one."

"Stalking me, Kate?"

"Oh, mind yer butter. Keep this project of yours grounded. Don't go running off and playing sheriff. I gotta go work fer a living." She hung up.

"There's nothing to be jealous of, Paula," I said to a corner in the room. "It's not what you think."

• • • • •

I was still reading the articles about the wreckage of Lloyd Carr and the Michigan football team after handing Notre Dame another victory last Saturday when my cell rang.

"We found Hanna's sister, Evangeline," Eddie said in a voice that sounded like a three-alarm fire. "Both parents are dead."

"Where is she?"

"Comins."

"Oh, right by the river," I said because there was a Comins Flats access not far from where we fished.

"No, it's about 15 miles due north of there," Eddie said. "Zac sent me some letterhead. I'm drafting a letter of introduction. Can you proof it?"

"Sure, send me an email."

"Can you come up for the interview?" he asked, "Assuming she agrees to it."

"You need me?"

"Yes, this is going to be sensitive, Art. There's a need for empathy. I got my hands full with the questions that need to be asked. You know empathy is not my strong suit."

"That's not entirely true. Can you shoot for a weekday?"

"Of course, she has a husband and two kids. They would complicate the questioning if they were around. Also, the husband works in the oil and gas business, up in Montmorency County, so check your conservation at the door. Understand?"

"I do." It wasn't a new thing for me. My job had involved interviewing people who strongly believed that natural resources should be consumed, and any type of environmental law or regulation was anti-American. One had told me that all conservationists should be shot on sight. I've always believed that he was behind some of my death threats for that book.

"Look," Eddie said. "I might be able to make it a two-fer. We found the bartender from that night at the Big Water Bar & Grill. It was easy. This guy has done several interviews over the last twenty years. He's the one who threw them out for being too shitfaced."

"Domino Clark," I said. "He was in Fountain's book."

"Yup, claims that he was quoted accurately. He owns a restaurant in Rose City called Targets."

"How far is that from Spinnerfall?"

"Forty-five minutes. He's my next call."

"Set it up." Then I noticed Sammy looking forlorn by the door. "Gotta go. Dog duty."

Fall was clearly in the air as well as on the calendar as we drove through the countryside to the town of Comins, which was in a wide clear patch of flat land, rare for the area.

"When did they clear out the trees here?" I asked Eddie.

"Lumbering did most of it way back when. Then they had a bad tornado a few years back."

Downtown was about twenty buildings, some in better shape than others, a few were vacant.

"There's the only restaurant," Eddie said pointing to a building with a big sign proclaiming it *The Carrie James Restaurant.* "It's supposed to be haunted."

"Maybe we should interview the ghosts?" I said. "They'd know."

Evangeline Grey, now Evangeline Cooper, lived right off the main drag in a new house that stood out from most of the split log, Permalog, and dilapidated structures on the street. The oil-and-gas business paid well.

"Welcome," she said while opening the door. "Gee, you're right on time."

"We appreciate *your* time," Eddie said.

We made our introductions and met the family dog, Scout, a golden retriever, up in years with a face gone to white, who licked our hands, wagged its tail and then plopped at Evangeline's feet when we sat down in the living room.

Evangeline was ten years old when sister Hanna was found swinging in that tree. Now she was 32 and a mother of two, trim with dark hair tied in a bun. Her face was young but pinched. I think that was considering what we were to discuss. It couldn't be easy for her.

She offered us coffee, but we declined. There was a great sense of apprehension in the air. Both Eddie and I felt that this was a moment of truth. Evangeline was a lynchpin of sorts. What she had to say would direct any further investigation.

"Thank you for doing this, Mrs. Cooper," Eddie said.

"Evangeline," she said softly.

"OK," Eddie said in a matching voice, a trick, I believe, that he learned in the courtroom. "As our letter stated, we are here because of the Massengale and Parrish murders."

"Alright." Evangeline was clutching a throw pillow while she sat on the couch.

"There are two main things," Eddie said. "First, we are not certain that your sister's death was a suicide. Second, we believe that it may be connected to the murders in some way."

Evangeline considered this. She closed her eyes, inhaled, scratched her cheek, then focused on Eddie. I thought that she might be getting ready to ask us to leave and started to stir in my chair.

"I've always wondered that," she finally said. "I've *always* wondered that."

"Why?" Eddie asked.

"Hanna and I were very close." Her face showed emotion, the eyes were shiny, and her arms had a death grip on that pillow, but her voice was steady as a rock. "She raised me, took care of me." Then she looked across the room. I glanced to see what she was staring at, a set of pictures on the wall, family shots. One was the portrait of Hanna that had been used for the funeral notice. Evangeline reached down and petted Scout, then swallowed. "My mother drank. She was…not…always there. Hanna did a lot of the cooking and cleaning and everything."

I saw an opening, a chance at connection.

"People don't understand how difficult it is growing up in that environment," I said.

"Around here many do," she said.

"Hanna was the adult in the house?" Eddie said.

"My father was a good man. Strict, but he had a good heart. He drove a truck, mostly lumber but other things. Often, he'd leave after Sunday dinner and not get home until Friday evening. I don't think my mother could cope."

"Clearly Hanna was a responsible child. What else was she like?" Eddie asked, and I noticed how he'd positioned himself on the edge of his chair to be closer to Evangeline.

"Oh, she loved to draw and paint," Evangeline said in a cheery tone. "We'd spend hours drawing pictures. There were bird feeders out back of our house. We lived between Mio and McKinley, just off the river. Hanna loved to draw the birds, animals, wildflowers and trees. We played games, Chutes and Ladders, Sorry and cards like Go Fish. I didn't get to bike with her as much because we only had one bike and I was too young to ride it. By the time that I could, well, Hanna was in high school…and she changed. We weren't as close."

"How did she change?"

"She was becoming a woman, getting interested in boys, wanting to be popular. Han had some good friends in elementary school, but she was never the most popular girl. She didn't seem to care that much then, but by the time she was in eighth grade it became an obsession. She ditched her friends to try and be friends with the 'cool' girls."

"Who were the 'cool' girls?" Eddie was now head to toe in synch with Evangeline's posture on the couch and trying to match her vocal tone.

"Cilla May and Pam Naylor, especially Pam. She was the queen bee. They were the two who first started smoking, drinking wine, flirting with boys during school, all of that. Everyone else was still playing dolls and watching cartoons, but that all changed. By ninth grade Han was whining about clothes and makeup and going out at night. Now, she always made sure that I was fed and had clean clothes, but we didn't spend much time together anymore."

There was a moment of reflection. Eddie appeared to be Jonesing for a chew. He kept licking his lips and twisting his hands. Then he looked at Evangeline and leaned his body toward her.

"Junior high and high school can be tough," he finally said. "Tell me about Cilla May and Pam Naylor."

"Cilla's dad worked at Hoskins. It was a factory south of here, now it's shut down. He was a big shot. They had money. Cilla had a car in high school. Her own car. She wasn't pretty like Pam, but Cilla had nice clothes and could get liquor, pills and pot. That was her key to being cool."

"Pam was pretty?" Eddie said arching an eyebrow like Dr. McCoy from *Star Trek*. "Was she tall as well?"

"Oh, yes! She could have been a model or actress. In fact, I think she did some modeling. I remember Han talking about it. And Pam was going to go to Hollywood. Maybe she did, but I've never seen her on TV or the movies. She was the captain of the cheerleaders as a sophomore and junior. She was prom queen as a junior and should have been as a sophomore, but that wasn't allowed, I guess. I remember Han saying 'Pam got robbed! It's so unfair!' And here we were with a zombie of a mom who, when she was sober enough to speak in clear sentences, called us every name in the book and wished that we had never been born, but it was unfair that Pam Naylor wasn't prom queen as a sophomore."

"What did your father think of your mother's drinking?" I asked.

Evangeline gave me a cross look then cleared her throat.

"Mom didn't drink as much when he was around, so I don't know. I was only a child."

I decided to keep my mouth shut.

The interview went on. Evangeline Cooper drew a picture of Hanna that was not uncommon for teens. She was a bit shy, uncertain of herself, and wanted to be liked. She desperately tried to connect with the right people. Cilla May and Pam Naylor were those people. They kinda let her in, but it was never full membership in their circle. Hanna was a beta girl. She did endless favors like getting juice for them in the cafeteria, letting the girls copy her homework and being the butt of their jokes — taking it all just for a bit of reflected glory.

Han even joined the cheerleading squad although she was not athletic. Cilla and Pam made fun of her clumsiness and the fact that Hanna was not that pretty. Still, she soldiered on, trying, always trying to be accepted. Once, Hanna hurt her ankle but didn't want to miss practice, fearing the girls would have her kicked off the team. Cilla gave Hanna some pain pills that made her sick. She'd throw up in the high school bathroom between classes then go to cheerleading practice.

Cilla and Pam treated Evangeline with contempt on those two or three occasions that they came by the Grey house.

"Beat it, you little rat girl!" Pam would say. Hanna did not defend her little sister, who she otherwise cared for and protected from a delinquent mother. Instead, she turned on Evangeline to curry favor with Cilla and Pam.

"Yeah, go get lost in the woods," Hanna said, "We're busy."

"It hurt," Evangeline said. I could see it in her eyes.

Eddie sympathized, then moved on to the issue of werewolf parties.

"Did she go to any of those?"

"I think so. She mentioned the kids going to parties in the woods to get away from parents and the police, but she never went into details. Han missed some curfews, came home drunk a couple of times and got sick. Dad grounded her. It led to lots of shouting and tears.

"'They'll hate me, Dad!' Han would cry. 'They'll hate me if I don't go.'

"Then during senior year Han started staying over at the girls' houses. I think that was to break curfew. Cilla's folks weren't strict, and Pam's parents were divorced. Her mom was on the prowl for another husband, so she didn't care. Pam had an older brother. I think he bought them wine and vodka. But then Cilla and Pam started taking trips out of town on the weekends and they didn't ask Han to go. She was crushed and would sit in her bedroom crying on those Saturday nights."

"Were there any boyfriends?"

"She went to homecoming and prom in both her junior and senior years but there was never any one guy," Evangeline said looking a bit perplexed. "Oh, there were crushes on guys she couldn't get, mostly Pam's boyfriends. Pam could get anyone. Han said that Pam even had some teacher wrapped around her finger. The few boys that Han dated were nice guys, but I think she just went out with them because it was better than being alone."

"Do you remember any of their names?" By now Eddie had established a connection with Evangeline. She'd stopped grasping that pillow and seemed very relaxed given the topic. Even Scout was comfortable, getting up to visit with him.

"I don't," Evangeline said, sounding a bit surprised herself at this. "It was like they were faceless. She never talked about her dates much. We didn't even take a junior prom photo with… what was his name? Hmph." She sighed with frustration. "She went on more about Pam, but there was one guy that I remember. They didn't date, at least I hope they didn't."

"Who was the guy?" Eddie asked while scratching Scout's ears.

"His name was Denny and he only came by the house once," she said. "You could hear his motorcycle a block away."

"Motorcycle?"

"Yes, I don't know what kind, probably a Harley. Almost everyone rides a Harley up here."

"Did you see the guy?"

"Only through the window. He had long black hair, a black leather vest and he was thin with muscles, you know, lanky."

"What happened?"

"It was a Saturday afternoon in summer. Han was between junior and senior years," Evangeline said. "Dad was home watching the Tigers. He heard the bike. When the guy parked it and started toward the house Dad stormed out the door and said something like, 'What do you think you're doing, son?' The guy says he's there to see Hanna and Dad says, 'Oh, no you're not!' My dad was a big man who grew up in the U.P. and was a marine in Vietnam before marrying Mom. He did not fear anyone or anything! There were some other things said but not as loud and the guy got back on the bike and rode off.

"Han comes running around from the backyard screaming 'Denny! Denny! Why? Why can't I go with him?' and other stuff that I can't remember. Dad and Han come back into the house and Mom starts in on how Han had disgraced the family by being a biker whore. Han screams at her for being a drunk. Dad screams at both to settle down. I run to my room and hear Han say...and hear her say...'Sometimes I just want to kill myself.'"

Evangeline's chin was resting on one hand. Her eyes had a faraway look. She was in that summer afternoon, seeing it and hearing it all again. I don't believe it was for the first time.

"Let's take a break," Eddie said. He'd started fidgeting during the last part of Evangeline's description of events. It was as if he'd experienced something similar once.

"I need a cigarette," Evangeline said.

"I need a chew."

"Oh, my husband does that," she said and smiled. "But both of us do our tobacco outside, even in winter to keep the house clean and children free of smoke."

"Lead on," Eddie said, clearly needing to get some air.

I went out and walked around in the Coopers' front yard while Eddie and Evangeline tended to their nicotine needs. While the story of the biker intrigued me, I was certain that Hanna Grey had killed herself and that there was no true connection to Donny and Roland. Hers was an all-too-familiar tale of the overwhelmed teen unable to cope with an unhappy home and stressful school life. She saw only one way out. There was no one to save her.

We reconvened. Eddie asked about that spring in 1984.

"Oh, gosh," Evangeline said with a long exhale, "that was the worst of it. Han was either gone all weekend at Cilla's or Pam's or home pouting about no one really liking her. She had no friends. Life was terrible. She would retreat to her room and listen to music and draw."

"What kind of music?" Eddie asked. He seemed more composed now.

"Sad love songs," Evangeline said, "like *Tainted Love, Up Where We Belong, Don't You Want Me,* and *Tempted.* She was pining for somebody."

"No heavy metal?" I asked.

Evangeline gave me an unpleasant look. I hadn't learned my lesson to keep quiet.

"Did she have any plans after graduation?" Eddie asked.

"She wanted to go to art school. Mom thought it was crazy. She said that Han had no talent. Dad was concerned about money. Han had a job the previous summer at the hardware store in Mio. Dad said that he'd meet her halfway with tuition at the community college. So, I think, Han was going to work again that summer, maybe even in the fall, and go to some classes. She wanted to be a commercial artist. You know, do the artwork in advertisements."

"I know that this is hard to ask," Eddie said carefully, "but was there anything different in those last two or three weeks of her life?"

"There was," Evangeline said after thinking for a while. "Oh, um, the weekend before her last…weekend. Han was supposed to spend it at Pam's, but she called Dad on Saturday afternoon and asked to be picked up. That had never happened. She came home and said to me, 'Let's play some cards.' We did, then she made dinner and asked Dad if we could rent some movies. He let us. We watched *All the Right Moves* and *Risky Business* that Saturday night. Han loved Tom Cruise. Then she stayed home all the next weekend…her last weekend, and we did the same thing both Friday and Saturday nights."

Evangeline stopped, cleared her throat, and took a drink of water.

"We," she said and cleared her throat again, "we went for a walk on Saturday. It was a nice warm spring day after several days of rain. She told me to be careful about walking in the woods at night. 'Never do it alone,' she said, 'Always do it with friends. Stay away from strangers around here. There're some bad people.' On Sunday she made a nice dinner." Then Evangeline started to cry. Eddie produced a handkerchief for her.

We sat while she sniffed and blew her nose.

"The last time I saw her she was…she was…"

"Take your time," Eddie said, and he reached his hand out to her. "Something like that never really heals."

"It's better than it used to be, Mr. Fletcher, Eddie, but you are right, it's never easy," she said with the last word coming out in a hiss. "The last time I saw her she was doing the dishes. I had homework and went to bed afterwards."

I teared up at this. Evangeline acknowledged it. I gave her a weak smile in return. The last time I saw Paula alive she was… combing her hair?

"Do you think that she could have ridden her bike all the way to the spot?" Eddie asked.

"Yes, but she hardly used it anymore. She had not ridden it since the previous summer for work in Mio. That was a five-mile round trip."

"I see. We looked at the newspapers. The stories made it sound like Hanna was very depressed and out of control."

"That was my parents. They made it her fault. The only thing that I will ever hold against my father was that he went along with Mom's story about how troubled Han was. He should have told the deputies about Pam, Cilla and Denny, but I don't think he ever did."

"Do you think that they killed Han?" Eddie said looking a bit apprehensive for asking it. With him it was always in the hands. They were clasped tight.

"I think they were bad people doing some bad things. Drinking, drug use, sex or rough sex and other crazy stuff like those spirit boards, seances, occult things."

This drew sparks for us. Eddie sat straight up in his chair.

"Did Han talk about those occult things?" Eddie asked while rubbing his thumbs and fingers.

"Han said that she'd been to something by the river near Davis Landing where they tried to contact a dead lumberman. That was in the previous summer, '83. Han didn't like it. She just wanted to party and have fun, normal fun, not that."

"Only time she ever mentioned anything like that?" he asked, now his elbows were on his knees and those hands were flexing.

"Yes, but Han had a while when she was drawing all sorts of weird pictures…monsters, demons."

"Dragons?" I asked.

"A couple of those, but that was the previous summer."

Eddie had instructed me not to visibly react to any comments, but I shifted in my seat when she said this. Eddie appeared unfazed.

Then Eddie leaned over toward Evangeline again. He put one hand on her shoulder. "Thank you for being so brave in telling us all of that. Now, I want you to know this, Evangeline. We are going to investigate all those folks and anybody else that they knew and ran with. They've got a 20-year head start on us, but we're coming, and they can't hear us, and they won't hear us until we knock on their door. They might not have been directly responsible for Hanna's death, but they are going answer questions. There may be no connection with what happened to Hanna and what happened to Donny Massengale and Roland Parrish, but her death is not long after theirs."

"I think that Hanna might have heard about something," Evangeline said in a whisper, "I think it was the last straw for her…or maybe they killed her."

"It is time for some accountability," Eddie said.

"They are going to be hard to find. I haven't seen Pam in twenty years. She left the area in '85 or so. Of course, I only saw that Denny guy once, and Cilla's dead."

"Dead?"

"Yes, she died in a car crash. That would have been about ten years ago. She hit black ice out there on that turn on M-33 by Mt.

Tom Road, headed to Fairview. She was drunk, by then she was always drunk. Cilla became the town drunk and the town whore, in Mio and elsewhere."

Eddie considered this. He touched Evangeline's shoulder with one hand while tapping his brow with the other.

"You wouldn't happen to have Hanna's old high school yearbooks, would you?" he finally asked.

"I do," Evangeline said. "They are in the other room. Do you want to see them?"

"Senior year?"

"Yes, let me get it."

She was gone for only a minute or so. Scout followed her into the other room. Evangeline came back and handed the yearbook to Eddie. It had a blue cover with Mio-AuSable High School 1984 in yellow letters. Eddie quickly thumbed through the pages to the Senior Class profiles. He stopped on a page and started tapping it with his index finger, then making circles on the page with the same digit.

"Look at this, Art," he said and handed me the book. It was Pam Naylor's page.

Her head shot was that of a girl with brown hair styled to feather around the face. Her features were oval, symmetric, pointed nose and chin, attractive but not stunning.

Then there was the full-length photo of her in a cheerleading outfit, skirt oh-so-short and sweater oh-so-tight. That was a different story. It triggered the dirty old man in me, a figure that had started lurking around in the back of my mind in the last few years. Her legs were long and toned — one could see almost all the way to the promised land. The hips and breasts were full and in perfect taper, ready to be stroked. The hair, in ribbons, was luscious and spoke of a pretty young wild thing just coming into season. Her expression, with pom-poms held high, was a coy come-hither featuring pouty lips begging to be kissed and chewed. It was a look that would make men both young and old do foolish, foolish things.

The writing in her profile mentioned cheerleading, drama club and her high school royalty. I was interested in the end part:

"Make that shovelhead roar! Ahhhwhoooooooo! M is The Master. W is The Watcher," she wrote. Adolescent code for something.

"She's only listed as cheerleading as a sophomore and a junior," I said. "And how come she wasn't senior prom queen?"

"Pam quit cheerleading as a senior, so did Cilla," Evangeline said. "It got in the way of their other activities. Also, Han said that Pam gained weight, or was having problems with it. I think that most of the school had had it with Pam and Cilla by senior year. They were feared but not liked."

"Is there a copy machine at the hardware store in town?" Eddie asked.

"Sure," Evangeline said.

"Can I go make some copies of a few pages and come right back?"

"OK."

We went to Breyer's Sundries and made copies of Pam Naylor's page, Cilla May's page — which had the same cryptic messages as Pam's — Hanna's page and several other pages that we thought might be useful. Eddie made copies in different levels of brightness, trying to get the best reproductions. In total, we had over 50 pages, many of them duplicates.

We went back to Evangeline Cooper's house and Eddie ran the book up to her door. She gave him a kiss on the cheek before saying good-bye.

"What a good person," Eddie said. "She found a way out of that shit. I didn't have the heart to ask her for permission to look at Hanna's autopsy file."

"Do we need it?" I asked.

"We might not, but I may go back and ask her anyway out of respect," he said. "I think we are making progress. I really, really do."

"Did you catch the part about drawing dragons?" I asked.

"Yeah, but let's follow Zac's lead on that and not jump to conclusions. Hanna Grey was troubled, likely depressed, and so desperate that she made some bad choices in the company she kept," Eddie replied, but he seemed preoccupied.

We rode the rest of the way in silence back to Spinnerfall. I imagined how dreary and dismal it must have been to be Hanna Grey.

Eddie charged inside the house when we got back. I started to get the dogs ready for a walk.

"Hold it, Art," he said. "The dogs can wait. There's something you gotta see." He was fiddling with some files on the table and arranging some of the pages that we'd copied. Then he slammed down his finger on one, then another. "See! Come here! Now!"

His finger was tapping Pam Naylor's senior photo.

"OK," I said.

Then his finger jumped to the photo of Roland Parrish at the fall rush party in 1983. It tapped happy-go-lucky Roland and then slid to the figure next to him, a woman…Pam Naylor.

"Holy Fuck," I said.

Then Eddie slammed down Cilla May's senior photo, tapped Roland again and slid a couple inches over to another figure, a woman, shorter than the first…Cilla May.

"Jesus Christ, Eddie. They knew him, or at least had been in his vicinity at a party. That's what those weekend trips were about?"

"The game's afoot, Watson," he said. The light caught his big eyes and bits of chewing tobacco stuck to his wild smile in a way that would have made any October pumpkin proud. "The game…is…fucking…afoot!"

CHAPTER 8

The Satanic Mechanic

Eddie called Zac three times while pacing around the room.
He got voice mail each time.

"Zac, Eddie, we just broke the case wide open." "C-2, stop
whatever you are doing and call me." "C-2, Zac, we've connected
Parrish to a local girl, the one Marshall ran into!" he said on the
calls. He grew more manic with each unanswered call.

I sat and fleshed out my notes. We recorded the interviews, but
I took notes as well. It was mostly out of habit or maybe a need
to do something while Eddie handled the questioning.

I had proved less than useful at the interview. My attempts
at empathy had only drawn the ire of Evangeline Cooper. Eddie
made the connection to her. He got the information we needed
and then landed the yearbook. Coupled with Marshall's interview

149

it was now a real investigation. We were on to something. Snipe hunts be damned!

Eddie finally stopped pacing. "I'm gonna go tie some flies."

"I thought the dry-fly season was over," I said. "Mostly," he said, "There's some small olives but I got about 50 of those. Nope, I need to tie some streamers for winter fishing. You need to come up and try it although you'll need to get your own waders and winter gear."

Before I could answer with something along the lines of "That'll be a cold day in Hell," Eddie's cell rang.

"Yeah, what the fuck!" Eddie said. "No, no bullshit. Let me get us on speaker phone."

"Hey Art," Zac said. "Should we tranquilize Fletcher?"

"Nope, he's got a right to be amped."

"Tell me everything," Zac said.

We did.

There was a long silence at the end of our description of events. I thought that we might have dropped the call. It had happened once or twice before. Eddie got fair cellphone service at Spinnerfall, but it wasn't perfect.

"Jesus," Zac finally said. "Have you got copies of those yearbook pages?"

"Yes, sir," Eddie said. "We'll mail 'em to you on the way to see Clark tomorrow."

"When's that set for?"

"Noon at Targets. He's bird hunting in the morning."

"Don't bother with events at the barroom. Everybody knows that by heart by now and nothing came of it."

"Copy." Eddie paused to pack a chew. "He may know who this Denny fellow was and who he ran with."

"Yeah," Zac said. "I'll get on those girls, see if there are police records, find out where Naylor is. If we can get her to talk then I think the fog of time may start to clear."

"It already is," Eddie said before spitting.

The ride along M-33 to Rose City was pleasant with woods

packed close to the road. The birches and aspens had turned bright yellow, and hardwoods were showing splashes of orange and red. The terrain qualified as foothills going up and down and up and down.

County Road 604 was at the bottom of one hillock. About 15 miles due east Hanna Grey died at the end of a rope.

We passed a local landmark known as The Pink Store about halfway to our destination. It was the quintessential northern Mom n' Pop place with everything from milk and eggs to oil and ammunition. A sign advertised, "We Now Have Pizzia" — spellcheck was for Downstaters.

Then the land flattened as we came into Rose City, which lined M-33 for nearly a mile. There were churches and bars for sure, but several restaurants, gas stations, and other businesses ranging from accountant firms and bakeries to mechanic shops and tailors. There was even a car dealership, McDonald's, Subway and Dairy Queen. The place was thriving by the standards of the hardscrabble North Country.

"Rose City is one of my favorite towns up here," Eddie said as we parked in the lot at Targets. "It's got a good karma. I had a fortnight fuck-fest with a waitress from The Rifle River Inn back in '84 after thawing out from a training mission."

"You were always having fortnight fuck-fests," I said.

"Only way to romance, trust me," he said.

The theme of Targets restaurant was hunting, hunting and more hunting. The "e" in the logo was replaced with the crosshairs of a gun sight. An impressive rack of deer antlers was bolted above the entrance. Inside there were mounts of all God's woodland creatures from fox squirrels to black bears. I didn't like this sort of thing but had to admit the work was well rendered. The ducks, geese, pheasants, grouse and woodcock all looked like they could fly off the wall at any moment. It turns out each creature had been felled by Domino Clark himself. He had a reputation as a first-class hunter. If it had fur or feathers, Clark had likely fed it lead at some point.

The lunch crowd was sparse, not surprising given that it was the last Wednesday in September.

"You must be here for Domino?" a youngish waitress asked. She had dishwater-blond hair and was cute but not overly so. My sense was that she couldn't be 20 years old but sported a wedding ring, nonetheless. "He just got in. Come this way. He wants to meet in the back room." She led us past the bar and down a hall to a room that likely was used for overflow customers or private parties.

"Gentlemen! Right on time! Such precision is rare in these parts," said a man dressed in fall camo, obviously Clark. He set down a coffee cup, walked over and extended his hand to Eddie. A beautiful Brittany Spaniel jumped out of her bed in the corner and greeted me with soft ears and wagging tail.

"That's Spirit," Clark said, "and she's mad at her daddy."

"Why?" I asked. Eddie was busy scratching Spirit's ears.

"Because Daddy shot like shit today," Clark said.

"You were hunting partridge?" Eddie asked.

"Right-o."

"They can be tough," Eddie said, "very tactical in flight."

"Right-o, again," Clark said and beamed at Eddie's recognition. "They are not the fastest in flight at all, but very adept at putting something between you and them. Plus, they won't flush until the last possible moment in most cases. They are up and in the brush before you can aim. Very sporting." He chuckled, then reached down and stroked Spirit's head. "I put a lot of pellets in trees today. She didn't get a feather."

"It's partridge hunting, not partridge killing," Eddie said.

"Indeed."

Eddie wasn't a hunter. He'd done his share of that activity tracing the enemies of the United States of America and various coalitions of the willing. His two recreational pursuits, fishing and skirt chasing, had elements of the hunt, but in the end involved a voluntary commitment by the quarries in question; fish chose to bite his hook, women let him know their interest with a proper glance or inviting smile. Besides, if everything went accordingly there was no death. Fish were released with a sore mouth and bruised ego, although some that did not survive the hook were kept for food. The women sometimes had broken hearts, but that worked both ways.

Eddie had quickly researched Clark, learning all he could about him. Then he delved into upland bird hunting. Clark was known for shooting anything in season. It was September so he would be on birds.

Eddie's approach fit with a time-honored tenet of communication going back to Aristotle: know one's audience. It turned out that Eddie had a copy of *The Rhetoric & Poetics* alongside his law books.

"And you thought I was just a warrior, Art?" he asked me once.

"Oh, I think you are many things," I said.

Eddie was ready to mirror Domino to gain his trust.

"Tell me about these mounts, Mr. Clark," Eddie said.

"Domino."

"Eddie."

"Well, this one here was a tough customer, Eddie," Clark said and pointed to a duck.

I sat down at the table and arranged my notebook, set up the tape recorder, ordered a pitcher of coffee along with some nachos and onion rings. Eddie was practically addicted to onion rings.

After a few minutes of war stories, Eddie and Domino seated themselves at the table. Clark was a big man of a half-century-plus who'd slightly gone to seed with a noticeable beer gut. Otherwise, he had broad shoulders and thick arms. As a young man he'd done eight years in the Coast Guard. His face was ruddy from ancient acne scars and too many hours under the sun. He tried to cover it with a thin beard of reddish wisps going steadily to grey. This matched his receding crown of hair. He took off his amber shooting glasses to reveal sharp green eyes. There was yet another predator in this sad tale, but as with Zac Phoenix it was not problematic. Domino Clark radiated good cheer.

Spirit stood by her human's side through all the mount descriptions — she may well have witnessed some of the kills. Now, she retreated to her bed, set her head on the pillow, and watched us intently.

"Hey Domino," Eddie said, "is that your first name or nickname? I love it either way."

"My first name is Willard," Clark said. "I got the name 'Domino' because I can drop 'em." He made a gesture of firing an imaginary rifle and clicked his tongue as he pulled the trigger, then burst into a hearty laugh. Eddie joined him.

I forced a smile and thought about what Paula would make of all this. There'd be some 'splaining for sure.

We outlined our intent, but Clark insisted on recapping those 20 minutes with Massengale and Parrish. After listening patiently, Eddie asked about the nature of the times back then.

Clark looked puzzled.

"Did I not come across as clear, Domino?" Eddie asked.

"No, it's just that, nobody ever asked me about that," Clark said.

"We're trying to establish that there was a group of bad people around here back then who might have had something to do with the murders, or know who was involved," Eddie said. "Does anybody come to mind?"

Clark thought for a moment and then began.

"Oh, yeah, there's some candidates, certainly," he said then took a sip of coffee. "This area has always been a place where people come to get away from the rat race, live free, do what they want, you know? Now some rats come up here as well. That goes back to the gangsters, The Purple Gang, even Al Capone had some of his guys around here. It's a great place to lay low from Johnny Law."

"I did not know that," Eddie said. But he did, having read several books on the Prohibition era. Eddie Fletcher wanted to know everything that ever happened from 1066 on, although he had a soft spot for the Roman Empire, too.

"Bad guys love these woods," Clark said. "Always have and always will. We had some back then."

"You show up in 1982?"

"Yes, end of January. Got out of the Coast Guard, got married, and had an uncle knew the owner of the Big Water Bar & Grill. He needed a manager. Some strings were pulled. That's how it was done 'round here. I did more bartending than managing."

"Who were the bad guys?"

"Well, there was a lot of petty theft, breaking into cabins, drunk and disorderly conduct, some drug dealing, but not much. Most of the criminal activity was getting paid under the table to avoid taxes and other government shit or disability fraud, a lotta that. Just about everybody was collecting on that and then sawing wood or doing a trade on the side."

"Who were the bad guys?" Eddie asked again. I could see his jaw clench. Domino Clark needed to be herded, otherwise we'd be here until dark. It was pissing Eddie off.

Domino Clark considered this. I sensed reluctance.

"OK, one name comes to mind for sure, but he's not around anymore, hasn't been for 20 years or so."

"Who is he?" Eddie asked then pulled out his Skoal and sought permission. Clark nodded and pointed to a table where there was a stack of paper cups. Eddie got up to fetch one.

"His name is Dennis Dunaway," Clark said.

Eddie dropped his cup; luckily, he had not packed a chew yet.

"You said 'Dennis,' did he ever go by the name 'Denny'?" Eddie asked.

"Oh, yes, but mostly with his friends."

Eddie sat back down and started tapping his Skoal can on the tabletop. I was experiencing a rush of adrenalin because we were once again in the chase. This was becoming fun in a guilty sort of way.

The name was also familiar to me.

"Like the guitar player for Alice Cooper?" I asked.

"Yeah," Domino said. "You a big Coop fan?"

"Oh, that's right up his alley," Eddie said, but he wasn't annoyed anymore. No, he looked very happy, as if he'd just received good news. "Now tell me all about Dennis Dunaway, and then tell me about all his friends."

Domino Clark's expression of trepidation turned to ebullience. Once again, he was the star witness. Over the next ten minutes he described Dunaway.

Dennis Dunaway was already in Mio when Domino made his bartending debut in early February of 1982. In fact, Dunaway was one of his first customers, drinking forty-cent drafts of Old Milwaukee.

"Stacking dimes is what we called that," Clark said. He seemed impressed by that tidbit.

Clark's description of Dunaway — tall, thin, muscled, long black hair to his lower back, sometimes tied in a ponytail, spit-gray eyes, pocky skin, angular face, and very bad teeth — was far more detailed than Evangeline Cooper's. But the similarities were there, including the leather vest.

"You could put everything that Dennis owned in his two motorcycle saddlebags and a standard backpack. He wore that vest all the time in warm weather. Otherwise, he had some shitty coat in winter, well, until he had a nice one, but that had to have been stolen."

"He had a motorcycle?" Eddie asked. He was looking at Clark with admiration because I believed that Eddie had sensed what I was perceiving; Clark liked being the center of attention and considered a Big Shot. We'd give him all of that to get the story.

"Oh, yes!" Clark said, then he started in on the details of the bike, mostly technical stuff that put me in a trance until I heard the word "Shovelhead."

"Like make that shovelhead roar?" I said, exchanging looks with Eddie.

"Oh, you must be a biker," Clark said.

"He was Hell on a ten-speed back in the day," Eddie said, "but not as fast as me."

This produced a good laugh, but so what? We were gaining.

"Dennis was a helluva mechanic and could have had a good career if he wasn't such a gypsy and all about sex, drugs and rock 'n' roll. He did some work on bikes locally, under the table, of course, but was otherwise without employment."

"But not really," Eddie said then spit in his dip cup.

"No, I don't think he stole much, but he was part of what passed for drug dealing up here, pot mostly. Dennis had to be careful. He'd done a few months' jail time over on the coast for an assault charge. I think that he was a person of interest in another case. Dennis would park his bike in the back alley because the Sheriff's was just a few blocks down. If he was really wasted, he would crash in a house or apartment nearby. Otherwise, I really don't know where he lived, probably camped a lot."

"Did he have a bad temper?"

"He had a reputation as a badass. Nobody around town back then would fight him. I never had any problems with him in our bar. He'd help with other unrulies, especially since I'd let him drink Old Mils the rest of the night on me. But I think he went to other towns and raised some Hell. There was a need in Dennis to draw blood from time to time."

"OK. What happened to him?"

"I really don't know," Clark said while scratching his beard. "Like I said, haven't seen him in about 20 years."

Eddie and I looked at each other again. Evangeline Grey had not seen Pam Naylor in 20 years. Massengale and Parrish faded into the night 21 years ago. The math wasn't perfect, but it was close.

"Was he here in 1984?" Eddie asked.

"Oh, yes."

"The whole year?"

"I think so."

"Did he ever talk about the missing boys?"

Clark thought about this. He waved to the waitress, made a gesture of pulling a beer tap and she went off to the bar.

"I need to wet my whistle," he said. "Had enough coffee. You, too?"

We shook our heads 'no.' We were on the clock.

"Dennis was not a chatty guy. He'd talk to his friends. He'd talk to me."

"What did he say about it?"

"Oh, he was pissed about all the police. Come to think of it…he was MIA for some of the spring, then he started showing up again, sitting in his spot at the bar, or a table in the rear with his buds."

"We'll get to them in a second," Eddie said. "So, he didn't like all the law enforcement being around. That makes sense, right?"

"Yes, sir it does." Clark thanked the waitress for his draft. "Really cramped his style, didn't want to be questioned, probably had to abandon his campsites, hurt his business opportunities. Dennis did not like cops."

"What part of the year was he MIA?"

"April and May, came back around fairly regularly by Memorial Day."

"Interesting," I said, but Eddie waved me to silence.

"Did he have any theories about the case?" he asked.

"OK, let me think. Well. There was an incident."

"Incident?"

"Yeah, some Flatlander comes into the bar and starts yakking about how the police got it all wrong. It's not a serial killer, it's local. The guy says something about how there are plenty of scumbags in the area who would have done the deed. The authorities should round them all up and grill the shit out of them.

"Dennis goes ape shit. He normally doesn't talk to strangers. He's not one of those guys who sits on a barstool and pontificates about everything. At first, he just glared at the guy, but finally Dennis stands up and says, 'You're full of shit buddy. You don't know anything about around here. I do. I know everybody and everything. Nobody I know would kill those kids. They didn't have anything worth stealing. They weren't muscling in. They were just passing through. Get your Flatland ass outta here.' It was something like that. I figured there was gonna be trouble. But the guy was spooked, got up and left a full pitcher of beer, a very rare thing around here. Dennis could spook just about anybody."

"You sure about the exchange?" Eddie asked. "That's more than just somebody's opinion. To me it sounds defensive, like Dunaway didn't want anybody exploring that path."

"Oh, I'm sure that Dennis said it because that's about the most words I ever heard him say at one time. He was reserved. It was his running buddy that was the big mouth, always going on about how unfair everything was or telling gross jokes, but that guy was gone by then." Domino took a sip of beer. "Good thing, he was a real creep, almost made Dennis look respectable."

"Let's talk about *that* guy," Eddie said with a smile.

"What was his name?" Clark said, then took a pull on his beer. "He was a mechanic at a shop north of town. A good one from what I remember. But a bad apple. He had a shaved head and Fu Manchu mustache — nobody had that back then. Had a real chip on his shoulder, you know, kept talking about his time in the Army. He said he was an Army Ranger."

"He did!" Eddie's face clenched, and he started rubbing those hands.

"Yeah." Clark appeared taken by Eddie's response. "He claimed that he could kill a man so many ways. Had a huge buck knife, wore it on his belt. I told him that he couldn't do that in my bar. Dennis convinced him to wear it in his boot because Dennis had a knife in his boot. A lot of guys carried knives. This was before everybody became so obsessed with guns. Knives were the thing."

Then Clark went silent. We waited for his next sentence. Along with Dunaway, Mr. Fu Manchu seemed like another potential killer.

"His name was Tony. He worked at Roscoe's. It's gone now. Owner died of a stroke in…1993 or so. Two sons were downstate. They sold it. New owner torched it for insurance. You know, Jewish lightning."

"Yeah," Eddie said flatly, "I've heard the term. What about this guy Tony?"

"Had a bike, similar to Dennis's. Everybody rode Harleys then. You see some Indians now, good bike, too. But back then it was Sturgis or Electra Glide and nothing else. Dunaway would give Tony tips on maintenance and Tony probably got Dennis some work at Roscoe's place.

"I didn't care for Tony. He was always bitching about the jukebox, wanted more heavy metal, wanted Black Sabbath and Van Halen. Always talking about those types of bands, most I've never heard of. Talked about this one group, Aphrodite something."

"Aphrodite's Child?" I asked. My high school friend, Jorge Cabrera, was a huge metal fan and had one of their albums.

"There was a band with that name?" Clark asked.

"Yes, their biggest album was entitled *666*," I said.

"That would fit with Tony," Clark said. "He had that personality."

I could see the gears turning inside Eddie. He was trying to figure out the next question.

"What do you mean by that?" Eddie finally asked.

"Well, his favorite song was *Runnin' with The Devil* and he talked about that kinda stuff a lot. Said Satan was misunderstood, but I think that Tony saw the whole thing as part of the party-hearty biker life," Clark said then took a swig of foamy amber. "Not sure what Dennis thought of all that. He was a loose cannon, but Tony's ramblings seemed too complicated for him. Dennis was amoral for sure. Some guy asked Dennis once if he was a 'one-percenter,' you know, like the Hells Angels. Dennis said, 'No, I'm less than that.'"

"Any others in this group?" Eddie asked.

"Yeah, the only other guy I met was a regular in the bar. Good guy, a bit strange, but that's the area," Clark said. "I know his first name was Rufus, but he went by the name 'Mr. Penguin.'"

"Mr. Penguin! Why?" Eddie asked.

"I don't know, but he'd always waddle into the bar and do a

bunch of 'quack, quacks,' kinda like that Batman villain. People loved it."

"He never caught any shit for that?" I asked. Eddie was packing another chew.

"Nooo, Rufus was six, six and nearly 300 pounds. Now, mind you, some of it was blubber. He had a pear-shaped build, but there was plenty of muscle. The guy had a Grizzly Adams beard and really long hair. But he wasn't a very bad guy. I think that he'd done a lot of acid back in the day. No, Penguin was a mellow guy, but capable of busting ass."

"Penguin and this devil business?" I continued.

"Can't see it, but he was a follower. Rufus was too fried to think for himself."

"When was the last time you saw Tony?" Eddie asked after finally arranging his load.

"When did the Bears play in that Super Bowl in the 1980s?"

"January of 1986," I said.

"Art's our football expert," Eddie said. "OK, so 19 years ago. Was Tony around in 1984?"

"Like I said before, no, that's what was so surprising about seeing him in the bar that day. He'd been gone for, maybe, two years, then he shows up to watch the game with Dunaway. Dennis was a huge Bears fan. He had money on the game."

"Any idea why Tony left?"

"I heard that police had questioned him about some robberies, and he bolted a few days later. He said to me that Super Bowl Sunday that he'd been offered better work in Montana."

"Is Penguin around?"

"Nope. Haven't seen him in…at least 20 years."

Eddie excused himself to take a piss. He was actually going to call Zac to confer about what we just learned. I decided to ask about the werewolf party angle.

"You've done your homework," Clark said. "It was a big deal in the '70s and early '80s. There would be a full moon or near full moon and people would howl, "Ahwooooooo!" like a wolf, you know."

"Did you ever go to one?" I asked.

"No, I was 29 in 1982, married and had a baby on the way. Those were summertime events. Mostly high schoolers, you know, go off in the woods, get away from adults, party hearty."

"Did our three amigos go?"

"They ran 'em."

Just then Eddie and the waitress came back into the room.

"Who ran what?" Eddie asked.

We filled him in and then the waitress took our lunch order.

Clark told us how Dunaway, Tony and Penguin organized the werewolf parties with some of the high school kids. It was a win-win situation. The kids got booze and drugs. The three amigos sold their wares and got access to young girls.

"Dennis really loved the young ones," Clark said. "His motto was 'old enough to bleed, old enough to breed.' Pretty common up here. The other two were up for it as well, but neither had Dunaway's game. Dennis was not handsome, but he could get the women, especially young 'uns. It was that 'outlaw thing.'

"Now, to be accurate, most of the action was blowjob, handjob because, in Dennis's words, 'You don't want some father with a shotgun coming after you because his daughter is knocked up.' But word was a couple of gals knew how to avoid all that, you know, the pill. One apparently would do anything, even with girls while the guys watched. The other liked to pull trains. It coulda been bullshit, but crazy stuff went on in those woods back then."

"Do you remember any of the kid's names?" Eddie asked while organizing a folder that he'd brought along.

"That's a long time ago. High school kids don't frequent bars, not ours, for sure. The cops were just down the street."

"How about Pam Naylor?"

"I've heard the name, but that's all."

Eddie slapped down a copy of Pam's high school yearbook page and pointed to her cheerleader picture. Clark studied it.

"I'd remember that, but I never saw it."

I thought this was an interesting take. He saw Naylor as an object, not a person. That dirty old man lurked in Clark's head, too.

"Cilla May?"

"Certainly," Clark said, "but after high school. She drank in here and everywhere else, sad, sad case." Then he fell silent for a moment. "You know that she's dead?"

Eddie nodded then went on. "Crazy stuff in the woods, does that include Satanic Rituals?" He had decided to ring the bell. I thought it was the wrong move.

So did the waitress who came in with our orders. She froze and almost dropped the tray. Eddie was out of his seat in flash to help her.

"I'm sorry about that, ma'am," he said. "Don't worry, we're talking about a long time ago. You weren't even alive."

"My grandma said stuff like that has always been around here," she said. "'People from downstate staining our woods with their black deeds,' she'd say."

"Thanks, Jas," Clark said. "That'll be all."

She served us and left with a polite smile.

"That's a taste of the folklore," Clark said after she'd gone. "She's a fifth generation local. They go on like that."

"Any truth to it?" Eddie asked.

"I heard stuff, but you always hear stuff," Clark said. "Christ! They did a huge investigation of Bigfoot in Foley Swamp up on the Au Sable, never found anything but the usual footprints. Anybody can make those."

"I live near Foley," Eddie said.

"Ever see Bigfoot?"

"I fish with him occasionally," Eddie said. "Terrible wader, pretty good caster surprisingly. Helluva night angler."

Clark laughed like Falstaff.

"Alright, did our boys do any of that?" he said after chortling. "I don't know. That Tony mighta been game. Dennis and Penguin mighta gone along for shits and giggles. It was the '80s. Most of the country was scared to death of all that. I guess a few thought it was just another way to party and flip-off the establishment. But there's the one guy I haven't mentioned."

"Jesus, this keeps getting more interesting," I said. Eddie agreed.

"I never met him," Clark said. "I don't even know if he's real, but he fits the bill as a very bad dude."

"His name?" Eddie asked.

"Hobbs," Clark said. "He comes into the picture in the spring of '82."

Clark told a story about how Dennis, Tony and Penguin supposedly met Hobbs at a bar near Curtisville where they went to avoid the local folks or possibly make a drug connection.

As the story goes, they meet Hobbs and have a few drinks. Turns out Hobbs is impressed with some medallion that Tony is wearing, probably a pentagram that Tony sometimes sported over his grimy T-shirts and biking leathers.

A bunch of bikers from some gang, maybe Midnight Riders, show up at the bar. Apparently, Dennis had some history with one of the guys, burned him in a drug deal or snaked his woman, something like that. The guy walks up to their table and wants to start trouble. He has about eight tough looking dudes with him.

Then Hobbs comes back from the bathroom. He looks at the biker and asks what's going on.

Domino Clark finishes the story: "The biker's eyes pop out and his jaw drops. 'You know these guys?' he asks. Hobbs nods. 'You with 'em?' Hobbs nods again. Then the biker guy says, 'Fuck this!' and the gang leaves. From that point Hobbs is the leader and the guys follow him."

"But you never met him?" Eddie asks.

"No, but I sure heard enough about him." Clark stroked his beard in thought for a moment. "He takes over the werewolf parties. I think that he takes over the drug thing as well. Speed starts showing up in Mio along with the pot. The whole vibe changes. It's darker. Everybody is acting crazier. It's a lot more on edge.

If there's anything to this devil thing that you're talking about then it might be this guy."

"This Hobbs fellow makes the rituals angle plausible?" Eddie asked in his best courtroom voice. I was expecting to hear an "objection" from some corner of the room.

"Yes, he does," Clark said, suddenly sounding a bit morose, "and now that I think about it, there's something else. Something from the following summer."

"1983?"

"Late summer '83, August or so. All three of them show up with tattoos on their left wrists. Dunaway says they got 'em downstate."

"What's the image?" I ask.

"A circle, some lines that indicate a pentagram," Clark said. "And a, and a dragon-like creature. It was in the middle of it and the work wasn't quite good enough to see if the lines connected or much detail of it."

"Can you describe the tail?" I asked, now knowing my hunch was correct.

"Pointed," he said. "It looked different than most dragon tails I've seen, but I haven't seen many."

"Was there a barb?"

"I can't remember."

"Let me guess," Eddie said, "It was Hobbs's idea?"

"Everything was by then. Even Dennis had changed. He'd always been independent, doing whatever, whenever. Not by then. He wasn't in the bar as much, always off doing something for Hobbs. Dennis was eating a lot of speed. He was almost skin and bones. Tony kept babbling about 'The Watcher' in the woods."

"W is the Watcher?" I asked with a dry mouth.

"How did you know?" Clark said.

"M is the Master," I went on. "Did the amigos ever say that as well?"

"Yes…How?" Clark shifted uncomfortably in his seat.

"We prepared, Domino. This is a serious investigation," Eddie said. "You've been very helpful. Is there anything else?"

"Jesus, I haven't thought about any of this in years. All the interviews by the police, journalists or Asa had been about *that* night, never anything else. I forgot about what came before because I never considered...now my mind's cluttered with it. I'd forgotten how unsettling it was back then. The murders were the culmination of it. Everybody was gone by February of '86. Are they responsible?"

"That's what we are trying to determine," Eddie said.

We finished our lunch and changed the subject to lighter things. Clark was less talkative as the meal went on. His expression when we parted was not quite that of haunted, but more like forlorn. Somewhere during our long interview his good mood and goodwill had vanished. Domino Clark left us to find our own way out. He chose instead to go behind his bar and pour a tumbler of bourbon.

"Art," Eddie said on the way to the truck, "just what kind of a bear are we poking here?"

· · · · ·

After dinner that night we called Zac and filled him in on the interview. Then he went into a long discourse about how things were heating up for his agency. They'd been hired by a pair of families to investigate the disappearance of two girls. One was found in Oregon living in a commune with some guy, a happy ending of sorts.

"She wanted nothing to do with her parents," Zac said, "not our problem."

The other case was not so fortunate. Zac's investigators found out that an ex-boyfriend had been carping for months about how badly the missing girl had treated him. Three witnesses claimed to have seen a man fitting his description around the girl's apartment complex the day before she went missing. Zac turned this new information over to the Illinois State Police. They brought the ex-boyfriend in, grilled him, he confessed, and the girl's body was found three days later.

"Justice and closure," Zac said, "but no joy in finding it."

Now the Illinois State Police wanted to work with Zac on nine other missing persons cases, in essence to do the footwork and gather information. They lacked the manpower and, by the private admission of the deputy chief of detectives, the expertise.

"We gained their respect," Zac said. "Now we are figuring out the billing."

"HOOAH! C-2!" Eddie said then smacked me on the arm.

"That's great, Zac," I said. Eddie had told me never to say HOOAH to anyone else but him.

"HOOAH! It's a big turning point for us," Zac said. "Law enforcement doesn't much care for PIs and rightfully so. A lot of them are fly-by-night opportunists. We've earned some bones. Wisconsin Staties are interested in a sit-down as well. It's all good but cuts into our resources on this case. I'm going to hire two more licensed guys, another case manager and more associates. But it's going to take time to run down Naylor and Dunaway. I had two folks doing nothing but that and now they're gearing up to assist ISP."

"ISP?" I asked.

"Illinois State Police," Zac said. "My new best friends."

"Can we parlay this with Michigan State Police?" Eddie asked.

"Apples and oranges," Zac said.

"Why?" Eddie and I asked simultaneously.

"The cases here are real-time investigations. We are working as a team. Massengale and Parrish involves sorting through some very old and very dirty laundry. I think the authorities in Michigan just want it to stay in the freezer. You guys should know why by now."

"But we're finding stuff," I said.

"Yeah, *we're* finding it," Zac said, "quickly, surprisingly quickly. Think about it, the SNAFU with the investigation when the trail was at least lukewarm, no evidence, none, the passage of time, Fountain's BS, then Bigfoot is captured and has an alibi."

"We're making them look bad," Eddie said.

"Copy, but when we do go to them, and that is getting closer, I think they will take us seriously."

"Why can't we go to them now?" I asked.

"We could, but here is what I think will happen. They will assign a detective to the case, or alert one who had this cold case in his portfolio. He or she will investigate it, recanvass the witnesses, ask the questions we asked, talk to law enforcement who worked it — many are now dead — and then go back to the dozens of other cases on their docket. Plus, they now have 15 other new cases, not counting our boys, because they had Bigfoot down for 29 unsolved murders and he cops to 12. Six families have already started screaming to whatever reporter is handy about how the police botched the investigations into the murders of their loved ones by lumping them in with Carl Lee's handiwork. Massengale and Parrish will get some refocus, but it won't last long or be as thorough as what we've done in six weeks. Think about that as well, the police don't ask Marshall or Clark the right questions, miss Hanna Grey's suicide and don't look more closely into who the boys might have known or met at a fraternity mixer. It will be a PR disaster."

"Gonna be anyway when we solve it," Eddie said.

"We'll need to be diplomatic, Leap," Zac said.

"I love it when you talk dirty, C-2."

"I'm getting moist, too. The wife wants to know when is the next three-way?"

"Get me Naylor and Dunaway. After I question them it's time to stock up on body oil."

"OK," I said. "Talk about losing focus. What do we do in the meantime, Zac?"

He told us. For me it was go through those 53 TV news reports I had obtained from Vanderbilt University. It would also be a good idea to look at the Iosco County newspaper for its coverage of the case and events during that era. I agreed to stay the next day to do that, and Eddie said he'd help.

For Eddie, his assignment was waiting on his email. It was the addresses and phone numbers for 20 people on his master witness list. Eight were local law enforcement, sheriffs and deputies, six were the surviving witnesses of Massengale and Parrish being thrown out of the Big Water Bar & Grill, three others had been quoted in local newspapers and the last three had been college friends of Donny and Roland, quoted or misquoted by Asa Fountain.

"That's likely all you are going to get from that list," Zac said.

"I'll work it," Eddie said.

"One more thing," Zac said after a lengthy cough (I think he'd been smoking while on the call). "Don't get carried away by Clark's foray into deviltry. My take is that these guys were hard partying, heavy-metal bikers. Old Scratch is just an emblem of that lifestyle."

"It could connect to the altars and animal sacrifices," Eddie said.

"Yes, Leap, but don't be distracted by shiny objects."

"Does it really matter why they killed the boys if they are the culprits?" I said, growing weary of Zac's cautions.

"No, Arthur. I just don't want to be stained by that brush."

The phone call closed with me agreeing to hire Zac and write a retainer check of $1,000.

I had skin in the game, and capital, too.

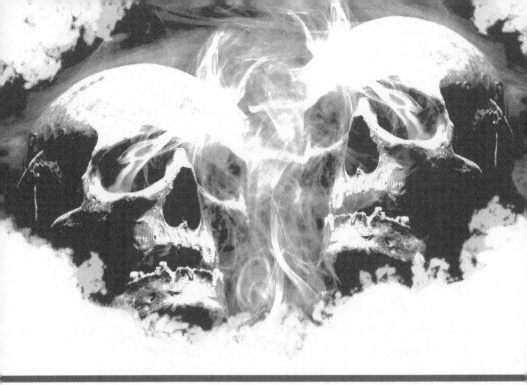

CHAPTER 9

October Country

Our plan the next day was to visit the public library in Tawas to look at their newspaper files. But that was interrupted when the dogs started barking during breakfast. Eddie bolted to the window.

"Shit," he said. "Police car just pulled in." He looked at me. "Give me a dollar, Art."

"Why" I asked while fishing one out of my wallet.

"Retainer," he said. "I'm your lawyer."

"What? Why?"

"You remember the cover story?"

I nodded.

"Good, follow my lead."

There was a knock on the door. I gathered up the dogs while Eddie answered it.

"Mr. Edward Fletcher," the voice from outside said. "I'm deputy Deke Snyder. Could I speak to you about a matter?"

Eddie agreed and suggested doing so on the porch because of the dogs. I shushed Sam and Sham then followed him outside.

Deputy Deke Snyder was baby faced, better than six feet tall and packed at least two and half bills of weight on that frame. I could imagine that in his younger days Deke might have played tackle for some high school tucked away in the pine barrens of Northern Michigan. Now he tackled backwoods crime.

"What county?" Eddie asked.

"Pine," Snyder said flatly.

"You're a long way from home, officer," Eddie said. "What's this about?"

Snyder fidgeted while searching for his words. "We understand that you have been interfering with an active investigation," he finally said.

"What investigation, Officer Snyder?" Eddie asked.

"The disappearance on Danny Massengale and Ronald Parrish."

Eddie looked bemused. "First off, it's *Donny* Massengale and *Roland* Parrish," he said. "And second, are you serious?"

"You're obstructing justice in an active case," Snyder said with his best law enforcement voice, no doubt designed to intimidate us.

"An active case, huh?" Eddie tapped his temple. "Do you even know what obstructing justice means?"

"Of course, I do." Snyder seemed annoyed. "I'm a law enforcement officer."

"Well, I'm an attorney, and you are way off base."

"I need to see credentials on that, Mr. Fletcher!" Snyder put his hands on his hips and glared at Eddie.

"Sure," Eddie showed him his membership card to the Ohio Bar.

"This is Michigan, sir!"

"Have you heard of reciprocity, Officer?" Eddie asked but kept his tone professional, at first. Snyder hadn't and neither had

I, but it turns out that many states recognize bar certifications from other states. In effect, Eddie had legal standing in Michigan. Something that he hammered home over the next ten minutes while also adding several other factors that could allow for recognition. After that lesson, Eddie explained both the legal definitions and practical applications of the term, "obstruction of justice." The whole thing was uncomfortable for me, and I wasn't in the line of his fire. By the end Snyder looked bewildered. Fifteen minutes ago, the deputy had arrived as an incredible hulk of sorts, now he looked more like Baby Huey with a holster.

Eddie paused for effect at the end of his lengthy statement. I remembered meeting a colleague of his several years back who said, "Sometimes Fletcher gets too intense in the courtroom. He can petrify juries with the power of his presentations. It can backfire so we keep him harnessed with cross." Looking at Snyder I worried what might happen.

"And then there's the aspect of the term 'active case,'" he said then licked his lips. I think that he wanted a chew.

"Yeah," Snyder said meekly.

Eddie went on to explain that newspapers are always reporting on active cases. "All the time, Officer, all the time. Ergo, that argument is invalid at worst, specious at best. Now let's turn to books and television."

"I get your point, sir," Snyder said, clearly exhausted by this. "But there are concerns. A book recently was published that got a lot of facts wrong." I felt that this was a reasonable argument.

But Eddie was ready for it.

"Exactly," he said with authority while pointing at me, "and that's why my client and I are investigating this to clean up Asa Fountain's shitstorm."

Snyder turned to me. "And just who the Hell are you?" He said with some bile. My sense is that having been verbally beat up by Eddie, Deke wanted to take it out on me, whom he assumed was a softer target.

I calmly introduced myself and explained the purpose of our

activities in depth, mostly to bore him into submission. I concluded that we were not planning to write a book, but a magazine article was likely, hinting that *The New Yorker* would jump at something like this (very doubtful), and that our findings would be turned over to the Michigan State Police at the end.

"How long before that?" Snyder asked. The tone was more neutral suggesting that my approach might have worked.

"A couple of months," I said.

"Now what's really going on?" Eddie asked. "Pine County is at least 80 miles from here. Does your Sheriff know that you're here?"

Snyder stared at him. "If he finds out there could be real trouble."

"Let's call him now?" Eddie stared back at him and held up his cellphone.

It wasn't much of a bluff because Snyder folded at once.

"That's not necessary," he said.

"OK, so what *can* you tell us, Officer?" Eddie had him, and everybody including the squirrels in the nearby branches knew it now.

Snyder visibly swallowed. I don't think that he ever saw this coming. He was used to getting his way, making everyone his bitch. But now the tables had turned.

"It's political," he said.

"Political?"

"That's all you're getting."

"The source," Eddie said. "In your opinion, not a person of interest?"

"Not in the disappearances," he said. "No way."

"But maybe something else that we've been looking into?"

"Can't know for sure, but this person didn't take those boys."

"Well, you got a long ride back to Pine County, Officer."

"I warned you," Snyder said as he headed back to his cruiser. "Somebody with power is not happy with what you are doing, gentlemen. That's your problem now, not mine anymore."

We watched Snyder drive out of sight, then Eddie punched in Zac's number.

After a three-minute rant dripping with profanity as well as some new-to-me military acronyms (SNAFU, FUBAR and BOHICA are about all I know), Eddie put his phone on speaker.

"Art," Zac said after a breath, "is that about right?"

I agreed that it was.

"So who leaked it?" he asked.

"Has to be Clark," Eddie said packing a chew.

"No other candidate," I said. "Cooper, Deacon and Marshall were very supportive of our efforts. Clark seemed disturbed at the end of our interview."

"He's a gasbag with backwoods connections," Eddie added. "Likely went quacking to somebody."

"About what, Leap?"

"Gotta be either werewolf parties or biker gangs," I said. "Those are the only two issues that Clark could have seen as new to the investigation."

"Beyond the ritual stuff," Eddie said with a spit.

"Political person of power?" Zac asked. "Where's Pine County?"

"Up by Big Mac," Eddie said. "I'm thinking somebody who was here back then might have gone to those parties or rode in a gang, maybe rubbed shoulders with Dunaway and his pals, but straightened up, went into politics and doesn't want this coming out."

"OK, gentlemen, send me information on your statehouse and congressional districts," Zac said. "We'll start there. I am interviewing some new prospective employees and will use this as a test."

"Is that wise, C-2?"

"Trust me, Leap, this is my world," Zac said, and I could hear the spark of a lighter and then some puffing. "And chill out, ya hear? Don't go punching anybody. You remember what happened in Norfolk."

"You're one to talk about punching people."

"Mine was justified."

"So was mine! The fucker was Navy!"

• • • • •

The Tawas trip was fruitless, too often small-town journalism is a not-so-clever copy of what big city and state papers had already reported. I went back to Chelsea the next day. My head was humming from our two interviews and the revelations of the photo. On the ride home I began to wonder if we could do a book, but it felt dirty.

"It'll be a report to the proper people," I said to the girls in the backseat. "Otherwise, Daddy only writes about protecting wild places that dogs like."

Sam and Sham both squealed with delight when I came off I-94 and turned on to our road. Just like me they had begun to feel at home here, although spending so much time at Spinnerfall had to be confusing for them.

After unpacking, replenishing the feeders, and playing a rousing game of tag with my pups, I went up to see Cam. Callie met me at the door wearing a Michigan State football jersey.

"We're gonna kick your ass tomorrow," she said instead of 'Hello.'

"That's right," I said, "It's tomorrow." The events of the last few days had diverted me from that week of the year when our state must choose sides, blue or green.

"Oh, typical Michigan fan, pretending it's not a big deal," she said and made a face of disgust. State fans were pissed at Michigan for a myriad of reasons, but lack of respect was at the top of that long list.

"It is a big deal, but I've been up north looking into that thing, Callie," I said, "and you're right, we're not good, you are. Is Cam around?"

"Working," she said in a somewhat friendlier tone. "Won't be home till dark. So, you admit we're gonna trample you tomorrow."

"After what happened to us in Madison last week it'll be on par with what happened in '67," I said. We lost that year 34-0.

"I cheered in that game," she said.

"I was in the stands."

"I'll let 'em know you stopped by, Art," she said. "Go Green, Go White."

"And it's time for me to go away," I said.

She waved as I did, sporting a look of confidence, or was that hubris?

As the kick sailed between the uprights and the ref signaled that it was good, I had an overwhelming desire to pick up my phone, call Callie Krenshaw and sing "The Victors." But I was a nice guy. Besides, Kody Krenshaw will do it for me and likely be pounding on my door in an hour or so when she disowns him.

God, I love beating those green-and-white bastards!

I took the dogs out then fed them a couple extra treats before heading to Ann Arbor to celebrate.

"Did you use the private lot?" Nick asked. There was a block of parking spaces for select employees of The Baron, a very necessary thing because the difficulty in parking downtown and on campus was legendary.

"Copy."

"Huh?"

"Sorry. I've been around Eddie and Zac too much."

"Did you solve it?" Nick asked while pointing to a table that needed clearing. A waitress quickly scurried over and began gathering glasses and pitchers. The bar was crowded but not packed. The game was in East Lansing, so things were not as crazy as if it been played in A-Squared.

"Closer. Any trouble?"

"We threw a bunch of State fans out when the game went to overtime. They went over to the All-American Café. I hope that their manager, Big Rick, sics his goons on them, and they never find the bodies."

"Don't say that!"

Nick was clearly taken aback by my reaction, but I didn't apologize for it.

• • • • •

September is the harvest month. It is a time to savor the fruits of one's labor. At 47 years of age, I now felt that I was living my September, or at least should be.

Ray Bradbury believed that October was a country unto itself. It wasn't just its long shadows, burning trees and Jack-o-Lantern grins. October was a time of transition from light to dark with a thinning of the veil at its end. I always felt there should be a black border around it. It was the month of dying. The dying of summer: that season of youth, living life in full stride, and believing in endless possibilities. Since Paula's death I knew that my summers were numbered and would never, ever be the same.

Now I stood at the frontier of Bradbury's October Country, no longer young, and troubled by the state of my own harvest. What had I put in the barn and silo? Would I get a chance to add to it before November came a-knocking with its cold winds and gray pallor?

By Monday morning my throat was raw and scratchy. I watched the DVD of those 53 newscasts concerning Donny Massengale and Roland Parrish. It was an echo chamber of frustration. "No new evidence." "Police are following leads." 'We still don't know where they are, or what happened." "Back to you."

"Back to you."

"Back to you."

"Back to you."

At the end of the stories my legal pad was empty. By sundown my sinuses were full. The next morning, I had the beginnings of a terrible cough. Hello, October Country.

Eddie didn't fare much better. I begged off on any trips north to help while mired in a beast of a cold. He made calls to all those sheriffs and deputies. The results were no-comments and hang-ups after he described the reasons for his call. The local witnesses did much the same. The three who talked said they knew who Dunaway was but didn't know him well.

"Christ, they never even heard of the werewolf parties," he said to me on the phone. I could imagine him rubbing those hands raw, stopping only long enough to pop another wad of chew in his mouth.

By the third week of black-boarded October Eddie's luck had changed. He'd sent letters of introductions to the friends of Donny and Roland — and probably should have done that with the other 17 prospects. I helped edit the missives. We emphasized the need to set the record straight and correct the errors of Asa Fountain. All three men agreed to talk, but two would have to be by phone because one was in Boston and the other lived in West Palm Beach. They both said that Roland had talked about some girl he'd met in the fall of 1983. Parrish had described her as a "hot blond with a killer, killer body who lives up north." Neither friend had met her, but both agreed that Roland Parrish was smitten.

"He was never great with girls," said one. "I think Rollie saw this as the chance to score big, but, I guess, she kept putting him off. She wouldn't spend the night with him in Mount Pleasant."

Zac was pleased. He'd feel even better after Eddie met with the third friend.

Steven Perkins had lived in the rental house with Donny and Roland during the school year of '83/'84. He'd smoked pot with Donny the night before the ill-fated trip. Now he had an accounting firm in Traverse City. Eddie met with him after business hours on a Wednesday.

He called me from the parking lot after the interview.

"The fucker met her!" he screamed. "ID'ed her picture! He was at that mixer!"

"Naylor?" I asked because it all seemed too good to be true.

"Yes!"

"What about May?"

"No, didn't remember her."

"What did he say about Naylor?"

"Well, first off, she called herself 'Jean,'" he said.

"An alias."

"We'll check about her middle name. Perkins said she was very attractive, but very immature, clearly a high schooler. She kept talking about how her parties in Mio were so much rowdier than the mixer. She kept saying, 'Come to Mio, baby cakes, and we'll show you how it's done.' Then, get this, she'd howl like a wolf."

"Wow."

"Also, she said she had a motorcycle, a Harley. Perkins said that she was flirty with a bunch of guys and Roland just put up with it, but she left the party early and just ditched Roland."

It was the only time Perkins met Naylor, and he did not remember Roland mentioning any plans to see her in Mio.

"He'd forgotten about it until I asked him," Eddie said.

That was the only nugget found in 20 potential interviews, but now we had a photo and an eyewitness to the fact that Roland Parrish knew Pam Naylor and was obsessed with her.

While nursing a cold, I busied myself with learning the history of Michigan environmental law in preparation for writing a regular column in *Michigan Hunting and Fishing*.

But my heart wasn't in it.

I missed Paula's voice. I missed hearing her tell me about her days, how the animals were doing or how the new pet tech was working out. Along with the Paw Palace, the other idea Paula was working on that spring was to offer high school kids a chance to intern at All Creatures and learn about the veterinary profession. She called them pet techs. There were hopes to expand the program.

I wondered how the hospital was faring. I thought about all my Florida friends, now long out of touch. I remembered my life before here.

Paula and I had both loved the fall. The temperatures dropped. The humidity lessened. She played more tennis. I wasn't fishing all night or getting up at 3 a.m. to stalk tarpon with some famous guide — all to chase another story just like a dozen that I'd written before. We lived a normal rhythm. There were evening "family" walks after dinner, followed by dog and human wrestling matches back home, which often led to me carrying Paula off to bed. On Saturdays we both cheered for Dear Old Floreedah, while I was left to root for The Blue Team alone since Paula would usually be on the porch gabbing with some girlfriends once the Gators were done playing. On Sundays, she'd make sloppy Joes and we'd watch the Dolphins.

"Who's the one that I liked in high school, Art?"

"Jim Kiick, you never stopped talking about him."

"He shoulda carried the ball more."

"You just liked watching him get back up after being tackled."

"Oh, I liked watching him do anything."

I took it for granted back then. It would always be that way, and just keep getting better. Life was an upward trajectory. I was all set.

The more I thought about it, the worse I felt about it.

And Black October had me in its clutches. I hadn't been to a meeting since mid-September. I didn't have a Michigan-based sponsor and rarely called Roger anymore. I banked my whole recovery on "learning that lesson after Paula's death" and Kate LeClair. The result was not a desire to drink, not yet, but a deepening depression and sense of shame for wasting my life, not appreciating what I had, running away from Florida, hiding in a cornfield, doing the same old job writing tired fishing pieces except for much less pay at an inferior magazine. And now chasing ghosts in the deep forests of Northern Michigan with a childhood friend going through his own crucible.

"Why the Hell did you have to die!" I yelled at the corner of the room, "and leave me with all this mess!"

But the corner of the room was silent.

I knew where this was headed and didn't raise a finger to stop it. That's alcoholism.

Then one gray morning the phone rang. It was Zac. He already had Eddie on the phone.

"We got good news and semi-bad news," Zac said.

"I could use some good news," I said.

It was very good news and fell along the lines that Eddie had predicted. Our visit from Deputy Snyder had been prompted by a member of Michigan's State Legislature., Cyrus Waxwell. His district included Pine County and Waxwell had known Snyder for 15 years. The deputy was doing a personal favor while likely expecting some future boon.

"Leap nailed it," Zac said.

Eddie interrupted by agreeing and claiming it was a "no brainer for superior brains."

Waxwell had grown up in Mio and graduated from high school in 1982. He had attended werewolf parties back then, just about every high schooler did.

"Did he remember any of our folks?"

"Only Naylor," Zac said. "Claimed she was 'the one on every guy's list, but a bit of a headcase' so he steered clear of her."

"He feared political blowback for going to a high school party?"

"Yes, if it turned out that it was connected to the murders," Zac said. "He represents a very conservative, God-fearing district and has future ambitions."

"Is he backing off?"

"As long as we claim that he played a crucial role in the investigation if we find anything."

"But…"

"Realpolitik," Eddie interrupted.

"His next move was to call in some favors with the Staties," Zac said. "You two would be getting pulled over every day, etc., but we came to an agreement."

"What is it?"

"Need to know," Eddie said.

"Come on!"

Zac drew in a breath before speaking. "My firm is going to do some work for him pro bono. There's an election next year."

"Oh, brother!" I pounded the tabletop and startled the dogs. "What's the bad news?"

"Fountain," Zac said.

It turns out that Zac had been "monitoring" Asa Fountain's website, Fountain-of-Justice.com. His operatives had hacked it and all of Fountain's emails and other digital files. He was completely inside Asa's computer.

"Be careful what you click, Arthur," Zac said with a bit of a sinister laugh. I didn't like this side of him. "Leap was right again"

"Always, C-2, always."

"Clark called him the day after the interview," Zac said. "Now Asa is sending some investigators to follow the leads that we developed."

"How soon?"

"Soon."

"We need to go double-time, Art," Eddie said. "Before they come in and fuck it all up."

"OK, where's Dunaway? And who is this Tony character?"

"We're getting close," Zac said.

The call ended shortly after that. My foul mood didn't lift completely but the thrill of the hunt was reignited. I had a fix of sorts for now.

• • • • •

I was trying to decide on whether to wear a costume that night — as a kid I had always been a ghost, but that did not sit well now — while handing out candy at the Krenshaws' when my phone rang.

"We found Dunaway," Eddie said. "He's dead."

This jolted me back to the case. The last two weeks had been free of sniffles and any thoughts about shovelheads, wyverns, psychopath cheerleaders and slimeball bikers. Instead, I'd dragged myself back to some meetings and was sizing up a new sponsor. It was progress of sorts.

"How long?"

"Since July of 1990."

"What from?"

"OD, Heroin."

"Well, that trail's cold."

"C-2 has his new case manager digging into everything about the death," Eddie said. "The ambulance responded to a call at the Twin Pines Motel near Brutus. They took him to a hospital in Petoskey, DOA."

"I know the area," I said. "It's on the way to Waugoshance Point — great smallmouth fishing there."

"I'll keep you posted. Happy Halloween!"

It was a touch frightening to imagine how Eddie might celebrate Tricks and Treats.

That night I came home from the Krenshaws' with a bag of candy and some dog treats. There was a message on my phone.

"We think Tony's last name was Galbraith," Eddie's voice reported. "He signed for the rooms, two rooms, three people, one was a woman. They were supposed to follow the ambulance on their motorcycles. They didn't. Now I've been promised a treat, good-bye." There was woman's laughter in the background before he hung up.

Eddie was celebrating Halloween at Shar's apartment. She was his somewhat steady squeeze in Birmingham, and also a second-year associate at his law firm. He had started staying with her during his manic forays into casework.

By Wednesday Zac had found Tony John Galbraith.

"He's doing a hard 12 at the State Prison of Southern Michigan in Jackson," Zac said on the conference line. "AKA Jacktown," voiced in his best soul brother tenor.

"Hard 12?" I asked.

"That's the minimum for his sentence regarding armed robbery, attempted murder, vehicular homicide and other things," Zac said staying soulful. "The fucker is a magnet for crime."

"How do we get at him?" Eddie asked.

"Why, Fletcher," Zac said with a flourish, "just ask for a meet." I guessed by now why he was in such a good mood. This case was close to going prime time again and The Phoenix Investigation Firm would have a huge pelt on its belt, plus a boatload of good PR.

"Can we get one?" I asked.

"I think so. But if the Michigan Staties aren't on our trail by now then they will be soon. I say, 'Let them come.'" Zac was giddy. Dunaway and Galbraith were a couple of Big Boy gets, even Marlowe would tip his fedora at that.

"Not necessarily a bad thing," Eddie said. "I'm almost out of the penalty box at my real job."

"We need a good cover story," Zac said. "One that is true but not overly so. Remember, Galbraith must agree to the meet. We can't spook him."

"What makes you think that he'll talk?" Eddie asked.

"Not certain that he will, but something tells me that he might speak to the time and place. Six months into his term at *Jacktown*," Zac loved saying that word, "Galbraith had kitchen duty. He's been a good skell as they say, so he'd earned that job. Tony gets alone in the kitchen, bolts the doors, and sticks his arm into a boiling pot of water. Keeps it in there for nearly two minutes before passing out."

"How'd he last that long?" I asked and remembered a lifetime of steam burns from the stove, especially when drunk or hungover.

"Vicodin. Galbraith had enough in him to OD in time had he not chose to call attention to himself by boiling his skin off."

"Let me guess, left arm?" Eddie said.

"Amputated just below the elbow," Zac said. "Prison doctors, prison medicine."

"Why did he do it?" I asked.

"He wanted to get right with God," Zac said. "He wanted to

atone for his sins. It'll all be in the brief that I'm preparing for you. Read it. Make a question list. Then saddle up. We need to get to him fast."

"After that?" I asked.

"We'll see what shakes out."

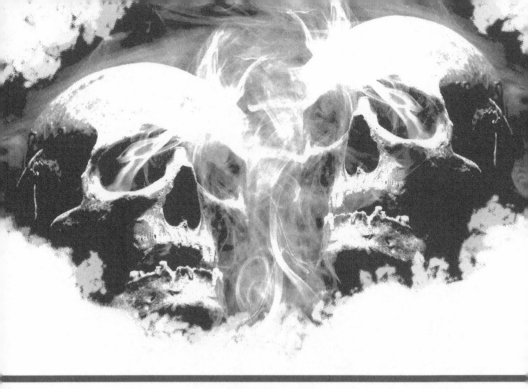

CHAPTER 10

Wyvern

Reading the brief on Tony Galbraith gave me a greater appreciation for Zac's skills. Had he not chosen a career in the military Zac could have been a fine journalist. He'd pieced together a comprehensive narrative through police, prison, and military service records plus a couple of interviews with people who had encounters with Galbraith along the way. Tony's story was one of tough circumstances, bad choices, and the road to ruin.

He was born in Flint, the son of a plant worker who helped make the transmissions for Chevrolet's muscle cars. Tony's mother died of breast cancer when he was only 10 years old. Unsupervised at home and living in a tough working-class neighborhood, he found a home on the streets with like-minded teenagers — all of them Hell bent on sex, drugs, rock and roll, plus a little petty crime for good measure.

He dropped out of high school in 1975, in part to serve six months in a juvenile offender center for stealing cases of Stroh's Beer. Time at Juvie Hall only sharpened his criminal skills. He was arrested for breaking into cabins in the Houghton Lake area during the frigid winter of 1977. For that offense, he served a year in the Roscommon County Jail.

After getting out in 1978, Tony Galbraith had a period of walking the straight and narrow. He joined the Army, served four years, and made the rank of E-4 specialist before leaving the service in 1982.

Galbraith used his savings to buy a Harley Davidson 1340 FXB Low Rider Sturgis motorcycle and moved to Mio. Once there, he found a job working at an automotive shop called Roscoe's just north of town. At this point it appeared that Tony John Galbraith had learned his lesson and grown up.

Perhaps not. Accounts claim that Galbraith had been a good soldier but a wild man when on leave. It transferred to civilian life where he was a reliable wrench, always on time, always willing to work late, and quick with a never-ending array of dirty and gross jokes, especially about dead dogs and babies. After the sun went down, Tony would prowl northern roadhouses like the Mio Saloon, Walkers, Linkers Lost Creek Lounge, Big Water Bar & Grill. He chased the local talent, sometimes screwing them right out back behind the watering hole. He rubbed shoulders with other bad men like Dunaway. At some point, those old habits started to feel appealing again. Schemes were hatched. Things were stolen. Mayhem occurred.

There had been a series of robberies in Oscoda, Alcona, Alpena and Iosco counties during 1983 as well as several strange acts of vandalism. Being an ex-con, Tony was a suspect. When an Oscoda County sheriff's deputy showed up at the garage, Tony claimed that he knew nothing about the crimes. His boss backed him up. The deputy left satisfied that Galbraith was not their man.

Two weeks later Tony quit and disappeared overnight.

Where Tony Galbraith went and what he did from the fall of

1983 until that June night 16 years later will never be known for certain. Perhaps Tony's actions in those years can best be summed up by his favorite song, Van Halen's *Runnin' with The Devil*.

Galbraith's run came to a crawl by the spring of '99. He was so broke that his beloved Sturgis was sold for parts because the bike wasn't working anymore anyway. He couldn't afford to fix it. By then, the mates he ran with after that '83 getaway were either dead, crazy or just too scary to hang with anymore. Drugs and drink had addled Tony's mind. Age was catching up as well, he was a world-weary 41 by then. Living in the woods, or with sketchy people, or in cheap backwoods motels was proving to be a grind. There were way too many "reasons" why he couldn't get a regular job and had to con, steal and scrounge in order to stay alive.

In June of that year, broke with no transportation and no decent shelter, Tony Galbraith decided to shoot for the moon. His plan, devised with an equally desperate colleague named Jace Durn, was to rob a major service station on I-75 outside Roscommon and use his share of the money to go into the drug dealing business where he could quadruple his stake in a fortnight, then do it all over again. The Fina store was a good choice. It did a lot of business because there was little competition either way for about 20 miles. It was also the only building around for miles.

Other than that, the idea was loony tunes.

First, they stole a gun from a "friend" who used the piece for his own heists and had even fired several shots into a bar in Waters the summer before just to "show how tough he was." Police had the slugs.

Second, they "borrowed" a 1992 Toyota Camry from a neighbor down the street from the hovel where they were currently crashing. Four witnesses saw Tony hot-wire it.

Finally, Jace decided to shoot the cashier, Stene LeDeucer, in both kneecaps to prevent him from following them. This was unexpected and completely freaked out Tony, the getaway driver, who gunned the car away from the scene in such a manic fury that he missed the junction with 75. Their plan had been to drive up to Wolverine and stay with some friends in the Pigeon River Forest. Galbraith's fear-addled brain didn't catch the mistake until they were almost back in Roscommon. He tried a 180 turn on Federal Highway to get back to the freeway. The Camry was not the kind of car to perform such a stunt and Tony didn't have that skill set anyway. The car rolled three times. Jace, who had not put his seatbelt on, was thrown from the vehicle and would die from internal injuries within minutes. Tony was banged up but otherwise OK. He got out of the overturned car and started searching for the money bag (the take was $426) but before he could find it the scene was bathed in blue light.

Deputy Sheriff Harry Regan thought that a Tuesday would lead to a quiet night. Then he got a radio report from dispatch that the cashier at the Fina out by 75 had been robbed and shot twice. On the way to the crime scene, he saw a pair of headlights swerve off the road in front of him and watched as the taillights begin to rotate.

"What the Fuck?" Regan said out loud, then radioed in before "lighting up."

Galbraith stood up to run but was met by a blinding searchlight and a crystal-clear command.

"Freeze now or I shoot!" Regan said.

Galbraith did just that, then followed further orders to get flat on the ground, spread out his hands and remain motionless.

Soon a second deputy showed up, then two Michigan State Patrol Cars. An ambulance blared by on the way out to the Interstate junction to attend to LeDeucer while Galbraith laid on his stomach cuffed and tasting asphalt. Durn was already dead.

Tony Galbraith would be questioned three different times for over seven hours in total. He would claim that it was Durn's idea, but that's not entirely true. He would claim Durn was the gunman, true but Tony still gets the assault with deadly weapon and attempted murder charge for being an accomplice. So, there's the robbery, assault, attempted murder and, for good measure, a charge of vehicular manslaughter for Durn's death.

Regan and a senior deputy, Dustin Shaw, questioned Galbraith. Tony quickly copped to the crimes and wanted a deal for it. Regan and Shaw wanted more for something that was already iron clad. So, Galbraith owned up to several burglaries over the last three years from Mackinaw City to Tawas City to Kalkaska. Some of the details matched over a dozen reported incidents. By Friday the Powers-That-Be were satisfied.

In the report Regan commented on how nervous Galbraith was when he was pressed on other crimes.

"He was surprisingly calm about the Fina robbery," Regan said. "But when we said that would not be enough for a sentence consideration, he started getting fidgety, dry-mouthed and sweated like a pig. There was real fear in his eyes, all the way until we asked if that really was everything? 'Yes,' he said. 'You got everything.' Then we left the room and came back and told him to write it all down. If was only after that he started to relax. I thought it was the power of confession."

"Great work, C-2, but they had this SOB in the box in '99 and fucking blew it!" Eddie said on a phone call.

"It was 15 years later, Leap" Zac said. "There was no reason to connect it. Galbraith is not in Mio in '84. Deputy Regan is a former MP, served in Germany, and seems like a sharp guy. He was very helpful. Remember, nobody in law enforcement looked at the antecedents in the Massengale and Parrish case. That's why we are."

"Well, it cost me a window!"

"What?" I asked.

"Yeah, I threw that coffee table through the front window when I read about the arrest in '99."

"Oh, Leap," Zac said.

"It's November," I said. "What are you going to do?"

"I boarded it up," Eddie said. "Got my buddy, Bernie, he

lives at Whippoorwill on the Holy Water, coming next week to put in a new one."

"Can we get back to Galbraith?" I asked.

"Keep your fingers crossed," Zac said. "I'm working on a meet."

We didn't have to keep them crossed for long.

Zac Phoenix, via his elbow grease, got us into the State Prison of Southern Michigan at Jackson. I don't know the details for sure, but I am certain that the Illinois State Police helped with the meet.

"We're for real, gentlemen," Zac said in our conference call. "They can't ignore us."

But we were drawing a lot of attention. Eddie had received two voice mails from a reporter from the *Traverse City Record-Eagle*. He was doing a piece on the missing Michigan trout fishers.

"I'm guessing that fucking Clark went to the press now," Eddie said. "What's going on with Fountain?"

"Well…" Zac said. "They were having problems getting plane tickets to the Traverse City Airport, Ha, Ha, but…, Hmm. They took down the website and went offline two days ago."

"They figured you out?" I asked.

"They figured out something, and my sense is that they will be here soon."

There was no time to waste. Eddie and I turned over our Social Security and driver's license information to the prison system for a thorough background check before being allowed access to Galbraith.

We held our breath, then received both clearance and permission to see Tony Galbraith on November 9th.

During this period of waiting there had been more breaks in the investigation. Zac's new case manager turned out to be a crackerjack computer sleuth, spending up to 20 hours a day scouting for information on Dunaway, Naylor and Galbraith.

"Song Rivera lives on ramen noodles, Skittles and tons of high-test coffee," Zac said. "Oh, to be 22 years old again."

"Is she a babe?" Eddie asked.

"She has purple hair, Leap."

"That's not a deal breaker, so what did she find?"

"Dennis Dunaway had several fresh needle tracks but did not show evidence of long-term IV drug use."

"He could have been snorting or smoking it," I said.

"The tox panel indicated a large dose of heroin, more than he should have ingested to get off. There were also traces of Methaqualone."

"Quaaludes," I said. "That's old school."

"It sounds like he might have gotten a hot shot," Eddie said.

"Galbraith is not gonna give that up," Zac said. Then he spoke to someone in the room. I heard him ask where the file was. There were some footsteps shuffling, then he came back on the call.

"Pamela *Jean* Naylor filed W-2's from 1985 through 1989 for work at two restaurants in the Petoskey area," he said. "Both are now out of business. She also renewed her driver's license all the way through 1994, but not in 1996 when it was due for a re-up. The address was in Wolverine."

"Cilla May died in a car crash in 1996," Eddie said. "Then Pam Naylor goes off the grid about the same time."

"Are you saying Cilla May's death was suspicious?" I asked.

"No evidence to support that," Zac said.

"OK," Eddie said, "but Dunaway's OD is very suspicious. Are you telling me that somebody couldn't have partied with Cilla May, slipped her a Mickey, and then crossed their finger's that she passes out behind the wheel?"

"Our evidence says that Cilla May was an accident waiting to happen. She had cirrhosis and other indications of long-term abuse of various prescription drugs. She was killing herself an inch at a time. I'll give you Dunaway. That's worthy of looking at." There was more shuffling of papers. "We should have talked about this already!" Zac said to someone harshly. Then there was a string of profanity before he came back on the line.

"Guys, I really fucked up," he said. "I should have told you about this weeks ago, but I forgot."

"Told us what?" Eddie said.

"The police report on Hanna Grey's suicide. There's two red flags, bright red flags."

"Why didn't you?" Eddie sounded very annoyed. For him, Hanna Grey was as much what this case was about as Donny Massengale and Roland Parrish.

"You know why! I've gotta business bursting at the seams, Leap! Shit happens!"

"What did you find?" Eddie said darkly.

"I'm looking at the photos of the scene." Zac cleared his throat. "You don't ever want to see those, trust me."

"I've seen bad shit," Eddie said.

"Then you know that you can't unsee it!" Until this moment Zac Phoenix, C-2, Black Zac had been the grounding voice in the investigation. He provided both a sense of direction and a reality check on the boundaries of the case. Now I think he was experiencing the stress that Eddie and I had already felt — it was like staring into an abyss.

"Her neck was broken clean," Zac said with an audible swallow. "Her head...was hanging below her shoulders, dangling."

"Jesus!" I gasped.

"Hanna was five foot two and about 105 pounds, not overweight," Zac said with a long exhale — I think that he had permanently broken the indoor rule on smoking. "The rope was 30 inches. She was out on a limb, likely dropped from a sitting position. The maximum drop she could have achieved would have probably fractured the neck but not broke it completely."

"Did you have experts review the file?" Eddie asked in a softer voice.

"Two, including the top guy for the ISP. Both agreed that Hanna would have died from the fall, but not instantly. In fact, they thought that she would probably have asphyxiated. The injury to her neck given the physics involved seemed highly unlikely."

"She had help," Eddie said. "Dunaway. What's the other flag?"

"The quality of the knot. It was described as 'tied in a professional manner.'"

"Couldn't she have learned to tie it in something like girl scouts?" I asked.

"Possibly. We'd have to ask her sister about that."

"Geez, that wouldn't be comfortable to do," I said. "Think about it if you were in her position."

"You learn to tie knots well in basic, C-2?" Eddie asked.

"I did, but we didn't do hangman's knots."

"The principle is the same. We learned to tie proper knots. That applies to any knots. People tell me that I should sell my flies to fly shops, make some money and a big name for myself. 'How did you learn to tie those so well?' they ask. 'You must have been tying flies since you were a kid.' No, sir, the Army taught me how to tie great flies over a decade before I ever sat down to a vise."

"Galbraith," I said.

"Copy," Eddie said, "So he was there, too."

"We don't know that," Zac said. "You can't go off on him, Leap. We'll lose access to what he *will* tell us. He's not gonna cop to any murders on Wednesday. For the sake of the victims, keep your cool."

"Oh, I will," Eddie said. "I'll do it for them, but I'll do it for Evangeline Cooper as well. She made it out of that Hell Hole back then. She made a good life for herself. She's the face of it for me. Galbraith ties a good knot. Well, so do I, and my plan is to rope him up and hand him over to the Staties. When I'm done with him, he won't be doing a hard 12, it'll be a hard forever!"

Eddie's words left me worried.

• • • • •

My cell went off as I was driving west on I-94. I pulled into the next rest stop. It had been the plan all along. Zac said to get plenty to eat and take several bathroom breaks because it would a long day. Once inside the prison, we would likely be forbidden from using the restrooms.

It was a message from Zac that a story had dropped in the *Traverse City Record-Eagle* about further investigations into the Massengale and Parrish case. It said that associates from the Chicago-based Phoenix Investigation Firm were looking into a local angle to the case that might involve a high school student who knew Parrish. The reporter claimed the firm could not be reached for comment. If Pam Naylor was alive and somewhere in Michigan, then she'd surely know soon that we were looking for her.

I had no problem finding Jacktown. It is the largest walled prison in the world and stood out like a raised dark mole on the flat landscape, now tanning in the blight of a midwestern November.

Eddie was easy to find as well. He was pacing back and forth in front of his Cherokee in the parking lot, cellphone glued to his ear. Even at a distance I could see the narrowed slits of his eyes and taut outline of his jaw. We weren't even inside Jacktown yet and he looked like a caged animal.

He didn't acknowledge me approaching him, just spat on the concrete. There was a huge bulge in his right cheek. This was a product of both nerves and the fact that he'd go hours before another chew. Eddie looked pale and drawn. His shoulders were a bit hunched as if they were carrying a heavy load. He was flexing his free hand and squeezing it until the knuckles turned white.

"Alright, then you confirm it!" he said. "Leave a message if that's his address. I will, OK? Don't worry. We got this, HOOAH." Then he hung up and made a sour face before spitting his entire wad at my feet.

"Fucking journalists," he said.

"We should have talked to that reporter," I said.

Eddie considered this. "You should have. We fucked it up, but there's some good news as well."

"Really?"

"We think that we've found Naylor's brother, and Pam was

alive as of six years ago," he said, then pulled a small package out of his coat.

"How?" I asked.

"Funeral notice," he ripped open the package. It was a nicotine patch. "Naylor's mom dies in the fall of '99. She is survived by son David Steven Brandon, then 37, and daughter, Pamela Jean Naylor, then 33."

"OK, how about location?"

No location for her. But David is in Houghton Lake and Zac has some ploy cooking to confirm it!"

"Will he speak to us?"

"Well, if it's his address in HL then we ambush him tomorrow morning before he goes to work," he said with a little smile.

"Great. Let's get this over with it."

"Copy." He placed the patch on his chest.

Zac's briefing made it sound as if our experience inside Jacktown would be a living Hell. I think that was on purpose. He wanted us over-prepped, so we'd adjust quickly to the environment. That way we'd be close to our best when talking to Galbraith, which was a good idea.

The State Prison of Southern Michigan can best be described as industrial. Its bones were steel and concrete. Its colors were pea soup green and faded gray. Everything was bolted down. There was the smell of disinfectant and a sense of despair.

The prison guards came in two sizes. There were the defensive ends, tall, lean but very mean looking, and defensive tackles, short, squat bodybuilders with warning in their eyes. All of them had bristly military cuts and were clean shaven. Nobody greeted us warmly. Instead, we were made to feel like invaders, a potential pathogen, because we were here to see a prisoner, in this case Number 799125.

We went through a metal detector, then had our IDs checked, then were searched, then had our IDs checked once more, went through metal detectors again and were searched for a second time. After that we were put in a room and sat for over an hour.

"Hurry up and wait," Eddie said, but he seemed calmer since getting inside.

There were two issues, one small, one big, both important. The small one involved our tape recorder, could we take it in? A guard seized it and took the device for inspection. It would not be returned to us for over two hours, but we did receive permission to use it with a promise to turn over a copy of the conversation to the prison authorities within 72 hours. Eddie signed off.

"That's for the Staties," he said. "We're doing their work."

The big issue involved getting a guard out of the room while we talked to Galbraith. Zac and Eddie were certain that Tony would be impeded in his comments with one present. We were not his legal counsel so there was no guarantee of privacy. Zac thought the issue had been worked out when he spoke to the assistant warden, but nobody was aware of that agreement when we arrived. Three different guards, including the supervisor, said they would look into it, but in each case, the individuals went about their other duties, some of which included just standing around.

Eddie took it in stride for an hour or so. Then he remembered another aspect of our agreement, we would offer $500 in commissary funds for Galbraith in return for speaking to us. That document had been seized with our wallets, watches and keys upon entering the building.

"I need to fix this clusterfuck now," he finally said, then got up and waved over a nearby guard. This one was a hybrid between end and tackle who also appeared to be a shift commander of sorts since he was giving out various orders to the others. Eddie engaged him in a moderately animated conversation. I couldn't quite hear any words, but after a minute the officer smiled and almost laughed. That would be the only sign of positive emotion I would see all day from the staff.

Finally, they shook hands and Eddie came back sporting a wry smile.

"I think it's settled," he said.

"What did you say to him?"

"Classified," he said and gave me a larger smile.

"Seriously!"

"I told him not to worry about Galbraith. We'd sign liability waivers, and he should sign one too because I'd fuck him up if he even farted loud. That takes care of the guard."

"What about the commissary shit?"

"We'll do it verbally. They are not comfortable with the document going in there."

Just before noon we were sent deeper into the Belly of the Beast, which required moving through one of the cell blocks, a large, long hall with five tiers of cells on each side stretching almost a football field in length. It was something out of *The Birdman of Alcatraz*. I expected to see Burt Lancaster in a cell using an eye dropper to feed a sick canary some medicine that he'd made from the shavings of matchheads. There were shouts from the prisoners, but I kept my eyes straight ahead and my thoughts somewhere else, anywhere but here.

Once through that gauntlet, we were placed in a small room with a table and two chairs on either side. There we would sit until almost two in the afternoon. Then, nearly five hours after we'd arrived, two guards brought in a man in leg chains and modified handcuffs because of his missing left hand and forearm. They took off the handcuffs.

"Turnbill says the leggings stay on," the one guard said to Eddie. "That's the agreement."

Eddie nodded. "Tell him thanks, OK?"

"We'll be right outside," the guard said, "Best behavior 799125. Understand?"

"Yes, boss," Galbraith said.

"You got two hours, sir," the guard said and handed Eddie back his watch.

The guards left the room.

Tony Galbraith was our age but looked a decade older. His head was a smooth egg, no Fu Manchu, with puffy eyes that were wrinkled at the corners. His complexion was chalky. There was a scar on his forehead and a sulk to his expression. His body was asymmetric, the right side looked strong, likely from weights, but the left side shrunken, and there was a rubber cap covering the stub on his arm.

He was probing us with those orbs, drab green in color, and likely wondering, "What can I get here?"

"So who are you guys?" he finally asked.

"You don't know?" Eddie asked

"Not a damn thing."

"Fuck!" Eddie said.

"Welcome to jail, Baby!" Tony let out a long unsettling cackle like a crow but with the staccato of a tommy gun.

Eddie looked at him while certainly recalculating his approach. Galbraith hadn't had time to prepare for us. As a result, the canvas for Eddie to paint our story was larger. He was reconsidering its landscape.

"First off, HOOAH, brother," Eddie finally said, "and thanks for this meet."

Galbraith's features brightened. He sat up from slouching. "Jesus, I haven't heard that in a coon's age. You military?"

"Copy that. Intelligence officer, started with the Big Red One in '82."

"Oh, yeah?" Tony seemed impressed. That was the plan, establish a rapport through a shared experience. "Hell, I was just 11 Bravo, a grunt with a rifle."

"Infantry is the backbone of the Army."

"Sure, like our motto 'Follow Me.'" There was some dignity in his words.

For the next 20 minutes Eddie and Galbraith talked Army shop.

"I had a 'Rican DI in basic," Tony said, "I can still hear him waking us up at O-Four-Hundred hours, 'Eye wan everee hun ah yoo swannging deeks to sheet, shower and shave by o-five hunnen,'" then he cackled again.

"OK, Tony," Eddie finally said. "Can I call you Tony?"

"Fuck yeah. Beats the shit out of 799125."

"I imagine." Eddie explained our cover story. We were investigating the work of Asa Fountain on the Bigfoot Killer with an eye at correcting the errors and establishing a sound set of facts for further examination.

Galbraith nodded. "How does that involve me?" His voice had a bit of a whistle to it, likely a product of poorly fitted dentures.

"Well," Eddie said, "Asa claimed that those two missing boys, the trout anglers, were Bigfoot victims. We now know that's not true."

Tony's eyes narrowed and he bit his lower lip. "So that's why you're here."

"Primarily."

"What's in it for me?" Tony said in a cool voice.

"We have an incentive."

"Sentence reduction?"

"Out of our purview. We're not law enforcement or part of the justice department, but, you know, Tony, they will be interested if what you have is useful."

"So what's the carrot, Bugs?" Tony asked in an even chillier voice.

"Five hundred dollars of commissary."

"No, shit, I want a whole yard."

This was going sideways in a hurry. Eddie and Tony argued for a few minutes, then there was a knock on the door. A guard came in with the receipt for Galbraith's commissary funds. He showed it to Eddie then Tony.

"This is your receipt 799125 for commissary," the guard said.

"Thanks, boss," Tony said. Eddie nodded. The guard left.

"I still want a yard." Galbraith glared at Eddie.

"We could do another 500 if you give us something." Eddie was clenching his fists.

"How can I trust you?"

"That works both ways, Tony."

Galbraith put his one hand on his chin and made a show of

pondering our offer. Finally, he laughed and said, "Sure, whaddya want to know, Eddie, *can I call you Eddie*, Eddie?"

"Sure thing," Eddie said in monotone. I could tell he was pissed at Galbraith's antics. "So why did you come to Mio in '82?"

Galbraith went into a lengthy harangue about the decline and fall of Flint. He didn't want to be a factory rat his whole life. He had seen what it did to his father and was watching what it was doing to his own friends, turning them into zombies. To Galbraith's eye it was a slow, soul-crushing death.

"This country consumes working people and spits them out," he said. "I wanted to go somewhere and be free of that. An Army buddy had said to head north and live like a man. I bought a bike and did just that."

"You got a good job almost right away."

"How'd you know?"

"Tony." Eddie's voice filled with gusto. "How did you think we *found you*. We've talked to dozens of people, lots of them *knew you*, and talked all *about you*."

"Really," he said with a downbeat.

"Yes, sir. We need your side of it, only fair, only right."

"It sure the fuck is, *Eddie*."

"Tell me about the bike." Eddie swung the conversation away from this revelation. Let it stew in Tony's mind that other people had been talking about him.

"Sure thing." Tony was off on a loving description of his Sturgis.

"Make that shovelhead roar," I said.

"It speaks," he said pointing at me. "You ride?"

"I got the bug after spending three months interviewing folks up in your old haunts."

"Me, too, Tony," Eddie said. "Always thought bikes were cool but never got around to taking the plunge." Then he made the motion of gripping handlebars. "Tell ya what. If there's time after, please give us a recommendation or two. You're a Harley guy, but I keep hearing about these Indians." It was bullshit, but Galbraith might well be bullshitting, too.

"Indians are not bad bikes," he said.

"Who did you ride with?" Eddie got back on point.

"What did they say?"

"I want your side."

Tony looked at Eddie, his wheels grinding inside. "I'm sure they mentioned Denny."

"Denny who?"

"Dunaway, come on, Eddie, meet me halfway, no Bullshit."

"Fair enough. Tell me about Dunaway."

Tony's description of Dennis Dunaway was practically gushing. In his view Dennis Dunaway was a biker god, a free and fearless man who did what he wanted when he wanted with whomever he wanted.

"The motherfucker coulda banged Farrah Fawcett or Jackie Bisset if he'd ever met 'em. I don't know how he did it because Dennis was uglier than a bag of assholes, and he rarely washed. Fucker could drive blind drunk in a snowstorm, too, nothing scared him."

"Tough hombre as well," Eddie said.

"Goddamn right." Tony was animated now that the subject was his world of yesteryear when he was young, strong and, maybe, homicidal. "There were guys who coulda kicked Dennis's ass, but they'd hadda thrown every last punch in their quiver. Not sure even then that Dennis woulda stayed down. Youda hadda kill 'im for that."

"You think Dennis would have ever killed anyone?" Eddie asked. I liked the look in his eyes. It suggested that he was engaged and in control. The rocky start was behind Eddie Fletcher, and now he would try to manipulate and squeeze Tony Galbraith for every drop of intel.

"Fuck you! Denny didn't kill those boys."

"Just asking, and how would you know?"

"Didn't fit the program of sex, drugs and rock and roll. Now

Denny was not what I'd call a peaceful guy, but the only way I would ever see him killing someone would be in a fight and that's self-defense, right?"

"You know that depends, but a good lawyer can move mountains. Thanks for that, so who else? We're on a roll."

Galbraith got a funny look on his face.

"Who else?" Eddie asked with matching face. "Let's talk about that guy?"

Tony was moving his jaw around. I think his dentures might have come loose.

"Quack, Quack, Quack," he finally said, and then did his creepy cackle. In his present state Tony Galbraith was not very frightening, but I could see how as a young man with both of his arms he could have been…disquieting.

"Mr. Penguin! Good job, now we're getting somewhere. Tell me about Rufus What-Was-His-Last-Name."

"Never did know his last name." Tony's rundown on Penguin was kind-hearted but familiar except Galbraith mentioned that Rufus had worked for several farms around the West Branch area. That was a new lead.

"He was handy with a tractor and a thresher. Rufus was not stupid, just kinda toasted. He needed to be told what to do."

"We heard that he was a follower."

"You heard right."

"So who else?"

Galbraith rattled off several names, but in each instance, we knew who they were because every one of them had been in the Big Water Bar & Grill the night of the boys' disappearance.

"Those aren't the guys, Tony."

"Can't think of anyone else," he said with a shrug.

"Let's talk about something different while your memory clears."

"What's next?" There was an edge in his tone.

"Werewolf parties."

"Ahwhooooo, Ahwhooo, whooo, whooooo!" Tony said glee-fully then cackled some more.

"You ran 'em?"

"That's a big 10-4, good buddy," Tony said with a giant, porcelain smile.

"Gimme your version." Eddie leaned back in his chair to listen.

Galbraith did, and he loved telling it. My sense was that it was the best of times for him. Along with Dunaway and the ever-faithful Penguin, they sold the high schoolers drugs and liquor while coaxing the pretty young things into all sorts of nasty acts. I imagined that he never got tired of telling his fellow inmates about those halcyon days, and likely never found the need to exaggerate.

"What about the guys?"

"They weren't gonna mess with the three of us," Tony said with pride. "Fuck! We could have kicked the entire town's ass if needed...and they knew it. Besides," and here he stopped for a cackle or two, and then readjusted his teeth. "We couldn't fuck 'em all at once. There were leftovers, but we always got first dibs." Then he laughed a far deeper and darker laugh. Tony's file said that he'd become a model prisoner, joined the prison recovery program, even went to Bible study, but that all washed away in this moment. I was certain that his black heart was still intact. He was just hiding it. This was a problem because I was now sure that appealing to any newfound sense of conscience in Galbraith was likely a fool's errand. I hoped that Eddie saw that too and had a plan to address it.

"They were afraid of you."

"Everyone was."

"Everyone?" I figured that Eddie was setting up a question about Hobbs.

But Tony threw us a curve.

"We had insurance. A Lucky Strike extra." He chuckled. "Bet she didn't tell you that, did she?"

"Who?" Eddie was delighted. In courtroom terms, Tony Galbraith just opened the door to a new line of questioning.

But Tony knew his mistake almost immediately.

"You tell me, *Eddie*," he said with that venom again.

"I need your version, Tony, because she tells a different version. One that doesn't involve statutes of limitation."

Both Tony and I were surprised by this statement.

"That cunt!"

Take the bait! I thought. Take the bait!

He rose to Eddie's offering.

"Pam Naylor was part of the whole deal, and so was her cunt friend Cilla May. Lemme tell ya what they did for us."

"Please do," Eddie hadn't looked this happy in weeks.

Galbraith painted his portrait of Pam Naylor and Cilla May. His words outlined a couple of dark-souled fellow travelers. We figured both to be bitchy mean girls common to every gathering of tweens and teens since humans left the caves. At best, they were just there for the party favors and a whiff of dangerous men. At worst, they were unwitting accomplishes to the abduction of Donny Massengale and Roland Parrish. As Galbraith made his bold strokes our perceptions changed. Whether Naylor or May were born bad or chose that path, they had gone dark long before Massengale and Parrish packed up Donny's Blazer that April in 1984.

Cilla May was an accident waiting to happen even back then. She was packing Mom's pills into her body daily. Then on weekends, especially Werewolf Weekends, Cilla would fill herself with booze. It made her pliable and Cilla was the girl who everyone fucked any and every way that they wanted, especially if it involved humiliation. But it was perilous.

"Fuck!" Tony said, "She nearly died out there on a couple of nights. We couldn't wake her up, had to stick her head in a cooler of melted ice. She almost drowned doing that. Some kid knew mouth to mouth. It was funny and scary at the same time."

"A girl dying was funny?" Eddie's demeanor was neutral. This had to take a lot of self-control.

"We were all fucked up. But at the time she was just some rich girl who wouldn't have given two fucks about us if we didn't have some goodies and didn't give her the thrills of slumming… you know what I mean, Eddie."

Eddie nodded.

"Besides. We got access to Mommy's pills and plenty of cash from zonked-out Cilla. She funded a lot of the goings-on, but probably didn't know it."

"What about Naylor?"

Tony bounced his head up in down like a bobble-head doll. Then he made a serious and somewhat threatening face before finally speaking. It only confirmed what still burned inside him: rage.

"Different kinda cunt altogether. Pam was a goddess, great body, knew how to use it, wanted to use it, and knew its power. She did need some coaching. Dennis took care of that early on. God! What a great fuck! But…you had to watch her, make sure that she knew her place."

"How so?"

"She wanted to control everything. Not at first. In the beginning she was an eager learner. We spent one entire night teaching her how to do a proper blowjob. She was all in, coughing, gagging, but ready for the next prick. It was impressive. But she started to use her charms to run her own game."

"Her own game?" Eddie asked. He was riveted now. Our working theory had Naylor playing cat and mouse with Parrish for the fun of it and maybe that went wrong when Roland finally showed up in Mio. Galbraith was adding credence to it.

Tony went on for some time about how Pam Naylor started out as the cheerleader who was, as so many young women were, star-struck by Dennis Dunaway. He had her wrapped around his finger, or somewhere like that, but along the way all that great sex with hot Pam began to change the power dynamic.

"I think that Dennis became a little pussy whipped. Penguin, too. They'd never had a woman like her."

"What about you?"

"She got to me, too, for a while. We had to be careful with her because she had this thing she liked to do, and we had to make sure that she didn't do it to us."

"What thing?"

"Pammie liked to dose people. Knock 'em out with some of Cilla's pills. She had tranqs, you know, and other stuff. Pam got ahold of some of it and mixed up a powder. She called it 'sweet dreams.' That was our Lucky Strike Extra. If some guy was getting out of line, then Pam would say, 'Come with me, Baby Cakes, we'll have our own party.' She'd go off with the guy and a couple of beers or a punch that we made and dose the fucker. Soon he was out cold. It would look like he'd had too much to drink, but we knew better. But she'd also do it on people just because she liked to watch them lose consciousness. She got off on that shit."

"What do you mean, sexually?" I asked.

"Absolutely. She went missing at one party and Dennis found her back near the cars with some guy, a football player. He hadn't done anything wrong, but she dosed him anyway. So, Dennis finds her with the guy all groggy and helpless and Pam's got her hand down her pants rubbing one out."

"That is a thing," Eddie said. I'd like to think he was just doing a bit of persuading by relating.

"For her, yeah, so Dennis asked, 'What the fuck, Pam? He wasn't doing anything wrong,' and Pam says, 'I love to watch their eyes go dull and heavy and they get soooo sleepy. Then they're helpless, Baby Cakes, we can do anything we want to them.' And Dennis says that she says it in an innocent little-girl voice with a 'supper's-ready' look on her face, so he finishes her right there by the cars while the football player guy snoozes away."

"No kidding," Eddie said.

"But Dennis said to watch your drink after that episode. We did, but she kept on doing it because it got her super horny."

"Do you think it is possible that she experimented on Cilla May to get the dose right?"

Tony thought about this. "That's a good question because Cilla was somewhat more manageable as the parties went on and Pammie got into dosing people."

"It was you, Dennis, Penguin, Naylor, and, to a lesser degree, Cilla May running the parties," Eddie explained.

Tony agreed.

"Cilla was the bank."

"We made some cash from the dope we sold. Maybe stuck an Andy-Jack in her purse at the end of the night to pay back some to her, but that bitch was outta pills fer sure between us an' Pammie-pie!" He let out his cackle and seemed very happy.

"Good times."

"Fuck yeah! Thanks for the memories, Eddie." It sounded genuine.

"Now we need to talk about the other guy," Eddie said.

Galbraith's features tightened.

"He leads to that," Eddie said while pointing to Tony's left arm. Galbraith immediately started rubbing the stub. "And, Tony, he's gonna lead to you possibly, possibly, getting out of here before...2012?"

"What guy?" Tony said apprehensively.

"Oh, you gonna let Naylor's story tell the tale? Cause that leaves you here...for maybe longer than that." Eddie pretended to write in the air with his index finger.

"You gotta say a name first."

Eddie looked back at him. "Ok. His name was Hobbs and when he shows up you all bowed down. He starts running the show. You're just his crew."

Tony blinked several times, a sign of stress, just like all those talking heads on television pontificating on Iraq, Katrina and prescription drugs for seniors.

"That's not entirely true."

"Then tell us how it really was. I need your version."

Tony adjusted his teeth and began to give it up.

His account of the Amigos meeting Hobbs fits that of Domino Clark's with a couple of exceptions. The gang's name was The Runners, there were only five of them ("Rough looking crew, but we coulda taken them") and Galbraith did not have a pentagram. It turns out that he was wearing a Van Halen T-shirt. Hobbs was a heavy metal-fiend just like Tony. In any event, Dunaway had pissed the gang off. Along with slaying sweet young things and driving through Albert Clippers while several sheets to the wind, Dennis made all sorts of enemies. Hobbs diffuses the situation, but as Tony remembers it was the Beretta pistol in the back of his jeans that led to the swift departure of The Runners, not some supernatural stare down.

That would come later.

Hobbs's ascension to leader of the group — Galbraith said that he had been the leader, but evidence suggests that Dunaway had a stronger claim — was due to better drug connections, stronger pot at a better price plus speed, which they called crank. This put more money in their pocket and a better high in their heads. It also improved the werewolf parties. The speed gave the kids more staying power which made for even better shits and giggles.

"What did Naylor think of Hobbs?" Eddie asked.

"She knew an alpha when she saw one. Didn't bother me. I still gotta piece of her ass plenty of times."

"How about Dennis?"

"He was liking the money. Dennis didn't have a regular job. I got him some work at Roscoe's but the old man, who was a good guy, didn't like Dennis being in his shop much. Dennis made enough dealing to get some good camping equipment and even crash at some places on a couch for a couple of bucks a week. That was high living for him because he'd had a ratty sleeping bag and a lean-to in the forest when I first met him."

Eddie's face brightened. I could almost see the light bulb above his head as he formed an idea.

"Say, Tony, was Dennis handy with knots?"

"He was," Tony said, looking a bit confused. "He built some pretty decent shelters back in the woods. I busted his ass about being some kinda Eagle Scout."

Eddie shot me a quick sideways look.

"OK, drug dealing, werewolf parties and a little thieving?" Eddie asked.

"Yeah, vacant cabins, idiots leaving guns, stereos, TVs and such. Hobbs had a good fence downstate. Sometimes there was a car or truck in the garage or outbuilding. Dennis and I knew how to hot-wire those. Dennis had a bunch of chop shops around where we could take them."

"Did he?" Eddie asked. This might explain why the Blazer was never found. "Hey, let's backtrack. What did Hobbs look like?"

"Black hair, black eyes."

"Black eyes?"

"Well, you know, deep brown. He had that bar tan, just like I have now, except it's a cell tan."

"Not getting out in the sun."

"Exactly. Hobbs was tall, but sometimes taller. He was always thin, wiry. His face was just kinda...a face, not a lot of expression, same with his voice, always flat, not a lot of emotion. He never got excited, or mad. Shit, he'd smile a bit but never a big shit-eating one. I watched him get blowjobs and he'd crack the barest of grins. His laugh was almost a pretend laugh. If you get what I mean?"

"A bit of a Mr. Spock?" I asked.

"Yeah, I mean, I know who you are talking about."

"You said taller," Eddie asked. "Could have been boots or lifts."

"He wore the same boots all the time. Shit, he practically wore the same clothes all the time."

"Did you ever get his full name?"

"I think it was Jack." By now Tony'd removed the rubber cap and was itching the end of his stub, a purplish-red knob. It was at this point that I realized we'd broken him, or as much as we would. Galbraith seemed to have lost some of his resolve. That black heart had faded. Now he was answering questions without attitude, which was a good thing because we were almost out of time.

"Did he say where he was from?"

"Back east somewhere, never said exactly."

"Did he start the rituals?" Eddie leaned over the table.

There was a long icy silence. Galbraith looked down at his feet while he shuffled them nervously. I could hear the chains rattle and remembered that line from *Cool Hand Luke*, "You never get used to the sound."

"Some of that pre-dated us. Dennis used to see stuff in the woods where he was camping. We thought it was kids."

"But you did some of it, too. Did Hobbs start it, or you?"

"I made one once. Dennis and Rufus helped. We made up some sayings from those devil movies and comic books, got really high and played some music. Pammie, Cilla and a couple other kids were there, nothing happened except a party. We laughed about it afterwards."

"Why the attraction?" I asked. "Was it just the music?"

"That was a big part of it, but I…I met a guy in basic. You remember all the different options for worship, Eddie?"

"I do," Eddie said.

"This guy was pissed because there were no services for his god."

"Satan?" I asked, ignoring Zac's warning.

"Called him The Morning Star. I didn't know what the guy meant at first. Sounded like a nature thing. Then the guy said, 'You know him by other names like Satan or the Devil,' and I didn't like this at all. But the guy said that was because Christianity had corrupted my mind with their bullshit. Satan wasn't evil. He just refused to be a bitch, always being told what he could do. He rebelled against God, who was a real pain-in-the-ass anyway. 'Think about it,' the guy said. 'The church is against all the things that are fun in life like sex, drinking, drugs, and are hypocrites about money and killing. Christians have been stealing and killing in the name of their God forever."

"And you bought into it?" Eddie asked.

"I thought about my life and where I'd come from. We had just enough to survive and work another week or two to get just enough to do it all over again and again." His empty eyes now had some spark in them. "Oh, if we were good boys, there'd be an extra crumb or two for us. A small raise, a bonus, a promotion, but nobody was getting ahead. We stayed right where we were at, born there, lived there, and died there. Somebody else got all the sugar, and all the rights."

"It pissed you off," Eddie said.

"Sure did. We were the trash that built the nation, died in its wars and got table scraps for our efforts. Teachers told us what to do. Preachers told us what to do. Politicians told us what to do. Television told us what to do. Policemen, wardens, guards, COs, POs, you name it, brother. We were in the yoke."

"So you pledged yourself to him?" I asked. This was enlightening because I'd never met someone who followed the Devil, although I'd once stumbled toward Hell all on my own, never understanding the danger.

"Satan, The Morning Star, was the First Rebel," Tony said, but not with affection. "He was the first one to say, 'Fuck You!' to the system. I really liked that! Hey, plenty of good tunes about it, too. I *still* like those."

"But the Army is all about following orders," I said.

"The Army was a choice. I didn't have many options and wasn't going back home because I knew that I'd be doing it all over again and again. The Army seemed like a way out." Then he smiled at Eddie. "And you get rewarded for being a bad ass, right, Eddie?"

"Copy," Eddie said. "So you decide to follow Satan in your own way?"

"Yeah."

"Hobbs shows up and he is a believer as well."

"Yeah, Hobbs knew more than I did. He said that we needed to set the circles up this way, draw these symbols and kill us some animals."

"Sacrifices."

"Yeah."

I had prepared for this moment and tried to go on automatic pilot — Serenity Prayer — while Tony talked about the animals killed in the name his beliefs. I hated it and I hated him, but showing any emotion, especially at this critical moment, had to be avoided. It was the second toughest thing that would happen to me during this investigation.

I stayed detached through Tony's descriptions of "decorating" the altars, one orgy that didn't go off too well because it started raining and an encounter with a bear that wanted one of the disemboweled cats. Hobbs shot at it with his Beretta.

Then Tony talked about the ritual that changed the whole equation from a group of scumwads and crazy teens caught in the tar of the Satanic Panic to something that may well have culminated in a double, or possibly, triple murder.

The now-four amigos plus Naylor, May and few other teens all assembled deep in the woods on the new moon. Werewolf parties were a full-moon event while these rituals always happened on the new or dark moon. They all did acid, performed their devotion, and proceeded to the after-party. Penguin would end up lost in the woods until the following day. Dunaway, Naylor and May would all get a serious case of poison ivy, and a couple kids got sick, but Hobbs claimed to have seen Satan's Servant, a winged creature with a barbed tailed.

"Wyvern," I said.

"That's what he called it. Hobbs said that we needed to mark ourselves so the creature would know us."

"The tattoo," Eddie said.

"Yeah, you know about that, too."

"Did Hobbs design it?"

"No, he had some girl do it," Tony was grasping the stub tightly now with his right hand.

"Some girl?" Eddie said.

"Yeah, man," Tony said in a conciliatory tone. "Some girl that Pammie knew who used to follow her and Dennis around. I guess she was an artist."

"You remember her name?"

"No."

"Does Hanna Grey strike a chord?"

"No, what did she say about it?"

"Nothing, she's dead, hung herself a week after those boys went missing."

"I'd look into that if I were you."

Eddie took in a deep breath, exhaled slowly, put his hands flat on the table and splayed his fingers. "Do you know anything about that?" he asked in a tone that could be described as seething. "Anything?"

"You read my file, Eddie. I get the fuck out of Dodge the fall before any of that shit happened."

"Why?"

"Cops came around and asked some questions about a few B&Es. Roscoe backed me up, but I knew it wouldn't hold. They'd be back, but that was the cherry on the sundae. Besides, I was fixing to leave anyway."

"Had your fill of the Devil?" I asked.

"They don't call him The Father of Lies for nothing," Tony said in a matter-of-fact voice. Then he did something different, unexpected, and enlightening.

Tony Galbraith closed his eyes and said The Lord's Prayer. Twice.

"OK," Eddie said when Galbraith opened his eyes. "You ready?"

"I guess," Galbraith said softly. "We go down and get these," he points to his missing appendage, "in Royal Oak. We pick up some supplies and go back home to sell 'em."

Tony Galbraith paused, his leg chains rattling, his body shaking, but he finally calmed down enough to continue the story in an unsteady voice.

Hobbs told the crew he had arranged a special ritual on the next dark moon. Members of a satanic cult would be coming up to perform it. There were certain instructions about how the site should be prepared, and several cats would be killed during the ceremony. Naylor and May secured the doomed animals from a shelter with a story that it was a surprise for an elderly aunt.

"These true believers, I didn't like 'em," Galbraith said. "They dressed too preppy; you know?"

"Not sure that I do," Eddie said.

"Well, they weren't like us, that's for sure. I thought that they were Narcs, you know?"

"You remember any names?"

"Not really, but Ida never pegged them for this thing. Anyway, we do the ritual their way, and it's boring. I mean, the killing of the animals was a clusterfuck. There are too many words, in some other language. It was too much like regular church. Even the festivities afterwards were…not up to our standards. Dennis was pissed because one of the true believers was a hottie. I think that she was a schoolteacher, but she wouldn't put out for him — seemed repulsed by him."

"No shit," Eddie said a bit surprised. "So, a real ritual by a real satanic cult was kinda a letdown for you."

"Fuck yeah! Way too structured. But the next day Hobbs says to me, 'TJ,' he called me that, 'we're sitting on a goldmine,' and he hands me a fifty-dollar bill. I figured that we sold them all our drugs but am confused because they didn't take any last night beyond a couple puffs of pot. Fuck! They brought their own wine and it tasted like piss! So I say something about another run downstate for supplies, but he says 'nope, somethin' else.' The true believers want to do more rituals up here, and they will pay us to help set them up. Turns out Hobbs got 'em to spring for this one, that's what the fifty was for: my share."

Tony stopped and licked his lips. "God, I wish there was some water."

"Me, too," Eddie said. "The guards said there would be some."

"And you believed them."

"Tell me what happened."

Tony let out a long breath. "I guess this is a long time coming: Hobbs says the leader, his name was 'Thorn,' I think. Well, Hobbs says that Thorn is pleased, that Thorn believes that this is the spot. Now Thorn was the only one that was kinda cool. He was dressed in black, didn't say a lot other than during the whole thing, brought a bunch of items for the ritual, wore some horns, took it all with him afterwards. Anyway, Hobbs says that Thorn could get us some big money for another ritual but…and I'll never forget the look on Hobbs's face when he said, 'We gonna have to turn up the heat.'"

"Turn up the heat?" Eddie said then cracked his knuckles, which startled Tony.

"Yeah, Hobbs says that Thorn told him that, 'It's all in the blood, and the best blood is human blood, and the ultimate offering is a human one. Animals only bring servants. Here, we could get Satan himself.'"

"You're shitting me?" Eddie said. My mouth dropped open as my mind quickly connected the dots. It couldn't be true. But then Tony went on to outline Hobbs's plan that unfolded over the next few weeks.

Hobbs apparently talked to this Thorn a couple of times over the phone before going downstate to see him in person. Then he came back to Mio and filled the three other amigos plus Pam Naylor in on it. Turns out, not surprisingly given what we had learned, that Pam Naylor took to satanism more than any of the others, even Hobbs.

"Hobbs said that if we could get a person for this purpose, we could make fifty thousand dollars all told for the sacrifice on the altar, draining the blood for future rituals and cutting up the body for relics," Tony said.

"Relics?" I asked. "Like the saints in the Catholic Church."

"Exactly. It would be a mocking of the saints. I think that's what Hobbs said.

"Did that happen?" Eddie asked.

"I don't know. I beat cheek in October of 1983."

"But what do you think?"

"I never believed they'd do it. It was too risky, and those true believers looked like they couldn't have come up with the cash. Look, I was a thief, a drug dealer, a con man, whatever, but you kill somebody, unless it's self-defense, and you're looking over your shoulder forever. You are not free. I wanted to party, to ride, to do what I wanted. I understood that some folks got into all the high evil of Satan but for me he was a liberator. I just thought rebelling was enough. I was living like him, telling The Man to Fuck Off."

"How come you never told the police any of this?" I asked.

Tony rolled his tongue around. I think that he might have taken out part of his dentures and sucked on them for a moment.

"I was out west when all that happened, didn't really follow it."

"When was the last time that you saw Dennis?" Eddie asked.

Tony looked at him. Both Eddie and I knew what he said next could be huge.

"That Super Bowl the Bears won in the Eighties," he said.

"So you did come back to Mio?" Eddie said. "What did Dennis say about the killings?"

"He said there'd been some shit a couple of springs back. It had been bad for business. He was thinking of splitting, coming out west."

"Did you see Rufus?"

"No, Rufus had died that summer, heart attack."

"He died!" Eddie said. "Did Dennis say what happened?"

"No, just that it was sudden. We drank a toast to him, poor Rufus, good guy."

"How about Hobbs?"

"Dennis washed his hands of him. They had a falling out.

Dennis wouldn't elaborate. Dennis was not talkative, even when speeding."

"Naylor and May?"

"Out of the picture. I gotta sense at the time that the whole thing had run its course. Rufus was dead. Dennis was in bad shape. Police were on the prowl. The good times were over."

"That wasn't the last time that you saw Dennis though, was it?" Eddie said.

Tony shook his head. "You tell me."

Eddie gave him the details of the time and place of Dunaway's OD. "Your name was on the motel ledger."

"He wasn't Dennis by then. He was a junkie."

"And Naylor was with him."

"I don't know why. Dennis was washed up, a skeleton, gray skin, no spirit, could barely ride his bike. Pam was playing nurse maid. She'd fix him, score the dope. I don't know why. She wasn't looking so hot herself."

"He OD's. You call 911, then book," Eddie said. "That's kinda looking over your shoulder. How long did you and Naylor stay together?"

"Not long. We sold Denny's bike. Pam took the cash, went back to Vanderbilt or Wolverine. She had connections there. I rolled over Big Mac and went west, never should have come back."

The guard pounded on the window and held up ten fingers.

"You get popped in '99. Why not tell the cops what you knew?"

"Because I didn't fully know it then. I was tired, stressed, fucked up, struggling to eat and sleep somewhere safe, warm and dry. There wasn't time to think about it, and I didn't know all the details. Prison got me sober, cleared my head, and gave me a chance to read about a lot shit that I'd missed in those years on the run."

"Why not then?"

"Because who'd a believed me? You asked all the right questions, know all the right players, pretty much figured it all out.

If Ida squawked, then my sense is that the cops woulda pinned it on me. I'm not sure any of my alibis for that time are still alive."

"Why that?" Eddie said pointing at Tony's left arm that he was still squeezing.

"I had a dream," he said. "In it my mother appeared and said to remove the mark and begin to heal. I felt that I could be saved if I did it."

"It had to hurt like a bitch," I said.

"More…still does sometimes."

Then the guard entered to say our session was over.

CHAPTER 11

The Abyss

We arrived well after dark at Spinnerfall, now sporting a board over its front window with pieces of the coffee table piled on the porch. The plan had been to go there after the Galbraith interview, debrief Zac, gather all our notes, and begin to write up the investigation. Finding Naylor's half-brother, David Brandon, had been unexpected. It was just one more thing.

"You confirmed it was him?" Eddie asked Zac while chewing on another fast-food French fry.

"We confirmed it was David Brandon," Zac said. "We think that it is our David Brandon." Zac had used a case manager posing as an official of Consumers Energy to alert Brandon via a phone call of a scheduled power outage while the company worked on the lines. His neighbors on either side were called as well. It was a short outage, planned to occur in the middle of the day.

While Eddie and Zac went over the cover story — we were investigating Hanna Grey's suicide as a potential murder — I stepped outside and called the Krenshaws to make sure that Kody had my keys and instructions for the dogs.

"I'll be back Monday, Cam," I said.

"Sounds good," Cam said. "Kody's excited. I think his girl-friend might be spending some time there, too." Kody's beau was Robin Goodall. I'd met her once. She was a pretty, petite brunette who didn't say much.

I thanked him but didn't elaborate any further. I was still processing Galbraith's comments.

Our working theory of the case had changed dramatically with Tony Galbraith's recollections. Zac may have been wrong. It now seemed possible that Massengale and Parrish had been chosen as victims for sacrifice and sale, a real satanic murder-for-hire. Furthermore, we now believed that Pam Naylor was a principal player in the atrocity. She was likely both the bait and the subduer, luring the boys somewhere and then dosing them.

It hung on the tenuous factor of Tony Galbraith's credibility.

"There's a lot of spinning wheels here guys," Zac said, still doubtful about the satanic angle. "Their plan involved at least four people, probably more, and one was a seventeen-year-old. Dunaway, and Penguin if he was involved, were drunks and dopers, very unstable. This sounds more like an impulsive thrill kill to me."

"Fifty grand sounds like a lot?" I asked.

"Yes, unless you are the mafia," Zac said. "Another reason I'm skeptical. What do you think, Leap?"

"I think it was a con," Eddie said. "I think Hobbs and this Thorn guy already knew each other. I think Hobbs was in Northern Michigan looking for the perfect dupes. If what Galbraith says is real then the true plan was to get these guys to kill somebody, secure the…goods, maybe pay them a little up front and then take these, ah, remains, somewhere, get a good price and then disappear."

"Hmmm," Zac said. I imagined his eyes tilted at the high corners. "It just sounds too incredible."

"OK, but what if it's just a couple of like-minded psychopaths, Hobbs and Naylor," Eddie said. "Hobbs was mysterious. I'm pretty sure he was using an alias, maybe even a disguise of sorts. I don't believe he ever saw any creature. That was made up. He knew that the drug use and these guys' relative idiocy would help with the deception."

"Maybe Hobbs and Naylor cooked up a plan for a thrill kill using these stooges as accomplices?" Zac said. "Still amazing, but more credible. Keep in mind that psychopaths enjoy using people, too."

"What about Galbraith?" I asked. "Do we believe that he was not there?"

"That'll be up to the authorities," Zac said. "It sounds like he might have seen the writing on the wall, didn't like it, and ran. That was maybe the only smart thing that he ever did."

"Besides enlisting, C-2," Eddie said. "He wasn't a bad soldier."

"True, he should have stayed in the Army," Zac said.

There was a long discussion about what to do if David Brandon gave us a good lead on Pam Naylor's whereabouts. It was decided that if it was anywhere within reasonable driving distance, on this Zac and Eddie went back and forth, we'd go there and try to confirm it.

"The interview should start about Hanna Grey and try to get Naylor to open the door to Donny and Roland," Zac said. "I worry about her bolting, if she hasn't already."

"Don't worry," Eddie said. "I can handle it."

"For God's sake don't eat or drink anything!"

"Relax," Eddie said. "I got this, right, Art?"

"I sure hope so," I said, and he gave me a dirty look.

We went to bed early that night, exhausted with plans to be on the road by 7 a.m. I didn't sleep well but hoped by sundown tomorrow all that would be left was to write up the case, copy our interviews to flash drives, and hand it off to the State Police.

• • • • •

We drove through a clear and cold November morning. The leaves had all dropped by now, turning the trees into skeletal figures reaching to the sky in anguish. Rifle season for deer started in five days. There would be more murder in the woods. We barely said thirty words between us on the way down I-75 to Houghton Lake while drinking McDonald's coffee and wading through our sleepy minds.

David Brandon's Permalog home was a couple of blocks off M-55. The yard was kept, but the grass was now brown, and the flowers withered. Two Jack-o-Lanterns lay collapsed and blackened by his door. Brandon answered it promptly.

"Are you from Consumers?" he asked.

"No, sir," Eddie said, and produced his Phoenix Firm ID. I provided my driver's license as well. "We'd like to ask you some questions about your sister, Pam Naylor. It won't take long."

Brandon looked at the IDs. He was already dressed in his work clothes. David Brandon managed a discount furniture store near Prudenville.

"You're not reporters?" he asked.

"No, sir," Eddie said, being formal and respectful. "And we understand why you would say that. We're aware of the article in the *Record-Eagle*. Clearly, the individual that I interviewed must have spoken to the press. They misrepresented it." Eddie was lying to keep the initial focus on Hanna Grey. Plowing right into Massengale and Parrish might spook Brandon and keep him from talking to us.

"It happens, Mr. Brandon," I said. "Our client," and here I was clearly stretching the truth as well, "hired us to investigate the case of her sister's suicide. Now, that happened around the time of Massengale and Parrish, but we have not found any credible connections."

"I remember that," he said. "She hung herself near 4001."

"Yes, sir, but we've found new evidence."

"May we talk to you?" Eddie said.

Brandon looked us over. He was a big man who'd gone to seed with a sizable gut, soft face and retreating hairline. I didn't see malice in his expression, but there was apprehension. I wasn't certain that he would agree.

"I expected something," he said. "Come in."

The home was comfortable with a large picture of two deer in the early autumn forest hanging over the couch. Eddie asked him if he hunted. Brandon said that he did and had been preparing his blinds, cleaning his guns and getting his garage ready for processing.

"I make most of it into venison sausage. My two boys love it."

"Great stuff," Eddie said, "partial to the chili myself." This was news to me.

"I make a batch of that. Gone by Thanksgiving Weekend." He smiled. I relaxed.

Brandon quickly went through his current life situation, divorced, sees the boys almost every weekend. Then he talked briefly about growing up. He was Pam's half-brother. They were never close. He was at Grand Valley State College during the time in question.

"I lived mostly with my father. My mother was not real attentive. She was always out and about. We were unsupervised. Pam liked it, but I don't think that it was good for her. My dad was strict, but he was there."

There were only two points of interest about Pam that David brought up. She was obsessed with being popular, even in kindergarten, and liked to hurt animals for fun. One of the reasons David lived with his father was to have a dog and not worry about something happening to it.

I expressed my interest in dogs. David said that he was planning on getting another one in the spring, maybe a golden. His last dog, a springer, had to be put down last summer.

"I had a mutt back then when I was at Grand Valley. His name was Simon. I came to Mio to see Mom and Pam, and Simon got violently ill. I took him to a vet there and he said that Simon must have eaten some chocolate. I didn't feed it to him."

"He made it?" I asked.

"Yes. I confronted Pam. She started crying but I could tell it was an act. Simon feared her. I went back on holidays but left Simon with a friend. Pam wasn't around much. She was clearly out of control, but so was Mom, both acted like a couple of teen-agers, really screwed up teenagers. I kept my distance."

Further questioning about that time was futile. We hardly talked about Hanna Grey. Eddie asked about the last time David saw Pam.

"Summer before last. She came by asking for a loan. I gave her two thousand dollars, knowing that I'd never see it again."

"What was her situation?" Eddie asked.

"She'd moved to Wolverine and was supposedly working in a bar making good money, just needed the loan for security deposits and furniture. She'd run through her inheritance. She'd gained a fair amount of weight, likely drinking. Pam was beautiful when she was young. She was also a talented actress in high school. Well, that's what she told me."

"Address?" Eddie asked.

"She would send me the payback."

"Letters, Christmas cards?"

"Not her thing," he said and laughed a bit but not in a jolly way.

Eddie started tapping his forehead. While he did this, I asked Brandon if he fished Houghton or Higgins lakes, giving Eddie time to cogitate.

"Oh, yes, for walleye and smelt."

"Good groceries," I said, and was about to tell him about my outdoor writing when Eddie interrupted.

"The estate settlement when your mother died?" he asked.

"Yes, we both got over a hundred thousand dollars. It helped pay for this house."

"Do you have it?" Eddie asked. His stare was intense.

Brandon went in another room and retrieved it. Eddie looked it over.

"Art," he said. "Paper, pen!" I gave him my legal pad and pen, then made a face at Brandon.

"I'm just the secretary," I said.

"Makes great coffee," Eddie said, "but has lousy legs." Brandon was amused by this but then turned serious.

"This is really about those boys, right?" he asked.

"She might know something," I said.

"And the suicide?" He asked rubbing his chin.

"Hanna Grey was in her social circle. Pam also knew a guy who kinda dated Hanna, bad guy. He might have killed Hanna. But he also might have killed Massengale and Parrish."

"We think that she knows who did these things," Eddie said. He was too busy writing something down to look up.

Brandon hung his head and scratched it with his left hand while making a fist with his right. Then he started shaking his head.

"Oh, fuck," he said. "I never really thought about it." He looked at me. "The police said it was Bigfoot."

"That's what they thought, and they concluded that too soon and stopped looking."

"Jesus, she wouldn't…" he said.

"We think that she knows who did these things," Eddie said while handing the document back to Brandon. "Thank you for your time." He got up and shook Brandon's hand. "We will let you know if we find her."

"And whether she was involved?" he asked with concern.

"Absolutely."

• • • • •

"Hack the motherfucker!" Eddie screamed into his phone. "I know, I know, we'll check the PO Box account. That's right, Jean Naylor! Scan for that name. She changed it. I don't know. You're

the guy with those skills. Get Song some more Skittles, on me!"
He hung up. "You ready?" he asked.

We had stopped at a rest area on 75 just south of Gaylord. Zac
wasn't in when we called him right after leaving Brandon's house.
This added to Eddie's frenzy. He was tired after yesterday, and
a bit disappointed by not breaking Galbraith completely. Eddie
wanted a confession and wasn't satisfied with the good stuff that
we'd obtained.

"That only happens on Perry Mason," I told him while he
ranted.

"Fuck Perry Mason."

The estate of Anne Marie (nee Curtis) (Brandon) (Naylor)
(Watkins) Glenn — alimony was her life's occupation — had
left Pamela Jean Naylor $107,536, deposited in a bank in Indian
River under the name, Jean Naylor. There was also a PO Box in
Wolverine under the name of Jean Naylor.

We arrived in Wolverine before 11 a.m. and stopped at a gas
station to take a piss and get more coffee. Eddie needed another
can of Skoal as well. We sat on the hood of his Jeep Cherokee
and tried to relax for a moment. I told a story about the Sturgeon
River, which ran through Wolverine. It had been one of Ernest
Hemingway's favorite fishing spots in his Michigan days. The
Myth of Papa claimed that he was late to his wedding with Hadley
Richardson in Charlevoix because the fishing was just too good
to leave. Hadley cooled her wedding day angst by taking a swim
in Lake Charlevoix.

"It sounds just like him," Eddie said. He loved Hemingway.

Then the phone rang, Zac again. Eddie put him on speaker.

"Somehow she changed her name," Zac said. "But we cannot
find any legal documents yet. She had a driver's license in that
name as of last year." He gave the address.

"She may have lied her way through it," Eddie said. "It fits
the profile. Anything else?"

There was a recent W-2 for a restaurant in Wolverine.
That was the first place we went to, but it was out of business,

another casualty of the Northern Michigan economy. Downtown Wolverine, only about three hundred yards in length on 27, the Straits Highway, reflected this fact. It was quaint with many of the buildings resembling relics of the 19th century lumber era, whether genuine or faux, but several storefronts were vacant.

We went into a couple of businesses and asked about Jean Naylor, but nobody seemed to know her.

Then it was off to the Wolverine Post Office to inquire about the PO Box, which was tough sledding at first. The post office matron, a slight, nervous woman of middle age, was, at first, reluctant. But then Eddie turned on a combination of charm and gravitas.

"Ma'am, we completely understand the rules," he said in a very sympathetic voice while leaning toward her. "But this is the case of a girl that, ah, Jean knew in high school." Eddie went on to give a very detailed and compassionate account of Hanna Grey's life and death. I could see that it was working as the woman, who was a good soul just doing her job, started injecting "Oh, dears," "Oh, mys" and "Poor things," into Eddie's tale.

At the end of it, Eddie paused for effect, then talked about heroic Evangeline Cooper, the younger sister that Hanna had mothered and protected. Thank goodness nobody came in to buy stamps or send a package of whatever to Aunt Ester in Ionia because the mood would have been broken in an instant.

"Evangeline has always wondered about what really happened," he said so gently that I even teared a bit. "That's what we are trying to determine." Then Eddie leaned back, stood ramrod straight and put his hands on the counter. "All we want is the truth."

The woman stared at Eddie blinking. She was both moved and concerned. There were rules after all. My sense while looking at the woman in her neat and finely pressed uniform (which was missing a name tag, although that might be simply because in small towns like this everybody knew everybody), was that she had always, always followed the rules.

But, maybe, not this time. It turns out that our post office matron, who finally introduced herself as Karen McClain, knew Jean Naylor.

"You know," Karen said leaning over in a whisper, "She's not well-liked around here."

"Really, Mrs. McClain," Eddie said, "Oh, or should I have said Ms. McClain? It's about half and half up here. I live in Luzerne." He threw her a rakish grin: Eddie Fletcher, woman killer, all shapes, sizes, ages, and occupations.

"Oh, Karen's fine," she said with a nice smile. I liked her. My sense is that everybody did.

"Eddie."

"Art."

We were getting somewhere.

"She's got light fingers," Karen said in a whisper again. "Lost two jobs for stealing…drugs, not a good person at all."

"You should make a copy of this and this," Eddie said setting his PI Associate ID and Driver's License on the counter. "As well as this and this." He produced his military ID and Ohio Bar Association ID. "Now I am retired from the military and my PI ID is as an associate investigator. You need to know that. Art, give her your driver's license." I did.

"My goodness," Karen said. "You are a lieutenant colonel?"

"Yes, Karen," he said. Somewhere along the line Eddie had dropped the bit about retiring as a Full Bird. I would never bring it up.

"Did you serve in Iraq?" she asked and gave him another look over.

"I did, eighteen months, Fallujah." The look on Eddie's face was telling, it was a mix of both pride and regret.

"Hold it," she said sounding preoccupied. "Hold it."

Oh, no, I thought.

"You're the one who blew the whistle on the awful company," she said with disgust, but not aimed at Eddie.

"I don't know if I'd characterize it that way, Karen. I just told the truth."

Indeed, he had. The Smutek scandal had broken wide open. Likely it was a pot that was simmering so hot that nothing could have kept the lid on it forever. Smutek's remediation tactics were the cause of the illnesses, not just at The Donkey and The Mule, but at 16 other sites in the United States alone. The number varied when other countries were included. The Bush administration was distancing themselves from Smutek. The Justice Department was looking into charges. The company's stock was down 47%.

"Let me make copies of these," Karen said. "You know, there's talk of problems with Smutek over by Onaway."

"I've heard that," Eddie said. The truth was that other than that first day back in August we had never talked of Smutek again.

Karen gave the address and directions to both places. In turn, we promised not to divulge how we got them.

"How can you do that?" Karen asked as we were leaving.

"Given time we would have found these anyway," Eddie said. "But it is a somewhat exigent circumstance. Thanks again, Karen, be well."

"Be careful," she said. "Jean Naylor hangs with a rough crowd."

• • • • •

The first address was a five-minute drive from the post office. It was a new two-story house that had used what nature provided, several monarch white pines plus a couple of mature spruce, to create pleasant surroundings. Its backyard was the west branch of the Sturgeon River, a smaller stream, not much more than 30 feet wide, that flowed smartly over rocks and fallen trees. It could have been the setting for a fairy tale.

"I could live here," Eddie said when we pulled up. "Any good fishing in that stream?"

"Brook trout for sure," I said. "That's what I saw in an article in *Michigan Hunting and Fishing*. There was something about big browns and rainbows coming up into it during the summer for relief from warm temperatures. It's supposed to be ice-cold water."

"This is a big house for somebody struggling to make ends meet," Eddie said.

"Maybe she used that inheritance," I said.

An elderly woman in a peach-colored bathrobe answered the door. We introduced ourselves and showed our credentials.

"We are looking for Jean Naylor?" Eddie asked.

"Who?" the woman said; she seemed confused.

"She might go by Pam Naylor," Eddie said. I could see his jaw flex.

"She's not here, but, but," the woman said and muttered to herself.

There was a tense silence.

"Doreen," the woman yelled. "Who's Jean Naylor?"

There were footsteps from somewhere in the house.

"I have to ask my daughter," the woman said, then smiled. This broke the tension.

A younger woman with black hair wearing jeans and a flannel shirt appeared behind her mother.

"What's this all about?" she asked. Her expression was guarded.

We explained.

She stared at us with narrowed eyes and a tight mouth. Eddie offered his PI and lawyer cards. She looked at both for a very long time.

"What is an associate private investigator?" she asked. But her voice was level.

Eddie gave a too lengthy reply about how private investigators were required to pass certain examinations regarding legalities and such. In his case he had not done so because of his law background.

"A PI and a lawyer looking for Jean Naylor," the woman said with a touch of contempt, "that figures." Then she looked at me. "What's your deal? His sidekick?" She asked and pointed at Eddie but smiled just a bit when she said it.

"I'm a journalist by trade," I said and showed her my driver's license. "My job is to take notes, document interviews and ultimately write up a report to our client." I was getting comfortable with the cloak aspect of our job, hoping never to see the dagger.

"Well, you could write a book about Jean Naylor," she said then introduced herself and her mother, Helen. "I've seen her about a dozen times in town, never actually met her, but lordy have I heard some stories."

We went inside and chatted for about 20 minutes, declining coffee while moving the conversation along as fast as possible.

It turns out that Pam Naylor had rented the house back in 2000 and lived there through 2003. It's possible that she was renting to buy, but Doreen wasn't sure. Whether Pam or Jean, Naylor's story had many twists and turns, and it was not certain what was real or grift. The cheerleader from Mio had created a pliable persona tailored to meet whatever con was necessary, but that just made her suspect in the eyes of the sober-minded.

"There were a lot of sketchy things about Jean Naylor," Doreen said. "She had a buncha people living here with her, wild parties, all sorts of vehicles, trucks, ORVs, snow sleds and motorcycles. She had a black F 150 and a Thunderbird plus a fancy sled, a Ski-Doo, I think. She threw her money all over the place."

"Then what happened?" Eddie asked.

"The money dried up," Doreen said. "She skipped on the rent and either sold her toys or quit meeting the payments. Then all the goodtime buddies split. All of a sudden she was looking for another place and a job and had all sorts of stories why. Claimed a buncha oil wells went dry or stocks crashed or something. She was always yakking that way. But what I heard was secondhand. I didn't like her, parading around like a rich bitch in town then holding out her hat."

Eddie asked about the people she hung out with, but Doreen said most of them were not local.

"If you hang around till Happy Hour there's some folks who could tell you more," she said. "But I've heard that people around here steered clear of her almost from the get-go. Too many of Pam's friends were scumwads or creepy characters. There was talk that she'd conduct seances and stuff like that. That's not something folks around here are going to cotton to at all. She left this place a disaster area, both a boon and a curse for us. Gotta good price but there's a lot to fix up."

"It's haunted," Helen said, until then she'd sat on the couch seemingly oblivious.

"Mom," Doreen said, "those are mice."

"Ghosts."

"You said that about our last house and the one before that," Doreen looked embarrassed.

"Ma'am, my place is just the same," Eddie said. "I want to believe it's just mice and the wood settling with all our temperature changes but some of it is hard to explain."

"He knows," Helen said pointing at Eddie and nodding her head.

"Is Jean still in the area?" I asked, trying to finish this so we could check the other address.

"Probably," Doreen said. "But I haven't heard much gossip about her in several months. I think she got a cabin out east." She pointed toward her backyard. "You can live cheap out there. I don't know how she makes her money now, don't want to, if you catch my drift."

Eddie showed her the other address.

"Yeah," Doreen said. "That would fit. That's the boonies and, Hell, we're the boonies, right?" she laughed. "You're sure that you don't want any coffee?"

We thanked Doreen and Helen for their time and left.

"I'd take anything that she tells you with a shaker of salt," Doreen said as we left. "That's my two-cents."

• • • • •

We crossed the bridge over the Sturgeon River and headed into the woods. Soon the pavement gave way to a dirt road. At first, there were several houses, a well drilling company and even a small city park, vacant now in gloomy November. After that… just trees, endless tall trees.

Two pick-up trucks passed us going back toward town.

"Deer hunters," Eddie said.

"Must be bowmen," I said, "or fixing up their blinds."

"I might try the bow thing next fall," Eddie said. "Lotta skill in that."

About two miles into the forest, we came to the last known address of Jean Naylor, a two-story house in need of a paint job. A rusting blue Dodge truck was in the driveway and a small boat on a trailer sat on the dirt lawn.

A dog started barking after we knocked. There were words and commotion inside, then the door opened. The head of a big black dog, likely some type of shepherd, popped out with teeth bared and snarling. It was mad, but I thought things would be alright because no person would allow this beast to attack us.

Then the dog came completely out of the door and lunged at Eddie. It just missed grabbing his arm. Eddie moved quickly, stepping back, and pushing me with his free arm into the yard. The force was so strong that I ended up on the ground.

"Hey! Hey!" Eddie screamed. "We mean no harm!"

The dog was on the doorstep trying to gather itself to pounce. As I rolled to my haunches, I saw Eddie in a defensive crouch ready to throw a punch.

We finally fucked up, I thought, and tried to remember Paula's advice on dealing with dog attacks. She'd been bitten more than once and had received some stiches on a couple of occasions.

Then a voice from behind the door yelled "Storm! Stay!" and yanked on a rope that was attached to his collar. After nearly a minute, Storm was dragged back inside and somehow secured. I could still hear some barking while Eddie and I repositioned ourselves on the withered lawn, more pine straw and sand than brown grass.

Then a small, wiry woman wearing a thick red Mackinaw and an orange wool cap came outside. Her face was a vast series of wrinkles surrounding two sharp blue eyes. I guessed her to be north of 60 years, but she was certainly fit, having wrestled that wolf back into the house.

"Who the Hell are you?" She asked in a tone that was not friendly. I noticed that she had a holster on her hip with pistol inside it. Eddie noticed it as well.

"We want no trouble, Ma'am," he said and raised his hands. I raised mine as well.

"Then explain your business," she said and put her hand on that holster.

Shit! I thought, now it's even worse.

Eddie calmly outlined our presence, thanking her for securing Storm, and promising that we were not a threat in any way.

"I can show you ID," he said.

"Those can be faked," she said.

"How can I gain your trust?" Eddie said with a feel that suggested this was nothing new to him. "Clearly you are concerned. What more do you need to know about us?"

"You smell of police."

"We're not. Private investigators, like I said."

"Investigating what?" She asked. Clearly, she had not been listening.

"Jean Naylor. She might be going by Pam as well."

The woman smiled, but it was not a disarming smile like those of Karen, Helen or Doreen. This grin had a touch of maleficence to it. The way a rattler or alligator might look just before striking.

"She goes by a lot of names, Mister. Can't keep 'em all straight."

"So you know her."

"Ah, yeah."

"We need to talk to her about the suicide of a young woman that Jean knew."

"What's in it for me?"

"How so?"

"I'm not giving that up for free, Mister Private Investigator."

"How much?"

"Two-hundred dollars."

Eddie looked at me. I got out my wallet and had just over the amount. I handed him ten twenties and made a mental note to hit an ATM in Grayling on the way home.

"What am I getting for my money?" Eddie asked. I noticed that as the conversation had moved along Eddie had moved closer to the woman. He was now only about five feet from her with his body on an angle that favored his right side. My sense was that Eddie had positioned himself to disarm the woman if things truly went sideways. He was flexing those hands while staring the woman down. She was starting to blink a lot. Eddie's expression was deadpan serious.

"I'll tell you where she's at and then some."

"A hundred now," Eddie said, "and a hundred after." He held five twenties in each hand.

"How do I know that I can trust you?"

"Works both ways. If she's nearby, then it will take only an hour or so. We come right back, leave the money at your door and leave."

"She's not far away."

"Have we got a deal?"

The woman nodded. Eddie handed her five twenties from his left hand, but not before handing me the other five with his right.

It turns out that Jean Naylor had never lived at this address, but instead had asked to use it when applying for the post office box number. The woman had agreed for certain considerations that she did not get into.

Naylor lived at a spot much further into the woods, a place

that she may have purchased or already owned before leaving the house by the west branch of the Sturgeon River.

"I'd seen her out here way back when. She and her buddies spent a lot of time in the deep woods."

"Do you think that anybody is out there with her?" Eddie asked.

"Could be. Men run through Jean's hands like water. She has her ways." There was a twinkle in her eyes that kinda disgusted me. "But if you go now, they're probably sleeping one off."

"Will Jean be awake?"

"Likely. She never sleeps much," then she made a sniff, sniff sound. I now understood how Pam Naylor went through a hundred grand; it went up her nose. "She's probably watching some movie on the DVD, chain smoking her Camels and having an eye-opener, of sorts."

"The directions?" Eddie asked.

Those were easy. We were to drive another five or so miles, cross two bridges and the place would be just after the second one on the left.

"This is the only way out, mind you," the woman said. "I'll be sitting on my porch with my 30-30, so don't try passin' without payin'." Then she turned and walked back to her house. Storm started barking somewhere inside — in a room that I never wanted to see.

• • • • •

Five minutes after leaving the house, Eddie pulled his Cherokee over. He got out and went to the back of the vehicle, opened the hatch, and fiddled around with something. He came back holding a small pistol.

"I know you don't like it, but we may need it," he said.

I considered his words. Now was the moment to speak up and say, "Hold it, this has gone too far." But I didn't. I couldn't. We had traveled a long way down this trail and couldn't stop because of an overly aggressive dog and hardscrabble biddy with a chip on her shoulder and an eye for an easy payday. This story had me in its clutches. I wanted to know the truth, the truth, the whole truth. I wanted to look Pam Naylor in the eyes, to hear her tale. Still, the smart play would have been to call Zac, I looked at my cellphone, no signal, not a surprise.

Eddie got back out of the Jeep and walked into the middle of the road. I watched him scan the trees, locate the sun, and then move around the road for a minute or so. Then he came back to the Cherokee, opened the center console, and took out a pair of amber shooting glasses and repeated the same exercise before returning to the vehicle.

"The sun is behind and over my left shoulder," he said. "These are a better choice than my shades." He put his sunglasses in a case then closed the compartment.

"What's that all about?" I asked.

"Preparation," Eddie said and put the Jeep in gear.

There was no sign of human presence other than the road we were on. The bare trees made it feel even more foreboding. This was a place beyond the mores of civilization. Out here, anything could happen, and the outside world might never know.

After we crossed the first bridge Eddie pulled over and handed me his second set of keys.

"If there is another bad dog or problem of any sort, I want you to run to the truck, start it and wait for me," he said. "I'll handle it and we head right to the nearest law authorities. Got it?"

"I do."

"We don't go inside."

"What about that woman?"

"We'll see what happens."

After the second bridge we went up a hill and there on the left was a wood-planked cabin, weathered and grey with a large pile of cut firewood stacked along its sides and a black Ford Bronco near the front door. The truck was at least a decade old. The house seemed from another time and place altogether.

"This is it," Eddie said. He drove past the driveway, turned around and parked the truck in the middle of the road. Then he tucked that pistol into the small of his back. "Let's do this, brother." He slapped my arm, then held it. "You don't have to go up if you don't want to. You can wait with the engine running?"

"Not a chance," I said. My heart was pounding while imagining a pack of wolflike dogs tearing us to pieces. My mind was too noisy for a Serenity Prayer or any sensible thought.

But nothing was going to keep me from going.

We got out and walked toward the driveway. As we turned to walk up it there was a man waiting for us with a shotgun. He was tall with long gray hair in a ponytail, and a brushy beard to match. The man was dressed in overalls and a green and black checked shirt, but no coat. I couldn't get a good bead on his face because that gun barrel looked ten feet long and wider than a coffee cup.

"Just who the fuck do you think you are?" he said.

Fear for me had always been the sense of my guts dropping out of my body while bolts of electricity shimmered from my head to my extremities, turning my legs to Jell-O, and filling my mouth with the taste of pennies.

This is how it ends, next stop Rainbow Bridge.

"Relax now, sir," Eddie said, but there was tension in his words. "We are not law enforcement or trespassers."

"Looked like you were planning on trespassing, motherfucker!"

"I can show you my credentials," Eddie said.

"Fuck your credentials!"

"Our client believes that you can help us."

"What? Who?"

"Do you know Jean Naylor? She may go by the name of Pam."

The man did not immediately answer.

"There is some reward money," Eddie said. "We really need to talk to her. It's about…it's about somebody that she knew in high school who was possibly involved in some bad things."

"What things?" The gun barrel lowered just a touch.

"Drug dealing. It may have led to our client's sister getting addicted and OD'ing. She wants to know what happened and thinks that Pam might know where the person is now."

"What person?" the man asked, but his tone was less hostile and more curious.

"Her name is Cilla May, and we believe that she sold drugs to kids at three different high schools back in the 1980s." This statement was enough to shake me just a little out of my state of panic, if only because I felt the need to correct his words, but my lips would not move.

The man didn't know what to think of it either.

"*She* ran a drug ring in the 1980s?" he asked as if to challenge Eddie's account.

The gun barrel was now pointed more at our feet than at our heads.

"That's the information. Hey, we've got conflicting accounts on that, and, fuck, law enforcement's no help, buncha fucking yobboes. They weren't very good at that stuff back then, only slightly better now. She sure could help us straighten out this mess."

The man and Eddie exchanged stares for a long time, neither one blinked, but the gun barrel stayed where it was.

"My client will pay for the information," Eddie's eyes were straining as if he were trying to see something very tiny. I'd seen this expression before when he was watching the river for hatching insects. "Do you know where Jean Naylor is? It would be a big help."

The man considered this, but I was watching Eddie. He was giving the man a thorough looking over.

"If you can give us a lead and it pans out then there could be a couple hundred in it for you, maybe several."

The man lowered the gun barrel to somewhere between us and him. I was able to take a decent breath. "She split long ago," he said.

"Oh, really," Eddie said, and then he looked past the man for a moment. "Do you know where she went?"

The man did not immediately respond. Instead, he glanced over his shoulder to where Eddie had been looking, then backed up three steps, but raised the gun barrel up toward us again.

I thought I might faint.

"No tricky business," he said.

"Actually, I thought that you might have somebody up there in the trees," Eddie said. "Can't blame me for that?"

"I'm well protected, and I don't know where Jean is, and I don't want any reward money. Fuck off!" He backed up two more steps but kept the shotgun on us.

"Very well," Eddie said walking backwards while still facing the man. "Art, go start the truck."

As I turned to walk away, I saw the man lower his barrel to the ground and begin to turn back toward his house. The corner of my eye caught some motion. It was Eddie drawing his pistol.

"Jack Hobbs drop your weapon," Eddie said. "This is a citizen's arrest."

Before I could swing entirely around Eddie screamed, "Art, take cover!" I turned immediately, took two steps and dove for the tree line. I heard three pops, a blast, felt some type of impact, and then everything went dark.

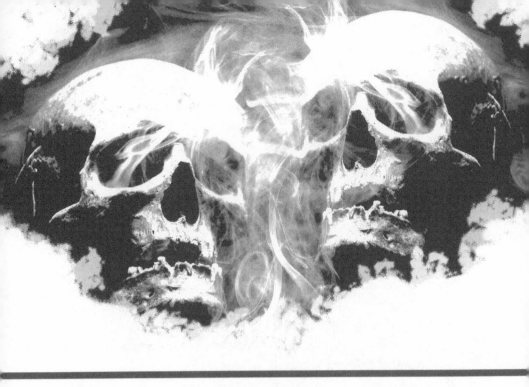

CHAPTER 12

The Woman in the Aqua Dress

There was a balmy blue sky. Several puffball clouds floated slowly across it. The high sun kissed my cheeks with warmth. A gentle breeze tickled my ears. I could smell the sweet aroma of orange blossom. Somewhere chickadees chirped friendly "Fee Bee Bee Bees."

I was in a boat, a sailboat, like the old Sunfish models that I sailed as a kid at a summer camp called Soaring Hawk. The sail was white with a distinct pink stripe. The logo was not a sunfish however, it was that line-sided quarry that was the totem of my Florida youth, El Robalo, Mr. Jutjaw, the common snook.

"When did they do that?" I wondered but liked the change in design. It's about time that backcountry brawler, the mayor of brackish water and mangrove cities, got his due. Tarpon were surely next in line. It would be a sports car for the Silver King.

I turned my attention to the water. It was a lake, navy blue in color, but otherwise very clear. I could see schools of bass, bluegill, mullet and one very large redfish cruising slowly above the edges of the turtle grass. This suggested that I was somewhere in the backwaters of the Everglades, a place where sweet and saltwater fish swam side by side in relative peace.

But the shoreline suggested otherwise. It was lined with giant monarch white pines. The type that had covered much of Northern Michigan before the axmen came and cleared them out. Woodpeckers and nuthatches climbed up and down the bark of the ancient trees. The banks were sloped at about ten feet. There was a small meadow in one spot where wildflowers grew, mostly black-eyed Susans with a few daisies of varying sizes. A red fox watched me from in between two tree trunks, just on the edge of the shadow line.

Two ospreys, likely a mating pair, flew above me. They talked back and forth in short screeches, gliding on the midday thermals, looking for a meal in the water to feed their brood. One hovered with head down and tail feathers splayed while the other circled around it. It was a beautiful cotillion in the air.

"Do you like it?" a familiar voice said to me.

I turned to see Paula in the bow of the boat. She had a captain's hat on her head and those blue eyes sparkled in the sunlight.

"I do, Bird, very much," I said.

"I thought you would." Her smile melted my heart.

"Did you arrange it?"

"It just sorta happened. That's the way it is here."

"Where's here?"

"You know."

"Do you like it here, Bird?"

"I do, but I've missed you."

"I've missed you so much." I could feel tears on my cheeks.

"I know, Honey," she said softly, "I know all about it."

"I was a fool," I felt the shame of that summer bender wash over me. "Can you ever forgive me?"

"I already did," she said sweetly. "Wally Cat did, too. It's OK. You were so alone, and I was so far away. There was no way to reach you." I could see the regret in her face, but knew it was not for what I had done, but for what had happened to her. In the crazy way these things go I immediately understood that Paula felt tremendous guilt. All this time, she had been grieving her own death and the way it happened — everything gone in an instant because of a defect in her heart.

This was an epiphany, my recognition of her pain, her loss. I hadn't been the only one to lose something that May morning. Paula had lost so much more than I had.

"I forgot about what it meant for you, Bird. I was wrapped up in *my* pain. It was selfish, but I see that now. You had so many plans. *We* had so many plans."

Her despair vanished at once. Paula's expression became almost beatific.

It was then I noticed that she was wearing the aqua dress, with Trinity glimmering around that delicate neck.

She sensed this.

"I like it. I would have worn it…" and here her words went into gibberish about some party at Christmas or maybe the Fourth of July. It didn't matter. She looked beautiful in it. I finally saw the truth.

"It looks magnificent on you, Bird."

"Thank you, sweetheart. That means so much to me."

"Is Wally here?" I asked.

"Oh, yes. So are Maggie and Mango and so many others, Artie. They're all here. They're all safe. They're all waiting."

"For that someone?"

"Yes, Dear. It's true for them, us and everybody."

"Where?"

"Oh," she said, and giggled as she did as a teen. Then a gust of wind turned the sailboat to port. I almost lost my balance. "Art, you're the helmsman, steer the boat!" I grabbed the tiller and righted the ship.

"There, Honey," she said, and pointed to a beach on the far shore. In a blink of an eye, we were just a hundred yards or so off the shoreline. Here there were no white pines but stands of oak, elm and maple, as well as a couple of Queen Palms (Paula's favorite), providing shade at the edge of a long expanse of sand as white as sugar. There were several floating docks and two towers with diving boards.

Dogs by the hundreds were frolicking along the beach, swimming in the water, and diving off the diving boards. There were barks and yelps of joy all over. Then I noticed the cats, sitting in the shade of the trees, some playing with balls of yarn and catnip mice, others batting paws at things hung by strings in the branches. The dogs were doing the same with their toys, squeaks from Busy Bees and other toys were mixed in with the barks.

"Don't forget the birds, Art," Paula said.

The birds, parrots and such, were flying over the action on the beach in a cloud of yellows, blues, blacks, oranges and greens. Some were enjoying a roost of sorts in the tree limbs, with the cats somehow ignoring them. I couldn't hear the chirps and caws because of the music. All of a sudden there was music!

"Is that Beach Boys?" I asked.

"Well," she said, sounding a touch coy, "it *is* a beach party."

"Who chooses the music?"

"Who do ya think?" she shot me a goofy mug.

Just then *Brandy* came on. It had been our song in the summer of 1972 as adolescence took hold and puppy love, at least for me, flourished. Paula, who had a beautiful voice but didn't always remember the words, started singing along. Most of it was incoherent or incorrect — this was getting sillier now that I noticed animals wearing hats and clothes — but one verse remained so very true:

Brandy, you're a fine girl! What a good wife you would be!

In that moment, I knew everything that really mattered. Paula was at peace now. She really did find Rainbow Bridge. I was forgiven for my sins following her death, for all of them, in fact, whenever those transgressions had passed. It was OK. Everything was going to be OK. This was the clean and well-lit place waiting at the end of it all, but I wanted to stay there now.

"Bird, can it always be like this?" I asked.

She looked at me and started to speak…

…and then I woke up.

"Mr. Jenkins?" a woman in a nurse's uniform said, then she took hold of my wrist.

I mumbled something, but as I tried to make words there was a sharp pain in my head.

"Ahhhh, what?" I said, my mouth was bone dry. "Head, head, hurts, hurts bad."

The nurse went around to the other side of my bed. I tried to turn but the pain increased. I saw stars in front of my eyes, closed them, and saw more stars in a red background. Then all at once a warm rush filled my body from head to toe. The pain dulled. I felt drowsy, and kept my eyes shut while the stars and red glare faded.

"Better," I said. "Better."

"Good. I'll get the doctor. It's nice to have you back with us, Mr. Jenkins."

• • • • •

"Mr. Jenkins, do you know where you are?" a male voice asked.

I opened my eyes. "Hospital," I said.

"Do you know what day it is?"

"Thursday?"

My vision was blurry, but I was pretty sure that the doctor frowned.

"And the month?"

"Novemberrr."

"The year?"

"2004."

The doctor frowned again. Then he turned on a light and

shined it in my eyes. It was like he was jabbing me with a stick, and I closed them.

"Does the light bother you?"

"Yesss."

The doctor mumbled something to the nurse. There was a shuffling of feet.

"OK, could you open your eyes just briefly please, as long as you can," he said.

I did and the doctor was quick about it, turning the light on and off while he studied me.

"How's your headache?"

"Not as bad," I said.

"Your vision?"

"Can't see clearly."

"Nausea?"

There was a bit of sourness in the pit of my stomach. "Some," I said and swallowed.

"Are you hungry?"

"Thirsty."

The nurse gave me a cup of water and a straw.

"When were you born?" the doctor asked.

"May 4, 1958. What happened?"

"You have a concussion," the doctor said, "Your head struck a tree with force, likely from a fall or jump," and then he went on to explain it in technical terms. I heard the words "Glasgow Scale," and thought of Kate LeClair as well as the term "moderate to severe."

"What is the last thing you remember?" the doctor asked.

I was confused and wanted to tell them about Paula and Rainbow Bridge but knew better — they would think that I was crazy. After thinking as hard as I could and sorting out what was real and imaginary, I finally answered his question.

"We were in the woods, after Jean Naylor," I said. "Could I have more water?"

The doctor nodded, then the nurse gave me another glass of cool water. It tasted like ambrosia.

"And the incident? Do you remember the incident?"

"Incident?" I closed my eyes to think hard. "We stopped at a house. Eddie asked me if I wanted to stay in the truck. There was a man with a gun...," I said, but everything else was fuzzy.

"Is Eddie OK?" I asked; something started to beep.

"Mr. Fletcher is fine," the doctor said. Then he said something to the nurse. She did something to my IV, but I couldn't tell what. The room started to spin when my eyes followed her around the bed.

"Could you turn off the lights?" I asked. The nurse scrambled to close some shades and then turned off any remaining lights in the room.

The doctor asked me some more questions about where I lived, my brother's name, who Zac Phoenix was, and the title of my book. I answered them all correctly.

"We're going to give you something to calm you down," the doctor said, by now I knew his name was Duncan. "I want you to remember these five words, onion, race car, mushroom, moonbeam and tennis shoes." Then he stepped away and consulted with the nurse and another person who came into the room.

After a minute or so, he came back to the bed. "Do you remember those words?"

I recited them to him. The doctor smiled.

"The nurse will check on you every few minutes," he said. "We don't want you going back to sleep. You've been out for quite a while. Just relax now, Mr. Jenkins, we'll take good care of you."

"Hey Doctor Duncan," I said as he walked toward the door. He turned to me. "I'm a drug addict, you might want to watch what you give me." I couldn't make out his reaction.

The next few hours involved nurses coming into the room, asking me how I was, asking me those five words, asking me if I remembered the ambulance ride, the CAT scan (I'd had one shortly after coming to the hospital's ER) and what I remembered about the incident. As the day went on, I remembered more and more in bits and pieces.

I was lying on the dirt road in the woods. Eddie was there. I could hear his voice but couldn't make out the words. There were sirens. Hands were touching me. I was lifted and shuffled. There was a bumpy ride. More sirens. I was on a gurney in a hallway. I was told to lie still. There were the hums and beeps of the CAT scan machine. I was rolled down a hall. People were talking, sometimes to me, sometimes to each other. There was Zac's face, very solemn, asking me if I was OK, telling me that it would be OK. Then there was darkness before light, before Paula and Rainbow Bridge.

Finally, after what felt like an eternity, I asked to take a piss. The nurse helped me up, the room spun as I stood and took a couple of steps. My feet buckled.

"You want to go back to your bed, Mr. Jenkins?" the nurse asked. "I can get a bed pan?"

"No. Give me a second." I took a couple of deep breaths and thought "one step at a time," then took one. The room held firm. Then I took another. The room held firm. Then I got cocky and tried to do two quick ones. The room spun. The nurse grabbed me.

"Are you sure?" she asked.

"Just gotta move slow," I said, then took my time, got to the rest room and, unfortunately, had to piss while she watched.

"This may take a moment," I said. "I'm shy by nature."

"It's OK," she said in a very supportive voice. "I'd feel the same way, anybody would. You're doing really well with the words and your pupils look so much better."

"Light is still a motherfucker," I said. "Sorry for the choice of words."

She laughed and said, "I grew up around here. That doesn't bother me."

I was pissing in the dark, but finally finished, probably decorating the room in urine. The walk back was easier, and I asked if I could stand for a while. She agreed, but watched me while

I took a step here, then stretched, then took a step there, and stretched again.

"I'm a little hungry. Can I eat?"

"Sure," she said. I could finally read her name tag. Her name was Betty. "That's a good sign."

"My late wife always said when animals start eating again that means the worst is over," I said while sitting down on my bed.

"Your wife was a vet?"

"A damn good one, had her own hospital!" The words were bittersweet.

"That's so cool. I'll try to get you the works since you haven't eaten in a day."

My eyes were working better now. She had brown hair in a bun and was kinda thin because her uniform seemed a size too big.

"I came in yesterday?"

"Yes, around three or so."

"What hospital?" The fog was beginning to lift from my mind, although my head hurt more now as well.

"Otsego Memorial in Gaylord."

"No shit, and my friend, Eddie, where is he?"

"Ah, I'll check," she said, and it sounded guarded. "Let me get your lunch."

She left in a hurry. I didn't like the vibe.

Hospital food is hospital food, but when one is famished it tastes scrumptious. Betty got me a second tray and watched while I gobbled both meals down with a pitcher of water.

"Is it possible to have a Coke?" I asked. My stomach started to feel a little squeamish.

"I'll see." She was writing something down on a clipboard. Then she asked me for those five words which I repeated, then did in reverse order before using each in as funny a sentence as possible before using all of them in one sentence.

"I was eating an onion-and-mushroom sandwich in my race car while wearing tennis shoes and dodging moonbeams on the road," I said then smirked.

"You're one of those patients," Betty said and returned the smile.

"What patients?"

"Overachievers."

"You've avoided answering my question about Eddie."

"The doctor will fill you in. Also, you have a friend here. I think he got here last night, slept on a couch in the waiting room."

"Describe him?"

She did; it was Zac.

"Son of a bitch."

"No, he's quite nice. Very concerned, too."

$$\bullet \ \bullet \ \bullet \ \bullet \ \bullet$$

"I'd like to get another C-scan and X-rays," Dr. Duncan said, then he stepped out of the room for a moment. I looked at the machine by the side of my bed. My pulse was 70 with a BP of 118 over 62.

"That's good," I said to Betty.

"Oh, yes, much better. How's your head?"

"It hurts." Then I raised my hands to touch my head. It was bandaged and heavily padded on one side, the sore side.

"How bad is the bump?"

"Imagine a tennis ball cut in half," she said. "It looked like that yesterday when you came in."

Dr. Duncan appeared and told me that they would be taking me to radiology within the hour.

"If I like what I see then we'll move you to another room."

"You want those words, doctor?"

"Sure."

I recited my sentence using all five words. He chuckled.

"Let's try some light," he said. Betty turned them on.

"Still uncomfortable, but not as bad as this morning."

"Any ringing in the ears?" he asked.

I closed my eyes and carefully put my fingers in my ears. There was a high-pitched whining that sounded like a dentist's drill in the next room. It had been there since I woke up, but I'd mistaken it for hospital noise.

"Some, not terrible."

In a few minutes I was taken to radiology for a picture session that went on for about an hour and then I lay on my gurney in the hallway for a long time before Dr. Duncan showed up.

"The swelling is down. We'll rebandage your head. Please don't touch it."

"My head does hurt more than this morning."

'We had to change your meds. I confirmed your condition with your brother."

"He knows?"

"Yes, Mr. Fletcher had called him from the scene. I think he's coming up on Sunday."

"It's Friday?"

The doctor nodded.

"Mr. Phoenix is here," Duncan said. "I may let him see you once we get you settled in."

"How's Eddie?"

"He was stabilized and referred to a specialist at Munson in Traverse City."

"Specialist?"

"Eye specialist, Mr. Fletcher suffered a gunshot wound to his upper head and right eye. Thankfully it was birdshot, but several pellets did hit him, and his eye was significantly damaged."

"Could he lose it?" I asked and felt my stomach tighten.

"We don't know," he said. "None of the pellets penetrated his skull. We got them out in the ER easily. His glasses kept it from being worse, but they were broken because of impact and some of the shards got in his right eye. There were at least two pellets as well."

"Did we get them?"

"Who?"

"The bad guys."

"Mr. Phoenix will know more about it, but that may have to wait."

I was moved to another room. I had been in intensive care, but the ward had been relatively empty with just one other elderly patient who was unconscious in his section as I rolled by for my X-rays and CT scan. The wing I was in now had more patients. There was lots of noise from movement down the halls, snippets of conversations ("Did you get meds for 109?" "The doctor wants more bloodwork for 107, bed 2") and televisions tuned to the evening news. It was dark outside my window. I asked them to leave the bathroom light on but otherwise keep the room dark. My dinner had the feel of a candlelight meal.

Duncan and a Dr. Turner, another neurologist, showed up as I was finishing my green Jell-O. We discussed what I remembered about Thursday. By now I could recall meeting the man with the shotgun and the gist of the questioning, but not when the shooting started. The doctors shined their lights in my eyes and gave me simple coordination tests like touching my nose. Then they tested me with a couple of tongue-twister sentences including a personal favorite, "How much wood could a woodchuck chuck if a woodchuck could chuck wood?" I said it twice and then added my own editorial comment.

"Just as much wood as a woodchuck could chuck if a woodchuck could chuck wood," I said and gleamed my teeth at the two doctors.

"Now," I asked in a serious tone, "what the Hell happened out there in those woods?"

Dr. Turner looked at me. "We need to make sure that you are safe to be exposed to information that might cause stress or a severe emotional reaction," he said. "TBIs are tricky. I think that the original diagnosis when you came in was incorrect. Your recovery since this morning suggests the injury was not as bad as the ER doctor thought. It was his job to stabilize you and that may have played a positive role as well."

"Not knowing can be just as bad, even worse. Isn't there some type of rescue drug if I begin to overreact?"

"It's not the ideal protocol," he said. "Besides, it would introduce drugs into your system that you shouldn't have. Imagine that your brain had a power surge or had the reboot button pressed. That's where you are at. It needs time to heal and reorganize. Fortunately for you there appear to be no complications."

"Clean living, and all that fish oil. What about tomorrow morning?" The doctor had made a clear case about my need to take it slow. I decided to surrender, it had helped me before.

"A good night of rest should help," Turner said. "You've improved rapidly today. I've downgraded your concussion to borderline moderate. I'll see you in the morning. If the improvement continues, then you can meet with Mr. Phoenix sometime tomorrow."

"Will you get me an update on Eddie?"

"Certainly," Turner said, then he turned to Duncan. "Did he get in at Munson today?"

"As far as I know," Duncan said. "But I'll make sure you know tomorrow."

"Some people get to go deer hunting," Turner said pointing his thumb at Duncan. "The rest of us work."

"Be careful out there, Dr. Duncan, that you don't become the hunted."

• • • • •

"How are you doing, young man?" Zac said. He came over and gave me a soft embrace before pulling up a chair. I didn't recognize him at first. Gone was the clean shaven, button down, spit polish C-2 that I'd met last August. Now there was a three-day beard. The eyes were tired and baggy. He was wearing a blue flannel shirt and jeans instead of a sharp suit. There was the smell of old sweat.

"Better," I said. "Do you want to hear the five words?"

"Huh?" he said, those hawkeyes looked puzzled.

"Never mind. Well, I had a choice, either you or the Michigan game."

"Who are they playing?"

"Indiana."

"Oh, they should beat them, and next week The Bucks will beat you."

"Fuck, that's right, you're a Buckeye."

"Through and through, O-H…I-O, Baby!"

"I'm not supposed to be stressed."

"Right, forget it."

"How's Eddie?"

Zac considered this. I think that he'd been coached on how to talk to me.

"He's got a significant injury to his right eye," Zac said. "There's damage to the cornea and maybe the retina. He's going downstate to your stomping grounds. I think it's the Kellogg Eye Institute."

"That makes sense. It's world class."

"Copy that, Arthur, it could have been worse, but the story appears to be a good one. It's still unfolding."

"Did we get him?"

Zac licked his lips. "We did. We really did. Eddie did. Fucking-A, he did!"

"Is he dead, who was that guy?"

"Jack Hobbs and he's stone-cold dead. Leapfrog hit him nine times including one in the neck, carotid artery, and one in the forehead — the old brain pan," Zac said with a smile worthy of a Pepsodent commercial. "Hobbs is an alias, of course. Leapfrog was right about that, too. Know what his real name was?"

"Jumping Jack Flash?"

"No man," he said and laughed for a moment. "It's worse, Maynard Junkquist."

"What? No wonder he went by an alias." But my head hurt too much to laugh.

"He had another alias that I think you'll appreciate, Randall Flagg."

"From *The Stand*?" Stephen King's first set of novels way back in the 1970s had been my favorites. "Are you serious?"

"It gets better." Zac's raptor eyes were engaged now. "They had him for two years in Jacktown back in '90 and '91, possession with intent to sell."

"Did you see the body?" I asked.

"No, but I got questioned for almost four hours yesterday. I turned over our notes. We still need to give them the tapes."

"Were they pissed?"

Zac sighed, then rubbed his hands together the way Eddie did. "Man, I don't know what they are. It wasn't contentious. It was like they were oblivious to it. They didn't even know that we'd interviewed Galbraith. I filled them in on him and Hobbs."

"Did you tell them about Pam Naylor?"

"I did."

"I guess she got away."

"Maybe," Zac said in a tone that suggested more.

"What? Tell me." It was clear by the expression on his face that he was hesitant to speak. "Come on, we could have died out there."

Zac bent his head in thought. "I tried to get out to the scene yesterday. They got the road shut off about 100, 150 yards from the driveway. I counted 14 vehicles, two CSI trucks, and get this, Arthur." He paused, then leaned close to me. "They had fucking cadaver dogs, two of 'em."

"How can you be sure?" I asked, my heart was pounding in my ears.

"We do all kinds of training in the Army, and in my line of work, we cross-train with law enforcement because you never know and need to know. Got it?"

"Sure," I said, and was pleased at how well I was following along with the conversation. Dr. Turner had told me to monitor my understanding of any new information. He also warned me that I might start feeling some depression. So far, I was doing OK in that regard, too. It helped to know that Paula was safe.

"So I know a cadaver dog when I see one. They're looking for bodies."

"Have they told you anything about it?"

"We have another meet set for Monday." Zac glanced at his watch. "I'm out of the allotted time. They'll let me know if I can come by tomorrow. I got more to tell you and want to hear about what you remember."

"Yeah, they said that I'm not supposed to get too excited."

"Your brother is coming up tomorrow. He's pissed at me."

"Why?"

"He blames me for this," Zac said with a down beat.

"That's bullshit."

"No, it's big brothers looking out for little brothers. I respect it. Look, we'll cover any bills that your insurance doesn't, including rehab. Same deal for Leapfrog. My lawyer is faxing me the papers tomorrow. That is, if the machine at the Holiday Inn Express really works." He made an amused face and threw his hands in the air. "Fuck."

"Don't worry, it'll be fine. I'll get Nick straightened out. Did somebody call Cam Krenshaw?"

"I did. Got your cellphone, too. It'll be waiting at the front desk when you check out. I'm hearing that might be Monday."

"Geez, everybody knows what's going on but me," I said feeling frustrated.

"Always that way for the guys who *are* the story," Zac said on the way out the door.

After Zac left, I napped until dinner then watched USC beat the shit out of somebody before turning in. In the morning, I remembered a snippet of a dream in which Eddie and I were walking in the woods when a spectral Hanna Grey showed up with a pack of cadaver dogs.

"I know where the bitch is," the ghost girl said. "She's mine now."

• • • • •

Nick came into my room around noon. I was just finishing my chocolate pudding — another fine product from Jell-O.

"How are you feeling?" he asked.

"A shitload better than two days ago," I said.

"That's good," he said and sat down.

"How'd we look yesterday?"

"You didn't watch it?" he asked. It sounded like an indictment.

"I was not supposed to be stressed."

"Not much to get stressed about. That's for this week."

"You know Zac is not to blame for what happened." I decided to get to the point.

"Then who is?"

"Me." I explained my decision to join Eddie in approaching the house.

"Who started it?"

"The shooting? The guy did, by the way, he was our target and Eddie got him. Keep that under your hat." By now I remembered everything but had decided to tell this version of the story. I was certain that Eddie would not be charged but would lie if I had to protect him.

"Why? It's in the papers."

"What?"

Nick filled me in on the media reports concerning a shooting in the Pigeon River State Forest involving an ex-convict and Iraq War vet. Both Eddie's and Junkquist's names and pictures were in the *Free Press* this morning. The speculation was that Junkquist had information on the Missing Trout Fisherman. My name did not appear although it was mentioned that another person had been wounded at the scene.

"What the fuck were you two thinking?" Nick asked. He had that look of intimidation that I'd seen so often from our father, who was quick to blame the victim in every instance. Try as he might, some of my father would always stick to my brother.

"Back the fuck off right now!" Rarely had I stood up to my brother, but I'd had my fill of this. My head started to ache.

Nick glowered at me.

"Eddie saved the day. We got the bad guy. There's only one more to get."

"You know he called me from the scene." Nick's voice suggested a lessening of tension.

"He did?" Then I explained Eddie's wounds.

"I'd a have never guessed that from the sound of his voice. It was so…calm. He said you'd been injured, nothing serious, and he had called an ambulance."

"What else?"

"That you had a suspect in custody, then he said he'd call from the hospital," Nick said. (Zac would be the one who made that call.)

"Yeah, Junkquist was apprehended alright. He wasn't going anywhere."

Nick smiled at this. "Eddie was always a piece of work." Nick's opinion of Eddie was mixed because he'd known Eddie's brother Donald and hated him so figured Eddie couldn't have been that different. Of course, Nick didn't know the whole story of the Fletcher household.

"Can we not fight about this?"

"Sure, we can watch the Lions, game starts soon."

"That's better than a sharp stick in the eye, but not much better."

I was discharged the following morning with a bicycle helmet, prescription for some meds to help the swelling, an appointment to see a doctor at the University of Michigan hospital on Wednesday, and a set of instructions on what I could and could not do for another five days — in specific, no physical activity and no stress.

"Let your brain heal," Dr. Turner said. "You're a lucky man, Mr. Jenkins."

Zac met us at the front desk. I'd forgotten that he was supposed to stop by on Sunday.

"Why didn't you come by?" I said. "Or did you and I had forgotten about it?" For a moment I felt some alarm.

"No, buddy," Zac said. "I was dealing with some other things. Eddie needed some counseling."

"Why?"

"He's upset about everything, and the media is after him. We got him squared away. He's seeing a doctor at Kellogg today. They're setting up a surgery."

"I need to talk to him."

"Let that wait, OK? He's not in a good place." Then he turned to Nick. "Can I talk to you for a second over here?" Nick agreed and they walked over to the waiting area while I signed some papers. I saw them finally shake hands and was relieved.

"All quiet on the western front," Zac said when they came back. Nick nodded in agreement.

"Oh," Zac added before walking toward the exit doors, "Staties postponed the meet until later this week." He held up both his hands with fingers crossed. "I think they're waiting on some forensics."

We swung by Spinnerfall to pick up my things but would not retrieve my truck for another two weeks. On the way home Nick and I discussed the upcoming Ohio State game. We both felt that it was possible to win. Talking about football, or any sports, was our way of saying that things had moved on. It was the Jenkins' solution to everything.

I received a hero's welcome at the Mother-In-Law. Sam and Sham danced and squealed and peed when I arrived. Cam was there delivering groceries, including a pot of venison chili, and supervising the addition to the house for a washer and dryer unit. His shirt-sleeve cousin, Terry, was doing the work.

"Arthur," Cam said, "How many times have I told you to watch where you duck?" He laughed and shook my hand so hard I thought it might dislocate.

Kody had left me a pile of DVDs of movies from the '80s and '90s, mostly comedies and action adventures. I emailed Kate

LeClair but got an out-of-the-office until the 21st message in return, talked to Adrian's voice mail for the umpteenth time and had a long discussion-argument with Roger about the role of ego in our decisions.

"Your hubris is gonna get you killed," Roger said.

"Maybe, but not this time," I said, and made a mental note to finally ask a fellow named Ron to be my new sponsor. He was a manager at a local bookstore and had good sobriety. Most importantly, he didn't find it necessary to look at every situation through melodramatic lenses. (His take on the shooting was that I should be grateful, but better prepared next time.)

My neurologist at Michigan was an overweight man named Pasricha who was pleased with my progress.

"You can resume moderate exercise next Monday, Mr. Jenkins," he said. "Are you planning on going to the game?"

"Nope, gonna watch on TV, no tickets."

"Good, probably too much, too soon. Can we win?"

"Anything is possible."

For the only time in my life the Ohio State game would be of secondary importance. By Friday we would know all that would ever be known about what happened to Donny Massengale and Roland Parrish.

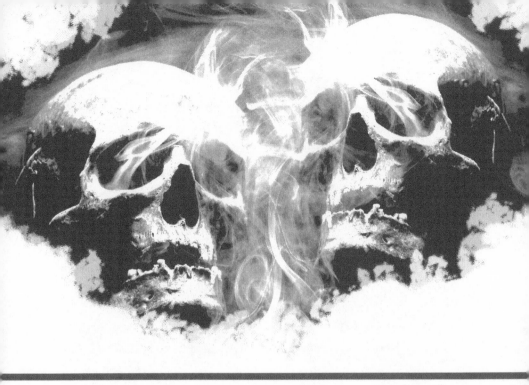

CHAPTER 13

Footprints in the Sand

On Friday morning, I met Zac and his lawyer in downtown Ann Arbor at an auxiliary branch of Eddie's law firm. Eddie had set up the meeting, though he would not be in attendance. He was under the knife a couple of miles away at the University of Michigan hospital in the first of what were to be several operations.

"I think that he'll be in the recovery room by the time we start our meeting," Zac said.

"How was he last night?" I asked. Eddie would not answer my calls.

"He's not taking any calls right now. It's not you, Arthur, it's all of us."

"They should be here soon," Trish Davis said. "My understanding is that officer Moon and Mr. Melbar are delayed in traffic."

Trish was the lead counsel for the Phoenix Investigations Firm. Her appearance, expressions and vocal tones were anodyne. Trish had an almost factory-issued form: average height with brown hair. I had met with her three times in the past four days and in each instance had to be reintroduced. It wasn't the concussion, I knew who she was, that she was very smart (Indiana undergrad, Michigan Law School), and a legal savant of sorts. But her face was just forgettable. I wondered if it was on purpose. Trish Davis had to do the legal dirty work for a PI firm that didn't have a problem playing in the paint and throwing a few elbows. She was good at her job, but probably didn't want to make anybody's revenge list, hence the gray suits, short "meh" hairstyle, no trace of make-up and a pair of glasses that could have come from the bargain bin at Lenses Are Us.

"Getting their ducks in a row, no doubt," Betsy Kentzarski said after checking her laptop for email. She was my counsel recommended by Nick, of course. Betsy had approved my agreement with the Phoenix Investigation Firm for medical reimbursements in the immediate term. She was crafting an additional document with another Phoenix attorney to compensate for any future problems. There the language grew a bit dense in legalese, but Betsy said they wanted to do right by me. She found Trish to be as inscrutable as I did.

"She's an automaton, Arthur," Betsy had said on the ride in that morning — she picked me up because I wasn't cleared yet to drive. "I think that it's by design and smacks of the military."

"Not surprising," I said between sips of coffee. Zac practiced what he preached by hiring as many vets as possible and running the firm with military precision. We were his only true FUBARS because a shootout was not part of the Phoenix plan of operation.

At five after eleven, the "other side" arrived: Darwin Moon, assistant chief of detectives for the Michigan State Police and Josh Melbar, a state prosecutor, and almost as faceless as Trish in a "G-Man" ensemble of black suit, white shirt, and black tie. The introductions were crisp, and the meeting got underway. It was time to talk of many things, of cabbages and kings, of Satanists and wyvern wings.

"First off," Moon said, "how are you Mr. Jenkins?" Moon was a large man with pale skin, light blue eyes and a porcine face. It gave him a soft appearance, but to assume that would be a mistake. Darwin Moon had risen through the ranks by quality field work, he was an elite interceptor in his days working I-96 in Grand Rapids, and he had led the successful apprehension of the White Lake Five, a group of white supremacists who prowled the state bombing businesses owned by people of color and their allies.

"The headaches are better, sir," I said. "Thank you for asking."

Moon gave me a regulation smile. "Good, then let's get to it." He shuffled some papers from a manila folder.

"A portion of this is an update on old business," he said. "You all know that the deceased was a Maynard Junkquist, 49, aka Randall Flagg, aka Jack Hobbs, who did two years on possession at the State Prison of Southern Michigan as well as a year in the Wayne County Correction Facility for assault in 1980." He stopped for a drink of coffee. "Mr. Junkquist was also a person of interest in a double murder in Port Huron in 1993." He paused again to look at us. "Until last Friday we had thought that he'd likely left the country."

"Nice to have him off the board," Zac said. He stared at Moon intently. "So, what was in the cabin, sir?"

Moon returned Zac's look with one of his own suggesting that Darwin held all the cards. I didn't like it. We'd solved this and bled for it. Moon should have more respect for that.

"We still need a statement from Mr. Jenkins about the shooting."

"That is on the table," Zac said. "Right after this meeting, right Mr. Prosecutor?"

"Are we still a go. Ms. Kentski?" Melbar asked.

"Kentzarski," Betsy said staring daggers at the State Prosecutor. "And yes, my client is ready to be questioned. Right, Arthur?"

"Copy that," I said. "What's with the attitude, Officer Moon? We're not the bad guys."

"No attitude, Mr. Jenkins. I just want to be clear about procedures." He turned to Zac. "You surely understand procedures, Mr. Phoenix?"

"What was in the cabin, sir?" Zac said with a bit of a growl. I was getting a look at old Colonel Phoenix, pissed that a charge had failed in a tail or had yet to find a person that the target might have known during an "experimental" period in college. I was hoping that Black Zac, the real Black Zac, born in a racist moment long ago, didn't appear because it would blow the whole thing up.

"Did Pam Naylor get away?" I said trying to move it along.

Moon smiled the way a big hog might before plowing into the trough.

"We found a body in the main residence." He paused for effect as if any was needed.

"Naylor?" Zac said breathless.

Moon went on as if he hadn't heard him. "The deceased was a female Caucasian, approximately 40 years old, approximately five foot seven inches, one hundred and forty-five pounds, brownish hair, green eyes."

"Do you have an ID?" Zac yelled.

"We do! It was difficult given the state of the remains. The deceased had been dismembered, stuffed in plastic bags and placed in a refrigerator. She'd been dead about 48 hours give or take…12. Mr. Melbar?"

Melbar nodded. It was only then that I noticed he was wearing glasses.

"And her name?" Zac said standing up and leaning over the table. My heart was pounding in my ears.

"The deceased was a Pamela Jean Naylor, aka Jean Naylor, 39, of Wolverine."

Zac pounded the table with his fist. "Now we're getting somewhere!"

I was light-headed at hearing this, and very disappointed. Pam Naylor wouldn't be interviewed. She wouldn't be prosecuted or sent to prison to rot and be abused by like-minded predators, many of whom were far more refined at violence and brutality than Pammie with her pills. Instead, Naylor's penance was to be treated like a common cold cut, sliced, diced, and packaged for a future meal. Was she headed to become a relic for Satanic worship like Massengale and Parrish? Only God and the Devil know now.

Melbar handed Moon another folder.

"That wasn't all we found out there."

"More bodies?" Zac said while sitting down.

"Did you notice the outbuilding when you were out there, Mr. Jenkins?"

"All I saw was a shotgun pointed at me and Eddie."

"Yeah, I could see where that might get your attention," Moon said with a smarmy grin. I was starting to hate him. "Did you know that he was cleaning his deer rifle? A few minutes later and he'd have met you with that and we wouldn't be having this conversation, I think. Did you know that he grabbed Number 4 birdshot rather than Number 4 buckshot when loading the shot-gun? Helluva difference in gauges, sir. That might have been a game changer too. Did you know he had a nine-millimeter in the next room? Another potential game changer. Did you know that he'd been drinking? Yup, blood alcohol of .18. Did you know that he'd been getting high? Did you know any of those things, Mr. Jenkins?" Then Moon looked at Zac. "Mr. Phoenix?"

"How could we?" I asked.

"But I thought you had all the answers," Moon said while standing up and sweeping his piggy hands across the table.

"OK, that's enough!" Zac said. "I see where this is going. You're pissed because we found 'em and you're catching heat in the papers. Got news for you, it's going to get worse. Get past tomorrow's game…Oh, Go Bucks," Zac winked at me, "…get past tomorrow's game and the press will really start to drill down on this, just in time for a long, semi-lazy Thanksgiving week where the public will be craving some murder porn to go along with those turkey sandwiches and another piece of pumpkin pie."

I couldn't have said it better myself.

Then it was Trish's turn.

"Browbeat us if you must in this venue," she said while pointing to a window and speaking in almost perfect monotone. "But one word like this one there and we will consider slander charges… as well as tell our *entire* story to the press."

This got Melbar's attention. Moon just fumed at her. His oinker face turned red. I thought of Ballpark Franks.

"What are you implying, counselor?" Melbar asked, but in an evenhanded tone.

"That you get all of the ranting out of your system now, give us the additional findings of the site, and then we formulate a plan for the public version of this," she said and put her hand on my shoulder. "Mr. Jenkins is an expert on public communication, and I am sure that he would agree with this approach." Then she turned to me while sliding that hand to the middle of my back and patting it like an old friend or prospective lover. "Wouldn't you, Arthur?"

I would know Trish Davis for years to come and this would be the one and only time that she ever turned me on.

"Yes, Trish, I would," I was a tad flustered, not expecting a seduction in the middle of the fireworks. I looked at Melbar because he seemed like the reasonable one. "You are going to get fire, no way out of it, but we can moderate the effect with the right narrative."

Zac caught my drift. "We're on the same fucking side here, gentlemen."

Melbar considered this. "We are," he finally said, but that was primarily directed at Moon.

Darwin Moon sat down and composed himself. His face faded from "plump-when-you-cook-'em" red to a shade more in tune with Porky Pig when the Merry Melody was over.

"What was in the outbuilding, Darwin?" Zac asked respectfully.

Moon sighed. "We initially found materials that could best be characterized as the type of objects used in dark rituals. We brought in two professors from Wayne State and UM who know a thing or two about these, ah, um, matters…There were boards with symbols on them, Satanic in nature, inverted crosses, a goat skull and posts for…mounting things."

I imagined those cat's heads, but it was worse than that.

Moon needed a moment. He was dealing with a dry mouth. This was hard for him. It wasn't our confrontation that had vacuumed up his confident spirit or softened that chip on his shoulder. Nope, it was the description of the items. It would have been that way for anyone in possession of a soul because this time all those worst fears turned out to be true.

"There was a…footlocker," he said in a broken voice. "We found inside…wrapped in plastic bubble wrap, you know, the kind for shipping things…we found, six human skulls. Their jaws were intact. In fact, they had been wired in place. There were more of those symbols drawn or carved on each of them. One had a bullet hole in the forehead, likely a nine mil. We didn't find the slug. The base of each skull indicated that they had likely been mounted at some point, perhaps even drilled into a post."

There were gasps in the room. My heart was in my ears again and I felt prickles on my skin. Zac's mouth opened so wide that it appeared as if he'd unhinged his jaws like a snake. Moon appeared frozen in time with a sheen of sweat on his forehead and neck.

Melbar, who had to have already known, rested his forehead on clasped hands as if in prayer. Betsy sobbed quietly while grasping my shoulder. Even Trish showed some emotion by tightly pinching her mouth, dropping her eyes, and then shaking her head, "Those monsters," she said in a whisper, "those fucking monsters."

"Any IDs?" Zac asked softly.

"We brought in two forensic dentists. One was from the FBI. We, of course, had some idea who to look for initially."

Then there was a moment that stood apart from all other moments in the last three months. It demarked "before" from "after." It was the case's omega.

"Three skulls have been identified," Moon said solemnly. "The first was Donald James Massengale, 21, of Dexter. The second was Roland Harper Parrish, 21, of Jackson. The third, which had the bullet hole, and we are less certain of ID than the first two, but have a high level of confidence in nonetheless, was Rufus Paul Young, 31, of West Branch."

"Mr. Penguin," I said, and my words sounded far off.

"What?" Moon asked.

"Read our report," Zac said. "Do the families know?"

"Massengale and Parrish, yes. Young's half-sister knows, but we are looking for other relatives."

"We found them," I said. "We found them." This was beyond that perimeter where there were no stars, as Morrison, The Lizard King, had once described. The surprise of confronting Hobbs had been lost in the backwaters of my concussion. Naylor's death was unexpected, but I knew that we'd find her. This revelation, however, had never been foreseen. As Zac had said three months ago, which now seemed like three years ago, those boys were completely gone.

I put my head in my hands, carefully because my left side was still very tender, and let out a long breath. There were no tears, just a deep sense of exhaustion. Something left me in that moment. It was heavy and dark and desperate. The sensation was like vomiting spiritually. I felt better, but completely spent.

"We actually found them," I said several times. Trish joined Betsy with a hand on my shoulders in comfort and support.

"We did, brother," Zac said. "HOOAH."

• • • • •

On Monday afternoon I was cleared to drive again. I called Eddie, anxious to see him and discuss everything. He picked up on the third ring.

"How are you?" I asked.

"I feel like a pirate, Arrghhh," he said.

"We need to talk."

"Yeah, I'm closer than you think." He gave me an address near the University of Michigan hospital.

It turns out that the Phoenix Investigation Firm had arranged for Eddie to stay at an apartment complex within walking distance of UM hospital and the Kellogg Eye Institute. It was a place otherwise occupied by medical and nursing students as well as interns and residents doing their grinds then coming home for long periods of sleep before another cycle.

Eddie's voice yelled to me to come in since the door was unlocked. I found him sitting on the couch in darkness listening to a cassette tape. The right side of his head was bandaged on an angle that ran from the middle of his forehead to just below his jawline, covering his right eye, ear and most of his right cheek. He looked like something from an old newsreel, a survivor of Corregidor or Dien Bien Phu. On the table were a bag of pistachio nuts and a bowl for the shells. There were also three Diet Coke cans, two packs of Wrigley's wintergreen gum and a pile of wrappers.

"Who are you listening to?" I asked.

"Audiobook, *The History of the Decline and Fall of the Roman Empire.*"

"Haven't you read that at least twice?"

"I gotta thing for Hadrian's Wall."

"Doesn't everybody?"

"No, about 99.99 percent of the population in this country doesn't know anything about it."

"Well, that's just the decline of *our* empire."

Eddie smiled a bit at this and made a motion for me to sit down.

We traded small talk about our recoveries interspersed with mentions of Emperor Constantine, Charles Martel (the only Frenchmen Eddie ever respected) and Alfred the Great (a distant relative of mine). It was all designed to feel each other out and delay the inevitable. Finally, we ran out of casual conversational steam, and it was left up to me to get down to it.

"I would have appreciated more of a head's up out there," I said, but not in a pissy way.

"I told you to take cover."

"Yeah, a beat before you started firing."

"Oh, yeah, I should have told Hobbs to wait a sec while I explain the plan to my partner."

"How did you know it was him?"

"How much do you remember?"

I explained to him my take on the story plus how I told it in my interview with the State Police last Friday.

"Close enough to mine," Eddie said. "They won't charge anyway. So how did I know it was Hobbs?"

"You were looking hard at him, like you watch bugs on the water."

"Remember when I looked over his shoulder?"

"Uh-huh."

"I was getting a confirmation. He wasn't wearing gloves, but the way that he was holding that rifle I couldn't get a good look at his left wrist for that tattoo. Getting him to look back over his shoulder moved that hand and gave me the proof that it was him. Plus it got that gun off us."

"For a moment."

"He'd lost his focus. I knew I could take him."

"The walking away was a misdirection of sorts?"

"I needed to get you out of the line of fire. I should have waited another second before making my declaration. You'd been far enough away."

"I stepped back toward you when I heard you declare a citizen's arrest."

"Fuck! Why'd you do that?" Eddie said in anger.

"Because I was hoping to incur a moderate concussion. It was experiential for me. I'm growing as a person."

"How's that going?"

"The headaches are much better."

"And short-term memory is functioning fine," he said while writing an imaginary note in the palm of his hand.

"Is a citizen's arrest even real?" I asked.

"Section 764.16 of the penal code says that I have that right if I witness a felony," he said. "Hobbs was brandishing a deadly weapon and making threats."

"You heard about the deer rifle?"

"Yes," Eddie said while grabbing a pack of gum. "Number 4 buckshot wouldn't have been pleasant either. We were lucky, but they'd had their streak of luck for way too long."

"What do you think of Naylor?"

"Fitting. Poetic justice, but I'd have relished questioning her." He unwrapped a stick of gum. "God! I wish I could dip!"

"Why can't you?"

"Blood pressure and surgery. Could fuck it up. I guess the eye could just pop out of the socket."

"That's pretty gruesome."

"Mm-hmmm," he said while chewing. "I wonder if it just splats on the floor like a meatball or bounces around like a superball."

"You're a sick puppy."

"Negative. Inquiring minds want to know."

"What happened after the shooting?" I asked. Eddie unwrapped two more sticks of gum and then told that part of the story.

Eddie emptied his clip into Hobbs, then made sure that he was dead. "I watched him bleed out from the neck wound while changing clips as fast as I could. Within a minute it was clear that he was gone." Then Eddie came over to me, checked my vitals, roused me to semiconsciousness, carried me to the Jeep and drove back toward Wolverine with one hand on the steering wheel and the other one on his cellphone waiting for a signal. He did this with blood dripping down his cheek, neck and into his shirt. "I went slow because I had only one eye functioning, and my face and head stung like Hell." He finally found a strong signal near the house with the woman and the dog. "I got out and called 911, Otsego County Sheriff, Michigan State Police, Zac, Nick and a couple of my buddies in Grayling." He got me out of the truck, covered me with his coat and two blankets that he'd had in the back and treated me for shock. "I sat talking to you and doing a huge wad of dip." At some point he'd put the pistol and clips on the hood of the Cherokee along with both our wallets. "I just waited until I heard the sirens." When he did, Eddie moved away from me and held his hands up, then put them behind his neck with fingers interlocked and waited for further instructions. "I told them that there was a shooting victim, likely DOA, about five miles east and that they should search the area for a blond woman in her early 40s. She should be considered armed and dangerous." Eddie was handcuffed and put face down in the dirt road while the ambulance took me away and more squad cars from the state and county started showing up. "I wouldn't get to Otsego Memorial for four hours. Just the way it went."

I didn't say anything for a long time after he finished, trying not to cry now that I knew the whole story. "What about that woman?" I finally asked. "The one with the dog."

"Fuck her! We left someone on the battlefield."

"Hanna?"

"We'll never know the truth now."

"Eddie." I reached out and grabbed his shoulder. "We did everything that we could. Some things just aren't meant to be."

"I hate that phrase 'we did everything that we could.' Fucking *hate* it!" He chewed hard on the gum reminding me of Nick. "And I'm haunted by the other one, too."

"I gotta ghost like that one rattling around my house as well."

He looked at me with that one very intense eye. "One of these days we gotta exorcise those sons of bitches."

"They tell me it's a process."

"There's one loose end. Maybe it might lead to that."

"What?"

"Thorn."

"Oh, yeah, "I said, "Do you think he's real?"

"I think he is, but whether he's still alive or in the wind or reformed...that I don't know.

"He musta got cold feet."

"You figured that out?" Eddie said with a slight smile on the left side of his face.

"Hobbs and Naylor still had the skulls."

"Yup, my guess that if the whole thing had been a real 'kill for cash' caper then the skulls would have been the prime goods." Eddie tapped the table. "What Thorn's role in this was or what the real motive was...I just don't give a Fuck anymore."

"Not our problem now. Let the State Police handle it."

"Copy that," Eddie said with a long sigh. "We've done enough."

• • • • •

After that day Eddie and I would not see each other until the following March. I think that was intentional. We stayed in contact through phone calls, emails and texts — it was the first time either of us started doing a lot of the latter — but there was a need for some distance. It was time to heal and put it all behind us.

Zac was right. By Thanksgiving Sunday, the state and local papers had made all the connections, thanks in part to the police leaking like a sieve at the local, county and state levels, and were having a field day batting law enforcement around the ballyard.

A common story line went something like: "How could a trio of amateurs solve a case in three months that the police our taxes pay for couldn't in 21 years?" There were front page stories above the fold, special inserts, multipiece investigations with plenty of salaciousness ("On Thursday: Part 3 — Satan's Seducer and Her Magic Potions") and endless op-eds and letters to the editor on the bumbling keystone kops as well as the whole thing being a sign of declining family values ("Mio Murders Show It's Time to Go Back to Church").

Darwin Moon became the face of police ineptitude until Zac Phoenix wrote an op-ed to every newspaper in the country asking the public to give Moon a break. "Assistant Chief of Detectives Darwin Moon wasn't even on the force in April of 1984, never had the case in his assignment file, and was not part of the Department's decision to put the murders in deep freeze back in 2000 because it was determined they could never be solved," Zac wrote. "Everybody involved in all those decisions is retired or working in another state."

From that point things cooled in Michigan, and Moon became one of our biggest fans.

Zac had a plan for that. He asked for Moon's help in keeping the press and TV off both Eddie and me. All of a sudden doctors were coming out of the woodwork explaining that Lt. Colonel Fletcher and Mr. Jenkins must be given privacy to recover from their grave injuries.

"These two men should be left alone by the media for now," said one doctor who neither Eddie nor I had ever met. "All this questioning could harm them!"

Eddie was pissed that Kim Gold, known as much for her long legs and honey blond hair as for her quality reporting, couldn't interview him. "Trust me," he texted. "She'd only help me recover."

The topics of eye injuries ("The Hidden Danger of a Damaged Eye — What You Need to Know") and concussions ("What You Don't Know About Concussions Can Kill You") became hot items on local TV news.

Zac took the lead and became our face in the media. He'd fly into Detroit Metro on Monday mornings with Trish in tow and then barnstorm the state all week in search of every available microphone and notebook. Part of it was to walk point for his wounded friends but part of it was also to recon the possibilities of setting up a Detroit branch of Phoenix Investigations. "Fucking C-2 doesn't miss a beat," Eddie said in another text.

It was all necessary. Eddie had a second operation in mid-December. He also started seeing a counselor, on the recommendation of Kate LeClair, for PTSD concerning the shooting. "I like your Dr. Scotty," he said in a phone call. "Is she single?" That comment alone told me my friend would find his way out of the thicket, although it also spurred some trepidation as well.

My recovery was easier. I finally spoke with Kate that Monday I saw Eddie. It was more heart-to-heart than therapist-to-client. "Don't ever scare me like that again, boyo," she said with a sniffle. "Never again, ya hear!"

I agreed to see a therapist she recommended for my possible PTSD. (I did so three times before we mutually agreed that I was doing fine.) The headaches subsided. The depression and moodiness never appeared. I believe that knowing Paula was waiting in Rainbow Bridge was the reason for that. I took a break from writing assignments until January, but by then felt that my organizational skills were close to the norm.

The only problem for me concerned two nightmares. Both would haunt me until the following spring.

The first involved that standoff with Hobbs. In this case he had that deer rifle. I watched him blow Eddie's head off in a crimson spray then turn the gun on me. With glowing red eyes and a mouth full of shark teeth, he laughed diabolically before pulling the trigger. I woke up screaming and clutched my dogs while waiting for my breathing to slow. Each time it was less frightening, but I could never change the outcome. Hobbs always won.

The second one wasn't as terrorizing but left a deeper mark. We were at Spinnerfall. I was getting ready to turn in when there was a knock on the door. It was Eddie.

"There's a bonfire in the woods out back," he said. "We need to go there."

We walked through a tunnel of trees to a clearing where a giant orange teardrop threw sparks and sounded crackles into the dark night. There were three figures by the fire who turned toward us. They were the pale visages of Donny Massengale, Roland Parrish and Hanna Grey. Their expressions were somber. There was disappointment in their eyes. Not a word was spoken.

I didn't wake up screaming but each time lay in bed while chills rolled over my body. In time I understood the dream's meaning.

Their story was not our story. There was no happy ending. For Donny, Roland and Hanna, the tale would always be one of tragedy.

• • • • •

By the New Year we were all on the mend.

Zac Phoenix would get a broader taste of fame that February, sweeps month, when the networks rolled out their versions of the missing Michigan Trout Fishers saga. One titled their program "Dark Deeds in the Deep Woods," and gave it two prime time hours on a Friday night. We'd cut a deal with all the networks to leave Eddie and me out of it. Our names were mentioned, no way around that, but pictures of our faces were kept to a minimum.

Zac Phoenix appeared in every program, usually along with Domino Clark, Evangeline Cooper, David Brandon, Wilbur Marshall, and several individuals who had refused to be interviewed by us. He explained our investigation but managed to gloss over the fact that we had close to the entire casefile from the start through an extensive hack. (It would only occur to me later that Zac's rescue piece for Moon might have been insurance against any charges of computer espionage.)

By February, the media had turned on us a bit. They had wrung our story of being heroic part-time Sherlocks for all it was worth and now wanted to cut us down to size.

First, they went after Eddie for challenging Hobbs and not just walking away and calling the police. It was suggested by more than one reporter that Eddie had PTSD and was a loose cannon. Veterans' groups went apeshit, and some newspapers retracted or allowed for rebuttal then dropped the PTSD angle like a hot potato. The Big Boys of nightly network television didn't, and it was left to Zac Phoenix to set the record straight on ABC, NBC and CBS.

"You thank us for our service ad nauseum, but if we step out of line or act in an atypical way then it's PTSD! PTSD! PTSD!" Zac said in so many words each time. "In reply I offer these facts for the record: Junkquist was a convicted felon and person of interest in at least six deaths. He was pointing a gun and making threats at Eddie and Arthur and finally opened fire on them. Was Eddie supposed to stand by and take it, so your sensibilities were not offended?"

The reporters would then pivot to the question on our unprofessionalism leading to serious injury.

"I feel terrible about what happened to my friends," Zac said. "But they are on the road to recovery and the case is solved."

"But Lt. Colonel Fletcher may lose his eye," the reporter would ask as if the very fate of the world hung on that possibility.

"You need to check your sources. His vision won't be 20-20 anymore, as it was on that day, but Eddie won't be blind. He might need a contact lens to correct some impairment. That's a far cry from losing an eye."

"So all in all," the reporter would usually say at the end of the interview, "How does it make you feel?"

The first time he got this question Zac gave a long-winded 10-minute answer that got edited down to a few seconds of mishmash. By the time he spoke for the final show Zac's response, perhaps at Trish's suggestion, was streamlined.

"Sanguine, Jane," Zac said. "Sanguine." Then he looked at the camera with confidence and just a touch of fury in those hawkeyes. I imagined that those piercing eyes must be something like what a doomed field mouse sees just before the talons close.

Eddie's mid-December operation was to reconstruct his right ear, shredded by birdshot, as well as his right eyelid, split in three spots by splinters from his glasses. In early January, he had another surgery on his retina. The results were promising. While there would by a third procedure in February, it looked like Eddie would have about 20-100 vision and some night blindness. He would have the choice of glasses with one corrective lens or a single contact.

"It'll give those big browns at night a fighting chance," he told me in a phone chat. "Besides, I can still track them by sense of smell."

"I wanna see that technique," I said.

"Sure, but it's top secret," he said. "Don't want a buncha' yahoos learning how."

His law firm came to their senses, in part because it was good PR, and made Eddie a partner in January. More importantly, he was back in the courtroom. In mid-March, Eddie was second chair in another fraud case involving double billing of veterans. He would even be doing some cross examination.

Eddie showed up with an eye patch. His ear looked fine but was a bit off color with the rest of his face. There were several indents on his forehead and right cheek from the pellets. Eddie likened those to dueling scars and would never have them corrected.

He questioned two accountants testifying for the plaintiffs and did a fine job. The defendants chose to settle.

I attended all three days of the trial. Zac and Trish were there on day one but had other commitments. There was a serial killer, dubbed "The Corn Stalk Slasher," on the loose in Iowa and Wisconsin. The state police in both places needed a helping hand. Zac and his team were ones that everybody in the Midwest was turning to for answers. One could see an expression on C-2's face now that suggested something far beyond sanguine, vindication. He'd found his version of that gold star.

"Good to see you, Arthur," Zac said to me with a firm handshake. "I don't know when it will be again. Black Zac is a busy man."

"You earned it," I said.

"We all found something more than we were looking for, copy?"

"I certainly do."

Eddie would sit second chair on five more cases in 2006. He would wear the eye patch in each of them, even though he really didn't need it by May. Some called it a charade or stagecraft but never to his face. I know why he kept wearing it. Eddie Fletcher wanted the world to know that when it was his turn to see the elephant, he met the challenge and saved the day.

My second Michigan winter went far more smoothly than the first. The dogs helped. Watching Sam and Sham frolic in the winter wonderland warmed my heart. They'd come into the house caked in snow and panting happily. Toweling them off after each walk, usually followed by a tug-of-war session, became a ritual, as did cutting wood and keeping those hungry chickadees, cardinals and woodpeckers fed. My Florida friends wondered how I could stand it. They made their choice and I had made mine. Let there be peace in the valley.

There were numerous calls and emails from friends, some that I hadn't spoken to in years, about the case. Adrian and I finally had a series of long phone calls, much of which involved a mea culpa from her for drifting apart.

"I got tied up in my business and a new relationship," she said. "Can you forgive me?"

"I was never angry," I said. "You got on with life. I chose a stranger path in that regard."

"Come out and see me in Denver this summer?"

"Sure," I said, but was already wondering how I could fit it in. Eddie had me perusing catalogs for fly gear. "We'll do the whole cycle, Hendricksons to Hex, smallmouth, mice on the South Branch and White Flies again," he said. "I expect a better performance now that you're not a greenhorn."

"Sir, yes, Sir!" I replied.

"Outstanding. Fly-tying will be next on the agenda."

"Can't I just buy my own or use some of yours?"

"Negative. I'm teaching you to be self-reliant, remember the advice of Emerson."

"He's not my first choice for fishing tips, not even on the list."

My January piece for *Michigan Hunting and Fishing* was a so-so effort about a team of conservationists restoring viable trout water on the upper reaches of the Rouge River, a stream pummeled by decades of pollution from the auto industry. I didn't feel my work was on par, but Bob Wills disagreed.

"I need you to look into that oil well scheme on the South Branch of the Au Sable," he said. "You know, the one on the Mason Tract, near that chapel in the woods." George Mason, the first president of American Motors Corporation, had donated 5,000 acres of wilderness to the state in 1955 to be enjoyed by everybody forever.

"When do you need it?" I asked.

"May issue, 2,000 words. We've got to educate our readers. If the oil and gas industry drills there, then they will drill everywhere. It'll be a disaster for wild places. You're the guy to tell the story." He gave me a dozen names to contact.

"I can do it, but my plan is to go to Florida for a couple weeks in March."

"You're taking your phone?" he asked.

"Yup, I can interview folks in between…some other things, and have a copy to you before April."

"Good. I want fire and brimstone, Arthur. I want the man who wrote *The Outgoing Tide* to ride again. We need that guy!"

"You got him!" I had waited years for someone to ask.

I hung up the phone and felt the old adrenaline start to churn. There was a tugging inside me toward a new crusade. Perhaps this time, in Michigan, my pleas would not be ignored.

"The game's afoot, girls," I said to Sam and Sham. They sharpened their ears and wagged their tails. The pack was ready to go.

• • • • •

Few people ever pay attention to the tides, even those folks who spend their whole lives by the sea. In most coastal areas there are four tides each day, two highs and two lows. The flows vary in size based on the moons and seasons. The major moon phases, new and full, cause larger tides. Eddie and I had always called these the Big Moons and fished them religiously. Ironically, in

Florida, the biggest tides of all, called spring tides, occur in the fall, while the smallest tides, called neap tides, happened in the spring. Weather can play a role as well. Wind can delay a tide or speed its arrival. Rain can add volume to the flow while a drought will starve it.

All tides have set characteristics, almost personality traits. High tides are robust crystal blue water that teem with life. Low tides are dingy brown liquid, stinking of decay and almost stagnant. For better or worse, none of them last for very long. There is always variation, always movement, and the tides are ultimately unstoppable.

The same can be said of life, although there will always come an ending for each of us.

It was velvet twilight on the vernal equinox, and I was walking the beach, south of the House of Refuge. There was a slight breeze out of the southeast, just a hint of salt in the air. The waves were patting the sand in an easy cadence. A couple of intrepid crabs scooted back and forth along the shore, showing remarkable agility by not getting sucked out to sea as the surf retreated. Some jacks or blues were running greenies in the trough, cutting the surface with splashes here and there. A great blue heron squawked at me when I got too close, then took off in flight somewhere into the night. The new moon smiled over the sand oats and buttonwood. This was vespers on still-sacred but ever-diminishing ground.

I was grateful. The trip had not been a certainty. It was in doubt right up to yesterday morning. Did I really want to go back there? Finally, it occurred to me that cutting this place out of my life for good was, in effect, staying in grief.

Kate LeClair helped me find that perspective.

"It's time to leave the prison bars, Arthur," she said on the phone. "That only happens by coming back and standing tall where you were once laid low."

"Ironic," I said in response.

"Psychotherapy is more ironic than anybody is willing to say on the record."

We were meeting for lunch tomorrow at a restaurant overlooking the Jupiter Inlet. It was time to move past the therapist-client dynamic to something else. I thought about bringing her flowers, white roses to be sure, but decided not to. It was complicated. Kate was too button-down, too professional, and too much a stubborn Scot to accept such a gesture. I was still too loyal to a woman, now dead nearly two years, to do it anyway…at least for now.

I trudged the wet shore for a long time, thinking about nothing, and leaving one thing behind while in search of another. Then I wondered what had become of the turtle I saw on that night long, long ago. Was she still out there somewhere?

After a while, I turned around to walk back and noticed that my footprints were gone.

They had washed away in the rising tide.

ACKNOWLEDGEMENTS

I owe a mountain of gratitude to Mike Magnuson for his comments on this and other manuscripts. No other person has done more to help me develop as a writer. Anything good in this book has Mike's influence baked in.

Ed Hoogterp also added important insight to several of the themes in the book. He helped me to ground the narrative and keep things real.

Mark Hendricks, longtime friend, and fishing buddy offered a granular review of the work. He has edited my writing for over 15 years and knows all my shortcomings. If Mark's not happy then I'm not happy.

A great thanks as well to Ellen and Tom Baird, Judy and Chris Guest, Marvin Roberson, and Bill Buhr for their thoughts on the book. Kathy and Rick Buhr were there from the beginning, wading through ten years and three iterations of the main characters' journeys. I could not have done it without them.

Lindsey Potter knocked it out of the park with her photos of me out at the House of Refuge. She totally gets it!

Josh Greenberg and John Bebow must be mentioned because their writing showed me the way to the next level. I'm still walking that path.

Working with Mission Point Press has been a joy. Doug Weaver, Heather Shaw (She said "Jump," I said, "How high?"), Sarah Meiers (Killer Cover!), Tricia Frey and Darlene Short are all stone-cold professionals. God willing and the creeks don't rise, I look forward to working with them for years to come.

Finally, thanks to John D., Raymond C., Dashiell H., and all the others who lead me to the land of shadows where choices must be made with souls hanging in the balance.

ABOUT THE AUTHOR

Thomas A. Buhr is a native Michigander and lifelong fisherman chasing everything from bluegills and bass to snappers and snook. At 14 years old he moved to Boca Raton—a place nobody had heard of yet—and fell in love with Old Florida. Watching "progress" steal away this magical land also spawned an interest in conservation.

PHOTO BY LINDSEY POTTER

While working his way through the academic thicket with degrees from Miami (FL), Central Florida, and Michigan, he found time for freelance writing. In over 30 years he has written scores of articles in magazines including Field & Stream, Florida Game & Fish, The Fisherman, Michigan Out of Doors, Midwest Fly Fishing as well as several pieces for academic journals. He was editor of *The Riverwatch* and won an Award for Conservation Journalism from the Sierra Club in 2011.

Buhr founded the Au Sable Big Water Preservation Association in 2007 and has been a member, often serving on the board, of several Michigan-based conservation organizations.

When not fishing, writing or protecting wild places, he cheers for his favorite sports teams: Leicester City Foxes, Michigan Wolverines and Miami Dolphins.

He can be reached at PO Box 300, Luzerne, MI 48636 or tombuhr@prodigy.net.